DARKLY BEGOTTEN

T STEDMAN

ACKNOWLEDGMENTS

I can't believe the series is complete. I want to thank all my readers who have stuck with me from the beginning, without whom there would be no meaning in all the hard work. Nicky Lovick, my fabulous editor, who has helped me grow as a writer, immensely, and to Jane Harrison, who has done a marvellous job taking over as my first critical reader.

ALSO BY T STEDMAN

21st Century Sirens Series

Soul Breather
Blood Sister
Shield Maiden
Tiger Lily
Night Goddess

Dark Valentines Collection

The Watchers
Diablo

The Novellas

Protector
Lost Moon

Non-Fiction

My Migraine Story

THE ROYAL FAMILIES OF ATLANTIS

The Royal Families
Of Atlantis

Dubonnetti
Bonaci
Santalini
Florianna

Of Murrtaine
Borge

PROLOGUE

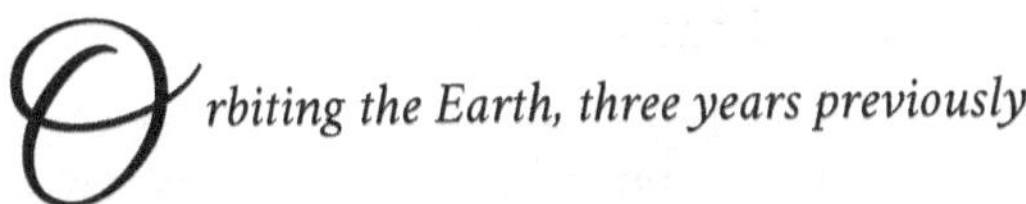

rbiting the Earth, three years previously

SETI FELT warm and comfortable before he became conscious. He blinked and heard the gentle hum of the clear lid opening on his pod. The sentient, water-filled ship had awoken him first. As commander, he must take control now they had arrived.

He took a moment to let the feat of what they'd accomplished sink in. They'd crossed a galaxy to judge a colony visited less than a handful of times and few lived long enough to tell the tale.

Now more alert, he waved his hand in the air and a holographic panel appeared. He moved the images around with his hand and settled the vessel into its resting orbit. Then he stood on wobbly legs and summoned the panel again, waking his twenty high-ranking officers and the rest of the crew.

No one had time for greetings. Time was critical. His

Twenty, barely awake, followed him to the Bridge and climbed into their egg-shaped pods, still dressed in the grey shimmering suits they'd worn to cross the great expanse of space. When they finally assembled around the viewing oracle, he looked at each of them one by one. They had all passed the journey well and looked young and in their prime. Their hair was either sleek black or pure white, their skin pale and covered in the dark stripes of Atlas. Their eyes were black pools, giving nothing away, but he knew they were in awe and thinking the same thing as him; that they'd safely reached their destination, destiny could finally be fulfilled, and the Earth be judged. Something their forefathers had begun long ago. It was monumental. Today the real work would begin. The Sirens had passed eighteen and they would commence The Watching.

The clear lids of the twenty pods closed over them. Then they rose and tilted forward to overlook the oval pit where they would spend the duration, until the time when they would intercede. Each person knew they couldn't leave their positions until judgement day. Except for one volunteer. The chosen one would leave at the appointed time to live among the Atlanteans.

The water pod began to fill with the bio-nutrients needed to keep them alive and the nanites used to neutralize waste. Pictures immediately began to hit their frontal lobes and holograms grew and floated in front of them. They had been chosen and trained because they had the highest IQs, the best memory and the greatest level of concentration. They would need it; they mustn't miss a thing. Evidence was crucial to the judging process. They must watch every instant of the Atlantean players below on Earth. It was literally life or death for them.

The journey had been made every five hundred years,

when the Sirens were scried to be born. Then, after a short viewing period of around five years, the crew of twenty returned home, passing the baton to the next crew, who'd set off immediately to be there ready for the next generation. Even with the use of wormhole travel, it was an epic journey.

Excitement buzzed through their joined consciousness. Never before had they reached the point where the Earth's orb and the Fates pointed to the end being in this generation. The stage was set. The five ancient Atlantean royal families were never more prominent. Each had many sons and the Sirens were hidden in their individual lives on the Earth. All it needed was for one to be found and the others would soon follow. Then a single king would be crowned. It only remained to be seen what manner of a male he was and whether he could hold it.

Ashaya, a young female of Seti's Twenty, flashed him a sensation of impatience. He knew what she meant. *Let us practise human thought patterns. The Atlanteans use it and it would be advantageous for us to be proficient and ready for the appointed time. Ask your question, Ashaya.*

I want to know what we are waiting for. We have seen the history of this planet over the years we slept. The hybrid race of Atlanteans and the humans have no ability to rule themselves, Ashaya projected to everyone's mind. *Every past generation of Soul Breathers has only served to prove this.*

What of the pure race of Borge? For most of that time they have remained beneath the sea, cut off from Humans, another young man named Ragnar said. *They follow the old ways.*

That may be true, but it is unlikely for them to rule effectively from beneath the sea. It is more likely to be an Atlantean who can live below the surface and on land. But no Atlantean has ever held the crown. Each ruler becomes corrupted by power and never follows The Way, she argued.

Seti nodded. *You are both correct. Our job is to decide whether there is enough good in the inhabitants to allow them to continue. However, this must be for the last time. The Atlanteans must have made every mistake and taken every advantage of ruling for themselves. There can be no argument when we exact judgement. The Way has not been followed and they have become debauched and tainted by their host planet. However, the time is not yet. Our job is just beginning. There is a main player yet to emerge.*

They all waited and looked at him expectantly to explain.

The Darkly Begotten is emerging. Only then can prophecy be fulfilled.

A large hologram appeared in the center of the oval pit. It depicted two solid gold rings engraved with the writing of Atlantis. *We know who it is. We've always known. It is the offspring of an unholy alliance and fathered by yet another. Its power is great but can only come from the darkness because of the tarnish of whence it came.*

What are the rings for? Ashaya said, speaking the mind of all of them.

They are the slave rings that will bind the Darkly Begotten to its purpose. Made of a gold alloy and protected by ancient charms, the Orb herself placed them in the catacombs on which the Bonaci castle was built, at the time of the sacking of Atlantis. They were put there knowing this time would come and would have but one owner. No other can touch the metal.

When they meet the chosen figurehead – the Darkly Begotten – they will meld to his skin and become one with him, so he can never escape what he represents. Then all will have to know where we are in point of time.

However, it is prudent to note, if there is the smallest chance that the Atlanteans can progress and learn The Way, we must decide whether we can give them that chance. It is for that reason alone that Ashaya will live among them, staying particularly close to the pure family of Borge.

And if they can't? Ragnar asked.

Then we have the correction code for the Orb of this planet, and she will carry out the sentence.

And what is the sentence?

Complete annihilation. Every man, woman and child of all species will be destroyed. Not a stone will be left upon a stone.

CHAPTER 1

Ballygowan Castle, west coast of Ireland, present day
"Long live the king!" someone shouted.

A few chanted it in response, but most just muttered it under their breath. There was a handful of claps, some boos and even a hiss. A less-than-enthusiastic response from a crowd of at least fifty people.

Tia was still reeling. Malleven, prince of Florianna and master of the ancient mystic order of Magi, had swept in with his fearsome, black-robed men and simply taken over. And just moments after they'd learned of the destruction of Murrtaine. She stood frozen, still gaping from the shock.

Malleven was tall and lean, as all Atlantean men were, but he was dark and mysteriously dangerous, with such a perfectly angled face that it should be on the cover of a magazine. The black symbols under his cheekbones only served to accentuate them. It was an awful slow-motion dream. A dream within a dream that kept getting worse.

Tia watched helplessly as her sister Lacy meekly moved over to stand with Malleven, the usurper, as if she was under his spell. She seemed distracted and unaware of the enormity of what she was doing.

Keenan Santalini, her husband, was dragged away kicking, screaming and biting like a wild animal. The rest of the once-strong Santalinis were disordered, arguing between themselves. Keenan was their brother, but their role was to guard the new king, even though every one of them wished him dead. The world order had shifted and no one knew their place anymore.

As her husband Dante, the deposed king, was escorted out, Tia felt the weight of a permanent storm cloud settling over the castle. Those that were left stood silent, visibly stunned, looking at each other for anyone to take the lead in what to do next.

Tia was dragged from her stupor by a whimper. Little JJ, the smallest of her sons, clung to her legs. She bent to scoop him into her arms. He was bewildered and tired, his chin trembling as he tried hard not to cry. She kissed the top of his head and pulled in the other four of her children to huddle closer to her legs.

Tia realized then that she was shaking. It was that white-hot fear that left a person sweating and the same time freezing cold. The sort of visceral fear you get when you think you and your loved ones are about to die. Her mouth was dry and her throat filled with gravel. She prayed that Dante got away safe. Worry about what could be happening to him threatened to paralyze her thinking. She had to get a hold and concentrate on her children and sisters, otherwise she'd go mad.

Lacy was her favorite; the one she shared most in common and found first. Back then she'd been the only family she had. They'd both been brought up by the British care system, although separately and shared a love of dance music. Tia had been a DJ and Lacy a club dancer. They had a similar build, but whereas Lacy had brown hair, Tia's was blonde. Their eyes were green, but Lacy's were Human-looking while Tia's were darker and unnaturally large. To Tia, she looked and felt the most like a sister.

Keenan was the love of Lacy's life and was utterly devoted to her. For Lacy to end up like this, Malleven must have done one hell of a number on her.

At least the big Murr, Darres, was close by. He felt the fear and need to protect the same as her, Tia was sure of it. She could tell by the tautness in the sinew of his arms and the tension in his jaw. He hugged her sister Isla, his bonded mate, into his chest as if he'd fight anyone who came near her or their two boys, sheltered behind him.

Isla and Darres were inseparable. They'd met at the same US army base, where they'd been held since they were children. They'd been trained as special ops killers for the American government in a deal cooked up between the two races. It was easy to believe of Darres at almost seven feet tall out of water and with the look of a Native American brave, but Isla couldn't look more opposite. She was a blonde, pale-skinned pixie-looking girl who seemed to have no street smarts. As it turned out, she may not be the first one to get a joke, but she was lethal. An expert in knives and martial arts without breaking a sweat, while at the same time managing to be kind and devoted to Darres and their two sons.

The Sirens seemed to have gravitated together around Lacy, who seemed weird and spaced-out. Even her sister Lily, and she was the one Tia got on with the least. She was actually married to Malleven. None of them understood it, putting it down to the fact that she had to be dumb in some way—and not just because she couldn't talk.

Lily had taken after their mother, who was pure Murr and none of the Murrs could speak; they had no vocal cords. She looked nothing like the rest of them. She was boyish, yet petite, and had the tightest brown corkscrew curls that sprang from her head all over the place. She stood holding hands with Lance, her mate. Their story was complicated. He was a human. A surfer dude with ties to the race. He was cool though, everyone liked him and looked around him, a lot more nervously than her.

Phoebe's howl of grief had almost split the rock ceiling and pierced all of their hearts. You'd have to be made of stone not to feel for her. The last of her five sisters, she had learned with the rest of them that her partner, Drew, was dead. She looked drained of blood, desolate and broken by grief. But *she* was the one who'd started this mess. It was hard for Tia to keep sympathy when *she* was the one who'd defected from Dante out of spite and given Malleven his way in.

OK, Dante had taken Drew with him for his summit in Murrtaine. And Drew's decision to stay behind so the pure-bred Murr inhabitants could escape before its destruction did have Dante's mark all over it, but Tia knew Dante and there had to be more to it. But it was easy to see Phoebe wasn't interested in details. To her it was simple; her lover was gone and Dante was to blame.

The thing was, Phoebe looked human enough, with her red wavy hair and hazel eyes, but she wasn't like the rest of them. They called her a Nix. Whatever that was. She freaked Tia out by being able to change into something else—something monstrous. She grew fangs and drank blood. She'd even changed something in Drew's DNA so that he could do the same.

So Tia felt for Phoebe, she really did, but she also hated her for starting all this. It was pretty hard to forgive her for blowing her life apart and terrifying the children at her feet.

Everyone was beginning to emerge from their shock. They turned to the person standing next to them and whispered behind closed hands, asking what they all wanted to know: What the hell was going on and was it even legal? The whispering grew and the mood became restless, more troubled and fearful.

Tia's best guess was that it *was* legal. As much as she hated to admit it, Duke Ormond Delissi, the Atlantean diplomat from Washington DC, had arrived with Malleven to make it so. It was probably why he had been brought along.

Tia's only hope was the huddle of men that gathered around him. They were the leaders and respected elders of the race. It included her father, Sebastian, her uncle, Alfonzo, Vionne, Lord Advocate of Murrtaine, and other leading dignitaries. Voices soon became raised.

"Can we at least defer till after the crisis of Murrtaine has been settled?" Her uncle was saying.

"Yes, the timing has caused chaos," someone else said. "Is he even eligible?"

"He is mated to only one Siren."

"I've heard his ring is red."

"You saw for yourself, all Sirens pledged to him," the duke said. But in the end, he wasn't given the chance to answer their protests. Malleven approached and the wave of hush that went through the waiting crowd reached their group and they immediately halted what they were saying. Everyone around them waited for some sort of reaction, but from where Tia was standing, it was hard to tell. The strain showed on her father's face. Smiles looked painted on and the duke behaved as charmingly as ever. It was clear there would be no reversal of events today.

Tia looked around for her Murr mother, Naomi, and she was nowhere to be seen. She must be helping her people settle into the catacombs after their home city of Murrtaine was destroyed. She hoped her father had the sense to mentally warn her to stay there, out of harm's way.

Tia shuffled a little closer. Malleven's Magi brotherhood continued to pile into the Great Hall and stood alert, waiting for any signs of trouble. Roman, one of her youngest children, whimpered. She hugged him closer to her leg, while balancing JJ on her hip. The men were terrifying, imposing figures with ancient symbols daubed on each cheek. Most were human and appeared to be unarmed, but they were famed, powerful mystics and proven fighters under the ceremonial black robes. They were overrunning the castle, outnumbering the Santalini guards at least two to one. Some guards had stayed loyal and gone with Keenan and Dante. She was glad of that at least, hating to think of Dante all alone. Those left behind seemed anxious and overdressed in their finery, now spotlit by the harsh light of the chandeliers and hemmed in by the shadows cast by the flames in the alcoves. The vast cave they'd lovingly called the Great Hall, had laughed, feasted and lounged in for years, now felt like a holding pen; danger hung in the air like a butcher's axe and no one knew when or where it would fall.

MALLEVEN LISTENED to the so-called elder wise men clustered around him, pleading their individual cases, desperation barely disguised as advice. He remained still and attentive, schooling his features to look at them directly and not survey his new kingdom in boredom. Each one of them was an experienced leader. He knew they saw him as the only one who wasn't. He should thank them. After all, their arrogance had handed him a kingdom. The truth was, he'd planned for this since he was a poor boy from an insignificant branch of the Florianna royal family and knew exactly what he must do. The nation needed holding together with a rod of iron if they were ever going to become great.

However Malleven did recognize that some changes

needed gentle handling until he was securely on the throne. While the voices melded into a dull rumble, his heart rejoiced, just for a moment, while he took it all in.

This part of the castle was below sea level and opulent in the old Atlantean style, but Malleven thought it a little dated. Too many large sofas and tables were cluttered into the space. It detracted from the sheer scale of the vast cave and magnificent window whose vista was the underwater sea. It was the breathtaking focal point of the room.

An equally impressive classical fountain made from black marble concealed a water route out of the castle and reminded him of a once-grand hotel. Everything was designed to bring water inside and was luxurious, larger than life and very definitely alien. Not that he was partial to the water, because he was not. As an Atlantean, he'd just always wanted a home like this. It conveyed to the world something money couldn't buy: stability, breeding and station. Real Atlantean residences like this almost never came onto the market. He inwardly smiled. *Unless you were king.* Then they came remarkably easily.

Before he joined the conversation, he signaled to the chief of his men who instantly became alert. With a flick of his wrist, and a nod of his head, he gestured to the group of three nervous men waiting at a respectful distance from the Sirens. They were the Protectors, sworn to serve them for life and no doubt hoping to remain unnoticed. They would never be loyal to anyone other than their Siren and for that they must go.

Six of his men stealthily approached and surrounded them, silently bundling them to the side of the room to the shadows, with the minimum of fuss. They outnumbered them two to one and easily contained any pushing and shoving and a shout of, "Get your hands off me." By the time anyone around them turned to see what was happening, they were already gone. The Sirens didn't notice; they were too preoccupied with each other. Two of the Protectors he recognized: Cash Reynolds and Sean McPhearson. They were Tia's. The other he'd been vaguely aware of as Phoebe's. Connor, he believed was his name. He was an Irishman who'd been with her for much of her life. The Protectors were easily banished from the castle, leaving their charges without protection as was his right as king.

Malleven let out a long, satisfied breath and turned his attention back to the big Murr, Vionne, now speaking. Vionne was his greatest threat. He was a born leader the people would naturally follow. He needed him onside to manage the purebred Borge family. Given that their society was permanently underwater, sheer genetics made ruling without a Murr impossible.

Vionne held up his left hand, revealing his purple divining ring. Malleven knew what it meant even before Vionne said the words, "I am Phoebe Ray's most compatible mate. Whoever her human was, he died in Murrtaine when the Orb destroyed it and its invaders. We now have a state of emergency, with several thousand displaced people."

Malleven had received news of the destruction as soon as they'd landed. It was an astonishing turn of events he hadn't planned for. He walked over to the impressive bank of CCTV monitors, set up in the corner, next to the great window and his entourage followed him. Dante and his closest advisors had been studying them moments before his arrival. They showed as far as the eye could see, a great biblical exodus of a weary people, carrying what they could and filling the catacombs of the castle beneath them. It was a huge complication. The fact the Murr prince had now found his Siren made him even more of a threat. However, the concern for his people was evident in the tense way he held his body and would be useful. Something he would consider more carefully later.

As Vionne spoke, Malleven continued to assess the man. His appearance was in stark contrast to that his brother, Darres. His hair was white blond to his shoulder, while his brother's was black to his waist. Vionne was the diplomat, putting his duty to his people first, while Darres was an unpredictable killer who thought of no one but his immediate family.

Vionne slammed down Malleven's scan and he reciprocated when Vionne attempted to do the same. Murr mental blocks were renowned as unsurpassed in their strength, however so were Magi and Malleven was a Magi master.

One thing quickly became apparent; Vionne was not to be underestimated. Malleven decided his plan of action was to keep him busy and on side—at least for the time being, until he thought of another plan.

His eyes tracked to Phoebe, standing alone and looking lost. Her once-lustrous red hair was lank and unkempt, her skin sallow and inner glow somehow faded. She'd been his prisoner only a few months before where he'd forced a full bond on her and cloaked her memories until today, but she was no use to him like this. He communicated wordlessly to one of his guards, who nudged her and brought her over to him.

He waited, not pressing her to speak. After a long moment, she raised her eyes to meet his. They were empty, desolate; the change in her was quite shocking. *You remember me?* he said, switching to projected speech which was easy through their mutual bond.

"My kidnapper," she said wearily on an exhale. She sounded exhausted, no anger left in her.

Vionne is your mate by ring.

Her face began to crumple and he caught her before she

fell to the floor. He held her to him and put his mouth close to her ear. *I can feel you have no great love for him.*

I hate him ... he killed my ... he killed... She became a dead weight in his arms and almost sank to the floor. He renewed his grip, keenly aware of the spectacle they were becoming. His mind raced even as he touched her cheek tenderly. *Listen to me, Phoebe. I want you to go with Vionne for now, but know that you are mine, Phoebe Ray. You work for me. I must secure New Murrtaine and you will come back to me.*

He turned her away from the onlookers and passed his hand across her eyes. He had woven a glamour around her when she was with him before. It only took a second to bring her back to his will.

She nodded, resigned. It was difficult to tell if she was in his power or had lost all interest and will to fight. It mattered little. All he wanted was the desired outcome. She was the perfect sweetener to buy the Borges' support and cooperation.

He put her away from him and picked up her limp hand. Then he led her to Vionne and held out her hand for him to take. For a moment, Vionne looked unsure.

"Here. Such is my hope for continued good relations between the crown and the Borge, that I give my treasured Siren into your care."

Vionne paused as if he expected a reaction from Phoebe. When there was none, he quickly took her hand and bowed his head. *His majesty is both wise and compassionate,* Vionne projected. *Will the council operate as before?*

Phoebe yanked her hand from Vionne's and escaped in the direction of the bedroom corridor. Malleven narrowed his eyes. Because of the lack of facial movement, it was hard to gauge Murrs for emotion or sincerity without a scan. This one had obviously spent some time with Atlanteans. It was clear how Vionne felt for his Siren.

However, his aura was honest enough and it was a good question.

Dante had introduced a council to include a representative from all the families—even the Humans, so all would have an input in government. He'd felt it would keep them sweet and invested. To Malleven, it was weak and one of the reasons he was standing there today. The families looked after their own. There was simply too much paranoia and ambition to ever make it work. All it served was a fracturing of power. Malleven did not intend to make the same mistake. He looked Vionne directly in the eye. "No, it will not. It is a dispensation, only for the Borge."

Malleven watched the male stand unnaturally still, as the purebloods often did. He was calculating what to make of it.

There was, of course, only one answer, and Vionne bowed his head graciously. *The Orb has chosen a new site for Murrtaine. Will you support it?* he projected. Again, the shrewd look. Vionne was sizing him up as a leader.

"Of course. It will be my first duty as king to stay close to our power source and my purebred cousins who guard it."

Vionne looked visibly relieved. In fact, Malleven thought him most expressive for a Murr. He had already guessed that his sole purpose in staying was to secure the safety of his people. It was an admirable thing to do, but he would not forget the friendship Vionne had had with Dante. Nevertheless, his sense of duty to his people would be useful leverage, if needed.

As Vionne went to turn back towards the fountain, Malleven said, "How long will your people need here?"

A few days at most. My people need to rest and prepare for the long journey ahead of them.

"Very well. Every comfort will be afforded to them while they are here. But I ask for one thing in return."

Vionne straightened as if he were to receive the catch he

was expecting. Again, Malleven was struck by his Human-like mannerisms.

And what is that?

"That when you leave, you take your brother with you."

Vionne went to protest and then stopped. Malleven watched him closely. Isla was his own most compatible mate, who'd chosen Darres over him. If Darres stayed, it would mean an inevitable fight, one that would not happen unless he was sure to win it. Vionne bowed his head and projected, *As you wish.*

Malleven was impressed. Instead of risking his displeasure by reminding him that he'd been rejected by Isla and standing with his brother, Vionne had chosen diplomacy. A true leader indeed.

I will remind my brother of the importance of his support for his people as a Borge prince of Murrtaine.

Malleven tilted his head. "I can see we will have a fruitful working relationship ahead of us." He smiled. "After all, the Siren, Isla Snow, is capable of handling herself." It was the very thing that made Isla irresistible to him and impossible for Vionne to argue. Isla's mind was as strong as his and she was a trained killer. Darres was simply not needed.

Vionne bowed from the waist this time, signalling that the conversation was over. Then he turned and went with two of his brothers, Dax and Caan, towards the fountain. All Vionne's brothers were strong, disciplined lieutenants and were a formidable force. Even the two youngest. They were carbon copies of Vionne, right down to the whiteness of their hair. Malleven continued to watch as they followed their brother and, one by one, stepped over the fountain wall and jumped into the deep pool that led out to sea.

Malleven was confident that Vionne understood his meaning. If Vionne wanted Darres to keep his life, then he must convince him to leave with him. He smirked. It suited him either way. Tia Storm was without her mate, the former king, Dante Dubonnetti. Lacy Rain's mate, the volatile Keenan, had been banished with him, and Darres Borge was to go with Vionne, leaving Isla. It would be a simple thing to exchange the necessary breath to bind them all to him. Phoebe was his, albeit broken by grief, and would be leverage with Vionne, so that just left Lily and she was already his legally witnessed wife.

He allowed Lily to keep her mate, Lance McCabe, for the time being. Lance was Human and weak. Malleven had access to Lance's mind because of the bond they both shared with Lily, so, in effect, he had them all. His takeover was complete.

Malleven turned his attention to the two elderly brothers hovering with uncertainty nearby. Sebastian and Alfonzo Bonaci were father and uncle to the Sirens and stood close to the Duke Ormond Delissi, waiting to hear their future.

Malleven approached. "Go back to Washington DC, Lord Duke."

The duke cautiously bowed his head.

"Let them know we have entered a new era of stability."

The duke looked uneasily between Malleven and the brothers. "Do you wish them to know all the Sirens are accounted for?"

Malleven understood perfectly what he was driving at. The human governments would know that the return of their ancestors was imminent and would descend into panic. "We cannot delay it forever," Malleven said, looking Delissi in the eye. "They are responsible for the attempted genocide of a whole city. Let them shit themselves at my displeasure and know they will need to kneel at my feet if they want any part of negotiations with Atlas. They now need us more than ever before."

The duke nodded and let out a breath. He would know the truth in his words. The brothers remained quiet.

Malleven reached out a hand and rested it on the shoulder of Sebastian, the Sirens' father. His scan was quick, bringing with it only surface emotions, but it was enough. Fear and sadness came through loud and clear and were natural responses. He smiled and reached out his other hand to Alfonzo and did the same. "Never fear. It is my wish to be a good king. I ask that you both stay here and advise me as you did for Dante." They were the king-makers. Everyone knew that. And for that reason alone, they would never be allowed to leave.

Alfonzo was a devious, complex character and more of a spokesman, but Malleven didn't underestimate the quiet determination of Sebastian. They were a formidable pair and had to stay where he could see them. They both dipped their heads. "Of course," Alfonzo said. "As always, we work for the good of the race." Then they bowed and went in the direction of their apartments.

Delissi remained. Malleven was fully aware that without him he could not have made his bid for the crown. "I have much to thank you for." He was also acutely aware that while Delissi was a diplomat, he was also a Dubonnetti and they had lost their king tonight.

"I'll leave for Washington, DC right away," Delissi said. "They would have suffered heavy losses in the destruction of Murrtaine. I will report what I find out."

Malleven nodded, still amazed at the man. "Thank you, Lord Duke. I would especially like to express my gratitude for your support."

Then Delissi completely surprised him. He came closer until they were almost nose to nose. "Never forget that you won a great victory today, Malleven. You deposed a good king and won all five Sirens. That is something that has never happened—not long enough for any one man to keep them, anyway. You must be strong. But, above all, be wise. It is almost the end of the eleventh hour and you don't have much time to secure the race."

He was referring, of course, to the imminent, foretold return of their ancestors from their home planet of Atlas. It was a prophecy that he and all the princes knew well. The judgement they would one day pass on them was always at the back of everyone's mind. Now he was king, the buck stopped with him. "As I have always maintained, I want nothing more than the strength and prosperity of the race." Delissi was right, but it annoyed him that he felt he had to keep hammering home the point. He was not a useless playboy like Dante was when he first took the throne. He couldn't be more the opposite—*a fact that everyone in this damn castle would soon know.*

By the time Delissi bowed and left him, the crowd had thinned out. It seemed those not immediately affected had used the opportunity to slope off to assess their future. However, before he turned his attention to the Sirens, one man caught his eye, hovering in the shadows. *Antonio.* A Dubonnetti, a brother of the deposed king and his lover of several years. Although it had been a while since he'd seen him. Too long. Antonio hadn't answered any of his calls. He scanned the heads of those left in the room; Antonio's father and brothers were nowhere to be seen. Antonio had come here just for him. Malleven's spirit lightened and he made his way over to him. "You came," he stated, leaning in and kissing his lover's face. "I thought you were avoiding me." He tried to keep the satisfaction off his face. Antonio had irked him by keeping his distance. It was the first time he'd ever done it and he didn't like it at all.

"How could I not?" Antonio said quietly. "You are, after all, my king."

Malleven had an overwhelming urge to embrace him, right there in front of everyone. Antonio had travelled much of his journey with him, and victory was sweet. "Don't let someone as insignificant as Phoebe come between us, Antonio. She is just a necessary means to an end." He didn't know exactly what Antonio was making a point over, but it was an educated guess that it was over Phoebe. It was during the month he'd kept her hostage that Antonio had disappeared from his home in New York. His jealousy simply overcame his good judgement.

"Oh? What about your wife, Lily, or your great love, Isla? Your other abductee, Lacy, or perhaps your newest project, Tia Storm?"

Malleven almost laughed at Antonio's snarky list. And, he had to admit, he knew him pretty well. However, he would do well to learn his place. Antonio would always be at his side as long as he knew what that was. Malleven picked up one of Antonio's hands and looked him deeply in the eyes. They were angry, hurt and full of sorrow. "Go to your chamber. I'll come later and we will talk. You are and always have been the closest to me, Antonio." It was gratifying to see him soften in front of his eyes. An easy conquest. Antonio loved him completely and that was how it must be. "Go!" he said with a flick of his hand, attention gone already.

The Great Hall had almost completely emptied while he'd been preoccupied, leaving just a small huddle of people—the Sirens and the besotted partners who refused to leave them. Silence descended as Malleven approached. They turned to face him when he came to a stop a few feet away. He looked into each face of the remaining four Sirens in turn and smiled. "I wanted to say thank you before you retire. Without you, this joyous day would not have been possible."

No one said a word but continued to stare at him. A movement made him drop his eyes and he took in the children for the first time. They were fidgeting, but watching him with interest, already sensing at their young age that their world had changed. "Hello," he said without smiling.

The four bigger children said hello back cautiously, but the smallest one looked up with eyes of understanding way beyond his years. Malleven adjusted his stance to look at him more squarely. "And who do we have here that doesn't see the need to greet their king?"

Tia, his mother, came and stood behind him, protectively. "He is young and doesn't understand."

The expression on the boy's face said that he did. He said nothing and didn't look scared. Indeed, he was summing him up. His scan touched the corners of his mind a couple of times. Malleven narrowed his eyes and a single blast of laughter left him. The boy could be no more than five years old.

"He is a quiet, serious boy," Tia said, increasing her grip on his shoulders and pulling him back into her legs.

Malleven smiled at him. "A wise one, I see." He looked around at the other Sirens. "I want you to know that this is a new era. I value loyalty above all things and if each of you give me that, we will enter a new period of prosperity and stability such as the Atlantean nation has never seen before."

"The human governments have suffered heavy losses in their attempt to take Murrtaine. They will not forget this. Nor will they let the new kingdom live in peace. No one will be safe. The return is imminent. They know this as well as we do. To remain together is the safest course of action."

Tia seemed unsure and looked at her sisters. Lacy stared blankly ahead of her, still in his thrall, and Isla moved closer to her husband—the most unpredictable of all the Borge brothers, Darres. Lily looked the most relaxed, standing with her Human lover, Lance.

Malleven grinned and held open his arms. She went

straight to him. He laughed, kissed the top of her head and looked over it at the others. "Loyalty," he said, "is always rewarded." His eyes went to Isla, who shifted uncomfortably. Her discomfort was gratifying. She knew what was to come.

He put Lily away from him and held her by the shoulders. *Are you happy I'm here, Lily?* he said, switching to projected speech. She was mute and he didn't want her to feel embarrassed in front of the others.

Of course, congratulations. How's Antonio? she said raising her eyebrows and making him laugh.

She was behaving like a jealous wife and it was delightful. *And your human?* he said, mimicking her expression.

She nodded. *It's all good now.*

He searched his favorite Siren's face. He had been most fond of this one. She would keep her man for now.

Alfonzo came up to his shoulder. "Excuse me, Your Highness, we need to make a statement to the White House."

Malleven gave Lily one last, lingering look. This was it now. No time for dallying with girls. "Very well … Rest!" he said as an order to them all. "It has been a tiring day." He bent and scooped up the smallest boy. The boy surprised him again by sitting quietly in his arms and continuing to study his face.

Tia immediately reached out her hands to take him. "JJ, come to Mummy."

JJ. Jay Junior. Jay Gardiner's son, Malleven quickly deduced. Foolishly, she'd given away the biggest weapon against them —their weakness was the children.

He poked the boy playfully in the stomach. "I will keep him with me. I like the little fellow." He smiled into Tia's eyes and watched the understanding seep slowly into them. She was well known to be the most troublesome of all the Sirens and she would be brought to heel.

All she could do was bow her head, stiffly, clearly using

every ounce of her strength to hold herself together. He admired her for it.

Then he moved on to Lacy. He waved his hand in an arc across her face and she seemed to come out of her daze. She looked around, as if awareness of her surroundings was returning to her. "Look after your sister," he said, turning back to Tia. "Bring her to my chamber this evening." The horror on her face was immediate, but, before she could protest, he cut in, "Then you can collect your son." Her anger morphed into hatred and then contempt. He smiled at the rainbow of emotions she couldn't hide.

He decided he liked her honesty. "We will talk of your guardianship, as you have no protection of a mate."

Tia looked around her, no doubt looking for the two faithful men she always kept around her, long gone by then.

"All Protectors have been dismissed, as is my right while you're here with me at the castle." Her defences had been taken, one by one, just as he'd planned. Terror flashed behind her eyes as she audibly swallowed.

Satisfied with her reaction, he turned and left them, safe in the knowledge she understood how vulnerable she was now. The boy was the key.

CHAPTER 2

$\mathcal{D}$ante was grateful that Cesaré still had use of the Florianna jet. They headed straight for the airport in three SUVs at top speed. They were directed straight onto the tarmac, exiting the cars to jog up the steps of the plane. The Santalini guards had their weapons at the ready. It had been his own biological father, the Duke Delissi himself, who had banished him, but no one could be sure Malleven wouldn't send an assassination party to eliminate him as a threat, now they were away from official eyes at the castle.

Dante headed for his usual seat towards the back. Keenan slumped in the one opposite him. "I can't believe they took any of that bullshit as being legal. Lacy would never have done that in her right mind. Never!"

Dante was too bewildered himself to console him. He gazed out of the small window, re-living the events of the day over and over. The look in Tia's eyes as she walked to his arch enemy as he'd watched, paralyzed with shock. He knew she'd had no choice and it was to protect her sisters, but it ripped out his heart nonetheless. Then having to leave his children; that alone made his palms sweat and his heart knock against his ribs.

As they waited for their slot on the runway, others from the castle were turning up at their private jets. Through the small oval window, he could see those without a jet arguing with officials; he guessed for helicopters to the nearest international airport, *Shannon*.

Then his phone, then Cesaré's and even Keenan's, started to ring. A constant stream of relations from around the globe, asking if it were true and where that left them. The phones quickly went unanswered. It wasn't that he didn't care. God knew, they'd only just got used to having him on the throne. There hadn't been a kingdom for five hundred years and, just as it began to prosper and become stable, it had been taken over. Dante needed time. Time to process it all. He'd lost everything: Tia, the children, home, his belongings, even who the hell he was. And, this time, Tia's father and uncle weren't there to help him pick up the pieces and rebuild.

Cesaré eased into the chair next to him. "The pilot needs the destination for Air Traffic Control."

Dante looked across at him, still not really seeing him until he registered what he was asking. "Malta. My cousin, the prime minister, will be expecting us."

Cesaré nodded and headed for the cockpit.

The Maltese prime minister had promised them safe haven months before when the threat to Murrtaine had escalated and Dante no longer felt that Ireland was a safe place for his family. It had been reassuring at the time. Now it seemed inspired. His study of Atlantean history had revealed it as being the probable site for Atlantis before it was destroyed. It felt like fate had brought him full circle. On a practical level it was remote, well protected and the last place Malleven would think of looking for him.

He watched Cesaré heading back towards him to sit down. No one knew if the council still existed and where that put them within their respective families. Cesaré was supposed to be head of the mighty Florianna royal family, but with his enemy, Malleven, now king and part of the same family, it was unlikely he'd remain.

Dante sat brooding while everyone filtered on and preflight checks were made. They were a surprisingly large party and it warmed his heart a little that they had all left the comfort of the castle to stay with him. It could have been so much worse. He could have been left penniless and alone, or worse still, executed. He just couldn't believe he'd been broadsided like this. He should have known and been prepared. He should have seen the trouble with Phoebe coming.

Phoebe Ray, the last of the Sirens, had made no secret of her month of unaccounted-for time. It had been a niggling mystery at the back of his mind since they'd first met and they'd had many discussions about it. Her answer had always been the same: "I have no memory at all" and he'd believed her. Even now he wasn't sure she'd been lying. As it turned out, her so-called blackout had been spent with Malleven, merrily sharing her breath with him the whole time. That meant he had a full bond and her power and that qualified him to make a bid for the crown.

Then the worst thought hit him like an executioner's blow. If Malleven was bound to Phoebe, he would soon have a link with all the Sirens. He already had Lily, which Dante did not. Dante tutted and shook his head. With all the illegal blood bonds going on, he was probably linked to them all already anyway.

His mind went back again and again to Tia and the children he'd been forced to leave behind. Delissi had enacted the banishment law and he'd been allowed to leave with just the shirt on his back. He guessed he was lucky to be alive. Left to Malleven, he was sure he would not. His heart pounded and he could barely breathe. Not having contact with Tia and the children was enough to send him into a panic that would be the downfall of them all. He had to keep a level head. But it was hard and took all his power. At the very least, Malleven would use the children to control her. He tried for the hundredth time to contact her telepathically, but it was as though the bond had been severed. That terrified him the most and he gripped the arms of the chair until his knuckles went white.

He closed his eyes and took some deep breaths to get a hold on himself. When he opened them some moments later, Cash and Sean entered the plane. His heart sank into the pit of his stomach. They were Tia's Protectors and even though he wasn't surprised they'd been dismissed, he kind of hoped they'd slip under the radar and be another level of protection for his family. They headed straight for him, sitting at the back of the plane, reading the anguish on his face.

They stood in front of him, guiltily, and Cash shook his head. "Literally ten minutes after you left."

Dante pointed at the two seats across the way. "Sit," was all he could say. He was too sick with worry to say anything else. Malleven would dismiss all the Sirens' bodyguards and the mates that remained were on borrowed time. He doubted they'd be released to go free. Still, he'd hoped for longer than this. He looked into both men's faces, looking as distraught as him. They were good men and loved Tia. "Please," he said, almost choking up.

They went to take the seats offered.

"I'm glad to have you." And he was. He needed all the support he could get. Keenan sat opposite, watching, eyes churning red with blood. Two of Keenan's brothers had accompanied him to stop him giving in to his animal side, fighting his way back into the castle and getting himself killed. The three men he'd grown up with, Vince, Rick and Dan, were with him too. They'd been inducted into the Santalini family and were Lacy's Protectors. That meant she was also under Malleven's influence and without protection too.

He thanked the Five Moons that the big Murr, Darres, was there with Isla and Lance was with Lily. It was something at least. "You think he will make a pretence at continuing with the council?" he asked Cesaré, sitting next to him. The doors of the plane were closing and the crew finally getting ready for take-off.

"Honestly, I don't know, but I suspect not. He will want ultimate power to rule. He'll squash any possible threat to his image of strength."

"I thank the Orb for Darres and Vionne being there," Dante said.

Cesaré tipped his head, but didn't look him in the eye.

"What is it?" Dante asked, cautiously, knowing he wasn't going to like it.

Cesaré turned from the window to look him in the eye.

"Please, Cesaré, you know him better than anyone. I need honesty."

Cesaré took a deep breath. "You want the truth?"

Dante nodded, dreading and needing to hear it at the same time.

"I think Vionne will agree to a deal to keep Murrtaine tied to the crown. Darres, if he hasn't been killed already, will die, as Malleven will see the threat immediately."

Dante swallowed. He was voicing what he knew already but didn't want to face. "And Lance?"

Cesaré bobbed his head and protruded his bottom lip in a very Italian way. "He has a destiny to fulfil, it is true, but I'm yet to see the worth of it. Malleven seems to have a regard for Lily. It is hard to say. He will use Alfonzo, Sebastian and Delissi to manage his position with the Humans."

"And the sisters?" Dante's heart pounded when he saw the light go out in Cesaré's eyes.

"Talk to your wife while you still can, because as soon as he cuts across your bond, he will separate you."

Dante had already tried, but as soon as he'd left the castle boundary their connection was lost. He shook his head and Cesaré sagged with disappointment. "I was hoping it was just me." Cesaré had a bond with Lily and had tried too. "The Magi must have placed ward charms around the castle, making all psychic links useless."

Dante understood. Cesaré knew his cousin, Malleven; they had been brought up together. The Florianna were the mystics of the race, and, with his Magi training, Malleven was a master magician.

Whichever way he twisted and turned it in his head, it always came back to the same thing. The sisters would not be permitted to renew their bonds. He, Cesaré and Keenan would be cast adrift to weaken and eventually die. "We need to speak to Vionne urgently," he said. They all needed some of Jay's medication to live without a bond, before it was too late and they became useless. Malleven had the woman Dante loved more than life itself and his five children. *Where the hell was Jay?*

Dubonnetti Estate, Ireland

Jay didn't go to bed at all that night. Ruby, his wife, had given up and left him closeted in the study with Christian Dubonnetti, the head of the Dubonnetti royal family.

Jay had virtually been brought up by the man since he was a small boy, with Dante, as brothers—although, Jay had never called him father. Throughout their childhood, he'd told them stories over and over of Atlantis and the five Sirens that all the princes needed in their race to become king.

Dante had been drunk most of the time, maintaining it was all a crock of shite. Jay simply listened. He knew his place as the tag-a-long of the family. Although when Dante referred to Christian as being mad, he'd had to go along with him on that—particularly as Christian beat Dante unmercifully.

In a cruel twist of fate, just as Dante had got the crown, Christian had disowned him for not being his biological son and adopted Jay, now professing Jay was. He still couldn't fully believe the sly old bastard was his father, although he was the only one he'd ever really known.

Christian had a connection to his mother, considering her some sort of psychic. Whatever happened between them, Jay would never have believed he was half Atlantean. He still didn't really. There were so many unanswered questions.

"We must make a plan, Jay, and tread very carefully if you're to take the kingdom," Christian said, dragging him from his thoughts.

"You invited me here to keep me away from the castle, didn't you." Jay said, flatly, trying to keep the anger from his voice. He should have been there to support Dante. He couldn't even entertain the thoughts of Tia and the children that boiled aggressively at the edges of his mind the whole time.

Christian put up his hands, placating him, and conceded with a nod. "I did. I admit it. But don't you see? You have to be completely unsullied by the events of today. You have to be nothing to do with it."

Jay's heart dropped into his stomach and he immediately went to walk to the door.

"Wait, Jay! He's already gone."

Jay whirled around in abject terror. Christian, immediately reading the murderous look on his face, quickly put his hands up and madly backtracked. "Banished. I promise you."

"You know this for sure?" Jay's mind was already racing to Tia and the children and how he would get them out.

"Antonio is there … Listen, Jay. Slow down and think," Christian said, regaining control of the conversation. "There is nothing that can be done here but regroup."

Jay shot him a scathing look. "My son is there and my—" He didn't say her name. The satisfied look on Christian's face said he knew exactly who he meant. "Friends," he amended. "I can't just stand idly by."

Christian was smiling now and came a bit closer. "That is why the only sure way you can guarantee their safety is by taking the crown for yourself." He finished by laying his hand on Jay's forearm.

Jay looked down at the long, elderly fingers and the Dubonnetti crest ring. He was right. Atlantean politics were complicated and there were several plays at work here. First, he must establish that Tia and the children were safe and then take a leaf out of Christian's book and use him to his advantage. He didn't like what Christian was suggesting, because he had no doubt that Dante was the true and rightful king. And, despite his shaky start, he was a good king. However, that wasn't what Christian wanted to hear. "You already have four other legitimate sons," Jay reminded him.

But he knew as he said it that it would immediately be brushed away with a watertight argument: "No one that anyone would follow."

He stared into the old man's face and wondered at the extent of what was going on in his mind. He was right, of course. Antonio was aligned to Malleven, Paulo too weak and Stephan too young. His hackles rose at the thought of

Marco. He would kill him himself before anyone ever backed him. The guy was a snake.

He couldn't help feeling that Christian's wish to champion him was rooted in so much more. Like spite at Dante for being the only one worthy, vengeance at Delissi for fathering him or some narcissistic need to win it for himself. Whatever the reason, he had no choice if he wanted to help Dante.

Malleven had a reputation as a wily, ruthless bastard. It was earned by the way he single-mindedly went after the things he wanted and always managed to remain in the shadows until it was too late. He wouldn't have pulled any of that off by being stupid. And now Tia and the children were in a man like that's care. A rare flash of panic threatened to bubble up from his gut. Jay flattened it fast, as he often did where Tia was concerned.

His lapse in control was unseen by Christian as he breathed through it and relied on his natural ability to deal in cold, hard facts. "What do you suggest we do?"

Christian straightened and perked up immediately, as if he was expecting much more of an argument. He walked briskly to the well-stocked sideboard to pour them both a whisky, neat. Christian would judge him by his own standards and assume he wanted the crown for himself, with him merrily pulling the strings in the background, no doubt. *Let him think on.*

He passed him a glass. "We need to get you inside the castle. You are a Santalini, which gives you the right to be there as a guard. Then you will be able to seek out Tia and find out how well they are being treated."

Jay nodded. It was a good plan. "Does this guy have much support?" He doubted that very much. He didn't want to waste time and wanted to move quickly to get Tia and the children out.

Christian shook his head and went back to sit behind the desk. He threw back the contents of the lead crystal glass and smiled tightly as the burning liquid went down. "You haven't had many dealings with Malleven, have you?"

Jay shrugged. He knew all he needed to know. He'd heard the rumors and knew he was a clever bastard.

"Well, I can tell you that I've never met anyone his age with so much power and presence. It's unnerving. He is ruthless and he will stop at nothing to get what he wants. The Orb requires the king to have five Sirens with him out of love and respect. I can guarantee you that isn't the case here. And yet look where he now sits."

Jay slowly paced the room while he absorbed what Christian said. That was something Dante inherently had. The Sirens all had a great regard for him, even as crazy as he was. "OK. I'll need to stay here for a while."

Christian smiled like he expected nothing else. "Your old room has been made up for you."

Jay stopped pacing and shook his head. "No, if I'm going to do this, I'm going to have to get close to Tia. I can't be around Ruby while I do that." It was more than guilt out of disloyalty; it was the blood that sung to him in Ruby's veins. He had a blood habit, one that he desperately needed to break. Tia had only just renewed their bond to help him and he felt the strongest he'd been in a long while. He didn't want to put himself in the way of temptation by sharing a bed with Ruby.

Christen nodded slowly. "Wise … Maybe I can find a use for her to get her out of the way."

Jay looked into Christian's crafty face. He wasn't sure what he was up to, he didn't want to know. If he could keep her away from him then he could focus on what he needed to do. He had to admit, a huge part of him relished it; the chance to do something, the chance to be close to Tia.

He took a deep breath. He was actually doing this. He was young and had already carved out a formidable business portfolio. He just had to think of it as a hostile takeover. One that he would flip and resell as soon as he had it. It was a better pill to swallow than stealing the wife and the kingdom from his best friend. Christian's words of the Darkly Begotten prophecy echoed through his mind.

Ballygowan Castle, Ireland

Malleven's limbs felt like lead weights and his head ached behind the eyes. He showered, put on a loose robe and flopped back onto the wrought-iron bed. Dante really had made a superb master bedchamber out of the subterranean catacomb. The neon-green water gently lapped the beach of yellow sand with only the wrought-iron four poster bed to disturb it. Flaming torches flickered in small alcoves carved into the rock, creating the perfect ambient light.

He took a moment to savor his achievement. He'd come from the poorest branch of the Florianna royal family, worked hard, graduated Cambridge with honors and been inducted into the Magi mystical brotherhood at a very young age. Now he'd become King of the Atlantean nation and had the choice of five beautiful Sirens to serve his every need. Life was good. He deserved to wallow in his victory for a while. He knew he needed to prepare for the return of his ancestors. All the star signs and prophecies were pointing to it being very soon. But just for now, he would enjoy the spoils of his lifelong battle.

He felt the instant he wasn't alone. Tia and Lacy hovered at the entrance to the cave. "Approach. Don't be afraid," Malleven said.

There was no other furniture in the room, so he gestured for them to sit on either side of the end of the bed. He sat back against the pillows and watched, amused at them perching uncomfortably. "Welcome." He studied them closely. They were both very beautiful. However, apart from the similar build and perfect facial features, they couldn't be more opposite in coloring and character.

Tia shifted impatiently, no doubt desperate to see her son, whereas Lacy looked sloe-eyed and still in his thrall. Sadness shrouded Tia, subduing her usually spirited nature. Perhaps she was remembering times spent here with the former king.

"You made a wise choice today, Tia," he said softly to draw her out.

She didn't appear to be listening as she began to fidget and look around her. "Where is my son?" Her chest rose and fell noticeably and her frown deepened.

"He's with the nanny. She's putting him to bed with the others."

Tia scowled at him, clearly trying to work out whether she believed him or not.

"I can assure you he went back to his siblings quite happily." The truth of that still surprised him. It had been disconcerting how calm the boy was in his company. "Life in the nursery is unchanged," he added, seeing her mind immediately switch to the other children.

She absorbed what he'd said for a moment. "I only chose you today so my sisters weren't alone," she said, looking him directly in the eye to wound him.

Malleven bowed his head. "And that is admirable. But that tells me a lot about you; that despite your sisters' strength, they look to you for guidance." When she didn't reply, he added, "I hope, in time, you will look on me more kindly." It surprised him that he genuinely thought that. He'd always thought he'd want to crush this one as she was so wayward. Then he looked at Lacy, confused and looking between them. "Both of you."

"I love Dante, and she loves Keenan," Tia blurted.

Malleven smiled at her ruefully. "As you do his best friend, and brother, Jay, do you not?"

Her face dropped and, for a moment, he didn't know what she would do. His pulse kicked with excitement as he waited for her famous temper to rear its head, but she seemed to get a hold on it and he was left disappointed.

"What do you want?" she said in the end, resigned, as if the fight had gone out of her.

He studied her a moment longer, a little surprised by her reaction. "It is my aim to get to know you all better. After all, you will be pledged to me shortly."

Tia cast a furtive look across at Lacy, who looked back at her, alarmed. "I don't think my sister can cope with this at the moment. You did something to her when you kidnapped her," she said, glaring at him, bobbing her head in Lacy's direction. "Isla's terrified of you and Phoebe is grieving. The only one OK is Lily, and she's not exactly bright, that one."

Malleven laughed. He was enjoying himself with this Siren, and what she said was true. Then he became serious. "Events cannot be undone." He smiled, turning to Lacy and waving his arm. "A simple glamour spell was all. It's completely gone; she'll be fine."

He took a deep breath and looked directly at Tia again. "I like you, Tia. So I'll make a bargain with you. I'll release your sister to her bedchamber, if you agree to spend some time here with me alone."

Tia stared at him and Lacy hitched a breath. "No, Tia, don't. You don't have to do that."

Malleven grinned. "Or you can both stay, it's up to you."

Tia looked over at Lacy, who was watching her anxiously. "You don't have to," Lacy said again.

Tia switched to projected speech. *He controls us all, Lace. Let me just suss him out. I'll come and find you later and we'll work out a plan. I need you to make sure JJ's OK. God knows what damage it's doing to him, being with him all this time. I haven't seen any of the kids since this afternoon.* She fought to keep the tension out of her body. Malleven was clever at reading people and she didn't want to give away her desperation any more than she had already.

Lacy sighed and shook her head, defeated. "I'll go and check on the kids. I don't trust this guy," she said, giving Malleven one last dirty look as she slid off the bed and stood up.

Tia let out a ragged breath and watched her trudge across the soft sand to the corridor that led to the lift. At least she'd have trusted eyes on the kids.

When she turned her attention back to Malleven, he was watching her closely. "Thank you," he said.

The nicer he was, the more he unnerved her. She expected him to throw his weight around. With a single derisive breath, she said, "What for? I haven't done anything yet." She studied him. He was outrageously good-looking in a dark, clean-cut kind of way. He had warm brown skin and the bluest-black hair she'd ever seen, sharply cut so a hair never looked out of place. He was tall and lean but filled out his clothes in all the right places. Even tonight, when all he had on was one of those long Middle Eastern robes and his perfectly manicured feet were crossed at the ankle in front of her.

His grin widened as if he followed her train of thought and enjoyed her evaluating him. "Relax," he said, eventually. His voice was deep and sounded very sexy with his Italian accent. "I won't force you to do anything you don't want to do."

"No, sure you won't. I've heard of your hocus pocus crap."

He laughed loudly then. Tia couldn't help thinking just how good-looking he was. She had to mentally slap herself and remember that all Atlantean men were gorgeous. And he did kidnap two of her sisters. "You still haven't told me what you want."

He relaxed back and eyed her shrewdly. "Let's talk. That's all. I have one other person to see this night." He put his hands up in front of him in surrender. "I would like to get to know you."

Tia shrugged and flopped down across the foot of the bed, holding her head up on an elbow. She was determined not to give in and chat with him like they were best buddies. She rolled onto her stomach and rested her chin on her folded arms. All the while he silently waited. "So who do you love the most out of your two men?" he asked eventually.

She was shocked at his directness and lifted her head up, glaring at him from the nest of her arms.

"Come, you can tell me."

The familiar guilt pierced the center of her chest and she frowned, slowly sat up and crossed her legs. She was no longer comfortable lying down with a question like that. She shrugged moodily. It was none of his business, but it was creepy how he seemed to know the heart of her. "I could never choose," she said, picking at a loose thread on her jeans. "That's always been the problem."

She glanced at him and he seemed to be thinking deeply about what she'd said. "But you were destined for the former king and because of that you couldn't leave him?"

He was asking her stuff she barely asked herself and refused to dwell on. It irritated her. "But I did, frequently."

He laughed. "So you did." He narrowed his eyes in that calculating way she was beginning to recognize. "So if it weren't for fate, you would have remained happily with Jay Gardiner?"

That was the oversimplification of the century. "You make it sound like it was up to me." She couldn't help remembering how happy she'd been with Jay right at the beginning, but it felt like a lifetime ago and it had been the closeness that had made him pull apart. He was a frozen land that thawed only rarely, with hidden hot springs that pulled you in for warmth and the search to find them would captivate her for ever.

Then there was unpredictable and passionate Dante. He'd been wild and spoilt, but had channelled an unrivalled determination into being with her and the children and, above all, learning to be a good king. And still, he always felt second best to Jay. That made her angry for him even now. "I love Dante. I've had four children with him."

Malleven bobbed his head in agreement. "And one with Jay. The one I take a shine to. Some might say that should be impossible with a Human?"

He was annoying her now. "Look, I don't know what you're trying to say, but we are bound, the three of us. I care for them both, but we're trapped together. To separate would make us ill." Then the horrible thought hit her. "We all have bonds." She thought of her sister Lacy, and Keenan being carried out. "All of us," she said, thinking of the implications it had for all of them. Her heart sank when she saw quite clearly that he knew exactly what she was talking about. "It affects us as badly as the men, you know. If we don't replenish the bonds, we get ill as well," she said, trying to salvage the turn the conversation was taking.

Malleven was listening, but he didn't look very perturbed by it. "I believe the Murrs have certain medications for this?"

So far, only Jay had used them. She was hoping Malleven hadn't found out about it or even the need for them. Her heart sank further. She guessed a guy capable of taking a fully fledged kingdom would have done his homework—particularly if he didn't want them to have contact with bonded mates. She was becoming more convinced that was what he intended to do. Even though some of them had their partners at the moment, it wouldn't be for long.

"That isn't what I brought you here to talk about. In order for the kingdom to be successful, you will all need to pledge to me. I have Lily and Phoebe; I just need the remaining three of you. Then I hope we can all live in peace at the castle."

She shouldn't have been surprised that was what he wanted. It was what all the princes bloody wanted; to be a strong king. "What about the return? Won't that put a downer on us all living in peace and harmony?" she said, not able to keep the snipe out of her voice.

Malleven tilted his head as if she'd made a very valid point. "All the more reason for us to find a way to work together, is it not?"

Tia studied his face. He was right, of course, but the more she got to know him the more she knew he wouldn't let any of them keep the freedoms they once had—especially her. Life was about to get intolerable. Dante always understood how much she needed freedom. Her heart twisted at the thought of Dante and tears brimmed in her eyes. She had no idea where he was and whether he was even safe.

Malleven didn't miss her emotion. He seemed very tuned into her, even without a bond. She wiped away her tears with her fingers and tried to get a hold on herself so he didn't think she was weak. "So how's it going to be, then?" She found she couldn't look at him. "Will you take a wife?"

He didn't answer right away, which finally made her look at him. He was studying her closely as if he found her interesting. "I have a wife—Lily," he said, as if she should already know that. She did, but she never thought of Lily with anyone other than Lance. Then, "As king, I will marry you all."

CHAPTER 3

ashington, DC

The Duke Ormond Delissi, ambassador for the Atlantean nation, was led into the president's private sanctum. Two Secret Service officers moved to the hallway, leaving just one at the edge of the room. The president was sitting in his black leather winged-back swivel chair, behind his large mahogany desk. He seemed to have aged since they last met, with dark circles around his eyes and more grey hair at his temples.

He held out an arm to indicate to Delissi to sit in the chair opposite him. The atmosphere felt stiff and awkward this time instead of their usual informality in each other's company.

Delissi sat in silence and waited. The president sat forward and stared at him for a full minute before he spoke, as if the answer was hidden somehow in his face.

"One thousand, four hundred and fifty-two!" the president said.

Delissi said nothing. He knew this meeting would not be an easy one. Despite US troops attempting to take

Murrtaine, he had a great respect for the man, often spending time teaching him Atlantean ways so he had a better understanding of them.

It had been the president himself who had warned him that the discovery of Murrtaine was imminent. A religious sect known as the Scythians had tipped them off with the exact coordinates of their underwater city.

"That is the exact number of American and Allied personnel who died in the mid-Atlantic," the president said.

"Nine thousand, three hundred and sixty," Delissi replied. "Is the number of Borge pure-blooded men, women and children that inhabited Murrtaine, now just a layer of crystalline dust on the seabed."

The president sat back in his chair and absorbed what he'd said as if the air had been knocked out of him. "They perished?"

Delissi left it a moment before he answered. It would have been an easy thing to lie and let the leader of the free world believe the inhabitants had been destroyed along with the city, but that would mean the kingdom would disband as there would only be four royal families. The reality was that the return was a very real threat and the president needed to be aware of it. "Thanks to you, only one person died. A brave young man, Drew Stone, who volunteered to stay behind."

For a moment, the president seemed overcome with emotion. "The people are safe?"

Delissi nodded slowly. "For now."

The president put his hand to his forehead. "And your power source?"

Delissi didn't tell him that if she had been destroyed, the Earth would have been plunged into events so catastrophic it would probably have been knocked off its axis and life on this planet would cease. "It was the Orb herself who destroyed the city so no secrets could be found. She has chosen her next resting place. It will be blessed and a great people will grow from it."

"You always refer to it as a she," the president said, smiling.

Delissi simply bowed his head.

The president continued to study him. "Thank you for your honesty," he said, eventually. "I knew casualties could not be avoided."

"There is more I wish to impart to you, but first it must be with the condition that you tell me all you know of the religious order you made the deal with in exchange for the coordinates."

The president summed him up for a moment and then nodded. "The Agency has been investigating them since they first made contact."

"You have their location?" Delissi said, sitting up straighter.

The president hesitated before answering.

"This is a far-reaching organization with hands in every strata of power, who solely exist for the eradication of the Atlantean nation," Delissi said. "I don't need to remind you of the danger that poses for both our peoples."

The president relaxed back into his chair. "I will give you the location of every cell of the Scythians—including their headquarters—if you give me the new location of Murrtaine."

"Impossible!" Delissi said immediately, swiping the comment away with a hand. It was unthinkable. It had only ever remained safe through the centuries because the humans had no idea where it was.

"I give you my word that no harm shall come to that city."

"You don't understand. It is Atlas that governs the secrecy of Murrtaine in order to guard its purity."

"And where is Atlas? Are they here?" the president said,

cleverly steering the conversation to another vital piece of information he needed.

Delissi let out a deep breath, bowed his head and prepared himself to deliver the information that was the reason for his visit. "The king has been deposed, Mr President. There is a new king that holds all five Sirens who will be pledged to him any day now. So I will say to you something I haven't said to my own people yet, and that is that I believe Atlas is already here. I think they are watching … waiting for an appointed time." The truth was he had no idea when Atlas would come to Earth, but he needed the upper hand in this situation. He would not give the Humans Murrtaine and he needed the Scythians wiped off the face of the Earth.

The president was clearly in shock. "This happened recently?"

"It happened immediately after the destruction of Murrtaine."

"And this kingdom will hold?"

Now he was getting the picture. He was well versed in Atlantean history and prophecy. He himself had seen to it. Each previous kingdom had been precarious and eventually fallen. The only hope for them all was stability—Human and Atlantean. "I believe that it will. He is a strong and driven male and has all five Sirens. That has never happened before. A strong kingdom is better than a weak one when Atlas returns." He thought momentarily of his son and all he had done to make a good and fair government for all. The president was studying him and he wondered whether he saw the regret in his expression.

The president rubbed his face wearily and let out a deep sigh. "So it's finally happening." He looked Delissi in the eye and straightened in his chair as if his resolve was strengthened. "Will you work with me to meet this king and help me to give a good and fair account of ourselves with the Atlasians?"

Delissi bowed his head. It was the sole reason he had come to Washington, DC and built a relationship with this man. The president was in an impossible position with billions of lives in his hands. "I give you my word."

The president reached down into a drawer of his desk and brought out a brown envelope. He pushed it across the table towards him. "Everything we have on the Scythians is in there. They have camps just outside London, Berlin, Paris, Budapest, New York, Salt Lake City and the headquarters in Washington State, in which I believe you will be most interested."

Delissi picked up the envelope, opened his briefcase and, without looking at its contents, pushed it inside. "Thank you, Mr President. I will personally convey to the new king your valuable help in the matter.'

The president smiled and bowed his head. They shook hands and Delissi left wondering how King Malleven would deal with the first real task of his reign.

Full memory returned to Drew the moment he was aware of the salt stinging his eyes, gravel biting into his knees and the white water crashing over him. *Murrtaine. The Orb. The destruction.* He turned over onto his back, spat the bitter water and looked up at the stormy sky. He could barely swallow for thirst and his head hurt too much for him to be dead. Somehow he'd survived the blast, or, more precisely, the Orb had saved him. The question was, where the hell had she spat him out?

He rolled back over onto his knees in an attempt to get up and hissed with the pain. Blood seeped into the water in tiny wisps, mingling with his long hair, inhibiting his movement.

He struggled to his feet, almost stumbling over, and tried to get his bearings. It was no use; he didn't have a clue where he was. The rugged beach was almost deserted; just a line fisherman and a dogwalker in the distance. He remembered where he was the last time he dressed and glanced down at the shimmering gauze that barely covered the lower half of his body. He had to get out of sight before someone saw him. He staggered up the craggy beach and when it flattened out to grass, he tripped into a jog. He needed water, food and shelter, urgently, and some time to rest and think. He could die of exposure out here.

He came to a line of cabins. A couple had washing out, which he jogged through and stole a change of clothes. Track pants and a navy-blue t-shirt; he hurriedly put them on. Then he guzzled water from a garden tap and jogged on until he found a cabin a little more closed up than the others.

Memories came back in sudden flashes of déjà vu. Covert ops, survival tactics, everything he'd learned at the Scythian camp to prepare him that had been lost before. He scouted the building, and, when satisfied that it was an empty holiday let, climbed up, removed the gauze screen and dove in head-first through a pantry window.

His landing wasn't pretty, but it made very little noise. In just a few moments he'd checked the rooms, was satisfied he was alone and was rifling through the kitchen cupboards. An envelope in a drawer revealed he was in Maine, which was mind-blowing when he contemplated the explosion in the middle of the Atlantic. The distance he'd covered was staggering. He was lucky to be alive.

He soon had a coffee pot on the stove, opened a can of beans and felt human again.

He'd lie low just long enough to build up his strength and process what he remembered. Everything made sense now. He hadn't realized just how many gaps had been in his memory before. All he'd known was that he'd played in his band, met Phoebe and entered the fantastic, unbelievable world of the Atlanteans. Then he'd discovered he'd been a plant by the Scythians, with a tracking device in his leg that had led to the destruction of Murrtaine. He couldn't risk Phoebe getting hurt because of him and so he'd volunteered to stay behind. He'd met the Orb and she'd confirmed what they suspected. That Phoebe had changed him; changed his DNA into something like her. It was laughable because the Scythians had spent so much time and effort training him and had hand-picked him because of his one hundred percent human DNA. They'd drilled and trained him into a fighting machine that, coupled with his new strengths, made him more of a threat than ever. Now his job was to turn that threat on them. Then he was free to go back to Phoebe, get her away from the big Murr and hope she would still have him.

Drew left the cabin after the third day. With his memory restored, he had the operatives' PIN the Scythians had given him, meaning he could now draw cash, buy clothes, supplies for the journey and a car. It would alert the Scythians to him, but he didn't care. They would think they could control him as they'd always done, but things were different now. Thanks to Phoebe, they would have no clue what they were dealing with.

As he drove across the country towards Washington State, craggy shores gave way to pine-lined highways and then the burnt copper trees of new England. Green snow-capped mountains, stunning pastures, plains and lakes followed until he reached the familiar fir trees shrouded in the fine mist of his childhood.

At one time he would have associated it with the comfort of home. When he wore blinkers. Now all he felt was the weight of the camp. The dark-green forest, dotted with glacier waterfalls, echoed with a bone-deep sadness at the loss of his youth. Nostalgia was replaced with anger, at the life of exhaustion and fear he could never show or else it was beaten out of him. There were scores to be settled on this trip.

Throughout the long drive, he'd mulled over all that had happened since he'd left and what he needed to do now he was back. The tracking device that had led the humans to destroy Murrtaine was still in his leg, so he had to assume they knew he was coming. He'd have to pretend he was still their man while he formulated his plan to destroy them. They had other camps that would need to go as well, but he needed to get a message to Phoebe first. She would be thinking he was dead and the big Murr would swoop in and take the advantage.

After two days of solid driving with only short stops in country towns, he reached the barrier to the Scythian compound on the outskirts of North Cascades national park, near the aptly named Diablo lake. He stopped at the barrier and wound down his window. The guy in the box looked him in the eye. "Two three six five coming in," Drew said, remembering his operative number perfectly. There were no names at the camp. Every boy was given a number to take away the importance of self.

The guy picked up a handset and talked into it. Then he nodded and the barrier came up. "Go straight to the office."

Drew drove the length of the shingle drive to the building he remembered with a stomach-churning feeling of dread. The bleak cabins came into view, parade ground just visible behind it, where he'd been drilled and trained.

Two cadets approached as soon as he pulled up. They were around twelve or thirteen, the age he was when he was sent out into the world. They had the same dead look in their eyes; that they had no will of their own and had seen every kind of atrocity, things no one of their age should see. Drew recognized it because he'd lived it. He'd been dead inside once too. They told him to follow, then took him inside the main building to where the warden's office was located. Boy A knocked on the door, then they marched away. The door opened. He recognized Seville, the principal monk, straight away. The man who'd singled him out and made his existence more miserable than it already was.

He'd changed little. Maybe a few more bags under the eyes and a little more gray, but he was still the same wiry man with slicked-back dark hair. He looked scholarly in his robes, but Drew knew the tattooed, lean, muscular arms underneath, because he remembered them being exposed when he'd caned him. This was the guy who'd taken it upon himself to make him his special project. The one he would kill before he left.

Drew averted his eyes before he betrayed his contempt and stepped into the room. Another, familiar, man was with him and introduced himself as Croll. It took a moment to place him, but the buzz-cut head and the huge muscular frame were hard to forget. There was nothing meek about these monks. They were all about aggression. Croll had been higher up and more of a decision maker, so he'd had little to do with him personally. However he'd been fully aware of the tortuous regime.

Drew bowed his head and punched his own shoulder with the flat side of his fist in salute. Things were coming back to him naturally, as if it was yesterday.

Seville came forward and gripped the top of his arm. "You survived," he said. "I felt sure the explosion would have killed you."

Drew fought the urge to recoil and looked curiously into the man's face, searching his eyes—eyes that were glassy with emotion. This man had pushed him almost to breaking point relentlessly throughout his miserable childhood and here he was, choked with emotion. It was astonishing that their viewpoints could be so different. He forced a small smile. "I was blown clear. Washed up on a beach. It has taken me this long to get back." Not a lie.

Seville turned his head to Croll, looking on from the back of the room. "You see what an outstanding operative he is? The jewel of our programme," he said, facing him again.

Croll walked forward until he stood almost nose to nose with Drew. They were of similar height, but Croll was much heavier with muscle. It was an action meant to intimidate.

A moment passed where Drew used all his willpower not to rip out his throat. He wanted to bring down the whole organization and liberate the boys before he showed his hand.

"Why did you come back?" Croll asked with narrowed eyes, searching his face with contempt.

Drew fought to keep the pupils of his eyes open. Any extreme emotion and they would narrow to the thin slits of a reptile. For now, he wanted him to believe he was the pure-bred human he was when he'd left this place. "The blast restored my memory. Where else would I go?"

Croll studied him a moment longer for any sign of a lie, then he stepped back. "You will have knowledge useful to us."

"Let him sleep. We will talk in the morning," Seville said, smiling and guiding him to the door. "Come, I will show you to your quarters."

Drew followed him outside, along a shingle path to the line of long wooden huts. It was dark now and the air smelled of damp earth and pine—a smell he associated with fear. He remembered the bare huts crowded with beds squashed in rows. The boys would be confined there at this hour. He tried not to draw attention to the ghostly faces appearing at the window to spy on him and then disappearing as quickly as they came. He didn't want to get them into trouble.

There were fewer faces at the last cabin, the one he remembered housed the older boys. He was struck by one boy who held his gaze longer than most. He couldn't see who it was, only that his look was direct and not scared at all. Seville pointed to the building. "We'll put you in here for now." By the time he looked again, the boy was gone.

They went up the wooden steps to the cabin, which was separated into rooms with four berths in each instead of one long dormitory. It was considered a privilege for being older, but there was still no privacy at all. They had communal cold showers and very few clothes. He was shown to a room that was empty and almost bare, so he knew he had it to himself. He had the choice of two double bunks on either side of the room. He turned a slow circle on the threadbare rug and absorbed the memories. None of them good.

Seville seemed awkward, like there was much he wanted to say. Thankfully, he opted for silence. He simply paused in the doorway before he left. "You are by far my greatest achievement." Then he turned and left him alone.

Drew was left standing looking at the place he'd been. His emotion shocked him; he hadn't expected it. He remembered very little affection from the man. If anything, he had pushed him harder than the other students. It made him convinced he'd done the right thing. Only by coming back here would he achieve true freedom from his past. Without it, the place would for ever be a specter in his mind.

He assessed the sparsely furnished room and grabbed the thin blankets from the spare beds. Memories of poor sleep from nights spent in the bitter cold had plagued his dreams for years. Now he knew they were real.

There was just one more job to do before he slept. He stooped and took out the mobile phone from inside his sock.

They hadn't searched him, but they would be watching and listening closely. He was sure Croll hadn't completely bought his story. He switched it on to check its coverage and swore at the 'No Service'. Wi-Fi would be password protected and the rooms bugged. The monks had always controlled their every move.

He went quickly to the window and was not surprised to find it screwed shut. He took out his car key and worked it loose so he could slip out easily from the single-story building. He ran, crouched low, to the trees on the edge of the parade ground. He found just a single bar of coverage on his phone and prayed the signal would hold to make the call.

He had no numbers to contact anyone except for one he'd managed to Google. It was the main landline to Ballygowan Castle: seat of power of the Atlantean nation, ancestral home to Phoebe's family, the Bonacis and home of the king. He prayed someone he knew would answer. His heart hammered as it rang and rang. He told himself it would take some time for someone to reach the phone if no one was in the king's study, where he knew the phone was situated. However it wasn't Dante who answered.

"Hello!" a familiar voice said. "Alfonzo Bonaci."

"Thank god," Drew whispered.

"Who is this?"

"It's me, Drew."

"Drew? Praise the Orb, we thought you were dead."

Drew looked around him, conscious that he would be heavily watched. "Listen, I don't have much time to explain. All I can say is that the Orb saved me to complete my mission. I'm at the Scythian camp in Washington State. Tell Dante I'm going to destroy it. I will need his help to bring down the whole organization."

There was a beat of silence that made him feel uneasy. "A

lot has happened, Drew. Dante has been deposed. Malleven Mancini is now king."

At first Drew couldn't believe all that had happened in such a short period of time. His heart plummeted and for a single moment he was hopeless with disappointment. The name was familiar, but he couldn't quite place him. "Does he have Phoebe?"

"No, not exactly."

"What, then?"

"Malleven has made a deal with Vionne. She is with him."

His fingers tightened around the phone and his vision went dark. "Where are they? Murrtaine was destroyed."

"The Orb has chosen a new place. They will leave for it soon."

"Where is Dante?" He feared the worse. He was the rightful king and the only one, other than Phoebe, who'd believed in him. He didn't know this Malleven character, but he knew a king wouldn't leave a competitor alive for long.

"He has gone to his safe place with a cousin."

Drew guessed the line was not secure to ask for details. If Alfonzo was loyal to Dante, he wouldn't want to compromise his position.

"OK, can you tell the new king that I am active and I need his help to bring down the Scythians?"

"I will."

"Can you give me a secure phone number so that I can text?"

Alfonzo promised to send that to him.

"OK, I need to get back in case I'm missed. Look out for Phoebe for me."

"Of course."

Drew ended the call and jogged back through the darkness, mind racing. How the hell was he was going to pull this off?

CHAPTER 4

Somewhere orbiting the Earth

The Twenty hadn't moved for three years. The living mechanism they were seated in had monitored their vital signs, kept a perfect temperature, discreetly removed toxins and made sure muscles were electrically stimulated to stop them wasting away. To be interrupted was unprecedented, but, nevertheless, the point the Atlanteans had reached could not be ignored.

The lids to each pod lifted and moved backwards on a whir. Ashaya blinked and looked around at the others all doing the same. Seti was the only one properly awake and looking directly at her. *I will speak in human-like phrases in preparation for what is to come.* Her heart quickened in expectation. It had to be her chosen to go amongst the Atlanteans.

Each of them nodded in response.

Let us examine the many violations, he mentally projected, waving his arm in front of him. Symbols began to appear in a holographic vision.

Blood bonds outside of the Santalini family. Humans included and welcomed into the inner circle. The seat of power destroyed. Blatant disregard of the destined mate system. And the most heinous of all: the tampering with the Fates. Sirens have been coerced to stand with a new king whilst his divining ring is red, disqualifying him from the position. He looked at each of them one by one. *What factors should we judge in this instance?*

They have proved incapable of governing themselves, one of the Twenty said.

The previous king had all Sirens genuinely, Ashaya said. *Despite his faults, he was respected by all, including his enemies. He even initiated a council to consult all families, including the Human hosts, in decision making. I say he is a king worthy of consideration.* When she finished, her eyes went directly to Seti. His aura told her she had answered well, but it was short-lived.

He is no longer king. His subjects have seen to that, he said.

She was immediately crestfallen.

Let us not forget the seriousness of such faults: the very inclusion of humans and blood bonds listed before, Ragnar said.

Seti nodded towards him. *A valid point.*

And who is to say that this new king doesn't have the necessary strength to lead a nation that refuses to be led?

Seti nodded. *The old ways have been flouted, that is true. We must weigh it in the balance.*

Not to be outdone, Ashaya picked up her argument again. *Dante was rightful king by First Breath of a Siren. If the old ways are to be followed, that must be foremost in our minds.*

Seti's aura smiled, but he didn't speak of it to her. *You are all correct, which is why we are twenty, to ensure judgment is swift and just. As soon as the five Sirens are married, we will descend. Then judgment and sentencing will begin.*

He addressed Ashaya directly. "The most important and dangerous matter is the relocation of our pureblood brethren. The

Orb and its people must be settled at all costs. The former Lord Advocate has passed and his son has not secured his Siren. You must go down as our emissary and ensure the relocation goes smoothly. Should anything go wrong, we will be watching and shall intercede immediately. You will have the advantage to watch the deposed king and see how he conducts himself at close quarters. Will he hold composure at the loss of his wife, children and his kingdom? Of that, I am not sure."

Ashaya bowed her head. She was being given an opportunity of a lifetime. It also meant all was not lost for the former regime, which, she had to admit, had become her bias.

The Atlanteans had been of great fascination to her even as a small child and she was being given the chance to live among them. It felt like her destiny. *I will prepare*, she said, and climbed out of her pod, legs stiff from lack of use. She steadied herself and walked awkwardly to her private quarters to pack. The rest of the party were covered again in their pods and returned to watching the events below.

The Islet of Filfla, Malta

Helicopter blades whipped above them and Dante grinned at Cesaré next to him. His spirits had lifted a little as he marveled on the approach to the little flat-topped island. It was just a single rock with sheer sides, no bigger than a football stadium and surrounded by the sea. It felt like he was descending into some kind of film set. The green-covered mountain opened and they slowly hovered down to the perfectly hidden helipad, easily a hundred feet below.

"To all outsiders Filfla is still the bird sanctuary it was before," the prime minister of Malta, Joseph Brincat, said from his seat next to the pilot.

Four helicopters had carried their party from Luqa

Airport, across the small strait from the southern part of the main island. When they had all settled on firm ground, a loud siren sounded, lights came on and the roof closed above them. "It's a supervillain's lair," Dante said, amazed.

"Come," Joseph said. "There was a hidden bunker here and I simply made some modifications. My army has been working on it day and night to get it ready for you. I think you'll like it."

Dante was intrigued. Cesaré and Keenan joined him and together they followed Joseph to a lift that went unsurprisingly downward. "It has catacombs rather like the ones beneath Ballygowan Castle," Joseph said.

"You've been there?" Dante said, surprised.

Joseph shrugged. "A couple of times as a child."

Dante knew he was a cousin of the Dubonnetti family. He was trying to work out by what connection when Joseph cut across his thoughts. "Your mother's sister is my mother."

Something in Dante sighed. It was as if the Fates had come full circle for him again. His enigmatic mother, who'd died when he was a child was still relatively unknown to him. "I should like to meet your mother," he said, his throat surprisingly constricted with emotion.

Joseph smiled. "Of course."

It surprised him just how close a relative the man in front of him was. The man he'd thought was his father had not kept up family connections for them as children. He chuckled. The Maltese people were completely unaware their prime minister was a royal prince from an alien race. He would be a useful ally. He put his hand on his cousin's shoulder. "Thank you for remaining loyal. Some might say you backed the wrong side," he said with a rueful smile.

"I would never follow the duplicitous Florianna charlatan."

Dante laughed, but his eyes strayed to Cesaré in case he took offence. The lift doors opened and the moment passed. He took a step out and the sight before him took his train of thought clean away. Before him was a room—no, a vast cave —to rival the Great Hall at Ballygowan Castle. He forgot all else and walked out onto the great platform. Fifty or more steps went down to the circular room below in three directions, like a pyramid. It was inspired by the Great Hall, but it was so much more. It seemed modern, bigger. No words he could think of fully described it.

For a moment he was overcome with emotion. All the events of the past days and then this. It was too much. If only Tia and the children were here to see it. For there was no doubt it was designed for an Atlantean king.

He became aware of Joseph at his shoulder and looked at him, words lost. "I used an old illustration of the great King Mettsud's palace, taken from his tome of *Atlantis*. I reproduced it to the finest detail. It was rumored to have bordered the north of these islands."

Dante still couldn't speak; just shook his head in wonderment. It certainly came from no human architect. The huge room could easily house two tennis courts with room to spare. It had a window to the sea as did all ancient Atlantean homes, Ballygowan Castle included, but this one followed the cave in a semi-circle. At around thirty feet high, the Orb only knew how they curved a piece of glass that large and that thick.

The fountain and gateway to the sea looked majestic and huge from his vantage point. It was easily three times the size of the castle's, and the water was an iridescent blue. The three tiers of the fountain rivalled the height of the window and the tumbling water more resembled a waterfall.

Large, modern sofas in watercolors of blues and greens were arranged near the great window and huge vines sprouted from the floor up to the ceiling and were interwoven with lights. With the blue light from the window and the small, twinkling stars in the vines, it really looked like an underwater fairyland.

"I haven't furnished it completely. I thought I'd leave the finishing touches to you," Joseph said.

Dante looked at Cesaré and then at Keenan, who looked as awestruck as he did. All previous conversation was forgotten with what was in front of them. "I don't know what to say," he said, pulling Joseph into a tight hug. He only released him when the lift opened and more of their party arrived. They all looked as excited and pleased with their new home as he was.

Joseph shook his hand. "Remember you are the rightful king. Many are still loyal and there are those just watching Malleven. The first mistake and they will flock to your banner."

Dante let out a long breath and nodded. He was more grateful than he'd ever know. "Any news of New Murrtaine?"

"Vionne has been in touch. He will set off in a marine craft when his people leave the catacombs of the castle. There is already seismic activity in the Mediterranean about ten miles west of here. The Orb has settled and begun her work below ground. As soon as the human task force has finished combing the area, the dome will go up. Then the real work will begin, undetected."

Dante thought of the thousands of people making the journey through the Atlantic and then the Mediterranean on their own steam. It would take them several weeks, however good a swimmer they were. "How long will the city take to be built?"

"I believe it will be ready," Joseph said. He turned and shook hands with the last of the men arriving from the lift and got in in their place. "Make yourself at home," he called as the doors shut.

They all descended the steps, marveling at the architecture of their new home. A small army of staff, dressed in black, appeared from behind the steps and asked them to follow them to their rooms.

The scale of the place was astonishing. A tunnel carved behind the staircase took them further beneath the island where a hundred rooms had been fashioned from the yellow sandstone that made up the whole of Malta. He knew it had been a bunker but, still, the work involved was astounding.

Dante admired his room. It was circular in shape and perfectly modern. It differed from the castle; more gothic and older in its decor. This, well its design, reminded him of Murrtaine before its destruction: all minimalist, clean lines in pale pastel colors.

The walls were the exposed yellow stone that he was becoming accustomed to. Huge painting-like sheets hung from them with moving images of the sea. The bed was huge and oval in shape and covered in cream fabric, with long whisper-thin drapes that hung down at its head. It gave it a majestic feel. The bathroom, consisting of a basin, toilet and shower, was hidden by a white opaque screen to the right of the room.

A knock at the door brought him out from behind it. "Come in," he called.

Cesaré came in and closed the door behind him.

"What do you think, Ches?" Dante said, smiling.

"A place befitting a king," Cesaré said, smiling and looking around him. "I have news, Your Highness."

Dante waited for him to walk further into the room before he spoke.

"I have just come from the study. It's been set up as center of communications to New Murrtaine and the outside world. It has a landline."

Dante frowned, sensing Cesaré had something important to say. "What is it?"

"Alfonzo just phoned. Drew is still alive."

CHAPTER 5

Malleven sat behind the large desk in the study of Ballygowan Castle signing an official paper using the seal he now wore on the little finger of his right hand.

"The boy, Drew, lives, sire," Alfonzo said. "He performed a great service for the Atlantean people when Murrtaine was destroyed and now he intends to do the same at the Scythian camp where he now resides. We should support him, Your Highness, and employ a several prong attack to crush them. They must not be allowed to recover and threaten us again."

Malleven pushed the paperwork away from him and sat back in his chair. He'd heard many of the details of what had happened to Murrtaine and the part the boy played. He'd unwittingly drawn the human world straight to them with a homing device embedded into his leg.

He'd admired Dante's decision to sacrifice Drew—an action bound to cause him endless problems with Phoebe, for the good of the nation so the Murrs could escape. The Atlanteans simply couldn't exist without the Murrs. It was a strong, decisive thing to do. It still made him smile. It solved

64

so many problems at once. With Vionne being her true mate, and Drew an interloper, his elimination saved Murrtaine, got rid of a tiresome rival and tied Vionne—the eldest Murr prince, to the crown. It was a tactic after his own heart. However, as amusing as that was, Drew's miraculous survival needed consideration. The boy was still a huge complication with Phoebe, who he'd already promised to Vionne. But Alfonzo was right. The Scythians were a real threat to the kingdom and must be destroyed.

There were also troubling rumors that Drew was a human that had been changed into something unnatural. That, in itself, mattered little to him, but if Phoebe loved him it was his death warrant. She must stay with Vionne to keep the Murrs bound to the crown. However, there was no harm in delaying his demise while he was still useful. "Contact the boy. Tell him that the new king will give him all the help he needs."

Alfonzo bowed, clearly pleased with his answer. It irked Malleven that the old man sought to control him. He was not one who would be molded. However, he was helpful in the handling of the Sirens and so he would allow him to think he was malleable for now.

"The Siren, Phoebe Ray, she is with Vionne?"

"Yes, Your Highness. They are preparing to leave. The catacombs are emptying as we speak."

"Do not tell her about Drew yet. He has dangerous work still to do. I don't want to raise her hopes only to have them dashed again."

Alfonzo bowed his head. "Your Highness is wise."

"And Vionne's brother, Darres?" He would like nothing more than to kill the Murr who Isla loved enough to betray him and leave for dead, but the time was not right. He needed Vionne and couldn't afford the rift it would create.

"He leaves with Vionne, albeit somewhat reluctantly."

Malleven smiled. He could imagine. "Send Isla to my bedchamber. I would have words with my true mate."

Alfonzo looked unsure for a moment, as if he was debating whether to say something. Malleven looked at him with a challenge to say one word, but the old man had the sense to merely bow his head and leave. He too was a wise man.

VIONNE WATCHED the rag-tag line of a once-proud people swimming out in a herd as far as the eye could see. The snake of people, four or five wide, carried their belongings, many in carts that were Human-like barrows that hovered a foot or so above the sea bed. Some carried huge packs on their back with small children on top. Older children excitedly whizzed around on the many small hover machines Phoebe had christened Bubble bikes and whooped with excitement. He smiled at their joy and wished them the best of it while it lasted. Such small conveyances weren't likely to last the journey.

The line of people were disappearing into the distance like a great cattle drive and Vionne was about to turn to go back inside when a group of five or six youngsters zoomed back into view. They came up fast to stand still in front of him, like seasoned bike pros, and sent an aura of greeting to him. What struck him immediately was that they were completely untainted by the human world. They were young and innocent to the harsh world plotting above them. A strong pain gripped his heart at the weight he carried. He simply stared at them and couldn't speak.

One boy, around ten years old, flashed an image of the old palace straight to his mind and hundreds of Murrs bowing their heads. It woke him from his daze and he sent his gratitude back. The boy knew who he was and flashed his images to his friends, who clicked their amazement back like dolphins. They were excited to meet their prince. The young boy ventured closer and beckoned him down to his level. Intrigued, Vionne did as he asked and remained frozen as the boy put his forehead to his. It was the gesture normally reserved for family and close friends. Some might view it as disrespectful from such a lowly boy, but Vionne was deeply touched and emotion rode him so hard he could barely convey what he wanted to say. Instead, he asked the boy's name. He answered with the representation of the imp god, Loki, from their folklore and adopted by human Norse peoples. He was often portrayed as a trickster and it totally suited the little fellow. He would remember the audacity of this one.

Vionne straightened up and, in the language of his people, in images and feelings, he wished them a safe journey. They turned and whizzed off to catch up with their parents and Vionne made a mental note to keep tabs on that young boy. Something about him had resonated deeply within him. Perhaps he reminded him of a happy, carefree childhood with his own brothers. To the boy it was a huge adventure, but he was in far more danger than he'd ever know.

Vionne turned back and gave the last of his orders to his lieutenants. Naomi, the Sirens' mother, had managed to avoid the madness of the castle and remained with her people. She was married to Sebastian Bonaci but was seldom there, preferring to live at the palace in Murrtaine. Malleven had overlooked her and it was fortunate for her to keep her freedom. He tried to convince her to come with them, but she preferred to stay behind to help shepherd his people through their long journey to their new Mediterranean home. She was a woman of worth and he charged his lieutenants with her care.

He, however, must leave to take Darres, Phoebe and a few high-ranking officials, ahead to see the way clear for their arrival. A fleet of small craft would follow, bringing the elderly and infirm. It was going to be an exodus of biblical proportions, taking about four weeks providing there were no problems.

The catacombs are now empty, Lord, his lieutenant projected straight to his mind.

Very well. I will do a final check before we leave. When you've set off, I will go ahead and return to you during the journey to pick up those falling behind.

The lieutenant bowed and left him.

The catacombs were a dangerous maze of caves beneath the castle, many below sea level. Vionne went from chamber to chamber wondering whether he could pull off moving ten thousand people, sixteen hundred miles, without being detected and without losing a single soul. The enormity gripped his heart whenever he thought of it.

He kept going until he reached the spiral stone staircase that led up to the dungeon level of the castle. It was small and built as an escape route many centuries ago. He and his brothers preferred the route that took them through the fountain straight into the Great Hall and rarely came this way.

Satisfied the area was empty, he was about to turn when he caught sight of a small boy coming down the staircase. He was looking up as if checking he wasn't being followed. Vionne recognized him straight away. *Prince JJ. Where are you going? Everyone has gone.*

The boy looked disappointed. "Can I come with you?"

Vionne smiled effortlessly now, in the way he'd learned from the Atlanteans and sat on a rock next to the boy. *We have a long journey to make to settle my people into their new home. Why don't you go back up? It's dangerous down here. There are many pools you could fall into in the dark.*

The little boy nodded, his blond hair falling into his

strangely luminescent eyes. A handsome little fellow, he looked no more than five or six Human years old—considerably smaller than his more full-blooded siblings. "I just need to go somewhere first," he said.

And where might that be, young man? Vionne thought him such a strange little boy. It was as though he saw so much more in the world than anyone else.

"I have to go to the place I dreamed about. The voices won't let me sleep until I find it. They promised there was something there meant for me."

It was an alarming thing for such a young boy to say. Vionne looked back the way he came. They would be waiting for him, eager to be off, but he couldn't leave the boy alone. *Can I come? I should like to see such a thing.*

The boy appeared to think about it. "OK," he said with a nod. "They didn't say no one else could see it, only that no one else could touch it."

Vionne grinned. A little politician already. *Shall we go?* he said, holding out his arm. *I would like to get you back before you're missed. Lord Malleven might not be so understanding.*

The strange little boy dismissed it with a wave of his hand and smiled absently. He was already walking off towards a tunnel when he said, "I wouldn't worry about it. He won't be here for long. When I find my treasure, no one—not even the new king—can tell me what to do."

His confidence was amusing, although it was a little disturbing for such a young child to speak like that. All he could do was follow him along, holding his shoulder, ready to grab him should he fall. He pulled a lighted torch from a wall holder as they began to get further apart and went through cave after cave. He steered him past sheer drops and pools that could have taken and swallowed a little boy. *You know where you're going?* he asked a few times.

Eventually they slipped sideways through a crevasse, the

boy finding it much easier than him. Then they went downwards, following natural steps in the rock. Vionne held the torch out further so they could see if the rock dropped off in front of them.

They finally reached the bottom of a cave with a large pool in the center, about three meters across. He halted the boy's progress by the shoulder. There was a strange green light below the water's surface. He didn't like the feel of it. There was no natural reason for the light to be there.

"We need to go in," the boy said, looking up at him. "My power is in there," he said, pointing towards the pool.

Vionne frowned, but he was intrigued and relaxed his hold. *Very well then, stay close to me.*

JJ nodded and slipped into the pool with Vionne closely following. He watched the boy open his lungs and they both dove down. It was disorientating, as the deeper they went the brighter the light got. They came out into another cave. Vionne swore they had not changed direction and yet it was filled with air. He climbed out and sat on the edge, pulling little JJ up with him. The cave was bathed in a green light which bounced off the walls that appeared to be covered in gems. The light was coming from a single large crystal in the floor. The boy went to move towards it, but Vionne held him back.

"It's OK. It won't hurt me. I dreamed about it."

Vionne reluctantly released his hold. The boy went closer and put his hand out to the crystal. There was a loud rumble and Vionne pulled back to escape, fearing the roof falling in, but JJ said, "The voices say you must hit the wall there." He was pointing directly at the wall in front of him where a crack had appeared.

Vionne climbed to his feet, picked up a large bolder and hit the wall twice. Two large pieces of rock fell away leaving a hole. Vionne went closer when the dust settled and saw a small chest. He went to reach for it, but the boy called, "Stop! Only I must touch it."

He turned. If it weren't for the boy's strange look of concentration, he would have ignored him. Instead, he stood aside figuring little harm could come to him.

JJ approached and Vionne lifted him to reach, but it was too heavy and JJ let it fall to the floor. It was the size of a large loaf of bread and opened on impact. Two large bangle-like rings now lay on the cave dirt. They were about three inches in length and not completely joined, ready to squeeze onto a small wrist. The gold was bright and gleaming and covered in familiar symbols, carved into its surface. They were the encryptions of Atlas, warning of destruction.

He went to move closer, but the boy threw up an arm to stop him. "No, Lord Vionne. They are for me alone."

The boy's assertiveness brought Vionne up sharp. He remained still while the boy put out his arms towards the bracelets. He wanted to snatch him away before he touched them, but, before he had the chance, the rings jumped as if snapped to a magnet and attached themselves around the boy's wrists. JJ yelped.

Vionne immediately dropped down to pull them off, but they refused to move. He turned the boys' arms to see the underside, only to find the rings welded shut. They were soon too hot to touch. *Are they burning you?* he projected in panic. It was as though they were joined to his skin.

JJ put his hand over his. "Please stop, Vionne. It's OK. They're mine. They've been waiting for me to find them."

Vionne stared into the boy's eyes while his words faded away. They seemed to hold a strange light, making them an even brighter aquamarine than usual.

"You must go now. You have people waiting for you."

Vionne didn't know what to do. He wanted to take the

boy with him, to protect him, but something in his eyes seemed so old, so ancient.

"And I must look after my family."

He was right. No good would come of him taking him away. Instead, he insisted on leading him back through the catacombs to the stairway where they'd started. His brain whirred with thoughts about the boy and how, even though he was small, he was going to be crucial to events to come.

The boy began to climb the steps and paused. "Can you tell Dante not to worry about me? He must work for the kingdom there and I must work for the kingdom here. There can be only one winner."

It left Vionne confused. He wasn't entirely sure what he meant. In the end all he could do was bow and promise that he would. *Who are you, little man?* he asked, straightening up to his full height with a grin.

The boy looked ahead of him as if he was looking at someone there. Then he continued to climb the steps. "I am darkly begotten, Lord. Do not ask me again."

CHAPTER 6

Isla stood on the beach of Malleven's subterranean bed chamber looking out at the water. She couldn't stop herself from shaking. She'd told Darres not to fight Malleven's order to go with Vionne as she didn't want him harmed. He'd reluctantly agreed as he knew she could protect herself—having once been a government assassin. She hadn't admitted that she had no defenses against the mate's pull that Malleven exuded in spades. It always beat her down until she was a quivering ball of want just waiting for his touch. Now she stood under Malleven's evil gaze as weak as reed grass, buffeted on the wind.

Malleven approached until he was breathing down her neck. He knew how her body reacted to him and she waited for her pulse to render her useless.

Nothing happened.

"I'm going to enjoy keeping you in a constant state of erotic agony," Malleven said, running a finger from her temple to her jaw.

Absolutely nothing physically happened.

The deep loathing she had for the man remained as sharp

as a hunter's knife and just as deadly. Her eyes traced down his arm to his divining ring on his left hand, but it wasn't there.

She wondered whether he felt it too or just read her preoccupation. "What?" he said.

Perhaps the rumors had been true. "I would like to see the color of your ring?"

She watched as realization and then a deep anger crept across his features. He could barely contain it. "Why?" he said, ominously low.

"It's been a long time."

He narrowed his eyes as if he dared her to continue, but, instead of making her wither, she felt stronger by the minute. "It's true," she whispered. "I'm free."

His eyes widened and his nostrils flared. Without saying a word, he went to turn, but, instead of walking away, he whipped around and backhanded her across the face with the full force of his weight. It happened so fast; she had no time to react. She was knocked several feet onto the sand.

He marched until he stood over her. "You think I need you? Look how weak you are at my feet. You are nothing!" he spat.

Isla scrambled upright and glared back at him. "I am not one anymore. I am five. You think you're strong, but you are alone. A king by his very nature must join us together, making us invincible. And for you, that will be your undoing."

Malleven lost all control, kicking her down and going to stamp on her. But she was too quick, rolling away and onto her feet, bolting for the doorway before he could get himself together enough to stop her. All he could do was shout after her, "Your Murr is as good as dead. I myself will see to it!"

She didn't stop to answer, running all the way to her bedchamber.

. . .

"RIGHT ... GRAB THAT END," Tia said to Lacy, ordering her to help carry the single bed from another unoccupied bed chamber.

Lacy huffed and groaned as they struggled to get the bed past the last door jamb. "I don't get it. Isn't there enough bloody bedrooms in this place?"

"Safety in numbers, Lace," Tia said. "Me, you and Isla. We can protect ourselves."

"I guess."

It seemed the logical thing to do with no mates or Protectors. None of them had genuinely chosen Malleven over Dante and she didn't trust what he might do.

On the way back to get the mattress, they stopped on the off chance that they could convince Lily to join them. Lily opened the door wide and they could see Lance lying back on their bed. He put up a lazy hand. Tia explained what they were doing and Lily looked at her skeptically. Without conferring with Lance, she projected, *No offence, but we have a perfectly good bedroom here with privacy*, with emphasis on the word privacy.

Tia didn't argue, just turned on her heel. "That girl is so dumb." Lacy shrugged and put her hand up by way of goodbye.

"I don't know why we bother," she complained as they walked straight past Phoebe's room. Phoebe had already been sent off with Vionne.

They struggled back with the mattress and dropped it down flat on the base they'd left next to the large double bed with an "Oomph!".

"Push!" Tia said, and they closed the gap to make one big bed.

They'd just finished admiring their handiwork when Isla

flung open the door, came in and sank down on the bed. She stared ahead of her with a dazed expression.

Tia looked at Lacy and they both went and sat either side of her in concern. "What is it?" Tia said, putting an arm around her shoulders, her heart automatically speeding up at what had happened. "Did he force himself on you?"

Isla looked at each of them as if she didn't understand something herself. "That's just it. Nothing happened. I mean … I didn't feel anything."

Both girls knew of the horrendous dynamic between Isla and her true mate, Malleven. Tia cringed every time she thought about how awful it must be. She noticed the redness and swelling in her cheek and frowned. "Well, not anything," she said, ruefully.

Isla put her hand to her cheek as if she only just remembered it. "He hit me when he realized that I'm free," she said, with a far-off, almost crazed look in her eyes. "Something's happened. I don't know what. It's to do with when I rejected him. It must be."

Tia looked at Lacy, who returned it wide-eyed. "I heard his ring goes red. That's why he never wears it."

"Yeah, Keenan said it means he can never get with a Siren again," Lacy said.

"Or make a bid for the crown," Tia added.

Isla shook her head. "Well he's done both of those things. No one will ever get him to prove it." She looked Tia in the eye. "All I know is that the magnetic pull between us has gone." she said with a slowly growing smile. "And I'm over the moon about it."

Tia laughed and hugged her. So did Lacy. They knew what it had cost her to be pulled towards a mate she hated. However, they soon sobered. With a man like Malleven, there would be a backlash.

"I'm terrified for Darres. This makes it so much worse for

him," Isla said, shaking her head as all the ramifications began to hit her. "Malleven is not a man to stand idly by while someone takes what he sees as his. It's the loss of power he can't stand."

Tia didn't really know the man but knew enough to know she was right. They huddled together for comfort. It seemed hopeless.

The silence was interrupted by a knock at the door. "Well at least he's out of the way for the time being," Tia said, as she got up to answer it.

She was still speaking as she opened the door, expecting it to be Lily or the maid. Instead, the sight of who it was stopped her dead. She stared into the handsome face of the man she'd loved from the first moment of meeting. The blond, sharply cut hair and toned body, filling out his clothes perfectly. A hundred memories came to her so fast, she almost collapsed in relief. "Jay," came out in a whisper.

He caught her in a single stride and his mouth was on hers. The kiss consumed her. Her arms went around his neck and she buried her nose in his shoulder, smelling him and hugging him for all she was worth. His wonderful scent enveloped her like another pair of arms. She wanted to dissolve into him completely and disappear, she'd missed him so much. It wasn't until then that she noticed he was in the full red and black Santalini uniform of the Honorable Guard. Another hammer in the coffin of how serious their situation was.

It took Lacy's cough to extricate her from him, but, even then, she kept a hold of his hand. She looked longingly into his eyes and saw everything reflected back at her. It was a good thing her sisters were there, otherwise their no sex pact would have been broken, she was sure. "What are you doing here? Malleven will kill you."

He smiled his slow, sexy smile and put up a hand of 'hi' to

both her sisters. Then he bobbed his head as if his death wish was of little importance and touched her cheek. His smile widened as he registered her impatience in him. "There's nothing he can do. I am a Santalini, so I have every right to be here as a guard." He grinned at her rolling her eyes. He was right though. He'd managed to be adopted by the Dubonnetti, Bonaci and the Santalini royal families during the course of his life, which had saved it on many occasions. Dante always said, people couldn't help falling in love with Jay.

Nevertheless, she doubted Malleven would honor any pacts not made by him and her blood pressure raised another notch with worry. So you've come to protect me," she said, knowing full well that he hated the label of Protector, seeing the life-long job as subservient.

He narrowed his eyes knowing she was trying to get a rise out of him. "I suppose … and to try and get the kingdom back for Dante."

Her sisters sat up straighter and she studied his face. He would risk his life for that; she had no doubt. And if the shoe were on the other foot, Dante would do the same for him. He looked tired. The furrows on his forehead creased with worry. "I know you love him too."

His face was hard and implacable. "You know how it is," was the only hint to any acknowledgement of feelings. Jay was closed off like that. He nodded almost imperceptibly. "I'll need your help and we don't have much time," he said, leading her over to her sisters.

Tia sat between them on the bed while he looked each of them in the eyes, doing the math of who was missing.

"Where is Dante; does anyone know?" Jay asked.

"He's gone to a cousin somewhere. Cesaré and Keenan went with him," Tia said. She didn't need to explain. Jay would know that they would be killed on some trumped-up charge the moment he left.

"Vionne has taken Darres and Phoebe to oversee the preparations of New Murrtaine. They've just left," Isla said, not betraying the worry Tia knew she felt. "All of his people are on their way to somewhere in the Mediterranean."

Jay looked into the distance as he thought about that. "Then Dante won't be far away. And Cash and Sean?"

Tia shook her head. "Dismissed. Only Lance has been able to stay. It's just us. That's why we're in here together."

"Yeah, it doesn't feel safe here anymore," Lacy said.

Jay reached out a hand and pinched her cheek. "Don't worry. We'll sort it out. Has he done the water thing with you yet?"

All three of them shook their heads. "He already has Lily and Phoebe," Tia said, reminding him that Malleven was married to Lily and had taken Phoebe for a month against her will. "But I doubt he'll leave it for long."

"I don't know how he got away with it. Have you tried to talk to Dante?" Jay said, pointing at his own temple.

"I've tried over and over. We all have. There's something stopping us. He's so strong, Jay. He's like some kind of master magician," Tia said.

"Cesaré is the only one who's a match for him in that department," Isla said.

"Then that's his plan. He's cutting us off from our mates to kill them." Tia looked fearfully at Jay. That meant him too. "You have your medication? Dante can just take that, right?" He would know as well as she did, how sick he became when she didn't breathe for him for ages.

"Some, but not enough for anyone else. With the Murrs on the move, it'll be a while before they're settled enough to make it."

Her heart ached with worry for them all. Jay was a strong man, but no match for an Atlantean like Malleven.

Jay's face hardened. He'd read her perfectly and hated anyone thinking he was weak. "There is something I need to tell you before I go," he said, pissed; she could tell. A muscle ticced in his clenched jaw. "I may not be as Human as we thought." He relayed the events of what had happened at Christian Dubonnetti's place and what he had in mind.

At first Tia wanted to rail and remind him Christian Dubonnetti was mad and it was suicide, but she bit it down. After all, nothing had happened yet and at least it had kept him away when Malleven had taken over. However, she was skeptical. They all were. "And you believe him?" There had never been any telltale signs. Like Atlantean stripes, for instance. And she'd almost killed him with her breath and came close to drowning him several times.

Jay shrugged irritably, as if his thought process had been exactly the same as hers. "It doesn't matter. Don't you see? If Christian has enough proof to satisfy Delissi, I'm then one of five sons and as eligible as Malleven for the crown."

"More so," Isla said. "If his ring is red."

Tia looked them all in the face, amazed that they were even entertaining any of this. They were shocked and intrigued and, even she had to admit, this was huge.

Jay was waiting expectantly for her to make up her mind. As always, it was left up to her.

"What do you need us to do?"

CHAPTER 7

Dante was kicking back with a glass of wine in the magnificent hall of his new home of Filfla. It was a good feeling to have this much support and there were worse places to hide out. It seemed like every hour clearance was requested from the airport to bring more people. Joseph, his cousin, had supplied a fleet of helicopters, permanently on standby there.

Keenan was oblivious, pacing like an animal possessed, and his boy, Vince, was trying to talk him down. The frustrating thing was, there was nothing to do but wait. Cash and Sean, Tia's Protectors, were talking strategies with Connor, Phoebe's Protector, who'd been released too.

The lift pinged and three guys stepped out, having the same reaction of awe everyone did at the top of the pyramid. Cesaré laughed loudly and jumped to his feet. "Welcome, Nathan, River, Mike. Down here!" Cesaré shouted. They jogged down with huge grins, clapped hands and embraced Cesaré, who met them at the bottom. He quickly introduced them as Lance's surfer crew, Lily's Protectors, who'd made the journey from California to show solidarity.

Dante welcomed them warmly. He'd met them once before. Cesaré was a keen surfer and knew them all, so they were already aware of the history between him and Malleven. He was glad to have them and issued orders for them to be shown to their rooms.

Cesaré flopped back down into a chair opposite him. "So why is Ruby on her way here?"

Keenan overheard and came and sat down on the sofas to hear better. "Ruby? Why has she left Jay?" He looked to Dante for the answer, accusingly, no doubt remembering the huge mistake he'd made by sleeping with her a few weeks ago.

Dante put up his hands in surrender. "It's nothing to do with me. Promise. I haven't seen her since. She called from the airport asking if she could come here and I said yes. Maybe she has news of Jay." He shrugged. "Someone trusted must have told her where we are."

"I know she's my sister, but I don't like it," Keenan said.

Dante knew what he meant. She'd dated his brother Marco and moved swiftly onto Jay. Then, as soon as Jay's back was turned, she'd got into his pool with him. They weren't the actions of a besotted wife. "Keep your enemies closer," was all he said.

A maid approached from the tunnel behind the staircase. "Mrs Gardiner has arrived, Your Highness," she said.

Dante smiled. "Thank you, Carmen. Please show her in." The staff all insisted on treating him as if he was still the king and it never failed to warm his heart. He heard the lift and stood and faced the staircase. Time to see Jay's wife again.

The chatter around him hushed when they became aware of the new arrival. As she stood, bewildered, surveying the room at the top of the stairs, it occurred to him that—apart from staff—she would be the only female there. He called over to Sean. "Where are Sarah and Ronnie?"

Sean was the only married one of the Protectors and had

a young son of similar age to his own children. Their marriage had been a bumpy one owing to his own devotion to Tia. She'd lived at the castle periodically, but they'd fought constantly.

"At her mother's," Sean called back.

All the while Dante watched Ruby take in the magnificence of the room and slowly descend the stairs in her shiny black heels.

He thought what an uncertain world they all lived in. Filfla was a fortress and probably the safest place for anyone loyal to him. "Send for them. They will live here."

Dante didn't see Sean's reaction. He straightened as Ruby's hips swayed closer in the black pencil skirt she wore. The scarlet blouse cinched her waist and hugged her breasts. Her raven-black hair fell loose around her shoulders. Her dark eyes were fixed on him throughout the walk, while her heels clip clopped on the shiny black-tiled floor. She came to a stop no more than two feet away. "Ruby," he said.

After a moment's pause, he picked up her hand and kissed it and then both cheeks. He wondered if her marriage had recovered since Jay found out about their steamy afternoon together. He and Tia certainly hadn't. Dante didn't trust her where her ambitions with his best friend were concerned. She'd given in to him too easily. "To what do we owe this pleasure?"

"I heard what happened and simply had to come and pledge my allegiance."

Dante kept his face painted on, but doubted that very much. However, there were only a very select few at the castle who knew where he was and what the Maltese prime minister had done for him. Someone had given her his location for a reason. "Where's Jay?" was the pressing question. He had been nowhere to be seen when he'd had to leave.

"When it all happened, Jay had been called to Christian's place. Christian is determined to adopt him as a son."

Dante frowned and nodded with mixed emotions. He was glad Jay was out of harm's way, but Christian would have known exactly what was happening at the castle. It was all relayed flippantly, but, between the lines, there had to be more to it. Jay was already an adopted son of Dubonnetti. Everyone knew that.

"Answer the fucking question, Ruby. Where's Jay?" Keenan said across his shoulder, in a directness only a brother could get away with. Dante hadn't realized he'd come to stand behind him.

When she went to open her mouth, he spoke over her again. "Stop playing games and tell us exactly what's going on." As well as being Ruby's brother, Keenan was very close to Jay. It was a fact that saddened him at times. Dante and Jay had always been like brothers, but they'd grown apart over the last couple of years.

Ruby huffed and rolled her eyes. "He's gone to the castle as a Santalini guard. He's watching things from there."

Relief rolled over him. It was perfect. Jay had every right to be there and it would have been him who sent Ruby to Filfla. It was still very dangerous for him there, even as a Santalini. Malleven knew of his bond with Tia and, judging by all the present company, he didn't abide bonds.

"He's going to contact me tonight. You can speak to him then," Ruby said.

Dante's blood buzzed in his veins and he looked Heavenwards in thanks. It was the best news he could have had in the circumstances. Jay was the strongest, most capable human he knew. He was cold and calculating and wouldn't hesitate to do what needed to be done, however hard the task. No contact with the castle had been driving him mad. Now he couldn't have a better spy to be his eyes and ears.

He turned his attention back to Ruby. "Thank you. You've done me a great service in coming here. Go with my servant and he will show you to your room. Rest. We'll talk later."

He watched her hips sway in the direction of the tunnel and the maze of rooms. Cesaré touched his arm. "Vionne is here with Darres and the Siren, Phoebe Ray, Your Highness."

His heart quickened and he turned towards the fountain. This was good news. It meant Malleven trusted Vionne with the Murr side of things enough to give him a Siren as surety. "Where is he now?"

"They're docking below," Cesaré said.

Joseph had thought of everything. There were already docking bays installed for easy underwater travel between New Murrtaine and Filfla. This would be good practice for its use. Just as at the castle, the fountain was the gateway, through a tunnel to the sea.

Dante continued to watch the darker water in the fountain's center. The water began to bubble until Vionne's white head emerged, followed by his striped, muscular body and two others he quickly recognized as Dax and Caan. The surface boiled again and one with familiar long black hair to his waist pulled himself out and reached down for a much-smaller girl. When she stood and pushed her red hair back, he could see it was Phoebe standing with the formidable male, Darres.

The men stood shakily in the shallow waters, expressed their lungs and sat on the wall at the edge. They needed to rest their legs until the lower half retracted into shape. It would be an hour or so until their bones solidified enough to walk comfortably and, still, they were never truly comfortable out of water. Phoebe was the only one who stood confidently, rubbing her hair with a towel handed to her by a maid.

Dante came closer and switched to projected speech for

the Murrs. They had no vocal cords and spoke in pictorial images and projected feelings, but for the sake of better understanding for Humans, they projected speech patterns in Human-like phrases. *Welcome, how's it going at the castle? Tia and the children?* Dante asked anxiously.

We left as soon as we could after you, but, of what we saw, they seemed well enough. Vionne said. *My people are on route. I will make several trips to gather the sickly and the older ones who will find the journey difficult. I'll be able to tell you more then.*

Dante nodded, gratefully absorbing the news. Vionne struggled to his feet and Darres stood with him. The lone wolf Murr was just as intimidating, even when unsteady on his feet. *Has the building of New Murrtaine started?* Vionne said.

My cousin said it has begun beneath the seabed. The Orb will commence above ground when the international salvage craft have finished combing the area for her, Dante said. The world's media had seen the comet leave the mid-Atlantic and land somewhere in the middle of the Mediterranean.

Vionne nodded, clearly relieved. Dante's eyes fell on Phoebe, the Siren he'd known the least amount of time. She stood apart with her eyes on the floor, a shell of her former self. The loss of Drew had broken her. "My servant will show you to your rooms to rest a while. We will assemble in the library. There is much I need to discuss with you. You too, Phoebe," he said, switching to normal speech so everyone could hear. She rolled her eyes and looked away, disinterested.

She has been this way the whole time, Vionne projected. *We will see you in an hour. There is something of great import I must tell you.*

Dante frowned at what that must be. Vionne had become very expressive of late. He watched the Murrs hobble awkwardly towards the tunnel behind the staircase and Phoebe went with them.

. . .

IT WAS late afternoon when Dante tapped his fingers on his desk, waiting for everyone to assemble in the new library. Joseph had seen to it that his family's personal collection of ancient books was moved there for safekeeping. It was an impressive collection and sat perfectly on the many shelves that lined the windowless room, right to the ceiling. Everyone was crowded in for the meeting, some on the large orange sofas arranged in a square and some preferring to stand behind them. Darres led Phoebe in and hovered near the door.

"I'll kick things off, shall I?" Dante said. "I just wanted to thank all of you for your loyalty. Some of you need a foot in both camps, but you're here and that means a lot. As most of you know, Alfonzo and Sebastian remained to keep an eye on things. They just contacted me to tell me they got a call on the landline a few days ago." He looked directly at Phoebe, who was still looking at the floor in front of her. "It was Drew." He waited to see if Phoebe heard him.

"What the—I thought he was dead?" Keenan said. The rest of the room fell into confusion, then grew quieter for him to elaborate.

"It was Drew, Phoebe," he said again.

Her eyes slowly rose to his. They were bloodshot and desolate, but seemed to slowly uncloud as if she was fighting to come to the surface of a fog. "Drew," she said, simply.

Dante nodded; still not sure she was following what he was saying. "Apparently, he got blown clear. He's at the Scythian camp that trained him. He said he's there to destroy it."

"He's alive?" Phoebe said, tears now brimming in her eyes.

Darres put an arm around her and pulled her into his chest.

How can this be? Vionne projected angrily so no one else could hear.

Dante continued on. It was a conversation he'd have to have with him in private. "He was unaware of what had happened at the castle, so in the end he had to ask for Malleven's help to destroy the other Scythian camps. Alfonzo said Malleven agreed. Thankfully, he sees the continued threat."

Phoebe was now openly crying. Her Protector, Connor, took her from Darres and she sobbed into his shoulder.

"Drew is by no means safe, Phoebe. Apart from the obvious danger of being discovered as a spy, I'm positive that Malleven will kill him. He has promised you to Vionne, has he not?"

Vionne's pissed expression confirmed it. It asked, in no uncertain terms, whose side he was on.

"I've asked for details as soon as Alfonzo has them, so we can join the mission to perhaps ensure that Drew lives."

"Yes! 'bout time," Keenan said. "I can't carry on sitting here doing nothing."

Phoebe stopped crying and lifted her head from Connor's shoulder.

Dante waited before he spoke, knowing she had something to say.

"I was under a spell when he took my breath … Malleven, I mean. I didn't even know it had happened. I had no memory of him or what happened until I saw him again at the castle."

"I knew it," Keenan said.

Dante nodded, relieved. He took it for what it was: A thank you and an apology of sorts. For offering to save Drew and for her part in losing him his kingdom. Sirens had to go to a prince willingly to make him king, otherwise it was tampering with the Fates; something that would upset the equilibrium of the Orb and be the downfall of them all. The Earth's weather patterns were already erratic and becoming extreme. He'd have to have a conversation with Vionne, but this woman was Drew's and she would never go to Vionne while he lived.

His eyes flashed to Vionne's and he knew he'd thought the same thing. He only hoped that he'd stay loyal without a Siren. "Vionne, what news was it you had to share from the castle?"

A long moment passed between them while they assessed each other. *She is mine by right of divining ring,* Vionne projected, so no one else could hear. *When the time comes, I will demand combat at the place of my choosing, as is my right.*

This was the absolute last thing he wanted; two valued princes fighting over a Siren, but he was right. Vionne's ring was purple. The Orb or the explosion had somehow righted the situation with Drew. He may now have Bonaci blood, but he was not Phoebe's destined mate. If he wanted her, he would have to fight; as Vionne was Murr, it made all under-water tests obsolete. Particularly as Malleven had already claimed her by force. The situation was a monumental mess. *Of course,* he answered. All the while, his mind whirred and his pulse quickened in the hope the Fates would intercede with the right outcome.

Vionne finally projected his thoughts so they all could hear. *Malleven admitted to me privately that there would be no council. He courts me because he has to, as no Atlantean can oversee Murrtaine ... And there is something else.* He shifted uncomfortably in his chair.

Dante took a sharp breath of alarm at Vionne's reluctance.

Vionne addressed Ruby sitting quietly on the end of one of the sofas. *What I have to say affects you. Are you happy for all to hear?*

She looked shocked when all eyes went to her.

"Is it about Jay?"

Vionne shook his head. *No, JJ.*

Ruby shrugged. "Say it."

Dante inwardly smirked and breathed in relief. Of course, there wasn't a maternal bone in the woman's body. He was relieved it was nothing to do with Jay. JJ he could handle. "You can speak freely here."

Vionne proceeded to relay the events that had happened in the catacombs with JJ.

"And you say the cuffs joined to him?" Dante said. It was the most bizarre thing he'd ever heard.

They did, Your Highness. And they seemed to change him. I mean, he was a serious boy before, but after, he seemed to grow in knowledge far beyond his years.

Dante thought about what that could mean.

That isn't all of it, Your Highness. He seemed to straighten as if he was gathering his courage. *As I was about to leave him to return to his chamber, he referred to himself as the Darkly Begotten.*

The room fell silent, horrified.

CHAPTER 8

Ashaya sat dripping, exhilarated with wonder, on the edge of the fountain. She couldn't believe she was actually there. It was a lifetime dream finally realized. It was also her first time breathing anything other than water, so she was glad of the medication she carried. Her eyes ran and her throat felt as if it was being stabbed with a thousand needles. The nausea was probably from excitement.

A pulse of light and she had landed in the sea nearby and simply followed the tunnel into the fountain. The whisper-thin material of her clothes would dry quickly. It was a silver-grey, figure-hugging one-piece that covered her from her neck to her feet, leaving her striped arms bare. Priestess of the Five Moons black ribbons criss-crossed the length of her arms and she looked as pureblooded as anyone could be. She went over her Human phrasing of what she would say, over and over, before anyone noticed her.

It was then she saw him storming out of the corridor behind the staircase in long, angry strides, heading straight for the fountain and that meant towards her. She shot up to her feet with her heart in her mouth and watched him pull off his shirt and undo the top button of his black pants. It was Vionne, just a few feet away—the object of her visit.

He stopped dead when he saw her. He frowned slightly, which was unusual for their kind. It gave her a chance to really study him: the well-chiseled face, framed in soft white curls, muscled torso and long legs, all covered in the well-positioned stripes of her people. He was very handsome.

His soft black eyes narrowed slightly as he regarded her with interest.

Lord, she projected, tipping her head in deference to him. Her black, silky, blunt-cut hair fell forwards into her face in wet clumps. He was a Borge prince; the first anyone from Atlas had spoken to in ten thousand years. It was a huge honor.

She looked up slowly, her jet-black eyes mirroring his.

He straightened and pulled his shirt back on over his head and hurriedly buttoned his pants. *Good day to you,* he projected, still studying her, no doubt, trying to work out where she was from. He would know she was pure bred and not from Murrtaine. *Welcome,* he said. *I am Vionne, Prince of Murrtaine. I don't seem to recall you, and yet I am sure I would remember such beauty.*

Ashaya admired the way he employed such flattery in Human-like phrasing of thought. Even his face moved to reveal his confusion. It made him even more handsome, if that were possible. Her eyes dropped to him tucking his shirt into the slim waistband of his very Human-like trousers. She swallowed, not able to resist the picture in her mind of him without them.

When she returned her gaze, his look was curious and enquiring, making her have to break the silence. *There is nothing to forgive, Lord. I am Ashaya, a priestess and daughter from the furthest of your colonies.*

Murrla, Axyl's city? Of course. Welcome! He seemed to emit joy at the mention of his brother.

She didn't deny it, simply inclined her head.

Do you have news to deliver? The king—I mean, Dante—is in the Library, should you need to speak to him. I can take you there.

Indeed. Thank you. I will, presently. Happy that such a plausible cover had presented itself, she walked stiffly towards a sofa nearby, surprised at how awkward her legs felt. It was one thing to watch from above, but another entirely to experience waterless air. When she'd sat down, she patted the seat next to her. *I am new here, perhaps we could talk for a while?*

He hesitated, then walked over and sat in the space offered, but with a gap that could fit another person. Atlasians had no concept of personal space. It was another taint from Humans. However, she had to admit, it was comforting when one was nervous. It allowed her to study him closely. The faintness of the stripes on his face that she'd learned faded when out of the water, made her wonder if hers did too. He seemed to be studying her as well.

Maybe you could tell me why sadness hangs over you like heavy kelp?

He looked surprised initially and then relaxed. He would understand that their kind were more alert and open to emotions, having no language of words.

She turned in her seat to face him and gazed into his black, pool-like eyes. In truth, she couldn't believe she was actually on Earth among the people she'd studied for so long. The whole of her adult life had been taken up on her mission. She'd been prepared from childhood and left Atlas at twenty-four years old and put in cryogenic sleep. In Earth years she was around two hundred and eighty years old, but hadn't aged at all. Every day of that sleep, her subconscious had absorbed Atlantean history from the destruction of

Atlantis to the present day. She felt like she knew the characters intimately, like a well-loved play.

She was born a seer from a very revered high priestess of the Five Moons of Atlas. She knew things that others did not by just being in the presence of someone, but this male was hard to read. She edged forward on the seat and reached out a hand to touch the side of his face. His eyes narrowed slightly, but he remained still. She ran her hand gently over the faint lines of his stripes that had lightened to grey. *You have a great pain in your heart,* she projected.

A range of emotions crossed his face and she couldn't help being in awe of them. She watched him swallow and look down at her other hand. He took it and held it in his. Her temperature rose and her heart fluttered.

You are a seer. I can tell. How does a prince deal with a destined mate that loves another? One that even if he wins in combat, will never love him. Her heart sank a little as she recognized he'd only taken her hand for a closer reading. However, it was momentary. His eyes looked so desolate when he finally looked into hers. *I made an oath to my father that I would marry my Siren.*

He projected such a great feeling of love and regret and yet it was clear he was a strong male. She found him more attractive than ever. For the first time she questioned her professional distance in the matter. Although there was no way she'd go back to Seti and admit failure. She must remember that he or any one of her peers could be watching her right now. *Do you believe in the old gods?* she asked.

He nodded. *The Way of the Five Moons is followed by my family.*

And you have faith in the Orb and your ancestors, set to return one day?

She found she wanted to trace the furrows of his frown.

I do, but—

She put a finger up stop him. *Then you know that a great leader will not be left unrewarded by the Fates.*

Then he completely shocked her by capturing her hand and kissing her finger. She became acutely aware of the softness of his lips. It had been a very long time since she'd had any physical contact and never from such a desirable male. Her heart raced and a pain hit her lower abdomen.

He held her hand and kissed the inside of her wrist. It amazed her that such small gestures could evoke such strong feelings. She pulled her hand away, suddenly aware of her indiscretion and how it must look. She had to get control of herself and the situation. It was the height of unprofessionalism and she would be rebuked, perhaps even punished for it.

He was studying her with a speculative expression now and when she pushed back a stray lock of her hair behind her ear, she was sure he noticed the tremor in her hand. She was a highly trained, strong female from a master race of beings and he'd managed to disarm her in minutes.

A cough sounded behind them and Vionne jumped to his feet, guiltily. Dante stood there, a mixture of amusement and interest. He looked between them and grinned.

The Atlanteans were a beautiful race, but the former king was utterly striking, with wavy black hair to his shoulders and mischievous dark grey eyes, mocking his old friend. The viewing oracle didn't do him justice.

"I wanted to talk to you about your Siren and how you would best deal with it." His eyes fell on her and his grin widened. "Then I see you are ahead of me already with an answer."

Vionne seemed to suddenly wake up and held out his arm to her. *Forgive me. This is—* His eyes widened in surprise and then he frowned and laughed nervously as he looked down at her. *Your Highness. May I introduce Ashaya from my brother's outpost of Murrla. She has made the great journey to pledge her allegiance.*

Ashaya stood, bowed her head and allowed the lie of where she came from to continue. *It has been a great ambition of mine to meet you.* Which was the truth.

Dante reached out a hand to shake hers, but brought it to his lips and kissed it instead. It threw her and took her totally by surprise. These Atlanteans were so tactile, however, it wasn't unpleasant. In fact, her heart fluttered again.

"Thank you for your support. Please stay a while on Filfla. Perhaps Vionne can see to it that you're settled in and comfortable." One of his eyes winked in Vionne's direction in a way she didn't understand.

It was a curious communication, as the corners of Vionne's mouth twitched and he bowed his head. *It would be my pleasure.* Gestures appeared to be another language entirely.

Vionne bowed and led her towards the tunnel behind the staircase. However, before he disappeared, he paused and turned back and projected. *I am truly sorry ... for everything.*

Ashaya looked between them, fascinated at the dynamics between the two strong leaders. Then she saw the familiar mischief cross the former king's face. "Ah, no bother. It's a dangerous man, with nothing to lose."

It was a curious thing for him to say. Something she didn't fully understand and would come to remember many times, but Vionne had no such problems and inclined his head in appreciation. *Indeed, it is. One must always beware.* There was a serious undertone to the strange conversation, but not without warmth. It preoccupied her long after they'd left.

She soon had to concentrate. She had to remember not to give away that she knew the exact layout of her new home. Before she disappeared, she looked behind her and saw

Dante watching her. She couldn't help feeling his mind working, deciding if she could be trusted and seeing the irony that he was the male she would have to judge.

Tia had been summoned to the Great Hall of the castle by one of the harassed, overworked, young male servants. They were always running this way and that. She couldn't be sure if they had more to do since Malleven took over, or if there were simply less of them. It was hard to say.

She strode along the bedroom corridor, furious. She wanted to see her children and Malleven appeared to be holding them to get them to do what he wanted. He had Isla's as well and she was now terrified after their last meeting of what he might do out of spite.

He had of course said they were well looked after, but she'd never had to go cap in hand to try to see them. She was almost there when a hand clamped over her mouth and she was yanked into a doorway. "Jay!" she yelped, as soon as he released her.

"Shh! Where are the kids?" Jay said.

"That's what I'm going, to find out. He's called for me. Does he know you're here yet?"

Jay shook his head. "I don't think so. I've kept in the background."

They'd remained separate in the castle to keep him a secret as long as possible, figuring Malleven's men wouldn't know him that well and the Santalinis wouldn't say anything.

"OK. Go ahead. I'll stay in the shadows."

She kissed him on the lips and left him, taking comfort that he would be nearby. When she came out into the Great Hall, JJ was playing cars on a mat on the floor at Malleven's feet while he was sitting in an armchair by the window to the sea. Antonio Dubonnetti sat reading a paper, nearby. It was the first time she'd seen Malleven's lover, her husband's brother, since he'd taken over. JJ seemed happy enough.

"Ah, my dear. Come and sit with us."

She went closer. It was a domestic scene to an unsuspecting bystander, but to her it was fake. JJ was being held as collateral and everyone saw Antonio as his pretty plaything that he dragged around with him and didn't exactly treat that kindly. Not a stage for happy domesticity.

Ignoring Antonio, she cautiously looked around her for any of Malleven's creepy Magi men. "Where are my other children?" she said. Alexia, her little girl, would be frightened. She hadn't seen any of them.

"In the nursery with the nanny. Sit!" Malleven said, closing down any further questions and indicating the armchair opposite him.

JJ jumped up and ran to her and she scooped him up. She kissed his cheek loudly and sat down with him in the chair. It wasn't till then that she noticed the cuffs. She sprang to her feet and immediately screamed, "What are these?" holding out his little arm for him to see, face burning red and blood pulsing her temple with anger.

Malleven sighed deeply. "I was rather hoping you could tell me."

She looked them over for a catch or a clasp, but the longer she touched the metal, the hotter they became until she couldn't bear to touch them at all. Realizing they were embedded into his skin, she quickly spun him around to face her. "Oh my god, is it hot, JJ? Is it hurting you?" She could barely get out the words as she clawed at the metal with her nails and anxiety robbed her of breath.

He put a calming hand to still hers and shook his head. "No, Mama."

She continued to try to get a finger between the gold and his skin, but yelped in pain. She couldn't prize it, even with a nail. "What is this? What have you done to him?" She looked down at her blistered finger and then glared at Malleven.

"I know nothing of it," Malleven said. "You bear the heat of the metal better than I. I was going to ask the boy about it, but thought it best that you were here when I do."

Jay strained to hear, in the shadows by the entrance to the Great Hall. He could just about make out what was being said. However, he could feel Tia's anguish loud and clear through the bond.

What's he done, Jay? Can you hear? she projected.

He couldn't respond because their bond was one way, but he heard just the same. Her not being able to contact Dante must be because he was outside of the castle.

Listen in case I call.

Jay moved further into the hall to hear more clearly.

"Come here, JJ," Malleven said.

He could just about see JJ look up at his mother and then slide down her legs and go over to Malleven. He stopped a couple of feet away.

"Can you tell me where you came by the bracelets on your arms?"

JJ looked down. Jay couldn't make out whether he was touching them. They didn't seem to hurt him in any way. "They called me to find them in the caves. They were hiding under the castle."

Jay knew he meant the catacombs.

"You went down there alone?" Tia said, raising her voice as if she were getting angry. Jay suspected it was for his benefit. "I thought you said they were being looked after," she accused Malleven.

"It's OK, Mama. Vionne helped me.'

"Vionne was there?" Malleven said, sounding angry for the first time.

"Yes, I saw him there. He was with me and went away afterwards."

Jay guessed that Vionne had stumbled on the boy. He'd thank him when he saw him. He edged further into the room as Malleven appeared to stay quiet for a while. He didn't trust the guy.

It was then that two men in black robes, *Magi,* appeared from nowhere in the shadows. They approached and he held up his arms in surrender. Together, the three of them walked out into the light.

Malleven saw them immediately and smiled. "Ah, Jay. Welcome. Perhaps you can answer the mystery of your son's apparel?"

Jay continued to approach, hiding the frustration he felt at getting caught.

JJ laughed when he saw him and rushed to him, arms raised, to be picked up. He looked over at Tia in shock. "I have no idea what they are," he said.

I don't either, Tia projected so only he could hear.

Jay knelt down so he could be eye level with his son. The boy touched his face and projected straight to him. *He's a bad man, Daddy, but I'm badder.*

"Do you know what the cuffs are, JJ?" Jay said, getting more worried by the minute.

JJ nodded and looked nervously at his mother. "I'm not sure you want everyone to know how bad I am?"

Tia dropped to her knees next to the boy as well and hugged him tightly. Malleven appeared to be looking on, as curious and dumbfounded as they were. Jay was convinced he had nothing to do with it. "You're not bad, you're a good boy," Tia was saying.

"It's not what the spirits tell me, mama. They say I'm born dark and I had to find the bracelets to know myself."

It was such an odd thing for someone to say, let alone a young boy. Unease slowly crept up Jay's spine. Tia continued to cuddle JJ. "It's just dreams, baby," she said over and over.

A weight of understanding was gradually forming in Jay's stomach and he looked over at Malleven. His eyes narrowed as he started to join the dots as well. *Could it be that Christian Dubonnetti had it wrong but right at the same time? Had the Darkly Begotten come though his line?*

The idea staggered him and broke his heart at the same time.

Malleven's eyes went to his as he reached the same conclusion.

CHAPTER 9

Drew fell in quickly with the routine at the camp. He remembered it well: endless drills, combat training and indoctrination class, against Atlanteans, of course. Somehow, he'd always known it was bullshit. But just the same as with these boys, it was accepted as normal as there was nowhere else to go.

He was the oldest, so Seville introduced him as a successful graduate of the program that had come back to teach. It was perfect for them as it gave the impression that there was a goal to all this shit, and not that they were thrown into the world without a care for their happiness or their survival. It suited Drew, as it gave him the opportunity to build a relationship with the boys so they'd follow him out when the time came.

Thankfully, Seville had put him on fitness training, martial arts and hand-to-hand combat. Now he had his memory back, he remembered he'd excelled at anything physical. It had helped him stay sane in the harsh, unloving environment. He hoped to do the same for these boys.

Nowadays, there were only about thirty in the camp. There had been at least three times that when he'd been there. Times must be hard for snatching unwanted children.

Every morning their exhausted, dreamless sleep was interrupted by upbeat brass band music, played loudly over an old British Tannoy system, that sounded more like it belonged in the former Soviet Union. He guessed it was chosen more because it was loud, and unable to ignore, rather than any musical value or enhancement to the inmates' miserable lives. Sleepy, shivering boys silently filed to the wash huts and hurriedly dressed in their inadequate PE shorts and t-shirts. They were quiet and serious and ranged in age from about eight to fourteen. They made their way straight to the playing field where they waited expectantly in the darkness.

Drew jogged to the huddle, which quickly separated into drill lines. He was grateful for the extra layers he'd brought with him to keep out the pervasive, freezing damp that hovered near the ground this time of year. Drizzle began to coat the side of their faces and threatened to block out the tiny glow of orange creeping over the line of trees behind them.

He found he prayed the dawn hurried every morning. He wanted it to cheer the boys up a little with its optimism, if not its warmth from the feeble light. He had to remember everything had to go on as normal, at least for a while. It wasn't for much longer. The boys would have to bear it, just like he had.

He immediately got them jogging on the spot to keep them warm while he scanned the area. The monks were arriving and standing sentry, ready to pick out a boy and punish him for any minor misdemeanor.

"OK, I'm 2365 … Laps," he said on his first day, sending them off at a run with his arm. He kept his words abrupt and to a minimum so as not to attract suspicion from the boys or the guards. Any compassion, such as even giving them his name, would alert them.

Drew moved on to give them the hardest circuit training session of his life, to push them to breaking point. He hated doing it. All he wanted to do was take them somewhere, feed them up and get them warm. But to save them, it was necessary for the monks to trust him enough to start to take their eyes off him and the boys grateful for any small crumb of attention and make them follow him anywhere. It was basic stick, carrot training.

After a few days, it was clear there was an elite group of about six boys. They kept up, without complaint, with a steely determination, the whole time. They were right there with him on runs and came back for more, no matter how many times he blooded their noses when they sparred.

They wanted to learn what he had to teach and quickly became his crew. He grew to like them and watched over them as unobtrusively as possible. Two stood out. One was 361. A dark-skinned, dark-eyed boy so damn likable, that, despite the back-breaking training, he never failed to lighten the boys' world with a subtle sense of humor that kept them all going. He was walking gold as a leader.

The other, he guessed, reminded him of himself. A tall, blond, skinny bag of bones, who never shied away from leading from the front and excelling at everything he put his hand to. Always at his side, even by the end of the toughest training. He couldn't wait to give the determined face a name.

Drew soon rewarded the six by giving them responsibility over the other boys. A chain of command would be the most effective way of assimilating orders and ultimately trust. He made them work hard, but, unlike those who'd trained him, it was also with fairness, so they'd pass it on to their charges, who would unquestioningly follow them and trust them implicitly. It was these six boys who must trust him enough to follow him out of there when the time came.

After keeping with the same plan for several days, and after much-needed showers in freezing cold water, the boys trooped into the mess hall for their meagre rations. It usually consisted of some sort of broth and crusty bread, but at least it was hot. It was barely enough fuel for a child, let alone to send a warrior into battle. He'd come to suspect it was to keep them too weak for any idea of escape. However, he remembered Seville had slipped him extra. Pieces of bread and cookies to store in his dorm. He'd taken it without question. It had helped him grow to the six feet three he was today. Seville had merely explained that he would need it for the difficult road he would travel in the future, for the good of the Human race.

Yeah, he remembered it well. It was what had made him stop at a truck stop on his way there and fill his trunk with energy drinks and bars, which he used as rewards for the six boys to keep them strong. They were suspicious for a trap at first, but soon took what was offered as the lifeline that it was. He couldn't blame them. It was definitely something the monks would do to see who was weak. However, philosophy class, apart from teaching hatred of all things Atlantean, had drummed into them the importance of obedience and being grateful for what they received—even if they didn't immediately understand it.

Drew led the table's grace. He wondered how he felt about God now he knew they weren't alone in the universe. Maybe ancient humans had worshiped the visiting Atlasians as gods come down to Earth. Maybe that was why the Scythians hated them so much, because it messed with their idea of a vengeful God. Whatever it was, it mattered little to these boys. They trusted him and they were ready. He ended with an, "Amen," and the boys ate their soup in silence.

"Are you happy in your training?" he asked, making sure the patrolling monk was going in the opposite direction.

He wasn't surprised one boy in particular had the guts to answer. The one he'd come to refer to in his mind as His Boy. "Of course, sir. It makes us strong."

He glanced over to make sure the monk was still walking away from them. "Do you remember your lives from before?" He continued to eat and watched the boys silently look at each other in his peripheral vision, deciding whether to answer him or not. When they didn't answer, he kept his voice and eyes down. "Know this. I was one of you. I will not betray you. You are my troop and I am your captain. I would give my life for you in battle. Do you understand?"

After a moment's pause, they all nodded. His Boy looked around him before he spoke in the same low tone. "We each came from group homes or the street. We are grateful for our training and purpose," he added, to cover them.

Drew understood perfectly. He himself had come from a group home and had it drummed into him that he should be grateful for this hate-filled regime. They probably had traffickers to find and zero in on the most vulnerable. They would need to be found and rooted out too when all this was over. "What if I were to tell you that you are about to fulfil your purpose; that you have been chosen for a secret mission for the glory of mankind?"

Their eyes widened, and they looked around to gauge each other's reaction. None of them wanted to appear to think the wrong thing, but they were unanimous in their enthusiasm. His Boy nodded for them.

Drew spotted the monk heading back in their direction. "Eat!" he ordered.

They all immediately obeyed and ate in silence. The monk continued on past them.

"What is the mission, sir?" His Boy whispered.

Drew kept his eyes down. "I can't tell you the details in case you are captured and tortured." They didn't understand that the danger came from their own monks extracting the information from them. "But it is enough to say that we will be leaving the camp and you must prepare your platoons to follow." Each boy had five younger boys under his supervision.

There was silence. Not one boy asked a single question.

"When do we leave?" His Boy spoke for them all.

Drew found he couldn't speak for a moment. A flood of pride flowed right through him. He welled up with emotion for all the boys looking at him with expectant faces. Their eyes had filled with a new light of hope. Each one of them knew he was being given the opportunity to escape and they were willing to take it, just as he had been, no questions asked.

Except, when it had happened for him, instead of destroying the Atlantean nation, he had been taken in by them and the most beautiful woman in the world. *Phoebe.*

He stopped his mind freefalling into memories of her. Instead, he resolved to save these boys and find a place for them. All of them. "In two nights' time. In the early hours."

"What about the monks, are they coming with us?"

His Boy was bright. As their eyes met, His Boy knew that whatever the mission was, it was one way and the monks were not in on it.

Without taking his eyes from the boy's, Drew replied, "They will remain here. Don't worry about them. Our orders come from higher up. You will take the boys out of the compound to a place I will tell you, and I will follow."

The boys all whispered between themselves, but His Boy continued to gauge him.

"Remember, you are my platoon and I will not abandon you. If you follow me, I swear on my life to protect you," Drew said, still addressing the one boy. He recognized that it all rested on him and he knew damn well they were on no mission for the Scythians.

He waited a long, agonizing moment, until the bell rang for the end of the lunch break. They all began to stand with the scrape of chairs. Drew followed them as they walked out in single file. Drew was just about to think he'd read the situation all wrong, when the smallest boy he was following, at the back, whispered over his shoulder. "We will be ready."

Drew's heart pounded in relief. All he had to do now was set it up with the Atlanteans.

MALLEVEN'S MIND whirred with possibilities when it became obvious that the boy was telling the truth. There was just no other explanation for it. He'd studied the Darkly Begotten prophecy for years and had the meaning totally wrong. He'd deduced the power was hidden and probably in Ireland. Then, by a process of elimination, he'd suspected it was probably at Ballygowan Castle, but he'd assumed the power was in the object itself. Now he understood that it was channeled through a person and that person was a small child who now wielded extraordinary power.

There was nothing else for it, he would have to keep him and win over his confidence. He hated that it was so out of his control. "Come to me, boy," Malleven said, holding out his arms.

Tia immediately snatched him to her and Jay stepped in front of them in one adept move. "The boy is mine. He is a

Santalini. You insult us if you take him against his will," Jay said, readying his stance for a fight.

Malleven laughed. He liked Jay. He was a suppressed ball of masculinity wrapped in a beautifully attractive exterior. If it wasn't for the shit storm it would create with his lover, Antonio, he would be very tempted. "Come now. On the contrary. It would be a great honor to be a favorite of the king. I will not hurt him," Malleven said.

For a single moment, there was indecision on the human's face. He had a fearsome reputation for calm assertiveness. It was interesting to see his weakness for the boy. He casually approached, so they were almost nose to nose. "Tell me, I am interested to know, where are your loyalties to your best friend?" He'd grown up with the former king and had been nowhere to be found when he'd been deposed. And yet here he was with his best friend's wife and the son Dante had adopted as his own. "I find it hard to determine."

And there it was, the perfectly contained anger, only just visible by a small tic in his jaw. He really was an outrageously handsome man. "I am a Santalini," Jay said in a clear, low voice. "I have every right to be here."

Malleven smiled and searched his face. Then he brightened. "Well then, you will have no problem in entrusting your son to me, will you? These are dangerous times, you will agree. It is safer for him." He left his veiled threat floating on the air between them.

Jay looked over his shoulder at JJ and something unsaid passed between them.

"It's OK, Daddy. I don't mind," JJ said, looking up at his father.

After a long moment observing the sincerity in his son's eyes, Jay looked over at Tia and she reluctantly let him go. "I entrust you with my son's life," Jay said, turning back to him, face flushed with suppressed anger.

Malleven inclined his head and noted the threat with admiration, but wasn't greatly perturbed by it. The last thing he intended to do was let any harm come to the boy.

JJ went quickly to Malleven and, without further thought, he bent, scooped him up and walked in the direction of the exit. "Have his bed sent to my bed chamber," he ordered to one of his men as he went. "He now stays with me."

He left the boy's parents, feeling them gaping after him, while he rushed as fast as he could along the corridor and to the lift to his subterranean bedroom. All he could think of was getting the boy far enough away to question him.

JJ sat quietly in his arms, studying him disconcertingly the whole time. It was a relief when the doors finally opened and he marched across the sand and dropped the boy to land roughly on his bed. For a moment words failed him and he glowered and paced while the boy showed no sign of fear. He merely watched him, expectantly, with those large blue–green eyes. "Have you always known what you are?" Malleven suddenly barked.

"No," JJ said, simply.

Malleven stopped pacing in annoyance, completely flummoxed at the boy's composure. He'd singled him out for it immediately. Although, when he thought about it, his father was like that. Maybe he was reading too much into it. "Are you here to destroy me?" he said more softly. It was a weak question, he knew, but it had to be asked all the same.

The boy cocked his head on an angle as if he'd seen it and found it interesting. He was disconcerting to say the least. He wanted to crush him, but he daren't. He had to continually remind himself that the boy had very weak genes, having been fathered by a Human. It was why he was foretold.

"Why would I want that?" JJ said. "I am darkly begotten, born of a line not of Atlas. I am apart from the politics here."

Malleven was astounded and exhilarated by the boy's maturity in his meaning. He knew the prophecy well. He was a cancer to the kingdom. However, if he kept him close and won his trust, he would be invincible with him behind him. After all, he hadn't won the crown by exactly fair means.

He walked over to the wall-mounted phone, just as the servants brought in JJ's bed. "Set it down over there, next to mine," he said, pointing.

Alfonzo answered the phone from the study above ground. "Have the necessary papers drawn up. I will adopt the son of Tia Storm and Jay Gardiner as my own." He put down the receiver and watched the boy happily swinging his legs over the edge of the bed. He knew he would be fulfilling the last part of the Darkly Begotten Prophecy: that he would be born of every family, but he didn't care. He wanted him to have all his powers when he worked for him. He was Dubonnetti and Santalini through Jay and Bonaci and Borge through Tia. By adopting him, it was the final necessary piece of the puzzle. JJ was now Florianna too.

The servants filed past him, having finished the bed. "Bring the boy soda and cake." His charm offensive would begin.

CHAPTER 10

"What?" Tia screamed. "He can't do that. I forbid it!"

Jay thanked the messenger, closed the bedroom door and sat with her on the edge of the huge makeshift bed. "Calm down. He can and he will."

Isla and Lacy stood close by, watching in concern. "He'll try to bend him to his will," Isla said.

Lacy nodded in agreement. No one disputed that Isla knew Malleven better than anyone.

Tia burst into tears, worry and fear taking its toll. Her hands shook as she covered her eyes. Jay pulled her into his chest and spoke into her unbrushed hair. "He's a strong boy and I have a plan while Malleven is kept busy."

MALLEVEN SIGNED the papers at his desk in the study. Then he ordered Alfonzo, "Announce to the Atlantean world that my first act as king has been to adopt the son of the former king, such is my regard and honor of him. And I invite them, two weeks from now, to celebrate my accession with the public pledging of my five Sirens."

Alfonzo bowed his head hesitantly. "And Tia Storm and Jay Gardiner are OK with this?"

Malleven cast Alfonzo a warning look. "I am king. I don't need their permission."

Alfonzo bowed again. "There is another matter to discuss, sire. We have the locations of the Scythian camps. Seven in all. Drew is ready to go tomorrow night. The US government is ready to take the New York and Salt Lake facilities and our own Santalini troops are in position to do the same for the four in Europe. Dante has asked for the go-ahead to send people in to help Drew at the headquarters."

Malleven sat back in his chair and thought about that for a moment. His first instinct was to snub his offer to reiterate his new lack of status, but then a list began to form in his mind of those with him that he would rather out of the way. "And Keenan Santalini will be part of his number?" he asked.

"I expect so. He was banished at the same time," Alfonzo said.

Malleven smirked. Cesaré was undoubtedly with him too. "Why not?" It wouldn't hurt to diminish Dante's supporters. He smiled. "Tell him I will allow it on one condition. That he takes Vionne with him." The perfection of it gladdened his heart. He would keep an eye on things. Then he would recall him and test his loyalties. Plus, he might just clash with Drew as his rival over Phoebe and save him the trouble later. The more he thought about it, the more he thought it was a great idea.

Alfonzo eyed him shrewdly as he bowed. No doubt following his train of thought. "There is one more thing, Your Highness. The president extends an invitation to meet our new king."

Malleven sighed. He hated being told what to do and his

first instinct was to deny it. He no longer felt safe outside the walls of the castle. Enemies would be circling to pick him off when they could. There was far too much to keep him there, and he certainly would not be at the beck and call of any Human—president or not. However, he did see the benefit of painting a picture of harmony for the Atlasians. Meeting the heads of state was a fitting part of his new status in society. But it would be on his terms. He inclined his head regally. "Tell the president I would be delighted. But find somewhere close, Alfonzo. I want to be there and back in an hour."

Alfonzo left it a second too long before he bowed. As if he was going to say something and thought better of it.

It irritated him immensely and he felt the familiar tremor in his hands. However, Alfonzo kept quiet and lived to breathe another day.

"Very well, Your Highness. I will see to it that the necessary communications are made."

Drew rose earlier than morning call every day, and, while it was still pitch black, he donned his sweats and jogged the perimeter. As far as the monks were concerned, he was a fanatical recruit, keeping at the peak of fitness and acting as a great example to the boys.

He soon located the spot to send the boys and mapped it by GPS coordinates. It was where the perimeter wall was high but scalable, with help. It was also the closest point to the road on the other side. There was just a small patch of forest between it, with enough of a clearing to park three buses. Then he scoped out the best places to plant the explosives to keep the monks busy and away from the boys. They needed to be at a safe distance and enough of a distraction to make their escape.

The first test text came from Alfonzo on the first day.

Then it was simple to send back short, coded messages with simple coordinates for the bus rendezvous and escape point and simple one word answers for the explosives. "Scholastic," went first for the building and then "4," for the number of floors, so they knew there was a basement level. And, lastly, "15 heads," for the head count of monks on the campus and, "30," for the roll call of the boys. The whole plan came together over the four days he'd been there and made little sense to anyone except Alfonso if his phone was found and confiscated. Finally, the last text for the go-ahead came that morning. "0300." Now all he had to do was let his Six know the arrangements.

He blew his whistle and pulled them into a huddle on the soccer field, keeping it simple. "Tonight's the night. Are you ready?"

"Yes, sir," they all said, one by one, as he looked them in the eye, holding His Boy's the longest.

Drew pulled away and blew his whistle again for the others to run another lap of the field, out of earshot. "I don't have to remind you of secrecy."

They all nodded, but seemed more controlled and uncertain than usual. Fear and anticipation were a tangible crackle in the air, as if a monster would burst out and capture them any minute. For a moment he wavered, worried they couldn't handle what he was asking of them. It was a lot. He met His Boy's eyes and they conveyed something only he could recognize. That unquantifiable thing he himself had when he was last at this place. That I'll-do-it-go-anywhere-do-anything-even-if-it-gets-me
killed-look, as long as it gets me out and makes me finally feel alive. It was enough to shake him out of his hesitance and he pulled the boys in as if he was discussing game tactics. "After lights out, you will remain dressed in your beds. The fire bell will sound. Then, in all the commotion,

you must get the boys out. You will head for the wall at the north perimeter. Someone will be there to help you. Go through the woods to the road. Three buses will be waiting to get you out of here. You will be taken to an airstrip. I will do my best to meet you at the buses. If I'm not there, you must leave with them and I will find you. Do you understand?"

They all nodded, but looked to His Boy, their spokesman, nervously. "What if we or the boys are caught up in putting out the fire?"

It was a good question. Drew wanted every single boy out of the place when they blew it up. "Don't worry about that. It will be in a place where only the monks are nearby. Just be strict on the boys being in their beds."

His Boy absorbed what he said, nodded, satisfied, and looked at the others. "Yes, sir," they all said.

Then he delivered the last piece of the puzzle that they were all aching to know. "This is a once-only mission and I want no one left behind."

It was 361 who voiced it for the boys. "Will we be coming back, sir, after the exercise?"

This was the time for honesty. Make or break. He hoped to god they all stayed with him on this and his intuition had been right. It was a huge undertaking for young boys that lived their lives under a constant yoke of fear. They would be risking their lives tomorrow night. In the silence, he asked, "What are your names?" It was time to discard the camp-issued number that took away any importance of self. He looked at each of them one by one. "I am Drew," he said to prove his commitment.

His Boy spoke first. "I'm Justin."

Their eyes locked for a brief moment and Drew smiled at him. He was surprised that he'd committed first and repeated the name in his mind. "Pleased to meet you, Justin."

Then the others gained confidence and followed one by one.

"I'm Luke."

"Mike."

"Gus."

"David."

Each name was said with a nod of hello, as if they were meeting for the first time. Drew smiled and rested his eyes on the very last one.

"Three six one," he said after a pause, making all the others burst into unprecedented laughter.

It was funny.

The boy shrugged. "It's what I was called before. Well, they added a zero here, but I dropped it."

Drew grinned. It was certainly a question for later and lovely to see boys acting like normal teenagers. But laughter was very definitely not encouraged and a monk stationed nearby was walking over. *Shit.* He blew his whistle. "Drop and give me ten then join the others."

As they recognized the danger and dropped to the ground, Drew stood over them and whispered. "I'm going to have to get hard on you, OK?" Then he shouted, "Run. Now. And keep your skinny butts running till nightfall." He hated having to do it, but he couldn't afford to look soft at this stage.

The monk came up alongside him as the boys ran off. "Problem?"

Drew shook his head. "Just high spirits that will be gone by nightfall," he said, looking into the dead eyes of the monk he vaguely remembered from before. "Don't worry. It won't happen again."

The monk gave one small nod. "You're needed in the study."

Drew watched the boys join the others and continue to

run. He felt bad, only bolstering himself with the knowledge that, after tomorrow night, the Scythians would cease to exist and the boys would be free. "Of course," he said, bowing his head. "Watch them, they can be lazy." Then he jogged off in the direction of the main building. It was for the necessary debriefing he'd been expecting. He'd promised himself that before he left this place, he would visit his mentors and teach them the lesson they deserved.

CHAPTER 11

*D*ante appeared to be relaxing in the opulent hall of Filfla, sipping coffee, while Nathan, one of the surfer guys, lazily strummed an acoustic guitar. He smiled and chatted, but, all the while, his stomach churned and his mind whirred, aching for news from the castle and how Tia and the children were faring.

His façade dropped and he put his coffee cup down when Cesaré came briskly into the room and walked purposely towards him. He obviously had news. He straightened in his chair. "What is it?"

"I just got off the phone to Alfonzo. We've got the go-ahead to go and help Drew."

"Yes!" came from several of the Santalini guards lounging around him. Keenan and his boys were straight on their feet, eager to do something constructive. Sitting and waiting was killing them.

"There will be a seven-pronged attack," Cesaré explained. "It will be on the same night at the same time so there can be no communication. We go in at 3 a.m. local time, so they can go into the European camps just after dark."

"How many other camps are in the US?" Keenan asked.

"Two. The president has offered troops to go into the New York and Salt Lake City camps at midnight and 2 a.m.

Dante had heard enough. It was a good plan, and, as much as he hated to admit it, one he couldn't have worked out better himself. "We leave right away."

"Not you, Your Highness," Cesaré said. "Malleven hopes for casualties. It's no doubt a trick to draw you out. You must stay here."

Dante wanted to protest, but knew he was right. "Then you must stay too," he said, knowing full well that any of the Sirens' mates could be picked off on this mission.

Cesaré looked frustrated for a moment, but bobbed his head in the end, knowing it made sense. "The only thing that Malleven stipulated was that Vionne must be included."

Dante frowned at what that meant. The Murrs were strong, but only in water. They weren't ideal soldiers on land. He looked over at Vionne. "You knew of this?"

No ... I think it is a good plan though.

Keenan sniggered. Everyone knew that the only reason he wanted to go was to make sure that Drew died during the operation. Keenan had no love for the guy either, making no secret that he never trusted him. His instincts had been right in the beginning, but, later, he was sure, it was just a case of him pushing his buttons. It had already ended in a fight where he'd had to put Drew down.

However, Vionne was his immediate concern and he continued to assess him. His first duty was to his own people and no doubt Malleven was playing to that, but he hoped his sense of honor meant he would remain loyal to him. "Remember what Drew did for us," he said, his eyes finally leaving Vionne. He looked at everyone around him one by one. "And if the Orb saw fit to save him then it must be for a purpose. By his blood, he is a Bonaci prince. So we owe him."

He looked at all the Protectors sitting together, then back to Vionne who sat with the new mysterious Murr female. *Besides, you seem otherwise occupied these days,* he projected, so only Vionne could hear. He shifted uncomfortably.

"OK!" Dante said, standing up and snapping everyone to action. "Be ready in two hours. Cesaré, Cash and Sean, you will stay here as my guard. Everyone else get to it!"

It felt good to be doing something. The wait was killing them all.

IN TIA'S BEDCHAMBER, Jay explained what happened with JJ and the bracelets and Tia wailed fresh tears. Their eyes widened in horror with each new piece of information. It was a blow to them all.

"I don't understand. How can little JJ be the Darkly Begotten? That's ridiculous," Lacy said, sitting down on the bed to comfort Tia.

"I sensed something in him straight away," Isla said quietly.

She wasn't sensationalizing it. Merely stating a fact. It was one of the things Jay admired about her; the ability to remain detached. He remembered the occasion they'd first met Isla. She'd attempted to scan JJ's mind and he'd slammed her down. He was just a toddler and she'd remarked that he was incredibly strong for his age.

"Rest assured, Malleven has a use for JJ. He will be safe all the while that's the case," Isla said.

Jay knew she was right, and he touched her shoulder. "I think I'm in more danger here than JJ. Has anyone managed to reach their partners telepathically?"

All three sisters shook their heads. It pained him that Tia still thought of Dante as her partner even though it was irrational. "Here." He took out a cell phone from his pocket and handed it to them. "It's a burner phone. They won't be able to trace it. Be discreet and use it one at a time above ground and only outside the castle, OK?"

They all nodded. Lacy was crying. Tia reached for his hand. He could feel how much she worried about Dante. It was impossible for him to speak to Dante himself, even though he wanted to. For his plan to work, he must think he'd abandoned him. "You must say no details about me here," he said, particularly to Isla. "Just that I'm here as a guard, nothing more."

Isla agreed, no questions asked, like the soldier she was.

Although he knew it would be hardest for Tia, she accepted reluctantly.

"What about me?" Lacy asked.

He'd left her out for a reason. "As far as Dante is concerned, say nothing about me, but you can tell Keenan to come here. In secret!" he emphasized. "If he can get here, I'll smuggle you out to breathe for him, OK?"

Her eyes were already brimming with tears of gratitude. She threw her arms around his neck and thanked him over and over. When he saw the other two sitting quietly watching, he kissed her forehead and put her away from him. "For Darres, we'll wait until he comes back with Vionne."

Isla nodded, satisfied. Tia looked at him sadly, knowing that it was impossible for Dante. He would begin to waste away until there was nothing of the old him left, if they didn't save him soon.

Jay began to pace. "Cesaré will get sick too because Lily is too loyal to Malleven to approach."

"It may not always be so," Isla said, guiltily. "Believe me, Lance does not have long. Malleven will not let her keep him."

Jay knew that Malleven guarded Lily closely like an investment. Her room with Lance was near his at the far end of the bedroom corridor. "You're right, but it's Dante this will hit the hardest as he is joined to all of you, except Lily. This will soon knock him off his feet."

"Please can I ring him too, Jay?"

Tia was pleading with him, but he knew her too well. She never followed instructions and she wouldn't be able to resist telling him that Jay was working for him here. It would be a death sentence for the both of them. So for that reason he had to shake his head. I'm sorry, Tia."

He pulled her into his chest as she cried softly. "If Dante knows me as well as I know he does, he'll understand I wouldn't abandon him." He hoped to god that was so, as he couldn't imagine how he must be feeling right now.

They relaxed after that. Jay had announced that he was staying in their room for extra protection and no one argued against it. Lacy had joked with a "Yeah, yeah, that old chestnut," insinuating that he was only there to get close to Tia. There was an element of truth in that.

The double bed pushed together with a single meant it wasn't too much of a squash for four to sleep together, but he soon grumbled when Isla and Lacy made sure it was him who slept over the gap with the single bed.

He shuffled closer to Tia, so he could push the strands of her hair from her face. "Are you sure you're able to do this?" he said. He knew how hard it was for her to hurt Dante.

"I can see there's no other way," she said, sniffing and wiping away a single tear. "We have to be fast though, Jay. He won't have long. And it's not just the breathing thing. I can't feel him at all."

"Neither can we," Isla called from the furthest part of the bed.

"Can you feel Darres?" Jay asked.

"No."

"It's like everything was cut, the moment they left," Lacy said, confirming for him that it was the same for them all.

It was very worrying. It had never happened before. There was only one thing it could be. "He must have done something to the castle walls because Tia spoke straight to my head earlier."

"Like a charm barrier," Isla said.

"They exist?' he asked.

"He's a Magi and a Florianna," Tia said.

He let that sink in for a moment. Then they had to speed up operations. There was simply too much at stake. "If I'm going to take the kingdom, I'm going to need to bond with you all before Malleven does." All the while he never took his eyes off Tia's. It had torn them apart when Dante had done the same in the early days of their marriage.

"What about Elixir, Jay," she said, drawing him back to the first time she'd ever breathed for him. She'd nearly killed him and it was one of the reasons he doubted what Christian had told him. His body had battled the Sirens' breath and needed Elixir to survive. He was a lot stronger now, but he'd only ever breathed with one Siren. Five or even three might kill him. He could only hope that what Christian had told him was true and his recessive genes would carry him through.

Thankfully, he had what he needed and tapped his pocket. "I have a supply with me." It was something Atlanteans only took for symptoms when around their most compatible mate. For him it would literally save his life.

Tia looked a little relieved at that. "Won't Malleven suspect if you get ill?"

He squeezed her shoulder. "You might have to cover for me."

Lacy giggled. "Keenan's gonna kill you."

Jay smiled ruefully. She was absolutely right.

"Darres is already going to kill Drew first, so you might

have a little time till he gets round to you," Isla said from her side of the bed, her wide grin evident in her voice.

Jay nodded solemnly. "You're cut off from your mates and Malleven hasn't bonded with you yet. The timing is perfect."

"Won't it be a bit conspicuous us all getting in the water together?" Isla said.

Jay understood they all overheated during the process and needed to be underwater. He looked at Tia, knowing she would think the same thing. "We'll use the shower." He looked into her eyes, forgetting the others, remembering the hundreds of times they'd done it before.

Three of us could kill you, Tia projected straight to his mind.

He picked up her hand. "There isn't time to stagger it. We might not get another chance." He pulled her up from the bed with him, to her feet, and began to walk towards the bathroom. The other two sisters looked at each other, got up and followed.

What about our sex ban? Tia asked, referring to the pact they'd made not so long ago.

"I'll do my best," Jay said, grinning as he pushed open the bathroom door.

Tia giggled and switched on the shower. Jay put his hand in and adjusted it to lukewarm. It was another mark against his Atlantean heritage. He couldn't take the cold. Atlantean's bodies ran a lot colder than humans.

It was a wet room with an opaque glass partition forming a large cubicle. It felt strangely awkward standing there with Tia and her sisters. The water pounded them all from a waterfall shower above their heads and they looked outrageously hot. Even standing in their PJs; made up of a vest and slouchy, low slung pants.

It was a good idea to stay dressed. When the euphoria hit, it lit up the libido like nothing else. It would be his only saving grace with their partners. Tia was a different story all together. She was the love of his life.

They all looked at him expectantly. He didn't know why he hesitated. His life had been filled with hard sex with a plethora of uninhibited women, willing to do anything for him. He guessed it was because it was Tia. Strangely, love and respect for her wasn't the main reason, it was more to do with the fact that she was married to his best friend and would go back to him when this was all over, ripping his heart out with her.

He wished he had the privacy of telepathic speech.

Tia looked at him enquiringly, no doubt wondering why he hesitated.

"Are you sure you're OK with this, Tia?" Dante breathing with other women had been a huge bone of contention in their marriage and here he was about to do the same thing.

She smiled and relaxed immediately. *It's not the same thing at all.*

He tried to process it without getting hurt, but he couldn't help feeling it was because he didn't matter. That she'd been married to Dante and so it held much more importance. His feelings were illogical, he knew, but that's what set her apart; she made him feel.

As always, she knew where his thoughts were going. *Jay. Stop! This is an emergency and you're risking your life for us. How could I get angry about that?*

After one last search of her face, he took a deep breath and nodded.

Tia pushed Lacy forward, so she was right in front of him. He was glad she was first. She was the most approachable out of her and Isla. "Come on, Jay. Like in the film: 'Just put your lips together and blow'."

Lacy giggled and Jay rolled his eyes. He guessed he was being a sap. He pulled Lacy closer, as if they were lovers, and held the tops of her arms. "Keenan's gonna kill me for this," he muttered as he moved in for the kiss.

"He'll have to get over himself," Lacy whispered, next to his lips.

Her eyes were closed when he covered her mouth with his. Despite the similarities, she felt completely different. He took one last look at Tia standing behind, who gave him a small nod. His eyes fluttered closed and he gave himself over to the stream flowing into his mouth. It followed its usual route, down his neck until he felt it lashing itself to his heart. There, any similarity ended. When it eventually exploded through his nervous system, he felt nothing but pure Lacy: warm, loving and sexy. He could even feel Keenan and Dante. The bond was truly an amazing thing. Then he rode out the wash of euphoria that always followed, in a torrent that robbed him of all coherent thought for several minutes. Arms helped him stumble back against the wall.

After what felt like hours, he opened his eyes and Lacy smiled at him. "Isla's turn," she said, chirpily.

He let out a breath of laughter, not sure how he could handle any more. He was slaughtered after just one of them.

"We can wait a while," Tia said, frowning with worry.

Jay shook his head and beckoned Isla towards him. His eyes were half closed and bleary. He was wasted, but they couldn't afford to delay. "Let's get it done."

He repeated the process with Isla. Her strength hit him instantly. He felt Dante, Darres and a hint of another that surprised him: Drew. But his thoughts soon jumbled into incoherence as her essence took him over; tangling with his heart and squeezing the life out of him. It blasted through his body and rendered him useless. He was wrapped in her and left wondering, for the umpteenth time, where that left him as an Atlantean. Returning the breath was something he'd never been able to do. He could only hope that a one-way bond with all five Sirens still made him a contender for the kingdom.

When, eventually, he slid down the wall to land on his backside on the floor, he blinked up at Tia standing over him. The sisters had left and her face looked flushed and serious. He hoped she wasn't angry or upset. She straddled his legs and sunk down to his level to sit on them. They were face to face, examining each other's eyes. Tia no doubt assessing his health and he, that she didn't hate him for what he'd just done. He was still intoxicated with their essence as if he were stoned. She brought him back to her with her hands on his shoulders. She was beautiful.

"Well, here we are, King Jay."

It sounded so wrong, it made him grin. "Here we are," he repeated, resting his head on the wall behind him. Her mouth descended slowly on his and he welcomed her wonderful familiar essence. He floated and bathed in her until the world went black.

CHAPTER 12

Vionne couldn't wait to get away. His ship was ready to go and he needed time to think. Drew was alive and he had almost ten thousand souls, vulnerable and reliant on him through the most dangerous undertaking of their lives. He must oversee the progress of New Murrtaine, but it was more than a need to ensure the safety of his people; it was a need to patch the bleeding hole in his chest that losing his father and his home had made in him. His ring was purple. Phoebe should be by his side through these dark days, but now Drew lived, with each passing day, it seemed increasingly impossible. He couldn't compete with a love like that. While he lived.

Preoccupied with the bitterness of what he must do festering in the pit of his stomach, he went to disappear into the fountain, when he spotted Ashaya. She was watching him, quiet and alone as she often was. *Do you have time for a tour?* he projected on impulse.

Her demeanor instantly brightened and she nodded. *Of course. I always have time for my lord.*

Her words pulled at something in his gut that he couldn't

explain. Maybe it was because it was sincere and not flattery at all. He smiled. *Come, then. We don't have much time.*

Vionne took a much smaller craft parked in the dock and they soon zipped the few miles to the New Murrtaine site. He watched her profile a few times while she observed the wonders of the clear sea that whizzed past the transparent sides of the craft. They didn't speak, but he found her presence comforting. He looked ahead and there it was, the newly constructed dome. A huge, opaque saucer that disappeared into the seabed. Undetectable from above, there was no technology in this world that could determine or trace what was inside.

It affected him utterly and completely, like a punch to his chest he wasn't expecting. His heart ached with a longing for something lost that was impossible to find, because it was a time not a place. It hit him in a single moment and only subsided with a gentle hand that rested on his back. The craft moved slowly through the membrane that blurred out the sea and he turned to look into Ashaya's eyes. They seemed to understand perfectly what he was feeling. *It is stunningly beautiful,* she said, saving him from any embarrassment.

It is, he answered eventually.

The dome is a great wonder.

No one will ever detect Murrtaine. He didn't know why he was explaining like a proud architect. She would be completely aware of its benefits from the one that covered Murrla. But there was something about her that always seemed like she was seeing things for the first time. A wonderful suppressed excitement, as if she was privileged to witness any of them. It was very inspiring and humbling. *You are one of life's beautiful souls,* he found himself saying.

She simply stared intensely back at him, until Vionne broke the laden moment by holding out his arm for them to leave the ship. He stood in a daze; somehow sure she was as affected as he was.

He allowed her to step through the funnel membrane in the floor first and then followed, leaving the marine bug and any awkwardness behind. *We can't be long. I just needed to see its progress,* he explained as they swam along. He was still so surprised at what had passed between them that he wasn't taking in his surroundings at first. Then the scale of the work undertaken started to filter through to him. Many of the buildings were already begun; footings and walls, floor bases in some. Even the new palace was clear to make out in its center.

The Orb alone was the great architect, plans and early work solely undertaken by her. Then, gradually, as more of his skilled subjects arrived, they took over the finer points and the real building work began.

They swam slowly through what would soon be streets. Tall, able Murrs nodded from scaffolding. Each was carrying the blue-green crystalline material in cupped hands from piles stacked next to them, to form the walls that made up the whole city. It fused together the moment it made contact with the wall to form the glazed finish and was amazing to watch. The material, designed in Atlas, was still a wonder, as the original Murrtaine had been built centuries before he was born.

He took Ashaya's hand, feeling the warm glow it gave him, and together they swam on.

Space had been allocated for gardens and parks, already lined with Murrs waving a greeting as they sowed seeds. Great trellises and rockeries were already taking shape for the production of food or simply for their beauty.

Much of the layout of the great city was still like a film set, but it was easy to visualize what it would become. Production would speed up too as more people arrived.

Turning slowly in the water, taking it all in, Vionne felt himself breathe a little easier at how far it had come. His people would be safe and it was going to be a magnificent city on an epic scale. Built from nothing in weeks. An overwhelming emotion came over him. He wished his father could see it. Just once.

Ashaya came closer and touched the side of his face. It drew his attention from the cacophony of emotions that threatened to overwhelm him. *You will have the city you were always meant to have because you are a great lord,* she said. He stared at her, dazed, and found himself falling into those pool-like eyes. He only just stopped himself kissing and crushing her to him.

He rationalized it as being overcome by the heat of the moment and quickly swam a step back. He had to swallow and consciously slow down his heart. *What was he thinking?* It was selfish. She was a gentle priestess, merely offering support and his life was a hopeless mess. His heart belonged to another. He bowed his head to disguise his turmoil and held out his arm in the direction they came. *I am satisfied with the building progress, shall we?*

She didn't argue, but her bright aura that always lit a room, appeared a little dimmer. They swam back, he even more troubled and subdued.

DESPITE THE WEIRD dynamic between her and Vionne, Ashaya felt the most alive she'd ever felt. They emerged from the fountain and Filfla was full of activity. It began to feel like the walls themselves emitted excitement and hope. It seemed that everyone was preparing to leave to go to the aid of Drew, the human turned Bonaci by his Nix Siren, Phoebe Ray. Ashaya felt like she knew them intimately and couldn't wait to meet them. She had to make sure she was in the party that went with them and so she hovered to seize her chance.

Santalini soldiers in black fatigues, full packs, with heavy weapons on their shoulders mingled with smaller, more human-looking Protectors and discussed strategy for the mission. Their bodies were taut, movements fast and their laughter a little too loud, showing clearly their coiled excitement. Tall, handsome Murrs were pouring in from the fountain all the time. Their deference to Dante was very clear and telling. Even in their stillness, in their groups, the pictorial speech was vivid and bright with anticipation. Everyone seemed at one in their eagerness for battle.

Her attention was taken by a commotion next to the staircase. A Protector, Connor, appeared to be trying to restrain the Siren, Phoebe Ray. "You can't stop me. I'm going!" she shouted, struggling against him. Her eyes churned in and out of their Nix form and she gnashed her elongated teeth. A circle of space cleared around her.

Ashaya wasn't afraid. She'd watched this Siren's development for three years and knew that a Nix could change living things around her. It was how she'd unwittingly changed Drew. It was a great power borne from her darkness.

She took a step forward into the space Phoebe had created and seized her chance. *I could come and keep Her Highness at a safe distance,* she projected so all could hear. This close the narrowed orange eyes looked directly at her. *That way, she will see the young prince as soon as he is liberated.*

Dante had observed from the opposite side of the circle. He tipped his head in a gesture of gratitude, but looked intrigued nonetheless. An active mind was always hard at work behind those lively eyes. Nevertheless, he seemed to quell it with more pressing matters. "Very well, she can go with you as long as she remains at a safe distance." He stepped forward and addressed the whole assembly more loudly. "The first party, led by Keenan, will be travelling in the Dubonnetti Industries' plane. Vionne will lead the second and travel in his Hyperneedle by sea." He turned to her. "You and the princess will go with Vionne."

Ashaya nodded. She had seen examples of the craft. Their extreme aerodynamics meant they could achieve super speeds under water.

"Because of the transfer times to and from airports, Vionne's crew will arrive only a little time after the aircraft. You will rendezvous and go into the camp at exactly zero three hundred hours. All the other camps will be attacked at precisely the same time. Don't be late!" Dante said, turning a circle as he spoke. "Myself, Cesaré, Cash and Sean will stay here, in contact the whole time.

Sudden laughter ran through her mind and made her turn to see the source at the fountain. Everyone seemed to do the same. Vionne was rushing to greet three strong Murr latecomers, breaching the surface and climbing out. He embraced one with black hair and touched his forehead with his. It was easy to see he was Axyl, the twin of the Murr, Darres. Her heart froze when both males turned to look directly at her.

Axyl shook his head as she knew he would, telling Vionne that he didn't know her from Murrla. Her cover was blown and Vionne would know she'd been lying. She watched nervously as Dante approached them. There was more embracing, and she held her breath while the two called her over.

She walked slowly, fearful and bitterly disappointed to have been discovered so quickly. She would be recalled by Seti and another sent in her place. She had failed her task.

She came to a standstill in front of them, bowed her head and waited for the accusation of being an imposter. She held her breath, waiting. However, instead of angry accusations,

Axyl bowed deeply and said, *Forgive me, Lady of the Five Moons, but I do not recall you in Murrla. The governing of the city takes much of my time, and, because of this, I am to blame for not socializing and neglecting my worship of late.*

Ashaya immediately dropped into a low curtsey, cheeks blushing, mind racing in relief.

You see what breeding she has, Brother, and a female of the Five Moons too, Vionne projected so she could hear.

Axyl took her hand and put his forehead to it. *Indeed, Brother.*

She almost swooned with the compliment and daren't look Vionne in the eye.

I will collect my men and Phoebe, and we will leave straight away, Vionne said, addressing her directly. *My craft is fast, but we have greater miles to travel by sea.*

Her heart was still pumping at her near-miss, but she managed a regal bow. *Of course, my lord. I am ready.* She decided the two of them were either keeping their own council or they were giving her the benefit of the doubt. Either way, it was a reprieve.

THE SANTALINI GUARDS and Protectors said a hasty farewell to Dante and headed for the helicopter bays. Ashaya stood with Phoebe next to the fountain waiting to dive down into the tunnel. *Ready?* Vionne said to them both.

"Let's get on with it," Phoebe said, hopping over the fountain wall and jumping into the deeper water, without hesitation.

Ashaya took a one last sympathetic look at Vionne. She understood the flicker of pain in his aura at Phoebe's eagerness to rescue another man. He gave her his weird crooked-looking smile and she jumped in and followed her. His presence behind her emitted heat, all the way through the tunnel, until they eventually came out to the clear Mediterranean sea.

The Needle was docked in a special cradle nearby. It was a marvelous feat of engineering, aesthetically beautiful, resembling a pearl in color and tapered more at one end like a long, smooth pencil. It didn't look wide enough to fit any people, but, in fact, it was probably the width of a private jet, although at least three times as long. It was easy to see how it cut through the water so fast.

The others would waste time getting a helicopter to Malta airport, a long plane journey and then driving when they reached the other side in Seattle. They, on the other hand, would go full speed across the Mediterranean to Gibraltar, then the Atlantic and slip through the Panama Canal. Then, once in the Pacific, they would head north along the western seaboard to Washington State.

Vionne held out his hand and Ashaya followed Phoebe, pushing up through the membrane hatch. The craft's fuselage was a cream-colored living organism that originated on her planet. It solidified and changed color to fit its surroundings.

The bridge was where you would imagine it to be; at the pointed end. Soft, powder-blue, wide swivel seats were arranged facing four to a table at the front half and blue curtain- covered bunks to sleep in were three high towards the back. Ashaya went to one of them to store her bag that held her vacuum-packed Human clothes. The thin, shimmering clothes she was wearing were suited to underwater and too conspicuous and inadequate on land.

The device to make moving through water like air was switched on and they moved off, reaching a speed that didn't feel like they were moving at all.

It was a relief to move freely and Ashaya made her way back to the seating area. She found Phoebe sitting at a table on her own, and she didn't look up or speak. Vionne seemed busy managing the running of the craft, so she took the opportunity. *May I sit?* she projected.

Phoebe shrugged like she couldn't care less and looked out at the sea, which became visible at a wave of the hand. Ashaya assessed her aura and stayed at the edge of her consciousness, now understanding that a full scan was not polite on Earth. What she found shocked her. Murrs emitted feelings and were easy to read, but Phoebe proved appearances could be deceptive and how little of reality they really understood from above. She was sweating, her heart palpitating and she was frantic with worry. *You love your human hybrid,* she said, eventually. It was obvious and troubling and would not be easily received by the kingdom she was soon to judge. *But you are promised to Vionne, are you not?*

Phoebe gave her a black look and, for a moment, her eyes flashed orange. *I do not love Vionne.*

Simple words said through gritted teeth and yet Ashaya couldn't help being glad of them. She told herself that she was rooting for her for the sake of love, but, deep down, she knew it was something far more troubling and selfish.

Nevertheless, it was true. She didn't love him. Hatred now rolled off her in waves. She'd seen them together. There was no pull for her towards a destined mate. A Nix was strong enough to follow her own path. It was disturbing and strangely thrilling at the same time.

He is a good man, Ashaya said.

Phoebe flashed her another warning look.

If it weren't for the fact that you were promised to him, you would like him, would you not? Did you not before?

The look Phoebe shot at her then was tinged with a frown. She was considering what she said.

For a moment Ashaya thought she'd given something of herself away. *Will you allow them to fight?* she asked, to throw her off. *Whichever one you love, Vionne has the right to challenge him.* For the Atlanteans it was a simple test of letting one of them drown, but for a Murr that was pointless—and she already had Vionne's breath.

She looked upset at that. *Drew is not the weakling everyone thinks.*

Ashaya tipped her head in agreement. *No, you have seen to that.*

Phoebe's eyes shot to hers again and they weighed each other up for a long moment. *You know a lot,* she said shrewdly.

Ashaya inwardly blushed. *I am a seer,* she said quickly, then abruptly changed the subject. *Tell me, if you hadn't thought that Drew was dead, would you have chosen to pledge to the new king?*

The question clearly took Phoebe by surprise, but then she considered the question. *I don't think so. Dante was OK and Malleven is a prick. He kidnapped me, you know. Made me do things.* Her brow furrowed as if her mind had gone to a very dark place.

I did know that, Ashaya admitted, having shown enough to her watching adjudicators. She stood and bowed her head. *I will leave you to your thoughts.*

Ashaya moved further down the craft towards where Axyl and Vionne were sitting. She paused before they noticed her. She felt a quickening in her heart whenever she came near the lord advocate and had to compose herself.

They noticed her exactly at that moment and stood up. *Join us,* Vionne said.

Actually, I need to take care of something, Axyl said, and left them to go to the front of the ship.

Ashaya sat in his place, feeling suddenly uncomfortable. It wasn't logical.

So, my lady, Vionne said. *What do you think of our craft here?* He held out his hand, encompassing everywhere.

It is very beautiful. They had indeed moved on in their technology since being cut off, but they were still behind what had been achieved on Atlas and she hadn't been there for five hundred years. *A most efficient use of power.*

Vionne looked at her with interest at her technical knowledge. As he began to talk, it was clear it was a subject close to his heart and she would have to tread carefully. She quickly excused herself, explaining her father was an engineer. A fact that was true, although she omitted that she herself had graduated top of her class. It was easier for him to think that she was intuitive and clever because she was a mystic of the Five Moons.

She felt him studying and trying to read her the whole time. His aura was gentle, speculative and interested. A little puzzling for a betrothed. *Tell me, what are your thoughts on the new king?* She knew he had already made a deal in exchange for Phoebe, but somehow it was important to know what he felt deep down.

He looked at her quizzically, as if he wasn't expecting her to talk politics. *It is a shame. Dante is spirited and unorthodox in many ways, but he sought a fair government.* He sat back in his chair and shook his head. *This one, I fear, will rule alone.*

Isn't that what the nation needs, a strong leader?

He tipped his head in a mannerism that was completely human, showing all that were watching that the taint was already seeping into the pure race. She found she wanted to stop him doing it, and yet it only added to his attractiveness, which made no sense. *Maybe,* he said. *But we hold sway over a host planet that outnumbers us many thousand to one. To be a successful king, you must have a symbiotic relationship with its leaders.*

It was an astounding comment for a purebred to make

and she found she wanted to protect him and get him to clarify. *You're not suggesting complete assimilation of the races, are you?*

Thankfully, Vionne shook his head. *No, what I'm saying is, there is beauty in this world and its people. And on a planet where we hold most of the power and wealth, we owe it to them to take them into account when governing them. It is the wise, far-sighted thing to do.*

Ashaya felt herself gushing like a proud parent, admiring his insight. He was indeed a wise and just leader.

A rod of iron now, could mean unrest or even revolution later, he went on.

He was right. She would remember Vionne's case for the Humans when judging and hoped those watching noted it too. It made sense of why Dante made a friend of Lance and many of the Sirens' Protectors. *Thank you for explaining your perspective so clearly,* she said, bowing her head, and thinking for the umpteenth time what an unusual Murr he was. She found herself looking into his endlessly deep black eyes. *Will you challenge the hybrid, Drew?*

His demeanor changed instantly. He looked down and played with the purple ring on his left hand. It proved that Phoebe was his and was close by. *It doesn't matter what I want. I promised my father on his deathbed. He was a great man.* Then he looked up, directly into her eyes. *Even though she hates me and loves another, I must for him.*

She could see he was conflicted. He had a great regard for Phoebe and didn't want to hurt her, but felt he was under an oath—one he couldn't break. It was an impossible situation.

They talked of New Murrtaine after that, and how it would rival the cities of Atlas when it was finished. His eyes shone as he described his old home and how he would pay homage to that in its construction. He had no idea she knew it intimately. That she had studied nothing else for over five hundred years.

He spoke of his people making the arduous journey and how anxious he was that many of them wouldn't make it. *We owe it to the children,* he projected, his mind moving away to produce an image of a playful bunch, zipping about on marine bikes—homing in on one particularly. *We build a future for them,* he said wistfully.

It was said more to himself than to her and she found her heart shifted a little more as she studied him. She knew it was unwise, but couldn't help herself. She had to admit her regard for him was growing with every interaction. It would be hard to keep a level of professionalism, but she must at all costs for the safety of all concerned. She must not be recalled as she firmly believed she was the only person truly qualified to judge these people. A destiny not even Seti knew was at play.

Time passed. The two of them chatted companionably, while the hyperneedle cut a swift path through the ocean and Vionne had no idea how woven their fates had become.

CHAPTER 13

$\mathcal{K}$eenan's phone rang with an unknown number just minutes before boarding the Dubonnetti jet at Luqa airport. He walked away from the restless Santalinis, clustered together, and answered the call. "What?"

"Keenan?"

"Lacy? Is that you? Are you OK?" He paced as he ran his fingers through his hair.

"Yes, Keenan. Baby, listen. I don't have much time."

Keenan froze with dread. "What's happened? What's he done?" Anger threatened to sear right though him so he could no longer hear. "I'm coming," he said flatly, already striding back to the main building.

"No, it's nothing like that. Jay is here helping us and he's going to smuggle me out to breathe for you. How soon can you get here?"

Keenan turned to look at his cousins while he walked backwards. Reeve was staring after him. *Shit!* He was meant to lead this mission.

He immediately jogged back and pulled Reeve aside while

Lacy still waited on the phone. "It's Lacy, I have to go," was all he needed to say.

Reeve simply nodded and said, "Go! Don't worry."

Keenan gave him a brief hug, grateful he was every bit as capable to take over the mission, and half walked half jogged back to the airport building. "I'm on my way," he said and ended the call. He wanted nothing more than to keep her talking, but he didn't want to compromise her in any way. He took one last look over his shoulder as he slid into the building and saw Reeve ushering their group up the steps of the plane.

He waited an agonizing further three hours for the next commercial flight with nothing but his spiraling paranoia to keep him company. He finally boarded, but even getting in the air lasted a lifetime. His foot tapped, his heart raced and he flicked channels. He hated Coach. His sheer size and coiled aggression kept any passengers or stewards away; a businessman unfortunate enough to be seated next to him soon asked to be moved. All the way to London and then onto Galway, he chewed his nails and told himself over and over that Jay was there. Bringing him back to breathe with Lacy was a good thing and didn't mean that things at the castle were dire.

The journey took him the best part of the night. Then, as soon as he hit Irish soil, he risked texting, *1 hour away*, and was immediately texted back a place at the edge of the grounds.

At last, he parked the hire car in the lane and jogged the last part to the boundary wall of Ballygowan Castle. It would soon be light. He hid in some bushes and took out his mobile phone. *Here.* He waited for what felt an eternity, crouched and straining his ears for the slightest sound, until he heard the soft whistle that told him they were there. He came out from his hiding place, took a couple of strides backwards and ran at the wall. In a couple of bounds, he threw himself up, put his leg over the top and slid down the other side. A move all too familiar for a kid who grew up on East London's streets.

He landed noiselessly, on his feet. Lacy ran and threw herself at him and he caught and kissed her hard. *God, she felt so good.* He held her to him, inhaling her scent, until he heard the familiar cough in the shadows.

He reluctantly put her from him and held the sides of her face. "Are you OK?" he whispered. "Is he treating you right?" He kissed her again until Jay stepped out from the shadows to where he could see him.

Keenan finally let Lacy go to hug his friend, holding him an extra moment, grateful for what he'd done for him. "I knew I could count on you. Thank you," he whispered, pulling apart and picking up Lacy's hand again. "I'm taking her back with me," he said, turning back towards the wall.

Lacy dragged her feet.

He tugged her again. "Come on, Lace, we can go to Dante. You'll be safe there."

She was shaking her head. "I can't leave my sisters, Keenan. Not yet."

Keenan looked at Jay anxiously. "Tell her it's best, Jay."

"I've got a plan, Keenan. The girls are helping me."

It made no sense. He was there now. Something in his friend's demeanor made him feel uneasy and he turned and faced him square on. "What you playin' at, Jay? You know she's safer with me. I'm not leaving her here."

Jay took a threatening step closer. "What about the others, Keenan? The kingdom. We're fucked if we don't do something."

Keenan glared at them—particularly Lacy, who was taking Jay's side over his. He swore and began pacing in front of them while he thought. He was torn. He loved the sisters, but this was Lacy, the woman who was his life.

"I need you to swear to not say anything of this to Dante, Keenan. Only that I'm here protecting them as a Santalini soldier."

Keenan stopped pacing. "Why? Why would you want to do that?" he said, narrowing his eyes at him.

"Look, just breathe with her and I'll explain. We've got ten minutes, tops, before Malleven's guards come around again, so be quick!"

Keenan watched Jay walk off and became conscious of the blush of orange rising over the tops of the trees. It then sunk in; the risk he'd taken to arrange this. He pulled Lacy with him behind a huge oak. The grounds were patrolled, and he didn't trust those creepy Magi bastards.

He backed Lacy up against the trunk of the tree, pushed her hair out of the way and ran a thumb along her lips. "Are you OK, really?" he asked. There was so much he wanted to say. His body was screaming to take her and get the hell out.

She nodded, tears brimming in her eyes. "Let's breathe for each other quickly, Keenan. Jay's risking everything. Malleven wants all the mates to die without it. That's why Jay called you here."

A sense of relief mingled in with his worry and he kissed her. He knew Jay would help in any way that he could.

When she came up for air, "Isla couldn't reach Darres."

"He's underwater. They've all gone to Washington State to help Drew. It's where I should be."

Lacy nodded and smiled weakly, but he could tell she was still worried.

"What is it?" he said.

"Shh." She pulled his mouth down to hers and immediately let loose her essence. It was so strong, so sorely needed that he didn't stop her and his knees gave way for a second. They were out of water and his temperature soared.

Lacy guided him down to sit and straddled his legs. "Quickly, Keenan," she said, desperately.

He answered her instantly with his breath. Then, as soon as she gasped with the strength of it, he plunged his canines into her neck and pulled hard. His temperature was hot, but her purer blood meant hers rose dangerously. Blood loss always reduced it. However, he only kept it up for two or three seconds. Normally, he'd be lost in the ecstasy of closeness, bathing in the afterburn of euphoria followed by lust-filled lovemaking, but, this time, his mind came to a standstill. The moment her breath lashed around him, he knew.

Someone else was on the bond.

Somebody very familiar. A close friend. *Jay.*

Lacy was watching him closely, knowing full well the moment he would reach the answer.

As he went to erupt and throw her off him, she clamped onto him and hissed, "Stop! Please, Keenan. Listen!" She held the sides of his face to fix him with her eyes.

He was struggling to keep his temper. "Get off me, Lace." His eyes churned with blood and his teeth descended.

She held him fast, shaking with the effort. "Please listen, Keenan. He's trying to help."

That was about right. Protecting him. He roughly moved her off him so he could get to his feet. "Where is he?" he growled through gritted teeth.

"Shh, Keenan, you'll get us all caught."

In his mind he couldn't think of a single reason for this that didn't make him want to rip Jay apart. He strode out from the group of trees. *And there he was, waiting. Expecting him.*

It was getting light and Jay was standing with his back to them a little way off. He immediately sensed them and turned to read his expression. "Back under the trees," Jay said, walking quickly towards him. He knew exactly what the problem was. His blood boiled and he fought to keep it from his eyes. Lacy was his weak spot and this was the one guy he thought he could trust.

As soon as they were under cover, Keenan threw Jay against the trunk of a tree by his shirt, ripping off the buttons. To his credit, he didn't fight him. Instead he looked at him directly in the eyes. For a moment Keenan's eyes clouded with blood. No toying this time. He was struggling to keep control. If he lost it, he'd tear out his throat.

Jay tried to get his hands up between them. "Stop! Keenan! Listen. I know you're angry but, believe me, it's the only way to beat him. Think about it. He won't see it coming."

Nothing was making any sense to Keenan's already anger-fogged brain. "What coming?" he demanded, slamming the air out of Jay's lungs.

"Listen to him, please, Keenan," Lacy said, hanging off his arm in tears.

Jay coughed and spluttered out the words. "Me … Taking the kingdom from under his nose."

Keenan went to slam him again when what he said finally filtered through and slowed his arms. He thought about what Jay had said and what he meant.

"It's true," Lacy said, sensing a softening in him. "He's already breathed with me, Tia and Isla. All he needs is Lily and Phoebe and he can steal the kingdom from under him."

That stopped Keenan's anger in its tracks, but then he shook his head and renewed his grip on his already ripped apart shirt. "He can't … he's human." He fixed his friend in the eyes and saw the blue directness in them. Then he felt him shift on *his* bond with Lacy and his anger fired up again.

Jay's eyes widened. "Christian Dubonnetti has proof that I'm his son," he said.

Keenan let that sink in for a moment.

"Look, I don't want it, but I have to try something to save the girls and the kids from him," Jay said. "He's already adopted JJ."

Keenan didn't know that and struggled to digest the implications. He studied Jay's face as if he'd changed into someone he didn't recognize anymore. He didn't.

"I'll help you come and breathe for Lacy in secret."

Keenan suddenly felt confused. He needed to work through everything it meant. "What about the others … Dante?" He didn't like the guy, but even he accepted him as the best-of-a-bad-bunch as king.

Jay shook his head. "I can't do anything for them. All I can do is move quickly. Then it'll work out for them."

Dante would be devastated when he found out Jay was shafting him in this way. It was wrong on so many levels. It had to be about Tia. The two of them had fought over her for years.

Jay leaned forward to whisper, "You have to trust me, OK? Go back and tell everyone what I'm trying to do here. That I'm doing it for the kingdom. Dante will understand."

As he coolly assessed his friend, Keenan doubted that very much. He didn't understand him or his friendship with Dante at all. But that was nothing new. "They'll all get sick. You understand that, right? Dante worst of all."

Jay nodded and Keenan slowly let him go. "I know. But it has to be this way. Malleven must think he's dying to take his eye off me. It's the only way we'll broadside him, Keenan. Believe me. I've thought through every angle. We've got to be as clever as him. He's too strong, Keen. When it comes to it, I have to be taken seriously."

Keenan let out a slow, deep breath and studied his friend's

eyes a long time after he'd finished speaking. Things were already a mess. They would help Drew and there would be the inevitable trouble between him and Vionne, which meant all the Murrs. Everything was already turning to shit. In the end he nodded, giving in and relaxing his hold at last. "I should fucking kill you, though." The thought of Lacy having to breathe with him on a regular basis made him grind his teeth. "You promise to protect the girls and the kids?"

Jay nodded, relaxing down and straightening his clothes. "With my life." He held out a conciliatory hand and pulled him into a brief man-hug. Keenan, still dazed, patted his back stiffly. "Now go. The Santalinis are here, but Malleven's men control the castle. They'll be passing on their patrol any time now."

Jay released him and Keenan hugged Lacy, not wanting to let her go. He kissed her shamelessly and held the top of her shoulders to look at her. He didn't like it, but recognized he had to go along with it. "Stay safe," he said, and Lacy nodded with tears in her eyes.

Voices were nearby. He let her go with one last quick kiss, leapt up on the wall and straddled the top. He looked down at Lacy standing shoulder to shoulder with Jay. "Stay close to him," he said, nodding his head to Jay. "Touch her and I'll kill you."

"Don't worry. "I'll look after her," Jay said, smiling. "Go!" he said, pulling Lacy with him out of sight.

With that, Keenan dropped down on the other side in a low crouch and jogged back to the car. He was still in shock. It wasn't purely that he now had to share his bond with his woman with Jay, it was more to do with an uncomfortable feeling he was getting, that in all the time he'd known Jay, he'd never seemed driven by power to the point he'd take it from his best friend.

· · ·

DREW HAD BEEN CALLED to the principal monk's office. He knew it was coming. He was surprised it had taken this long.

Everything was set for the boys to go in the early hours of the following morning. He felt twitchy and wished they didn't have to wait, but they were in the middle of nowhere and he needed the backup to get them away—especially if things went wrong. He knocked on the door to the office and his heart pounded as he wondered if that was about to happen.

"Sit down, 2365," Seville said.

Drew saw the wooden chair placed in the middle of the room and inwardly chuckled. It was designed to make the user feel like they were about to be interrogated. He did as he was told and looked ahead into the middle distance.

He was aware of Croll hovering by the window, watching, tattoos on his large crossed arms on full view. It just proved what hypocrites they were. Dressed like pious monks and yet plastered with their supremacy and hatred of the Atlanteans they'd sworn to annihilate.

"Sorry for the delay in our debrief, we had much to attend to," Seville said. "And you seemed so settled into your tasks here that we didn't want to disturb you."

Drew willed them to get the hell on with it. It was fascinating how he fell so easily into recruit mode after all these years: mouth shut, eyes front, showing no emotion at all. He guessed it must have been beaten into him. He just tipped his head slightly to acknowledge that he'd spoken.

"Out of all the inhabitants of that underwater city and the sum total of a thousand men, tell me, how did you manage to sit here today?" Croll said, striding forward to loom over him in his chair.

Intimidation didn't work on him as a fourteen year old and it didn't work now. Drew showed no reaction.

"Surely the fact that he is in this room at all proves his loyalty," Seville said.

"Silence! Let him speak. The other recruits trust him already. I would know what kind of instructor we have in our camp. He could be a spy."

Drew found he needed all his willpower not to stand and go toe to toe with him, but everything hinged on the Atlanteans coming and getting the boys out. He composed himself and proceeded to relay a very loose story of events that led to him gaining the trust of a Siren and going to the Atlantean court and eventually Murrtaine. Basically, everything they already knew.

"How were you taken to Murrtaine, when no human can do this?" Croll said, leaning closer, almost spitting out the words, his hatred so near the surface.

It was a good question. Even Atlanteans couldn't survive the journey, only those initiated to breathing the water by a siren. What the Scythians were unaware of was that it was just a very select few royals and, of course, he himself, who could do it. "My siren was taken there by the lord of that city. He wanted her for himself, but he took the queen as well, which ended up being a diplomatic nightmare for the king. A delegation was sent, and I managed to be included to go with them."

"Answer the damn question: how did you survive under water?"

The bastard was like a rat with a bone. He'd have to give him something. "The Murrs had some sort of face equipment for breathing and medication to cope with the pressure." He wanted to say that they had far superior technology, but Croll was already angry enough.

Croll paced and looked skeptical. "Why would they need this when they are already an underwater race?"

Shit! He turned and faced Croll directly, which wasn't

how a recruit would dare to behave. He knew this little inter-
rogation would go on until he himself brought it to an end.
"Very few Atlanteans breathe the water, sir, and none had
been to Murrtaine until that day. Only the Sirens and the
purebreds."

Croll glared at him, but Drew didn't avert his eyes. Seville
was becoming nervous. "Come, Croll, you can see he is a
good and loyal servant."

Croll was having none of it and leaned so close to Drew
he could feel his hot breath. He blinked away his distaste.
"And the whole Allied taskforce perished in the blast and you
didn't."

That was it. Drew slowly stood. The monk would keep
this up until he got a rise out of him and he didn't have the
time.

Seville rushed forward to try to break the standoff
between them, but there was no throwing the man off. He
was a tracker dog that had cornered his prey. There was a
large part of Drew that welcomed it. It had been a long time
coming.

Slowly, he allowed the changes his body ached for. First
his vision tunneled to the thin slits of a reptile and became
tinged in orange. Then his canines descended to their full
length so he could no longer close his mouth.

It was gratifying to witness the horror gradually seep into
Croll's face before he flew at him and locked down on his
throat. Sane thought gave way to pure blood lust and he was
governed solely by instinct. There was blood, several blows
to his torso, groaning and, eventually, gurgling. He could see
very little; only red. Then his thoughts momentarily
unclouded with a piercing pain in the back. Then there was
nothing.

. . .

DREW BLINKED at the brightness of the strip light and sat up slowly. Pain flashed behind his eyes so he had to hold his head for a full minute. When he finally let go, his clothes were covered in blood and he was on a cot in a cell.

Events came back to him from just before he lost consciousness. Seville must have tasered or injected him with something and taken him to one of the holding cells in the basement of the main building. It was the cooler where they put the new boys when they misbehaved to scare them.

A movement and he looked up. Seville was standing on the other side of the bars watching him.

"Croll is dead," Seville said, simply.

Drew looked at him insolently. *What did he want him to say? Sorry?*

"What have they done to you?" Seville looked grief-stricken. "You were human. I know this because all boys are screened."

"And any who don't make the grade are disposed of," Drew finished for him. There was no point in lying to this fanatic. "The Siren, Phoebe, changed me."

Seville looked desolate for a moment. Then his eyes widened and became crazed, filled with the same look of hatred that all the monks had there. "She has destroyed you," he said bitterly.

Drew stood and approached the bars. Seville took a fearful step back. "No, you're wrong. She made me and I welcomed it. She built me up after you systematically tore me down. And you do it over and over again to every boy who comes here. And all in the name of God?" Drew couldn't keep the laughter and revulsion out of his voice. Then he lowered his voice ominously. "Now, let me out."

Seville read the threat and took another step back.

"Yeah, be afraid. Because when I get out of here, I will kill you."

Seville's eyes widened in fear and then indignation. "I cared for you and gave you more support than any other boy, you ungrateful wretch!"

Drew fought to keep the changes from his face, dictated by strong emotion. His eyes reduced to slits and his voice came out in a snarl. "You did not care for me, only your mission to kill a people that are just settlers here. You punished me daily and worked me to exhaustion in a regime that would kill most boys my age."

Seville forgot his fear. "But you did survive and became stronger for it. You were my best, my greatest achievement. Everything you have done is because of my patronage." His voice was shrill and his eyes wild like the madman he was.

Then Drew jumped back to the edge of the room at the sound of a deafening boom. Seville brought his hands up to his ears. The building shook beneath their feet and plaster began to fall between them.

CHAPTER 14

Malleven watched little JJ swinging his legs on the red upholstered chair opposite him. He'd taken him to the library, his favorite room in the castle. The seat of learning for this family and, indeed, a whole nation, held together in antique shelves of dark wood and dust. He'd wanted to see his reaction to the sum total of knowledge and work in the huge collection of books and he wasn't disappointed. The boy was utterly captivated and equally fascinating. To all intents and purposes, he appeared to be like any other Human five or six-year-old; inquisitive and enquiring of the world around him. When, in fact, he was half that age, with an intellect matching most adults.

Even now he was thumbing through one of the oldest books as if he did it every day and understood it perfectly. "Do you like this room?"

JJ nodded animatedly. "It's my favorite place."

"Why?" Malleven asked, intrigued, sitting forward in his chair.

"It is a good place for hide and seek. None of the others would ever think of coming here."

Malleven laughed loudly. The boy had a sense of humor. His aura changed color with his attempt at a joke.

"What are your favorite books?" Malleven asked.

"The big tomes, of course. Particularly the ones talking about me … except I'm not big enough to get them down on my own," JJ said, looking up at the five large volumes in the protective glass cabinet. The white leather had aged to a mottled beige, but the gold and silver embossed symbols of the cosmos were still clear and magical.

Malleven could see what he meant. They were enticing and weighed almost as much as him. "Well, we will remedy that and see to it that they are on the lowest shelves."

The boy kicked his legs and smiled.

"So, who are you in the tomes that I might look you up?" Malleven's heart was already quickening in anticipation of the answer.

"I am Jason Themistius Enil Gardiner Bonaci Dubonnetti, but they refer to me as the Darkly Begotten son." He spoke the names confidently and apparently oblivious to the menacing implications of it.

Malleven smiled benignly, giving nothing away of the excitement he felt. "Don't forget Florianna. You're now my son."

The boy frowned and whispered his name again, adding Florianna on the end to see how it sounded. "Yes. It makes sense that I should be your son, you are the darkest of all my fathers."

Malleven blinked, unable to answer, and took a sip of a glass of wine he had on the pedestal next to him. Had he not been acutely aware of how dangerous the boy was, he would think him impertinent. Still, it was a fair assessment. "And why are you here—apart from fulfilment of a prophecy, that is?"

JJ looked up at the yellowed decorative plaster ceiling and

protruded a lip, all the while swinging his legs—a very child-like, fidgeting habit he appeared to have whenever he was thinking. "The books say that I'm here to destroy a kingdom and here to make one."

Malleven frowned. "That has already happened, has it not?"

JJ bobbed his head in a way that reminded Malleven of his biological father, Jay. "Yeah, but there is more than one pretender to a crown."

Malleven almost crushed the glass in his hand, but instead took a breath and composed himself again. He had to remember the boy was not mocking him; merely telling him things honestly, as he saw it. He topped up his glass, trying to hide the irritation in his voice. "I am now your father. You owe me your allegiance, do you not?"

The boy started turning the pages of his book again. "There are many kings and many fathers. I don't really care which one of them sits on the throne. It makes little difference to me."

Malleven sifted through what he said and decided that from a small boy's point of view, that was true. He felt slightly relieved and sat back into his chair again. He appeared to show little interest in politics. All he needed to do was keep him happy and close and he would be of use to him.

He decided to change tack. "What would make you happy here at the castle?"

The boy didn't hesitate and looked him straight in the eye. "I would like to be with my brothers and sister and cousins all the time. My father, Jay, made me live with him and I didn't like it. And I want to see my mother whenever I want to."

They were simple demands, very easy to give. It was also very telling that JJ asked to see neither of his two fathers. It lightened his spirits. However, the boy looked at him strangely as if he'd read his mind. "My mother is the constant in my life."

Again, the boy's mature insight into a less-than-ideal home life amazed him. It showed that he'd been very unhappy in the past and that would be of use to him in the future. "I will see to it that you want for nothing and all your wishes are granted," Malleven said with a smile.

Keenan arrived back at Filfla way before everyone else. There had been no time to join the mission. By the time he got there it would have been over.

He knocked on the study door and entered at Dante's command. He was in conversation with Cesaré.

Dante still looked surprised when he saw him, even though he would have known he was on his way from the airport. The helicopter pilot would not take off without getting his clearance first. "What happened?" Dante said, without any preamble. "Did everything go alright?"

Keenan just put up his hands defensively and shook his head. "I didn't go," he said and walked further into the room, flopping down onto the sofa in front of them. "It's OK, Reeve led the mission."

Dante and Cesaré looked at each other and turned to face him. Neither looked happy.

"Look, before you shoot me down, Lacy called me. She said Jay was there and would help me see her to breathe for me." He leaned forward with his elbows on his knees, defeated. "I'm sorry, I had to go," he ended, looking down at the floor.

There was stunned silence for a moment, for so long Keenan had to look up at them.

"So Jay is there working for us. I knew it!" Dante had the

light of hope in his eyes that hadn't been seen in a long time. Keenan immediately felt guilty.

"Can't we do the same?" Cesaré said, pointing between himself and Dante. "It could keep us all alive?"

Keenan was already shaking his head. "I already suggested that. Lacy, Tia and Isla are together for safety but Malleven has Lily separate and close to him. Until he makes a move on Lance, they can't trust her."

Cesaré looked at Dante somberly. "Your best chance is Phoebe. When she returns, she must breathe for you. It might buy you some time at least."

Keenan felt genuinely sorry for the guy. His only chance was Lily, and that was unlikely to happen any time soon. The clock was ticking on his life.

Dante nodded and looked troubled. He would have surmised the same thing. As much as he couldn't get along with Dante and he was very much Jay's man, he didn't want to have to deliver what he had to say next. He decided to lead with the good news. "Jay told me to tell you that he is guarding the girls."

Dante took a deep breath and nodded as if it was the good news he needed.

"But I also have to tell you that he has breathed with Lacy … Tia … and Isla. He's there right under Malleven's nose—"

"Stealing the kingdom," both Dante and Cesaré finished for him at the same time. Then they looked at each other. Cesaré sprang to his feet, his Italian temper more animated than usual. "I can't believe he did this. Your brother—your best friend. How is it even possible?" he finished, glaring at Dante as if he would know the answer. It did sound bad. He knew it would.

Dante was a lot calmer, but looked troubled. "He is," he said softly to himself, but his eyes darted as his mind worked.

"How did he say he got around the issue of lineage?" His calm acceptance was eerie.

"He has Tia, the children. Everything," Cesaré said in exasperation.

None of them saw this coming. Keenan inwardly cringed at having to deliver the final blow. "Christian Dubonnetti has proof that he's his son."

Dante closed his eyes. "Leave me."

Keenan was reluctant to leave him like this. They all knew the prophecy and that Dubonnetti being his father made him one of five sons, and eligible to go for the kingdom. He looked at Cesaré for guidance. He had been his closest friend since Jay left to become a Santalini. There had been a rift for a while. Still, even he was surprised Jay was doing this. "What do I do from now on?" he said at a loss.

"Stick by your friend," Dante said and turned his back. "Go!"

CHAPTER 15

Ballygowan Castle was no longer the safe and happy place it once was for its inhabitants. There was no relaxed chatter in the Great Hall, no callers from the outside world and the Sirens were separated from their children, except for short visits supervised by Malleven's men. Even the servants scurried around as if they were scared for their lives. It became the norm to feel you had to constantly look over your shoulder.

Isla had been summoned to the Great Hall along with her sisters. Even though he'd lost his hold on her, Malleven was a vindictive egomaniac and she lived in fear of what he might do to assert his authority.

The four sisters stood in a row in front of Malleven's throne. Dante never bothered with such things; there was no need. Something in his sheer presence separated him from other men. Strangers all respected him and yet he was nothing but easy and relaxed. He was firm, but always kept a lively sense of humor—like a hope-giving light.

Malleven, on the other hand, seemed impeccably severe and almost spiteful in comparison. His midnight-blue eyes were piercing, like a predator honing a kill. Without a greeting, he said, "A week from today we will complete the pledges in a public ceremony, in front of witnesses from the Atlantean world, to confirm my kingdom."

By that, she understood he meant in front of everyone that mattered. He was all about appearances.

"For the first time in history, an invitation has been sent to the President of the United States."

They were all visibly shocked at that. This was huge—and very clever. Malleven was firmly asserting himself on the throne, but not leaving himself vulnerable by going to meet human officials as Dante had once done.

"You all know what is expected of you. You are experienced in these matters," he continued. "However, before then, it is important we complete the bonds in private."

Of course it was. He would never leave such a vital thing to chance.

"You shall be called one by one." His eyes fell on Isla, dead like a shark's. She inwardly shuddered as her blood went to ice. He would have something special reserved for her, now he couldn't drown. Lily had a lot to answer for. She reached for Tia's hand next to her and held it, which she squeezed back for reassurance as she was shaking. How she loved her sisters.

"What if we don't want to, you know, breathe for you," Tia said, speaking up loudly. Then she turned her head to Lily and said, "We're not all fools."

It was Tia's turn to shake. Isla loved her for it, but willed her to shut up just the same. Lily scowled back at her, no doubt saying something straight to her head. "Everyone knows he'll get rid of Lance as soon as he gets the chance."

Lance put a protective arm around Lily, but no one argued with the truth.

Malleven kept surprisingly calm throughout the whole

conversation. Little JJ was on his lap, appearing oblivious to the tension around him. "You are here, are you not? You chose me in front of your former king and witnesses. Why not just finish the process so we can all be happy?"

Isla saw the threat instantly. They all did. He had the children and would use them if he had to.

Malleven put JJ down onto his feet and got up from his throne. He walked over and stopped directly in front of Isla. "You will stay and be first."

Even without the mate's pull, nobody affected her like Malleven. She was a stone-cold killer and yet she was terrified. Despite being her most compatible mate and spending many months with him, she had avoided giving him her breath. They'd had lots of sex, but she'd survived on excuses and now her time had run out. "I want my children with me," she blurted, and waited for his wrath.

But it didn't come.

Perspiration trickled down her neck. Then she noticed his gaze flicked to Lily a couple of times. He was keeping his cool for her. Now it made sense. Lily had been fooled because he'd been kind to her. The only one. She'd never seen the side that everyone else saw. It suddenly empowered her. She took a step forward so her body was a hair's breadth from his. "I want my kids with me, and then I'll consider breathing for you. But I can't promise. In fact, I doubt it very much."

She heard a sharp intake of breath next to her, probably Lacy, but her eyes never moved from his. His jaw muscles flexed while he ground his teeth and his chest moved up and down. She was walking a very fine line with his temper.

"The same goes for me," Tia said, stepping forward.

"And me," Lacy said, doing the same even though she had no kids of her own.

They waited for Lily. "I'll go first," she said, after a short pause.

Malleven took his eyes off her at last to glare at the other two. He took a step back and held out his hand to Lily. "Come, faithful wife."

They couldn't believe she went with him, leaving Lance standing there alone. She didn't see the moment of desolation that crossed his face and how it hardened afterwards.

Malleven left the hall holding Lily's hand, but not before one last, vicious look at Isla. It was the promise of what he would do to her when they were alone. She shuddered, vowing not to let that happen.

Tia and Lacy had already gone to Lance and stopped him walking off. "Come to our chamber," Tia said. "We need to talk to you."

THE NEEDLE CUT through the ocean as if it were flying through air. The deepest part was the darkest blue and there was very little to see at the speed they were travelling. Even schools of large fish went past like white dots on a radar. They were soon slowing down as they reached the Strait of Gibraltar, where the vessel negotiated the shallower, rocky terrain more carefully.

Ashaya gazed out in awe at the aquamarine seascape of rock, speckled with colored fish, too numerous to memorize, before the Needle left them behind to pass larger schools that flocked and dispersed like birds.

They soon left Europe for the land mass of the Americas —all the things she'd studied on her way to Earth. They moved faster, the view a darker blue till it greyed to an almost blank screen. Still, it was an emotional experience for her.

Have you travelled these seas before? Vionne said, next to her.

No, she said wistfully. *Just studied them.*

I can't believe my brother has never met you in Murrla. A huge oversight, Vionne said.

She suddenly felt nervous, as if they'd stumbled on dangerous territory and her eyes flashed to his. There didn't seem any accusation in his aura. *I live a quiet life of study and prayer,* she added with a bolt of inspiration. It wasn't a lie. She had to be careful with Murr abilities to read people and he was, without doubt, trying to read her as much as she was him.

You mustn't forget it is a dangerous mission you have decided to accompany us on, Vionne said.

She bowed her head slightly. *And a great honor.* Again, it wasn't a lie.

He studied her for a moment and she ached to scan his thoughts. *When we arrive, the Santalinis will meet us with the buses needed to evacuate the boys. When we go in you must stay there with Phoebe. I would not like any harm to come to you.*

Of course, she said, bowing her head, her heart swelling with the great compliment he'd paid her. It had been a very long time since someone had worried for her welfare.

VIONNE STUDIED the startlingly beautiful female. He had never come across anyone quite like her, and yet she was one of his race. Purebred in every way and preferring the old ways. He took in the ribbons of the religion of the Five Moons, convinced she was a real gentlewoman. All Murr women were composed and self-assured, but she seemed positively angelic. Almost like she was a world apart.

His mind went to Phoebe, which it invariably did, sitting

across the way. She was lost in worry for another male, *Drew*. It was clear she wouldn't even look back the moment she saw him, or give him a second thought. To her, he didn't exist. He became angry as it made no sense. She was his by right of ring. His promise to his father was still branded on his heart: he had to marry a Siren for the good of the Borge family and she was there in his sights. However, if he fought Drew for her and won, she would hate him forever. It was a pointless endeavor. He found himself wondering, for the first time, how easy it would be if Ashaya was his Siren, or he was free to court whoever he chose.

You are concerned for your mate, Ashaya said, dragging him out of his thoughts.

He turned to look at her; the sleek black hair, smooth skin and perfect stripes accentuating her already stunning face. She was a high priestess. It was obvious in her bearing. A young woman who completely knew her place in the world and where she wanted to go. How wonderfully natural it would be if she was his. She was purebred, where a Siren was mixed and notoriously fickle. She was far more suitable for him and Murrtaine than a troublesome Siren who hated him.

His heart ached in his chest. Yet the Fates and the Orb pushed him towards the one across the way. It made him wonder if they hadn't got it wrong on this occasion. His life felt in disarray. He was walking a tightrope between the former and the new king—either of which could turn on him at any moment—and all to secure the safety of his people. It felt a heavy burden to carry. *Life is of great concern at the moment,* he said, eventually, with a sad smile.

THE NEEDLE eventually slowed to a stop just off of Port Angeles, Washington State, at around 10 p.m. local time. Leaving just two of his crew to maintain the ship, Vionne led the party to swim the small distance into port. He sniffed the air, then he hauled himself up onto the small jetty and helped each of the others out one by one, paying special care with Ashaya and Phoebe. They expelled their lungs and sat on a group of benches until their legs hardened. He spotted the three buses waiting a little way off on the dimly lit road, their engines a gentle rumble in the quiet. There was just enough light to see the darkened buildings beyond and the black mountains looming behind.

After ten minutes, Vionne gave the order to move off. He led them onto the first bus and recognized several of the Santalinis and many of the Protectors who'd made the trip by air.

They settled into their seats and the buses moved off to make the four-hour journey to Lake Diablo where they would leave them to go in and destroy the Scythian camp.

Vionne had been disturbed by his feelings while talking to Ashaya. He made sure he sat next to Phoebe, who looked, unseeing, out of the window, her mind on the human he knew he would have to fight. *You must remain on the bus when we arrive and let us do our job,* Vionne projected.

She snapped her head round to him. "So you can kill him without witnesses?" she spat.

He rolled his eyes. Something he'd learned from the Sirens. They did it a lot when they needed patience. *I give you my word I will not hurt your pet Human. When we fight, I will indeed want witnesses.*

Phoebe scowled at him.

Ashaya will remain on the bus with you. His eyes drifted across the way to the fascinating woman, avidly watching the cars, shops and houses floating by. It was as though every building lit by streetlamps, every cluster of people going about their business, was of the utmost interest to her. Even as the town thinned out and was replaced by trees, she seemed to note them all one by one. He watched her, capti-vated, until all that could be seen was the blackness of the national park, too dark to appreciate, but her aura was bright and still one of wonder.

Vionne's mind buffeted this way and that, from Phoebe to Ashaya, to where his people were and how safe, throughout the entire journey. It was a relief when the road eventually narrowed and climbed, signaling the nearing of the end of their journey. The buses began to slow, until they eventually pulled off the road and parked between a thick line of fir trees. The headlights were quickly doused and everything went black. He nudged Phoebe, *Stay here,* and stood stiffly, not able to stretch to his full height.

Ashaya's eyes were on him. *Be safe,* she said.

He nodded once, then followed the others in single file and went down the steps at the front. He put the strange ache in his chest from his mind. The air smelled of earth and pine and the only light came from a magnificent star-filled sky. When their eyes were accustomed, it was remarkably light.

Seven Santalini guards and Keenan's three closest men alighted from the second bus. Keenan was noticeably miss-ing. "I am leading the mission in my cousin's place," the Santalini, Reeve, explained immediately. Vionne would have preferred Keenan, someone he knew, even though he was often disagreeable. However, Reeve was an able soldier and there was no time to quiz him. Connor, Phoebe's Protector and the three Santalini drivers, would remain with the women and guard the buses.

Vionne and the rest of the Murrs followed the Santalinis silently through the forest where they split and watched them run and bound over the seven feet wall.

The first of the loud explosions was their signal to go. The fire bell sounded and shouts were heard in the distance.

Vionne took his men easily over the wall because of their height. They landed softly and ran low into the trees at the edge of a field where he sent half his group off with their orders. They soon blended into shadows and waited in silence. His heart was pumping hard while he listened, keenly. Not long after, the many footfalls came. He looked at his men and they braced themselves to fight. Instead, they saw the group of boys run straight past them and amass at the wall. Then one gave a soft whistle.

JUSTIN LAY IN THE DARKNESS, fully clothed, ready for action, waiting. 361 was in the bed opposite. He knew he was awake too. There was no whispering, no discussion to calm each other's nerves. In the barracks you could never be sure who was listening. All he could do was count his breaths and calm his beating heart as much as he could. Drew hadn't come back after they'd last seen him on the field. He prayed nothing had happened to him. He'd warned them of the probability of having to meet them later. He just had to stick with the plan. His breathing quickened to almost a pant and he concentrated on slowing it down again. He had to get a grip.

The boom was loud enough to shake the windows in the frames. His eyes went wide, his breathing stopped and he counted. *One, two, three, four ...*

The continuous bell sounded, shrill and ear-splitting, acting like a release from a gate.

Justin jumped up and an eerie feeling of calm came over him like a suit of armor. Somehow, action was a lot easier than thinking about doing it. He knew his job. As head boy he simply had to take command; like any training session without Drew. They just had to follow the plan they'd discussed.

He called together his lead boys, already rising from their beds and signed for each of them to go to the other cabins. They knew the drill. Then he moved out the remainder of the boys without causing panic. Many were bewildered, half asleep and easily herded.

He wished he could have given them time to dress. The cold air bit them as soon as he steered them outside. By the time the others joined them, they groaned, fidgeted and shivered in their vests and shorts. "Soldier up!" he ordered. They immediately straightened and jumped into their lines. "We've trained for this our whole lives," Justin said, looking at as many as he could in the eye. He was aware of the growing orange glow behind them and didn't want them to turn around. "We are on our first mission. You must follow my orders exactly."

The edge to his voice seemed to wake them to the seriousness of what was happening and the general mood sobered. He put a finger to his lips and signed with his palm downwards and they understood. Crouching low, they crossed the road and nipped between the buildings, two and three at a time. "What are we doing?" one small boy asked too loudly.

"Following orders!" Justin hissed. "I am to evacuate the camp. We are under attack." Another series of bangs, sounding like fireworks, came from the main building to prove his point.

The boy looked terrified and crouched lower as they hid behind the last building. "Don't worry. Do as I say and we'll get out of here."

He wasn't sure if the others heard, but no one else challenged him after that. They were used to the older boys bossing them around. "Get ready to run on my order."

Behind them he heard the monks shouting. He guessed they were trying to put out the fire. The growing light in the sky and the acrid smell of smoke told him the fire was already taking hold. A spark deep in his heart rejoiced. Wherever this mission took them, they would never return, and he was glad. So would every single one of these boys if they gave themselves a chance to think about it.

"Now! Run!" he shouted, and they sprinted as fast as they could across the parade ground and then the large playing field, to the north where the boundary was set by a parameter wall almost twice their height. He headed for the trees and waited for the smallest boy to catch up. He allowed himself to look back for the first time and scanned the chaos hoping to spot his leader, 2365, but what he saw stopped his heart dead. Strange-looking men, a whole head and shoulders taller than the monks, were knocking them down without touching them; as if they were nothing. Some were different to them, but could not be called human. They were soldiers, stacked with muscle, huge extended teeth and eyes that glowed red like demons. They were shooting the monks with expert aim. His legs ceased to work as he couldn't take his eyes off one coming upon a monk and ripping out his throat with his teeth. No one was getting back up and he worried desperately for 2365. He wanted to go back and search for him, but his legs simply wouldn't move.

"Come on, before they see us," 361 said, pulling on his arm.

He still couldn't move or take his eyes off the alien men. The carnage continued and the world fell silent. He'd heard of people saying they were frozen by fear and now he understood in one slow blink.

"I know. Come on. 2365 said not to look back." He felt a hard punch to the top of his arm.

Justin finally turned his head and stared into 361's face, willing him to move. Thought and motor skills finally came back to him as if the volume on the world was suddenly turned up. 361 was right. They would die if he didn't move his ass. 2365 had known this was coming. He wasn't meant to think, he just had to trust that he knew what he was doing. He must obey without question, just like he'd been taught. He took one last look at all the burning buildings behind them and turned and ran with the other boys.

He ran until all he could hear was the pounding of his feet on wet grass and his breath. He concentrated on the rhythm, like a machine. A technique he'd perfected from the many years of laps they'd practiced. To fall or break down meant certain punishment. He kept going until he reached the wall, where, as if in a dream, everything ceased to be muted. He whistled and the world woke up to him.

The boys gathered around him, breathing hard. Some bent over, putting their hands on their knees. Then four of the biggest men he'd ever seen came out from the cover of the trees in front of them. Someone whimpered, possibly him. They backed up against the wall and some broke their training and screamed; they couldn't help it. They went to scatter, but found their feet paralyzed. The younger boys began to cry. One shouted, "Get away from us! They're the evil ones."

For a moment, Justin's heart fell away. They'd been tricked and had fallen into the hands of the enemy they'd been trained their whole life to fight. *How could 2365 betray them like this?* Then, just as his mind was about to spiral out of control, 361 took his hand and he didn't push him off. "2365 promised us a way out. Maybe this is the only way. Maybe this is the mission," he whispered.

361's hand became his anchor. He was able to slow down his breaths so he could think clearly. His heart lightened a little. No one had hurt them so far. He was right. They must trust 2365.

One of the huge men bent down on one knee in front of

him so he was on eye level with him. He had the whitest hair and the blackest eyes that were large and hard to read as there were no whites. *Be at ease. No harm will come to you. You are being liberated. We are going to help you over the wall and there is help on the other side. You must go through the forest to the waiting buses. They will take you to safety.*

It was said straight to his mind. He looked at the boys next to him and they nodded, proving they'd heard it too. "We must wait for our leader, 2365—er, Drew," Justin corrected. "We won't leave without him." It was partly out of loyalty and a lot to do with being left alone with these alien-like men.

The man smiled a weird-looking smile. *He will meet you on the bus. Our friends are helping him.*

Justin looked at the three expressionless men with him and then at 361 who nodded, cautiously. He swallowed and turned to his boys who huddled around him. "Do as they say. 2365 is meeting us."

The four strange men boosted them up and over the wall and two others helped them down on the other side. One stooped next to him and pointed at the path through the woods. He didn't need telling twice; he led the boys at a flat-out run, only turning back once to see the weird men hop over the wall as if it was nothing and disappear. He hoped to god 2365 got out to help them. Then he renewed his stride and ran as fast as he could through the trees.

As they ran the distance, the exercise cleared his mind. He began to feel a curious sense of elation. They were out and they were free. He began to laugh, and others joined him as if they were all feeling this mass hysteria. Explosions and shouts still echoed behind them and all they felt was free. The camp was destroyed and whatever happened to them tonight, each one of them knew they wouldn't be going back. The feeling that gave them was immense. Pure joy. It renewed them and gave them the energy to run and run without getting out of breath. For the first time in their miserable lives they felt excitement at what was to come.

Justin skidded to a halt when they came to the end of the forest path and they could see the three buses waiting with their engines running. Just as 2365 had promised. He looked either side of him and calculated their chances of running in another direction, but, before he could make up his mind, a big guy got out of each bus and beckoned them closer.

They seemed more Human-looking than the others, but he wasn't fooled. He remembered the ones with the huge teeth shooting the monks. They could run and some would possibly escape, but not all of them. He looked at his close companions either side of him and nodded. "Stay close together," he said. Then they moved steadily in a huddle towards the waiting men.

"Welcome," one said, with an American accent.

Justin looked in each of their eyes. They looked Human enough, although his adrenalin prickled as his blood pumped through his heart, ready to run.

"You're safe," the first guy said. "Split yourselves between the other two buses," he said, nodding his head towards the ones parked behind him. "We'll go as soon as the others are back."

"We won't go without 2365," Justin said, acting tougher than he actually felt. They needed him for further orders, but, if he was honest, he needed him to explain this. Otherwise, the boys would begin to panic and he wasn't confident he could hold them together without him.

The big guy looked mystified for a moment and then he seemed to understand. "He'll be here. Now get on the buses."

Watching the men get back into their cabs, he split the boys in two, making sure three of his head boys were in each bus to calm them.

. . .

ASHAYA SAT in the bus as quietly and riveted to the path from the woods as Phoebe. It was a dangerous mission and she didn't want anyone to get hurt. The thought of never seeing Vionne again sped up her pulse and constricted her throat. They both stared through the window, scanning the treeline in near silence, Phoebe only uttering, "Where the hell are they?" and "How much longer?"

It occurred to her while they were waiting, that they worried for different men to safely return. It was revealing and troubling.

Her thoughts were suddenly swept aside. "There!" Phoebe shouted. Her heart leapt in her chest when she saw the bedraggled group of boys. They seemed underweight and so small and unsure. Especially compared to the Santalini drivers who got out to direct them.

Ashaya knew they were weak little humans, but she thought them very brave. "He will be here soon," she said. But Phoebe continued to watch the path to the woods, now kneeling on her seat.

CHAPTER 16

The first explosion rocked the building around Drew, followed by shouts from outside. *It had begun.* He got up from his cot and rattled the bars. It wouldn't be long until the building was destroyed. He was in the basement and had to get out before he was trapped. Unless someone checked down here, they'd assume it was empty. He hadn't factored in being a captive when he'd come up with his plan.

Then he felt the mental push that made his blood boil. *Where are you?* The familiar voice said, *The Murr.* Drew paced his cell and kicked the bars in frustration. He didn't want to be a sitting duck, but the building would collapse on him any minute. *I'm in the cells under the main building,* he finally projected.

Feeling his mental signature reminded him of Phoebe breathing with the guy and it set off his changes. The guy's confidence, sense of entitlement and just how everything came easy for him, fueled his anger. He had to calm down.

I'm coming ... Stay put!

Drew let out a single blast of air, along with some of his tension at the Murr's pathetic idea of a joke, and scanned the room for a weapon for the inevitable fight to come. It was useless. The monks had already made sure he had nothing. All he could do was wait and listen for the slightest sound of him coming over the battle raging outside. The door to the staircase clanged, but instead of Vionne it was Seville.

Drew backed up from the cell door, not sure what Seville intended to do. Seville rattled a bunch of keys and undid the lock. "Come. You will perish here."

Drew hesitated. This man misguidedly assumed he was some kind of father figure in his early life. The hopeless years, as he called them. It was hard to believe he was so deluded, but Seville's eyes still held that look of fervent fanaticism that he knew would never change. However, he wasn't helping him out of any goodness of his heart, he just thought he could slip away with him and start again somewhere else. That couldn't happen. "No!" he said, flatly, then instinctively crouched. Vionne was there. His sense of perception amazed him even now.

Seville's face creased with confusion, as if he didn't understand why he wasn't pouncing on the lifeline he was offering him.

"You don't get it, do you? I would rather die in this cell than damage any more children like me."

Seville recoiled as if he'd been struck. "They've corrupted you to be one of them. I can fix you," he said, desperately, and went to the cell door. Again, he rattled his keys. Then Vionne stepped out into the open. *Drew. We must leave.*

While Drew processed the fact that Vionne could have simply walked away and left him, Seville turned and looked slowly up the huge body to stare into the full black eyes of everything he was afraid of, then screamed.

The shrill, unexpected noise shocked them both for a single moment and, in one adept move, before either he or Vionne could react, Seville jumped into the cell and pulled the door shut, locking them both in.

For a moment, Drew thought the idiot had just killed them both, when the Murr actually smiled. A little weird and crooked but there, nonetheless. He simply rested his eyes on the lock and it clicked open again. Another Murr he didn't know, with black hair, appeared and pulled the door open for him. *Say goodbye,* Vionne said.

Seville turned in his panic for Drew to save him, but all he met was a cold hard stare. There was no time left for recriminations. Explosions were shaking the building around them and ceiling plaster was falling in chunks. He allowed his emotion to rear up inside him. His vision turned orange, his teeth descended and Seville's ridiculous high scream only stopped when air was replaced by blood in his throat. Drew's mind went blank after that. He had no recollection of it until he was running in the darkness next to Vionne. As they ran, more joined them and explosion after explosion shook the ground.

"Is everyone out?" a Santalini guard shouted from behind. *It is done,* Vionne projected so they could all hear. *The boys are out and the monks are dead.* He turned his head to Drew, while he ran with a weird grace. It was a look that posed a question he didn't have time to process. In the recesses of his mind, he knew he was asking if they were going to fight, here and now, amongst the carnage. He was pounding the ground, barely listening, or taking it in. All he wanted to do was see Phoebe again.

Drew took care of the last one. Vionne said, eventually, and the moment was gone.

Drew didn't look at him again. What mattered was his former life was over. The slate was clean and he was ready to begin again. He bounded up the wall and was over in seconds. The others followed, some more elegantly than others. He felt strangely flat and not as elated as he expected to feel. He guessed it was shock.

The Murr the other side pointed to the path through the woods and he headed straight for it with Vionne soon next to him. His weird gait was compensated by the length of his legs. He could simply cover more ground.

"You could have easily killed me back there, or just left me," Drew said.

I can see that I shall have to train before our duel.

It was his second joke of the evening and it made him look up at Vionne. His breathing seemed labored. These Murrs might be huge and have amazing mental powers, but they were no good out of water. Maybe that's what he was telling him. "Where's Phoebe?"

Waiting on the bus.

Drew didn't need to know anything else. He quickened his pace and left the Murr behind, despite his extra height. He cleared the forest and she was there.

She came down the steps of one of the buses and ran towards him. She flew into his arms and he caught her easily. He thought he would crush her as he burrowed his nose in the crook of her neck and breathed. It was her.

He kissed her fervently for no more than a couple of seconds and opened his eyes. Justin was coming down the steps of the second bus. He looked wary at first, then strengthened in front of his eyes when he realized it was him. There would be questions to be answered. But for now, it was time to just enjoy the fact that they were all free. He nodded a thanks to the boy and he returned it. Then he walked back up the steps.

Get on! Vionne said. *The explosions will be seen and heard for miles.* We don't want to get caught up with emergency services when they arrive.

Drew took Phoebe by the hand and entered the bus. Then, one by one, the buses eased back onto the rough road and away into the night.

TIA TOOK Lance back to the bedroom she shared with her sisters. Lily had offered to breathe for Malleven when they'd all refused and the poor guy looked devastated. She'd seen Jay with the same look when she'd had to go to Dante in their early days. It had been there just for a moment, then he had covered it with his cool exterior. Now he was a master at never letting it show.

Lance put his hands in the pockets of his low-slung jeans and looked down. His mop of straw-like hair fell forward in his face so she couldn't see his warm, hazel eyes. He looked totally lost, like he shouldn't be there at all. And he was right. He should be surfing waves in southern California. "It's nothing personal, you know. He'll do it with us all eventually," Tia said.

"A king has to," Lacy added.

Lance rolled his eyes at their show of sympathy and began an agitated pace of the room. He shook his head. "Nah, this is different. It's like she can't say no to him. She cares for him and it's undermining us, you know?" he said, putting his hand to his own chest.

Tia exchanged a look with Isla. She knew. They both knew first-hand what that was like. Loving a man and being pulled to another. It never ended well.

"He's fooled her. She probably thinks she's indebted to him in some way," Isla said. "Don't be too hard on her. I've seen it. I was his most compatible. Only I have seen the monster he really is—and I suppose Antonio," she said, looking worried.

Lance was horrified. Knowing the strength of the mate's pull, he would feel the dread they all felt when they imagined what it must have been like.

"Yeah, have you seen Antonio's bruises lately?" Lacy said.

Lance sat down heavily on the bed and put his head in his hands. Tia felt instantly sorry. They weren't helping. "I just don't know what to do—how to act—how to deal with it," Lance said.

"You need to get out of here," Tia said.

His eyes widened as if leaving her alone with him was the last thing he'd do.

"He won't share her for long," Isla said. "He can't keep up the act indefinitely. He'll simply get rid of you."

"Like he's done with all the partners of no use to him," Lacy said.

He looked into each of their faces like he was weighing it all up. Then he shook his head. "No, I can't leave."

Tia felt exasperated with him.

He pointed at her and said, "You don't understand. It's the point of my existence. I've lived many lifetimes and, every time, we find each other and I protect her."

Tia hadn't forgotten that he and Lily had their own prophecy going on in all this. In every generation of Sirens, he got reborn to protect her. It was amazing and romantic, but his part always ended in death. He knew it and she felt desperately sorry for him.

He looked soulfully into her eyes. "But thanks."

Tia was about to open her mouth to tell him not to worry, that they had a plan with Jay and everything, when she saw the gold wash over his eyes. After a brief pause of shock, she said, "OK then. Be careful."

He nodded, now looking completely normal, then he slipped out of the room.

"Did you just see that?" she said, turning to her sisters.

They both nodded in shock, but Isla looked the most troubled of all. "It's too late. Malleven is in him. That's why he's still alive. He's just using him for intel and biding his time. We've got to be really careful now."

Tia was staring at them both, terrified. "And warn Jay."

CHAPTER 17

The warm, loving caress of Lily's breath seeped into every cell of Malleven's body and smoothed over his anger and humiliation in one long, tender stroke. Replenishing his bond with her was always sweet balm to his soul. It also lessened the ferocity with which he returned it, although he never failed in his need to own and dominate. He chose the shower in his room rather than the sea. It was impossible for him to drown, but he still hated being in its grip. It was the loss of power.

He kissed her soundly, and, shrouding her in a robe, carried her to his bed. She allowed it and lay languid in his arms. Her trust and purity of spirit continued to calm him, along with the fact that it struck a real blow at Lance. He hated that she valued him so.

However, he couldn't trust himself for long, for fear he would ruin the relationship he'd carefully built by unleashing the decidedly ungentle side of him. And so, he thanked her for her pledge, and said, "Go and find your male. No doubt he will need your attention."

Even then, instead of seeing the smug one upmanship he

clearly felt, her eyes softened, as if he was giving her a great gift by letting her go to him. He tapped her bottom as she went and watched her go.

His contentment didn't last for long. She disappeared from view and his eyes fell on his table of potions at the edge of his chamber. The memory of what happened earlier flooded back. He clenched his fists and ground his teeth. There was only one thing that helped when the whole world was determined to fight him. *Gold.*

Malleven pushed off the bed and went across the soft sand to his table. There, he took out the tiny beveled glass and the box of living liquid from its carved wooden box. He poured a measure, carefully, and lifted it to his eyeline to see the particles dance in the light. Then he threw it down his neck in one large gulp.

He staggered back to the bed as if he was drunk and fell on it while the searing pain racked his whole body. Thoughts of the hateful disobedience of his true mate and the other Sirens, Lily going back to the man she loved and having to placate a small boy to remain strong, raged through him, but were dwarfed by a pain so severe it flayed his skin inside and out.

It left him panting and sweating, face down. After some time, he sat up and wiped his brow with a handkerchief. The gold now lived and breathed inside of him. He felt its power. He took another moment and stood and straightened his robe. Then he trudged shakily in search of Antonio.

Upon sight of him, his anger returned with a vengeance. Antonio was in his rooms looking more and more like a frightened rabbit. The irony was, the meeker he became, the more it made him want to hurt him. It was his nature.

. . .

MALLEVEN LAY with Antonio replete in his arms and wondered what it was about the male that had held him for several years now. It was true, he was tall and angelically handsome. He had unruly blond hair and light grey eyes that were very disarming. He dressed well and had got himself disowned by his own father, Christian Dubonnetti, because of his relationship with him. He supposed it was because he was always there for him, despite sharing him with the Sirens. He knew he'd remained faithful because he'd tested him again and again and, still, he remained true. He guessed that was it: Antonio was loyal.

He looked down at him and could see him still shaking from the rather brutal sex they'd just had. Welts were coming up on his wrists where he'd restrained him and a new bruise was ripening on his cheek. He sensed him watching and looked up revealing the split lip he'd received for no other reason other than he'd felt like it.

There was scorn in the slant of the light-grey eyes, forcing him to ask as he always did, "Do you still love me?" It did strike him as strange why he always had to ask. It made him wonder whether his treatment of Antonio was a continual test of his love. It was perverse, he knew, to continually push him to the brink like this.

Antonio swallowed and nodded. "I just wish …" He trailed off and put his head back down on his chest. Then Malleven felt the quiet sobs against him that came even though they risked his anger. It made him wonder for the first time if he'd gone too far. He did love him. He was his.

He wanted all the Sirens, but he never intended to ever let Antonio go. Their relationship was based on an honesty that he could never have with the sisters—particularly Lily, his favorite.

He put a finger under Antonio's chin and pulled it up to look at him again. "The kingdom is finally mine, Antonio.

The Sirens are merely a necessity to keep it. You should feel glad, for you are favorite to the king." He knew it was only a roundabout, rather lackluster, declaration of his feelings for him.

Antonio smiled wanly. He understood he would wait a very long time for any direct words of love. *Wasn't it him he sought out at the end of every day?* However, he said nothing at all and that troubled him more than anything. He hoped he hadn't finally broken him.

THE NEXT MORNING, Malleven left Antonio sleeping and went and found the boy, JJ, playing with his siblings in the nursery. They were a charming picture, sitting engaged in various activities of gaming, reading or coloring on the large, circular rug.

Children had never really interested him, other than these—the knowledge of learning their names, parentage and where they fitted into the scheme of things. The girl, Alexia, seemed especially close to JJ, of which he noted. Xavier, Dante's eldest, would grow up to become a threat one day and there was Roman and Zander, the younger children and of little consequence to him other than being kind to them for JJ's sake.

Then there were Keefa and Dannon, Isla's pair. Too tall and awkward to sit with their cousins on the floor, they lounged on their beds. He sneered, not bearing to look at them. "Come, JJ," he said, sharply, wanting to get away from them.

JJ whined, but reluctantly stood and held up a sad half-mast arm of goodbye.

Malleven snatched his hand, roughly, and concentrated on lightening his demeanor before he scared the boy on the walk back to the Great Hall.

JJ seemed to forget and they were served a large breakfast. His high priest, Nasr, had asked for an audience and he wanted to see how the boy reacted in an official setting. Then he wanted to get on with breathing with the rest of the Sirens.

He knew why Nasr had made the journey all the way to Ireland from Syria. It was to call in a debt. The time had finally come and only one of them would be leaving this meeting today.

Malleven kept him waiting upstairs in the above ground part of the house for a full hour to put him in his place. Then, after he and JJ had eaten, he carried him to the small dais where he'd had a red and gold miniature throne made for him to match his own. "Sit, my son," he said, to reinforce his position.

JJ did what he was told with interest. "Are we judging one of our subjects today?" he said.

The use of the word "our" made Malleven pause. He didn't know whether to be pleased or annoyed. In the end, he just nodded. "One of my Magi brotherhood." It would be interesting to see how the boy behaved with the inevitable outcome.

Nasr swept into the room with two others by way of the lift and walked quickly down the marble steps towards them. He stopped just in front of the dais, touched the dark skin of his forehead and his heart and bowed low on his knees before them. Malleven rested his eyes with satisfaction on the purple disk on the top of his black, cylindrical hat, that singled him out as a high priest. The scarf that covered his balding grey head pooled around him like oil, mixing with his black silk robes on the dusty floor before him. His large hooked nose grazed the floor, just long enough to hear the strain in his breath before he allowed him up.

Two similar-garbed men bowed either side of him in

short formality. Malleven could not take his eyes from the brother nearest him. He detested him. Ghazi Sistani, the brother he no longer trusted. He had been guardian of the Siren, Phoebe Ray, since she was a small girl and he'd purposely not brought him with him because he strongly suspected his loyalties were divided. He was also the brother he'd given her to satisfy her blood lust while she'd been with him. He'd done it to divide them, but it hadn't worked.

However, he would wait. It mollified him, slightly, to see his brothers subservient to him—particularly Nasr, who'd enjoyed continually rubbing in his low birth since he was an inconsequential youth. He'd done enough bowing and scraping to climb the ranks of the Magi. Those days were gone.

Malleven held out his hand, bearing the king's ring, for Nasr to kiss. It was embossed with the great seal of Atlantis, proving his station. Nasr put it to his forehead and then kissed it. He inwardly chuckled at how the tables had turned.

"My king," Nasr said. "I have travelled all this way to convey my congratulations personally on your accession. As he stood, stiffly, his eyes fell on JJ. "And on acquiring a fine son."

Malleven inclined his head in thanks, knowing full well the real reason he'd made the journey.

"My brothers at the castle have kept me informed of your success here and that you have all five of the Sirens pledged to you."

Malleven bowed his head regally again, not filling him in that they were yet to follow through with their breath.

"And there have been whispers that you have also found the revered power of the Darkly Begotten."

While Nasr bowed obsequiously again, Malleven took a sideways glance at JJ. He was watching the scene quietly with interest, carrying himself as prince much older than his years. The boy impressed him already. "I have, High One," he said, turning back to Nasr while he stood up straight again.

Nasr's eyes widened, as if he expected him to lie. "And you remember our bargain? In exchange for our backing and having your brotherhood behind you to secure your beloved Siren, you promised me the power of the Darkly Begotten to wield—as High Priest, of course." His eyes darted, reminding him of an acquisitive crow.

Malleven's fell on Ghazi and the other brother with him. "Leave us. See the cook for refreshments while we conclude our business here."

Ghazi looked to Nasr who nodded and they both walked towards the corridor and the kitchens."

Once Ghazi had gone, he smiled and bowed his head. He was enjoying himself and excited about testing the boy. "I remember it well and do not wish to renege on our bargain, but certain information was withheld from me pertaining to the nature of the Darkly Begotten when I made it with you."

Nasr straightened and bristled. Anger was building in him as he readied himself for the fight he'd been expecting.

Malleven put up his hands to try to calm him. "It's simply that the Darkly Begotten is not a what, but more a who."

Nasr frowned. His crafty eyes shot to the boy, speculatively, then back to Malleven.

Malleven grinned. "Yes. You've guessed correctly. Meet JJ: The Darkly Begotten prince. Fulfilling all aspects of the prophecy."

Nasr took a foolish step towards him and Malleven immediately stopped his progress with his mind. Nasr fought against the invisible force. "He needs to be with me at the temple," Nasr ground out, as he struggled against his tightening bonds.

Malleven felt the gold surge through him. The heightened blood pressure pounded in his temples and brought with it the recognition that he was indeed a king. One that could do anything he wanted to whomever he wanted. Even a high priest. He slowly stood and walked to the edge of the dais where he could loom over Nasr and sighed. "The trouble is, you see, what I didn't realize is that the Darkly Begotten must choose himself who he aligns himself with. If he chooses you, then, indeed, he must go with you. I have upheld my end of the bargain. However, if he chooses to stay, then you must accept that." Malleven knew damn well that the Darkly Begotten was an Atlantean prophecy sent to impact this kingdom and would not be wielded by anyone. He could not be controlled, even by an Atlantean king. Nevertheless, he went along with the charade, so it could never be said that he went back on his word.

Nasr stopped struggling to listen and calculate whether the offer was fair. He gave Malleven a look of contempt, knowing exactly what he was playing at, and knelt in front of the small throne where the boy sat quietly watching them. He did the forehead/heart thing again.

Malleven observed the boy, curiously, taking all the homage paid to him as if it was his due. He wondered if the boy fully understood what was happening.

"I would ask that you accompany me to my temple in Syria and learn the ways of the Magi Brotherhood. There, you will be taught the wonders of the mystic world and become one of us."

Malleven fully intended to groom the boy in the ways of magic and alchemy himself. Nevertheless, he kept up the pretense. "What do you intend to do … Son," he said, dropping in the word to let him know how he saw him. "Nasr would know who you serve?"

The boy turned his head to him and then back to look Nasr in the eye. "I thank you for your offer of tutelage, but I serve no one; I am an entity alone. Without realizing it, you insult me and you insult this kingdom. You are not one of us and yet you seek to control me."

Malleven's smile widened with every word. The boy couldn't have made a better statement if he'd instructed it himself.

Nasr was already groveling out an apology, but then he appeared to pause and harden. "What trickery is this? You try to palm me off with a brat while you keep my spoils?"

Malleven had let the farce go on long enough. He didn't want him to scare the boy or bring his brothers back by the volume of his voice. Gold swept through his eyes and his mind until his power was in exquisite focus. It left him in a stream and gripped Nasr around the neck. This time, Nasr was ready and attempted to do the same. But he was no match for him. His body seethed with gold and the power of a Siren.

Nasr began to weaken and choke. He was the color of a dark berry and his eyes began to bulge. He would have loved to take his tongue while he writhed in front of him, but he looked at the boy. "Would you ever have gone to him?"

The boy shook his head as if he'd asked him if he wanted to play outside and he couldn't be bothered. He seemed completely unperturbed by the scene in front of him; one that would have traumatized an ordinary child. It was a little unnerving—particularly when the boy said, "You should take the body out to sea." He pointed to the fountain. "Your brothers will not find it there."

Malleven paused in awe. Nasr heard and made one last effort to struggle. The boy was absolutely right. Even Nasr drank the liquid version of gold. It was what enabled their sect to do their superhuman things. Once dead, the gold inside him would simply disperse into the sea, dissolving his flesh with it and, with no life left in him, it would never reassemble. His brothers would never be able to commune with it to find him.

"If you take it to one of the underwater catacombs it will not raise to the surface."

Malleven was amazed at his brilliance and above all, his coldness. Nasr was not yet dead in his arms. He couldn't help feeling exultant that the boy had so clearly sided with him.

"Go now. Someone is coming," JJ said.

Malleven wasted no more time and dragged the still-struggling Nasr towards the fountain, the gold bubbling feverishly inside him. He hefted him over the wall and took one last look at JJ swinging his legs in his throne as he pulled Nasr down into its swallowing depths.

CHAPTER 18

*D*rew didn't let go of Phoebe all the way to the port. They barely spoke. She cried silently into him a few times and he just held her. All she said over and over was, "I can't believe you're actually here." She'd thought he was dead along with everyone else, so he gave her what she needed and was just there for her.

Eventually, she looked up. "How are you still alive? I thought I'd lost you." She almost crumpled again, but he held her up.

"I met the Orb and she had a plan for me," he explained. He told her the full story of how she'd revealed everything about him and protected him in the blast.

It was late and she was wrung out from emotion. They both were. He borrowed a blanket and put it over them. He pulled her into his lap and the heat of his body and soon felt the sting of her bite at his neck, unseen under the blanket. It was a release in itself to be able to provide for her in that way. Eventually, he returned it. Her blood fortified him, filling his cells with everything her until they slept deeply.

He, feeling the burn of the big Murr's eyes on him the whole time. He'd let him live, but it was far from over.

They were woken up when they reached the small port and everyone alighted from the bus. The sun was warming the sky over a huge cargo ship that had recently eased into one of the three terminals. It was the first stop on the way to Pugets Sound and would soon be bustling with activity unloading. They would need to move quickly.

Phoebe wanted to pull him in the direction of the water, but Drew held back. He would have loved nothing more than to make the long journey with her, even with the dagger looks from the Murr. "I can't, Phoebe. The boys will be scared enough. I need to travel back with them."

"Then I will come with you," she said, taking a step towards him.

Vionne put out an arm, barring her way. *Have you forgotten we have a new king to which you have pledged yourself?*

"OK then, I unpledge," she spat over her shoulder, pulling out of his grip to continue on with Drew.

Vionne went to stop her more forcefully, but this time Drew was ready and stepped in the way. The Murr took a challenging step forward, eying him closely to see what he'd do. He was at least a head taller and Drew was no short ass at six three.

The Murr glared down at him. *Despite our grievances, she can't just remove a pledge. She must think of those relying on her. She must wait until New Murrtaine is built and its people safe within its walls. Until her own sisters are safe.*

Drew became conscious of the boys' stares behind him, but continued regardless. "You expect me to leave her with you when she doesn't want to go?" The change was seeping into his eyes and his teeth tingled.

Vionne appeared unfazed by it and took a step into him, bumping his chest. It seemed he'd learned a lot through

Atlantean interaction. *Never fear, you will have your chance to win her at the appointed time.*

Drew felt Phoebe pulling on his arm. "It's OK, Drew. I'll see you when we get back, I promise," she said, finishing with a filthy look at Vionne.

The tide brother, the black-haired Murr said from behind Vionne.

Drew looked back at the bus. Reeve, the leader of the Santalini guards, stood at the foot of the steps and tilted his head towards it. Time was up.

With separation imminent, Drew's mind raced. He hoped the blood they shared was enough to keep her going. He hadn't bonded with her in the traditional sense, with his breath. Being human, it had only been one-sided. But now, thanks to Phoebe, he was one of them and he was desperate to complete the bond.

However, the Murr was infuriatingly right. He turned and pulled her into his arms. He had a responsibility to his boys and Phoebe must bide her time to see that the Murrs were safe. He owed the Orb that much. "You must go with him."

She went to plead, but he shook his head. "I don't like it, but he's the safest person for you to be with right now." After searching his eyes, she reluctantly agreed.

The Murr immediately seized the moment and nudged her to the dock. Drew slowly went to go back up the steps of the bus, watching her the whole time; being pushed too fast like a small child and continually looking back. It broke his heart.

In the end, he had to physically get a hold on himself and go inside the bus. When he looked again, she was gone.

There were just a handful of Santalinis left on the bus. "Can I ride with my boys?" he said to one he recognized. "Sure. Be quick. We have a flight to catch."

Drew ran back out of the bus to the one behind and it quickly opened its doors. The boys looked up eagerly and he spotted Justin a few seats from the back. He bumped fists with them all as he moved along the aisle and the bus moved off. "Well done, guys. You made it."

He looked straight into Justin's eyes that said so many things: relief, worry, wariness. "Any casualties?" he asked.

"None of the boys were left behind, sir," the boy said, choosing his words carefully.

It wasn't lost on him, but he let out a deep breath of relief. He had a lot of explaining to do. Secret missions to save the world were not going to cut it any longer with these boys—particularly Justin. He put his hand on the boy's shoulder and gave it a squeeze. "You were brave." He could only imagine how terrifying it must have been to come face to face with all their fears and then have nothing but blind trust in him to go with. He stood, holding the corner of the aisle seat, his body swaying as the bus moved and he looked into the boys' eager faces. He would have hugged them all if they could handle it, but they weren't used to physical contact and it would freak them out. He remembered how hard that had been when he'd first left the camp. "You've all been brave."

Someone hissed, "Yes!" as if they wanted to celebrate. All eyes, including his, naturally went to the boy responsible and his face dropped. Drew felt immediately sorry. "It's OK. You can be boys now, you're free." How he would have loved them to cheer and pat each other on the back, but he doubted they'd ever do that. They still couldn't trust there'd be no reprisals.

The bus trundled on and the boys settled into their seats, looking tired and a little less anxious, although their eyes strayed to him for reassurance all the time. He sensed movement behind him and looked over his shoulder. The boys in the back seats were signing an OK and thumbs-up at the window to the boys in the bus behind. It almost brought him to tears.

"What happened, 23—er, Drew, sir? Where were you? We didn't see you after class," Justin said.

A boy got up to sit across the aisle and Drew slid into the seat next to Justin. He was a bright boy and he could tell he knew exactly what had gone down that night. "I was in the cells," he said, watching the boy join the dots.

"They're them, aren't they," Justin said.

Drew felt the boys all turn and kneel up in their seats to hear. There was no point in lying, but he must choose his words carefully. He wanted to avoid panic at all costs. These boys had been brought up to believe the Atlanteans were sent from the Devil himself. He nodded and watched the shock spread from boy to boy.

"Are we prisoners?" one boy said.

"No, it's a mission. We're agents," another whispered more quietly.

Drew smiled at them all and shook his head.

Then Justin surprised him. "They helped us escape."

He heard the sharp intakes of breath around them. Some looked excited, others terrified. He felt a wave of panic run through everyone except Justin. He looked calm and knowing, as if he wasn't surprised. Drew had to stand and put up his hands to calm them all. "Listen to me. You trust me, don't you?"

A few of the boys nodded.

"You've been lied to your whole lives." At the shocked faces he had to say quickly; "You must see that the way you were forced to live in that camp wasn't right?"

"We were being prepared to fight the Devil," one boy shouted.

A couple of Santalini guards at the front laughed.

Drew sagged a little in exasperation. It was going to take

more than a brief chat on the way back in the bus. They would need a proper deprogramming regime. "Have you heard of the word indoctrination?"

"I have," Justin said. "It's where you get an idea drummed into you so you believe it, whether it's right or not."

"Yes!" Drew said, pointing at him. "Correct!"

With awful timing, the bus was pulling into the airport. He needed to get these boys debriefed as soon as possible and hope none of them ran for it when they caught sight of the plane. He went to the front and asked Reeve if he could have a word with him.

The three buses pulled straight onto the private airstrip. The boys looked around them in awe. The Dubonnetti Industries plane stood on the tarmac, alone. Many of them would never have seen a plane, let alone been on one. Still, it was less scary than the Santalini troop carrier, which was doing a similar job in Europe.

The boys got off the buses and huddled together, nervously. Whispering what it all meant. Thankfully, their passports had been arranged by the President of the United States himself.

Drew quickly bumped fists with the boys off the rear bus to regain their attention, giving a big smile to the three of his six who had ridden with them. "Well done," he said, getting smiles of relief. How he loved these boys already.

"We're going on there?" one said.

Drew nodded. Then he bent forward and whispered, "Life starts here. We're going to Europe."

The shocked faces turned to wonder and then joy as what that meant began to sink in.

"Go on. Up you go," Drew said, pointing at the airstairs.

They walked hesitantly towards the plane. Then some began to quicken their pace until they all began to run, scurrying up the steps and squealing with excitement in their race for the good seats.

They were acting just like any other schoolboys on a field trip. It made his heart glad and fill with hope for them. He was so proud they were adjusting so quickly.

He climbed the steps behind them with the Santalini guards making the trip back with them. Three would return the buses and go back to their HQ in New York.

"You sure you want to take them all with you?" Reeve said, chuckling next to him as their heavy boots clanked up the metal steps. "The president would have taken them with the kids from all the other camps to find new homes."

Drew stood and watched the excitable boys being offered pop and chips by an already harassed stewardess. These boys were special. He couldn't ever imagine leaving them to the human care system. "I'm sure," he said more to himself. "I want them with me. At least for a while till they, you know, adjust."

Reeve nodded, understanding perfectly. "Sure gonna be lively about the place," he said grinning. "Not sure how Dante will take it."

Drew hadn't thought about Dante. He hadn't been to his new home yet. It would be strange for the boys, no doubt. He'd need to prepare them.

He went along the aisle with the stewardess, making sure all their seatbelts were on, then sat and watched their excited faces as the plane taxied then roared and took off. It was wonderful to see a rare first in their lives. Even Justin broke a smile.

When they were settled into the flight, eating and drinking, he unclipped his belt and signed for Reeve to come over. Reeve nodded, then got up and stood in the aisle in front of the boys. Chatter and the rustling of crisp packets died and they all looked up at him fearfully.

"Hi, my name is Reeve. I thought I'd just come over and say hi on behalf of the guards. And answer any questions you might have. Drew tells me we have a bit of a bad rep with you guys."

When no one spoke up, Drew played devil's advocate. "We've been led to believe that you are the Devil's children, thrown out of Heaven, and have stolen this planet to spread your evil and depraved ways," Drew said, trying to keep a straight face.

He felt Justin switch his gaze from his to Reeve, waiting for him to answer.

Reeve laughed loudly, and, in doing that, clearly showed the fangs that never completely retracted into his gums.

The collective gasp from the boys had Reeve bewildered. He looked at Drew for help, not knowing what he'd done. Drew tapped his own teeth.

Reeve said, "Oh," in understanding and leaned casually against a seat, not fazed at all. He was the perfect chilled-out guy for this. "OK, let's do question time. I'll lead by saying we were originally from another planet on the far side of the universe called Atlas and I've never been to Heaven … or Hell."

"When did you come?" Justin called out.

Drew was so proud. Only by starting them off, would all the other boys follow. Justin was a born leader.

"I was born here. My ancestors came ten thousand years ago."

"Are you a vampire?" 361 shouted. "And where can I get some fangs?"

Everyone laughed. The boys relaxed into a pleasant Q&A session.

"Not exactly," Reeve said. "You see, we came from a water world. I'm from a family of soldiers, and, when we first arrived, we were sent out first to scope the place. We drank blood to survive, but we soon settled, made a home and no longer needed to do that."

"What's your favorite food then?"

"Steak or a good burger," Reeve answered, which made them laugh at the normality of it. It struck Drew that many of them had not eaten food as rich as that for a very long time, if ever at all.

The questions came thick and fast after that. His six making sure all the important ones were covered. In the end it was Justin that asked the question that shut them all up. "Why are you different to the other guys?"

It was a great question and Reeve nodded in appreciation. "The other guys are from a different family. They are the Borge and live permanently underwater."

"So, they are the ones that came thousands of years ago," Justin said.

It was very insightful, that Justin should get it straight away.

Reeve nodded. "Yes, they are the purebreds. In the beginning we were all like that. Then the other four families went on land and mixed with the human population. We stayed on the land and became known as Atlanteans."

"Can you breathe under water?" another asked, amazed, and that sparked them off again.

Drew looked on, contented. They relaxed more with every question. The hours passed and, one by one, all the boys fell asleep. Except his six. He was so proud. Even now, when they were as exhausted as the others, they remained leaders of their platoons and kept watch. He went and leaned over their seats. "You did well, boys."

They looked up at him trustingly and he took in their expectant faces. He vowed then to look out for each and every one of them. "We're going to land in about an hour. Then we'll be going to the court of the king—the deposed king," he corrected. "Anyway, it's a secret place and you are going to be the only humans ever to see it."

Their eyes went wide. Only Justin quickly asked; "Are you coming with us?"

Drew nodded. "I want you all to know that I have requested for you to stay with me. All of you," he said, making sure he looked in each of their faces.

361 folded his arms and slumped back in his seat. "Until you rehome us."

There spoke the voice of experience. It was a sad fact of life for many of these boys, even before they were captured and indoctrinated by the Scythian organization. They'd already had a sad life that would take longer than a few hours to get over.

It made up his mind. He had an idea he'd been pondering on for some time. He just needed to put it to Dante. "Look, I can't tell you about it yet, but, if the former king agrees and regains his throne, then I'll make sure you stay with me for good."

The boys looked at each other, not able to hide the excitement building in their eyes. "That's if you want to," Drew said with a grin

CHAPTER 19

Instead of going back to Filfla and reporting to Dante, Vionne went straight to Ireland. He didn't like it, but he had to make sure the new king believed in his allegiance. Plus, he had to admit, it suited him to keep Phoebe away from Drew as much as possible. They hadn't breathed for each other yet and he wanted to keep it that way.

He did message Dante, however, letting him know the mission had been a success. He knew he was walking a fine line between the two kings.

He sent Axyl on in a small marine bug to check the progress of his people, and he, Phoebe and Ashaya entered the castle by way of the fountain; the latter seeming more enthusiastic than the former.

The sight that first greeted him made him pause in shock. The new king was sitting on a magnificent golden throne with several people prostrate on the floor in front of him, with Jay's son on a smaller one next to him. On sight of them, Malleven dismissed his trapped prey and they gratefully scurried off.

Vionne cautiously signaled for them to express their lungs and the three of them approached. He and Ashaya more awkwardly as their legs had not yet set.

They all bowed and Malleven flicked his hand, giving them permission to sit. His demeanor seemed a little impatient. Slightly erratic, even. Whenever Vionne had seen him in the past, Malleven had always seemed so calm and composed. He kept his thoughts to himself, however, and watched as a servant brought forward three chairs. Vionne's eyes rested on JJ. "Hello, Uncle Vionne," JJ said, seeming completely at ease in his current situation.

Vionne bowed his head. *Good day to you, Prince JJ. May I present a friend of mine visiting from our outpost of Murrla: Ashaya.*

She stood and curtseyed deeply. *May I say what an honor it is to meet you both.*

Malleven eyed her coolly, a little puzzled.

Ashaya is a priestess of the Five Moons, Vionne explained.

ASHAYA STUDIED MALLEVEN CLOSELY. She'd never seen him this close up. He was very handsome in a chiseled, shrewd, kind of way. However, there was hardness in the lines of his face that gave him an air of cruelty.

Malleven merely inclined his head and offered no polite enquiry of her. It was very telling of his character, particularly regarding his spiritual inclinations—or rather, lack of. JJ, however, sat up with interest. "My mother studies The Way," he said.

I should love to meet her one day and discuss such matters, she said, demurely. She couldn't, of course, let on that she'd watched Tia's development with interest. Vionne's eyes seemed to soften towards her and made her heart flutter. He distracted her a lot.

May she be truly blessed. Ashaya said, attempting to focus again.

Then the boy said something that shook her to her core. "I know who you are." Her heart literally fell from her chest into her stomach.

Malleven immediately turned in his seat to face him, suddenly interested.

JJ glanced at him and pointed at her. "You must be attentive to her, Father, so she forms a good opinion of us."

Ashaya's heart stopped beating as Malleven narrowed his eyes at Vionne. Thankfully, he looked mystified. Instead he changed the subject. *The mission in Washington State was a success. The camp was destroyed and the boys liberated.*

Malleven nodded, still distracted. "Delissi has sent word that the president's troops have been successful in New York and Salt Lake City as well. Our troops secured the European camps easily."

What of the boys? Vionne asked.

Ashaya listened keenly. It was a point of special interest for her, how he dealt with the human population.

"I am keeping them for collateral for now. They have been taken to a central holding camp in France. Europe's leaders need to know their place with their new king."

Ashaya absorbed the information, shocked. The president had offered them sanctuary in the United States and she knew that Dante would not have proceeded like that. Malleven was securing his power in the world, but she felt that Dante would have tackled it in a way to bring better understanding between the two peoples. She wasn't entirely sure how it would be viewed from above, and which of the two approaches would be favored.

Vionne bowed. *If Your Highness would excuse us, I would like to join my people to check on their progress and help the weak and infirm.*

Malleven was watching Phoebe, who hadn't said a word throughout the whole exchange. "Rest first," he said, still not taking his eyes off her. "Phoebe will replenish her bond with me and tomorrow you can get back to your people."

Ashaya felt the fear and doubt in Vionne, but he could do nothing but bow. Phoebe remained silent. Her unhappiness was evident to all.

PHOEBE KNOCKED on the bedroom door the servant said now belonged to three of her sisters. She could only assume they'd gathered together to protect themselves, as the castle had many luxurious rooms to sleep in.

The door opened and Lacy pulled her inside, where Tia and Isla gathered around them. "Is it true Drew is alive?"

Phoebe nodded, bewildered. She still couldn't quite believe it herself. The mere mention of him brought tears to her eyes. She fought it down and relayed the dangerous mission, spearheaded by Drew. "He stayed with the boys because they were scared," she finished, unable to say more as a lump had appeared in her throat that she couldn't swallow.

"He's such a good guy," Lacy said, setting her off.

"Now he's going to have to go up against Vionne to win me, in a place Vionne chooses. How can he win?" she said between sobs.

"Shush," Lacy said, hugging her and wrapping her in the scent of lilies.

Tia immediately cut in. "Look, stop crying. We've been working on our own plan. Has Malleven topped up his bond with you yet?"

Phoebe shook her head, pulling out of Lacy's arms. "No. I've got to go to him next."

"Shit!" Isla said. "I can't see how it can work."

"What?" Phoebe said, looking at each of her sisters in turn.

"Malleven is already in her. Can you hide another person, do you think?"

"I'm not sure. I suppose so," she said, remembering how Dante had no idea Malleven was there. She must be able to do that on some level. "Who do you mean?" she asked.

"Jay," the three said in hushed voices.

"We haven't got time to explain everything," Tia said. "But Jay is about to challenge Malleven. We've all breathed for him already," she said, pointing between her and her sisters. "We've been stalling with Malleven to keep him in the dark as long as possible. He's holding the kids against us."

Phoebe's brain was racing with all the new information. *Would Jay be any better than Dante in dealing with her situation? Would he let her have Drew?*

Tia seemed to soften, proving she'd followed her train of thought. "I know you blamed Dante for what happened at Murrtaine, but there wasn't really anything he could do. The Scythians had tracked Drew."

Phoebe smiled wanly and guessed she was right, but she wasn't convinced. "Vionne's more my problem now. He needs a Siren and I'm his mate by purple ring." She read their confused faces. The last they knew, Drew had the purple ring. "No," she said on a weary exhale. "It's a long story. Drew's blood had been tampered with. Then he met the Orb before she destroyed Murrtaine and the explosion seemed to reset everything. The Fates reverted back to what they should have been. Of course, I didn't know any of this. I just saw Vionne's ring was purple, and assumed Drew was dead like everyone else."

Tia looked at Isla, who seemed a little rattled. "One step at a time, eh?" She gave her shoulder a squeeze.

A knock made them all jump and they turned to look at

the door. Phoebe's heart began to thump in fear and she had no idea why. It was Isla who finally broke her paralysis to answer it. "What do you want?" Isla said, so curtly that they all gathered to see who it was.

A dark-bearded man in the black robes of the Magi stood on the threshold.

"Go! You have no business here." Isla went to close the door on him.

He quickly put out a foot and an arm, holding the other up to calm her. Isla crouched, ready to fight.

"I mean you no harm. I have a message for Phoebe and must give her this," he said, holding out what looked like a small jewelry box. "She has been called to Malleven's chamber immediately."

Before anyone could say anything further, Isla snatched the box, pushed him out and slammed the door in his face. "I will return in an hour," he called through the door.

"Don't bother," Isla said back.

Tia and Lacy's smiles faded. Phoebe was troubled.

"What is it?" Isla said, plonking the box in Phoebe's hand.

Phoebe wasn't sure, exactly. It was like a feeling of dread that settled in her chest. She had the same weird feeling before when she'd seen the Magi brothers. "There was something about him." She cautiously opened the cigarette packet-sized box. There was a necklace inside with an unusual tear-shaped gemstone pendant. It appeared to catch the light and shone in pastel colors on its many facets.

Phoebe staggered and felt woozy for a moment. Lacy quickly grabbed her arm to steady her. Phoebe shook her head. It felt heavy, like a fog was slowly lifting from her mind so she could see clearly for the first time in months. Her memory hadn't been fully returned when she'd seen Malleven again. Something had been held back from her: *Ghazi.* "I remember him!" she said, bewildered. "That man."

"Who is he?"

"Ghazi Sistani," she whispered, feeling how it rolled off her tongue, remembering herself saying it over and over as a young girl. "The guy at the door looked after me when I was kidnapped by Malleven. He's watched over me since I was a small child." She even remembered the pact they'd made when he warned her Malleven would take her memories. "I remember everything now," she said excitedly. "He'll help us."

Her sisters looked at each other, not so sure.

"Look he's a good guy. Malleven tried to have him killed a few times." Heat entered her cheeks at the memory. He'd used her to do it in a moment of blood lust. It was a deeply humiliating lack of self-control that Ghazi had forgiven her for and never spoken of. More than that, he'd vowed to serve her, something no one would understand. In the end, all she said was, "Believe me, Malleven hates him."

"I dunno," Tia said, still dubious.

Phoebe picked up her hands, all previous doubts now gone. "Look, I have to go to Malleven now. I'm not sure how long I'll be. But when Ghazi comes back, tell him I remember who he is and to bring Jay here for when I get back."

Her decisiveness was enough to satisfy Tia and the other sisters took her cue. All three nodded and she went off in search of her former kidnapper.

PHOEBE FOUND MALLEVEN LOUNGING on his four-poster, wrought-iron bed when she reached his chamber. It was a magnificent cave with its own sea and beach, that Dante had designed himself. There was a child's bed nearby, which made her raise an eyebrow. Thankfully it was empty.

Malleven sat up when he saw her and must have read her puzzlement. "The young prince is visiting his many siblings and cousins."

Phoebe had no idea why he would want a kid in his room, but, whatever it was, she could bet it wasn't a good intention. "Can we get this over with, please," she said, flapping an arm in the direction of the water.

Malleven slowly got to his feet, already calculating the reason. "You want to hurry back to Drew."

She suddenly lost patience with him. "Yes, Drew! It's always been Drew. But everyone keeps pushing me towards Vionne. I hate Vionne. Why can't everyone get that into their thick heads!" she shouted. "I will never accept him."

Malleven didn't answer, merely studied her, showing no signs of anger. He took her hand and guided her towards the water. "We will talk after," he said.

They waded into the water and stopped when the water lapped their upper bodies. "It is enough to keep us cool," he said.

She was glad. She wanted it clinical and over with as soon as possible, but when she thought about it, Malleven was never comfortable in the water, which was unusual for an Atlantean.

He wasted no more time, grabbed her by the shoulders, covered her mouth with his, and streamed his essence straight into her. It was sudden and overwhelming; she was overcome by the strength of it. Lily was there, but none of the others. It was unmistakable through the bond. She took heart from that.

However, she also felt all that was him. There was no hiding what kind of man he was: an egocentric megalomaniac, already powerful, with very little room for any real selfless love.

It shouldn't surprise her. She already knew a side of him could be a monster. She'd seen it first-hand. But she guessed she kind of hoped there would be some saving grace—a redeeming feature. Now she saw there really was none.

"Your turn," he prompted, when her dreamlike state began to subside.

She returned the flow of her breath in the same way and watched him stagger in the water. She held him up dispassionately, feeling nothing as he faltered. After a few moments, his eyes begrudgingly cracked open as if he was drunk and he smiled. "Such darkness," was all he said at the revelation of her. She didn't care.

She decided to tackle him while he was more disposed to speak to her and, possibly, a little weak. "What of Drew now he is alive? Can I be with him?"

Malleven sobered, straightened and narrowed his eyes at her. "Vionne is your true mate and the leader I must have for the Murrs," he explained in his most reasonable voice as if his hands were tied.

Despite understanding his position completely, she wasn't interested. "So you're saying no," she said, flatly, already turning in the direction of the beach.

Malleven made no move to stop her. "I have the power to make you pledge to me," he called after her.

Yes, he did. He'd already done exactly that when he'd kidnapped her. He literally stole her First Breath from her without her knowledge. Without it, he wouldn't be standing there today. "Yeah, I know. You're gonna have to do that with all of us—even Lily. Because without any of our mates, you haven't got a hope in hell of holding any of us." She grinned triumphantly, turned and stomped across the sand to get away from him before his anger hit.

Her mind churned all the way back to her sisters' room. She may have won a small victory, but he would now think and he would plan. Although, when she really thought about it, even if Dante regained the crown, he'd still have the same obligation to Vionne.

She refused to give in and vowed to never lose Drew

again.

again.

CHAPTER 20

Drew watched the wonderment on his boys' faces, satisfied he'd done the right thing. They looked so happy. The three helicopters descended into the center of the flat-top mountain that made up the whole islet of Filfla, just off the Island of Malta, in the middle of the Mediterranean. It was awesome, even for a seasoned traveler, which these boys very definitely were not. They'd needed several choppers to get everyone there. Just as with the buses, Drew had split his head boys into groups to supervise. Most of the Santalini guards would come last.

Drew stepped down and hunched over to run clear of the blades, with the first few boys on his heels. They squinted from the dust and covered their ears, while the wind whipped up the huge landing bay and the helicopter lifted off for the second to take its place. The next group ran to join them, followed by a third with a few of the guards. The boys instinctively grouped together, nervous and subdued, their eyes darting around them.

"Isn't it cool?" Drew said to reignite their excitement. "Like a Bond villain's lair." He finished doing his best evil laughter. They looked at him strangely and didn't seem convinced. They should be joking and laughing like boys of their age, instead, he knew they were scoping for exits and the best advantage to fight. He knew it, because he did the same thing when he walked into anywhere he didn't know.

Eventually, they heard the throb of the next helicopter getting closer and the last group arrived. The blades slowed to a stop and the boys piled out, followed by the last of the guards. They soon took the lead and told them to follow them down a spiral staircase, chosen as Drew insisted they stayed together and a lift wouldn't take them all. They were in enemy territory and he didn't want to rattle them by splitting them too soon. He was watching them closely as they continued downward. Justin was counting steps, which made him smile. He would certainly have his work cut out deprogramming. They went down so many, he wondered just how deep this bunker was.

They came out behind a pyramid-shaped staircase and walked around it to get to the front. What awaited them was so spectacular that it robbed them of speech. It reminded him of the Great Hall of Ballygowan Castle, but, at the same time, nothing like it. It was bigger and grander, if that was possible. It was modern, but that wasn't enough. He struggled for a better description. Foreign. Space age. Then it hit him. Alien was the word he was searching for. The sheer scale of it was breathtaking. The window to the sea was larger and curved at least forty-five degrees around the circular cave. The fountain was in sandstone and almost reached the roof. Living trees, laced with small lights twinkling like fireflies, climbed from the floor to the vaulted ceiling. It was magnificent and not at all Human in its design.

By the looks on the boys' faces, they were feeling the same thing. Someone said "Woah." Another, "Wow." Their minds were so blown by it that it overtook their fear. A few ran to the window to see the fish.

"Are we underwater here?" Justin asked.

"We are," a voice cut in from behind them before he could answer.

Drew swung around to see Dante striding towards them with Cesaré close behind.

Dante stopped in front of him and pulled him close, clapping his back loudly. Cesaré did the same. The boys filtered over to see who the strangers were and Drew was struck by Dante's pallor and the dark circles around his eyes.

He felt the boys next to him. "May I introduce to you my young friends from the Washington State camp?"

He watched Dante take a moment to take in their rag-bag appearances. "Welcome … I am Dante."

Drew turned to face the boys. "This is the rightful Atlantean king, boys," he explained. "You will address him as Your Highness." And he bowed to show the boys the correct etiquette.

They immediately copied him, but kept their eyes on him, cautiously.

Dante grinned, still with that same easy-going way Drew remembered. "So you couldn't be parted from them," he said, like it didn't surprise him at all. "Follow me. I expect you're tired."

Dante led them behind the grand staircase to a long corridor that cut through the sandstone rock that made up the islands. It soon split off into many directions to a hive of tunnels, too numerous to count.

"How many rooms do you have here?" Drew asked, amazed.

"My cousin tells me there'll be around a hundred when it's finished." Dante looked behind him at the boys following on, bewildered at the size of the place. "So I think we'll have space for a few boys," he said in his warm Irish accent, with a grin.

Drew was keeping his eye on the boys' reaction too. This was a lot to take in after the camp. The younger ones were in awe, but his six, he could tell, were mapping the way. "You OK?" he said quietly, to Justin.

Justin seemed uneasy and Dante was listening in with interest.

Justin cast Dante a furtive look.

"It's OK. You are free to speak here," Drew said.

"I need to know the route in case of fire," Justin blurted.

Dante looked into Drew's eyes with real empathy. He now understood perfectly why these boys meant so much to him.

Dante put his hand up and they stopped and waited for the stragglers to catch up. He looked at all the expectant faces. "Please listen. You are my guests. You're not prisoners here. There is an army of servants at your disposal who will tell you anything you need to know—particularly in an emergency. But for those who need to know now, all trade entrances and staircases if the lifts aren't working, are that way," he said, waving his arm to the left. This is the main corridor and you know that because of the blue lights in the ceiling. The others have different colors, so you can learn your route that way. This one will always take you back to the Great Hall." He smiled at Justin, then Drew, and continued walking.

"I guess, to start with, they will all want to remain together?" Dante said.

Drew nodded, impressed with how he was dealing with them. He wasn't patronizing them, simply giving them the facts. It was what they needed until they felt grounded. "Yes, Your Highness. If you can accommodate them like that. I would like to stay with them as well, if that's possible, until Phoebe gets here."

Dante frowned as if there was another conversation he didn't want to have in present company. They got to a metal door and Dante passed his hand over a panel. The door slid open revealing a huge, long, roughly hewn cave. "I thought, until we know what's happening with them, I'd put you all in here. There are no walls yet, but it has a large bathroom at the far end and will serve as a dormitory."

Drew surveyed the huge room and it was perfect. There were small cots and mattresses lined up either side against the wall, pretty much like they were used to. Except these beds had a proper duvet on each and looked warm and comfortable. The boys would feel in heaven on these.

"The bathroom is temporary, but there are four showers, sinks and toilets in there," Dante explained, pointing at the far end.

It was more than adequate.

"When we know what's happening, we'll move them to more comfortable accommodation."

Drew shook his head in amazement and gratitude. He held his hand out to Dante to shake. "Thanks, man. Believe me. This is the Waldorf to these boys."

Dante shook his hand.

"I can't believe what you managed to pull together in such a short time," Drew said, amazed.

"No problem," Dante said with a smile, already walking towards the door. However then he swayed and put his hand out to balance himself against a wall. Cesaré came to his elbow to steady him. It was worrying; *was he sick?*

Dante recovered quickly and looked over his shoulder at him. "Settle in and come and find me in my study," Dante said.

Drew bowed. "Yes, sir."

The door opened at a wave of his hand and Dante disappeared. Drew turned and grinned at them all waiting expectantly. "Sweet crib? What do you think?" When they all looked at him blankly, not sure what he wanted them to say, he waved his arm and said, "Well, go and choose your bed."

After a moment of inaction, they ran in every direction to bagsy a bed. They would be warm and comfortable tonight. The two older boys were reluctant to leave him. "It's OK. You can relax here, I promise. No harm will come to any of you."

Drew put an arm round their shoulders and pushed them over to three vacant beds nearest the door. "Here. I'll sleep right here with you."

The two boys looked at the beds with pillows and patchwork quilts. On top was a small pile of clothes for each of them: underwear, socks, PJs, slippers and sweats.

"We'll do an internet shop and get you some cool stuff," Drew said, suddenly realizing just how much these boys would need. Not just the boys. He literally had nothing to his name.

Just then, a servant came through the door carrying a holdall. He recognized it instantly as the bag he'd packed all those months ago when he'd left Seattle to enter this world. "His Highness kept this for you," the male servant said, placing it down in front of him.

Drew was forced to turn away. For some reason, emotion hit him hard. It was irrational; it was just stuff. He took in a deep breath. He guessed it represented the world he'd left behind to start a new life with Phoebe. It was a lifetime ago. Their plans had gone awry, but the king had seen fit to keep it, even when he thought he was dead. It felt like he'd kept the hope alive. A stupid thought really.

He swallowed his sappy thoughts away, turned back and took the bag gratefully. He thanked the servant and went to the bathroom for a bit of privacy. The room was basic white tile and porcelain, but he had it to himself. He showered and put on some old faithful black skinny jeans, ankle boots and a Blunderbuss band t-shirt. His old band. His heart felt heavy, but it made him feel his old self.

Privacy didn't last long when the boys discovered it had hot water and good soap. They were soon whooping and laughing and having a fine old time shooting the soap at each other with slippery hands. It was a joy to see. However, in the end, he had to shoo them out before the room became awash with water. He wasn't angry; it was good-natured and high spirits were a positive sign.

He was about to walk out when Justin and 361 got to their feet, dressed in their sweats, to come with him. Drew looked down and saw the inadequate slippers on their feet. They reminded him of inmates of a psyche ward. He walked back over to his bag.

"We want to come with you," 361 said, misreading his silence for anger.

"We need to know our future," Justin added.

Drew understood completely. He had planned on doing that later, but they may as well come with him now. He threw them each a pair of his white training shoes. "Put those on. They shouldn't be that much too big for you. They'll start you off until you have your own."

The boys looked at each other, sat down on a cot and eagerly put them on. Then Justin stood and signed to the remaining four head boys to keep an eye on the others happily giggling and running around. They understood and one whistled for them all to calm down, which they did, instantly. It was miraculous how they did as they were told. He guessed camp life would never truly leave these boys. Maybe that wasn't entirely bad. Order and obedience would keep them alive in an uncertain world. It was time to go and find out just how much.

Drew opened the door as he'd seen Dante do and a male servant immediately came to attention outside. He was dressed smartly in black shirt and slacks and wore a headset. He spoke into a mouthpiece that they were on their way. It was a rude awakening to where they actually were. As they moved through the labyrinth of corridors and up in the lift to meet Dante, Drew still had to pinch himself that they were now in an alien world. One which they could never really leave.

CHAPTER 21

The large double doors loomed high above Drew. "The study, sir," the servant said and walked off down the corridor. He paused for a moment to get his thoughts together. One step through here and he was back into the madness. Then his mind automatically shifted to what it was all about: *Phoebe*. His thoughts cleared and came back to the two boys behind him, with purpose.

Justin and 361 seemed to sense his attention was on them and took a step closer. "Enter," a voice said from the other side. Another servant opened them and stood back for the three of them to go in.

Drew moved inside more slowly than most would expect, with the boys at his back. Within precisely two seconds he knew they would have logged the head count, potential weapons and any other possible route of escape—of which there wasn't any. He knew this, because he did the exact same thing himself.

Dante was sitting behind an ornate carved desk on the far side of the room, and Cesaré was sitting to the right of him. Keenan was lounging on one sofa on the left and Tia's

Protectors, Cash and Sean, sat on the one on the right. Connor, Phoebe's Protector, who didn't like him very much, was leaning against the bookcase that ran the length of the right hand wall.

Drew nudged the boys out from behind him and Keenan moved his legs so that they could sit next to him. He was so proud because they swallowed their fear at his size and sat down anyway. A servant brought a chair forward so he could sit next to them in the middle of the room.

Dante smiled at them all, despite the strain etched on his face. Drew was shocked at how old he was looking. He'd always been so healthy. He worried about that for the first time. If anything happened to him, the nation would crumble.

"Well done, Drew. On behalf of us all, thank you for destroying the Scythian threat and what you did for us in Murrtaine. We thought you were a gonner," he finished with a smile.

Drew just bobbed his head, not sure what to say. He'd got rid of the Scythians more for himself and these boys than for any threat to the Atlanteans, if he was honest. The two boys were watching their interaction closely. He had to remember that they still didn't really know what he was and whose side he was on. At the moment they were just trusting him.

"So how did you manage it?" Dante said. "We had you written off."

When Drew thought about it, he still couldn't quite believe it himself. "I met the Orb. She saved me," he said, with a shrug and a shake of his head.

Dante sat back in his chair, amazed.

"She told me exactly who I was by my DNA. She recognized me as Bonaci. The blast knocked out my tracking device and evidently my claim to Phoebe," he said, ruefully. "The rest you know."

Dante didn't seem to dwell on the whys and the wherefores. Instead, he smiled at the boys next to him. "We meet again. Eager to learn about Atlantean politics, I see." Dante coughed suddenly and uncontrollably. Everyone looked at him in concern, but no one said anything.

Cesaré passed him a glass of water and he took a large mouthful. "Forgive me. I am not ill. It's just the lack of my wife's breath."

"And that of her sisters," Cesaré added angrily.

The former king closed his eyes for a moment, as if he was gripped by a pain that was a struggle to quell. When he opened them slowly, something in them told Drew he was right. The anguish was clear to see in a second long tempest that immediately cleared. "I haven't seen or heard from my wife and children in too long," he explained.

It all made sense. Dante was carrying on as best he could while Malleven kept them all apart from their mates to starve them to death. When he looked closely, Cesaré looked a little tired too. Although it was clear that, for Dante, the torture went deeper than that. He was being kept from his family and the women he loved. He completely got that and his respect for the guy grew. Keenan seemed to be faring the best.

"Introduce me properly, Drew," Dante prompted.

It woke him out of his thoughts. "Sorry, sir. These two are part of my six who led the boys back at the camp. I couldn't have done it without them."

"And you have come to learn your fate," Dante said with admiration. "What are your names?"

"This is Justin and 361," Drew explained, indicating with his arm who was who.

"361?" Dante said, puzzled.

"We were each given a number instead of a name to dehumanize us," Drew said, suddenly seeing the irony from an organization who prided themselves on one hundred percent human genes.

Dante got it too and grinned.

"I had the nickname from before, though," the boy said, bravely speaking up for himself.

Dante looked pleased and surprised. "What does it mean?"

"When I was small, I couldn't count. We used to play this hide-and-seek game, and, when it was my turn, I'd put my hands over my eyes and shout 3.6.1. ready or not."

Everyone laughed. "I used to play that game. We called it 40, 40." Keenan said.

Dante agreed. "So did we. My brother should have been called 30.90.100."

They all laughed again. That is, everyone except Justin. He was watching them closely. Drew could see his clever mind working. Comparing them to what he thought he knew. Looking for anything that would give them away for the monsters he'd been brought up to believe.

"So what's your real name?" Dante was saying.

"Marcus. But you can call me 361."

They all laughed again. All warming to the boy's cheeky nature that not even the sadistic monks could beat out of him.

Dante looked at Drew, shaking his head. "And you want to keep this lot?" he said in his very Irish accent, chuckling.

"That's what I wanted to talk to you about," Drew said, clearing his throat and sitting up straighter. "I've been one of them. I've lived the life they've just came from. They were taken from the street and care homes and I don't want any of them to end up going back there."

Dante sat back in his chair. "What did you have in mind? I am no longer king, Drew. My power is limited."

"I know, and I've been thinking about that. I don't want to

give this idea to Malleven. When you face the ancestors, I want you to put it to them."

Dante sat forward, looking intrigued. "Go on," he said with a wave of his hand.

"It's not just an idea for the boys liberated from the camps, but for all those kids that run the streets that have nowhere to go but a life of crime."

"That's a huge undertaking, Drew," Dante said.

"You could work with the country's leaders. It would be a charitable organization and work like a cadet camp, but they'd live in."

"Isn't that what you just left behind," Keenan said from the other side of the sofa.

There was no love lost between them and Drew narrowed his eyes. "Believe me, it was no boy scout camp."

Keenan raised his eyebrows and put up his hands in front of him in surrender. "What did you have in mind? I'll help."

"It would encourage life skills, camaraderie. All the things that managed to survive back there despite the horrendous conditions. It would encourage academic ability, offer apprenticeships, train techs and engineers. Anything they could take with them into the world. But, most of all, it would educate a whole section of society that we are not monsters. That we're like them and we give a lot to this world."

Dante sat back and seemed moved and impressed. He nodded once and looked at the boys again. "And you would like such a camp?"

The boys looked at each other and nodded. "If 23—er, Drew was with us ... We don't want to go back to a care home," 361 said.

Justin remained noticeably silent.

"Very well. Thank you, Drew. I will think further on this." Then he reached for his water again to stifle a cough.

Drew stood and indicated with a bob of his head for the boys to follow, then the three of them walked towards the door. He hoped to god that Dante had enough time to get his kingdom back to implement his plans. Taking one final look over his shoulder and seeing Dante dab blood from his lips with a handkerchief, he wasn't so sure.

DREW MENTALLY MAPPED the system of tunnels while a servant showed them back to their dorm.

361 chatted animatedly. "Wow, he's a real king. And he's so cool."

When the servant eventually opened their door, Drew held Justin back as he was about to go in. "You go," he said to 361. "We'll be in in a minute.

Drew studied Justin, who looked everywhere but directly into his eyes. "What is it?"

Justin just shrugged and leant against the wall. "It's none of my business."

"What?" Drew said, not believing the sudden attitude he was getting. He thought, out of everyone, he could count on this boy. His boy. "Talk. We're friends, Justin. What's on your mind?"

"You're one of them?" Justin said, looking him directly in the eye for the first time.

Drew sagged and leaned against the wall next to him. "It's not like that. Not like how you think." How did he explain to this kid what happened between him and Phoebe?

"What's it like, then?" Justin said, turning to face him, still resting on the wall. He wasn't going to let this go. "I mean, I'd like to know who it is that I follow into battle," Justin said, reminding him of his promise to lead them anywhere, back at the camp.

He took a deep breath and nodded. It was time to come

clean. "You know what the real program was at the camp: to train us and send us out in the world as agents?"

"Yes, of course. Find and alert them of the Devil's spawn. We all know that."

"That wasn't the program, Justin. I went through it, start to finish, remember?"

Justin looked suddenly confused. "What was it, then?"

Drew slid down the wall to sit on his haunches and Justin followed. This wasn't going to be a quick conversation. "The Atlantean world is based on five royal families and hidden on Earth somewhere were five prophesized, powerful princesses that each of those families had to find in a race to become king. That guy," he said, pointing in the direction they'd just came from. "Was the first. That's why he's the rightful king."

Justin was listening intently, cross-legged, as if it were a great campfire story.

Most humans have no idea they're even here, but some—leaders and those like the Scythians—hate the Atlanteans, because they colonized this planet and appear to have all the wealth. No Devils or fire and brimstone, Justin. Just plain old greed. I guess you could liken it to the Europeans who came to the Americas."

Justin frowned and nodded. "Where do you fit in?"

"My generation was brought up just like you at the camp, then, when we got to around your age, we had our memories taken and new ones implanted for whatever life they decided to put us in. But I can tell you, I went through all the DNA testing possible to prove I was one hundred percent human like you." All the while he spoke, he was gauging Justin's expression. He was shocked; that was evident. "Then, just before we were sent out, a tracking device was embedded in my knee. Any time they needed me in, it would hurt and I would unknowingly go to them at a specific medical center."

Justin was clearly trying to get a handle on it. "So you *were* carrying out the program."

Drew bobbed his head. "Not exactly. We were being sent out to find one of their princesses, to lead them to the source of the Atlanteans' power. That's what it's all about, Justin. That's what it's always been about."

Justin went quiet for a moment. "So you found one?"

Drew smiled at the memory of Phoebe working at the club in Seattle a lifetime ago. "Yeah," he said with a smile. "We were drawn together inexplicably." Then he hardened. "But what we didn't know at the time was that at my medical check-ups, the monks had been injecting me with Murr blood. The tallest guys, back at the camp," he explained. "That was why she was initially drawn to me," he said, bitterly.

Justin looked sorry for him then. "So she didn't really love you?"

Drew smiled. "Yeah, she did. You see, the Sirens have a power of their own and when we, er, made out—." He didn't want to go into the specifics of their vampiric relationship, so he kept it simple. "Something passed between us and she made me into something else. Because of the blood … her power … Anyway, I'm not entirely sure, what, but my DNA changed permanently and now it matches hers completely."

Justin looked horrified. "Isn't there anything they can do?" He pushed off the wall, outraged and stood up.

Drew followed him and touched his arm. "It's a lot to take in, I know, but I wanted you to know the truth. It's not a bad thing at all. Except the monks tampering meant it clouded who her true mate was. The big Murr at the camp."

Justin nodded in understanding. "And he's got her?"

"Yeah," he said with a deep sigh. "And if I want her, I'm going to have to fight him for her at a place of his choosing. Which will probably be underwater."

"That's it, you're dead then," Justin said, walking away and pushing his fingers up through his hair.

"I can breathe underwater," Drew said, stopping Justin in his tracks.

Justin turned to look at him. "You can?"

"Yeah," he said, haplessly. "That's another long story, one Phoebe's still angry with me about. Anyway, I haven't the first clue how to fight underwater. No one except the Murrs do." Justin was right. He was fucked.

CHAPTER 22

Phoebe wasn't at all surprised that the minute Malleven got what he wanted, he dismissed her. Interaction with Malleven always left her feeling hollow and confused. He manipulated her with his psychic powers, so she never knew what was real. She guessed the hollowness was her body telling her that it wasn't. It was a stark difference to Dante, who always got to know his Sirens personally and thanked them for their gift.

A pain shifted in her chest and she knew the feeling was guilt. Even though he had bitterly disappointed her with Drew, he'd always managed to be honest and upfront with her. She was sorry for her part in this mess; it was something she had to put right.

She quickened her pace and hurried to the bedroom that Tia shared with her sisters. She hoped Ghazi was waiting for her. She rapped three hard knocks and was let in immediately. There he was, standing in the center of the room looking every bit the Middle Eastern prince she remembered from her childhood. "Ghazi," she whispered.

"Phoebe," he said, and his eyes softened.

She ran to him and he caught her, embracing her tightly. Her teeth tingled in her gums, her body remembering and reminding her of her shame. The blood she'd taken, almost killing him in a rage of blood lust, orchestrated by Malleven. "You came," she said. With his wonderfully familiar smell came the memories he'd freed for her. He'd been the one who had taken her to Malleven and been her only friend when he'd witnessed his mistreatment of her. He'd promised he'd find her and break Malleven's memory spell and he had. Now she remembered everything that had happened during her lost month.

"As I said I would," he said softly, next to her ear.

Their private moment was interrupted by a cough and she became aware of their onlookers. Jay was standing looking on with her sisters. She reluctantly let Ghazi go, but kept a hold of his hand.

Jay came forward in the red and black uniform of a Santalini guard. Malleven, no doubt, insisting they wore it to emphasize his own importance and to tell them apart at a glance from his Magi brothers, who wore the black tunics of the Middle East. She didn't know Jay well but recognized him instantly. "He is a Magi, Phoebe," Jay warned, taking a step closer as if he needed to rescue her.

"I'm fully aware what he is, but I trust him with my life, and he can help us." She looked up into Ghazi's face, next to her. "He's my Protector." She chose the words carefully, knowing all Atlanteans viewed the title as a huge honor. She was bestowing it on Ghazi, so everyone knew his position with her.

She took a bracelet with a turquoise stone off her wrist and put it around his. It was one that Vionne had given her when she was stricken with grief. It would serve as a symbol.

Jay seemed unconvinced.

Ghazi bowed his head. "I would protect Phoebe with my life."

Jay bobbed his head in a way that said that might be the case. "But can we trust him with *our* lives, Phoebe. There's a lot at stake."

"Malleven is looking for an excuse to kill him. He wants him dead even more than you."

It brought a wry smile to his lips. "And you would go against your brother?" Jay said to him, skeptically. "I thought you had to be joined, or something, to do your magic."

Ghazi nodded with a deep sigh. "You are correct. Our magic is based on strong alchemic bonds. But there are grumblings within the brotherhood. Our high priest is missing. Many think Malleven has killed him. They are fighting between themselves as they wish to try and sentence him, but cannot because he is a king."

Jay looked thoughtful at that. No doubt seeing how their plan could all work in their favor.

"The Magi has never sought to be an enemy of the Atlantean nation. We have worked alongside each other for hundreds of years," Ghazi said.

Phoebe saw the perfect timing of it, they all did. The Magi wanted to depose Malleven as much as they did. If they helped them, Jay could hand them Malleven on a plate to do with what they wanted. They could be on the same side.

Jay seemed to come to a quick decision. "I need to breathe with Phoebe. Then that leaves just Lily."

There it was. The plan laid bare. It took Ghazi no more than a second to realize it was Jay who would come from the shadows to steal Malleven's crown. "It's perfect. He won't see it coming." He was thinking deeply on the implications. "But Lily won't be easy. She is his wife and he sees her as such."

Jay listened carefully and assessed him closely as to how

far he could be trusted. "Yeah, he has her fooled. We need to engineer a situation that will expose him to her."

"One that involves Lance. We'll need to warn him," Tia said, turning to Jay.

Now it seemed that Ghazi was summing up Jay. Phoebe guessed many would think the same thing: Who was this person, a human, that would steal a kingdom from a prince? "So, would you steal it for yourself?" Ghazi asked, half amused. It was a sharp question, one that she would like the answer to as well.

However, Jay wasn't going to elaborate and fixed him with a hard look that held a definite challenge not to continue in that vein. "It's the only way to keep the sisters and the children safe."

It wasn't a lie, but it didn't really answer the question. Phoebe looked up at Ghazi. He was thinking about it. "You set it up with Lance and I'll make sure Malleven is there for Lily to see his reaction," Ghazi said, eventually.

It was agreed, although they weren't entirely sure how they would do it yet. Her sisters were excited. Ghazi kissed her forehead. "I must go before I'm missed."

She nodded. Ghazi would have to look busy and, at the same time, keep out of Malleven's way. He slipped silently out of the room, leaving her face to face with Jay.

After a moment of awkward silence when Jay's direct gaze locked intensely with hers, Tia seemed to take the cue. "Come on, let's go and check on the kids." Her hurry to leave was stark reminder of the romantic entanglement there. She'd have to tread carefully. *Hadn't she been left devastated from Drew doing the exact same thing?*

She swallowed. She was left alone in the room with Jay. He wasn't imposing like some of the Atlantean and Murr men she'd met. He just had this presence about him. An innate confidence that punched you immediately and, of course, he was insanely good-looking. She totally got what Tia saw in him. On the surface he was tall and model beautiful with blond, clean-cut hair falling into one eye. Always impeccably dressed, he was the wholesome guy moms always wanted a girl to date. Even the uniform seemed to accentuate the angelic blue of his glacier eyes. But she wasn't fooled. It was there in the sharp glint. His proven reputation. That, beneath it all, he was a tattooed, cold, calculating, efficient killer, as dangerous as any Santalini guard. Everything opposite to Drew. "Do you want to do this in the bathroom?" he said, taking a step closer and looking intently into her eyes.

His directness disarmed her for a moment. Then she understood what he meant. "I don't get hot in the same way as the others."

He looked curious at that and stepped closer still, so his clothes brushed hers. This close, his eyes were the color of a cornflower, ringed in a darker blue. "So you don't need water to keep cool?" he said, sounding fascinated, while his warm, mint-scented breath touched her cheek.

"No, I don't," she said, having to swallow at how close he now was. She didn't know much about him personally, other than he was Dante's best friend and a trusted brother to him. He was human and married to Ruby Santalini. A marriage rumored to keep him away from Tia and supply him with a legal supply of blood; a habit that would be his downfall. He was definitely a very complex man.

Jay took another small step. His body was now flush against hers and his breath gently warmed the side of her face and her ear. His lips inched closer to hers and her temperature started to elevate. Not to overheat, but enough to initiate her physical changes. He'd seduced her with his presence alone. "Will you survive the breath of four?" she asked to stall him, her voice suddenly hoarse. He was a strong man, but a weak human nonetheless. He had no idea who he was dealing with, and she had no wish to kill him. The memory of Ghazi, a swift warning for her.

He was close enough for her to see a muscle flex in his jaw as it clenched. A small glimpse of his anger. "I'm not as entirely human as first thought," he said.

His chest was rising and falling in anticipation and his eyes were, surprisingly, not on her lips at all. They were riveted to the carotid of her neck. The shocking revelation made sense and was more acceptable to her. It appealed to the dark primal part of her, now unfurling, of which she had no control. "You go through changes?" he said gruffly, as if he had similar impulses he had to get a hold on. His arms came around her and his body began moving against hers.

He felt oddly in tune with her; wrestling demons just like she did every day. "I am a Siren, but I am also a Nix," she whispered, pushing back against him. "I can change things at will." Drew had been a happy accident. She'd never chosen to practice controlling her impulses. This man was opening up a world of possibilities for her.

Jay brought her thoughts back to him by gently nipping down the side of her neck. She got it instantly. He wanted her to lose it. It was intriguing and she couldn't wait to find out why. The answer would be in his blood—as it was always in the blood.

Her eyes zeroed to thin orange slices, focused solely on him and her teeth slowly elongated into her mouth. She was losing control. "I'll hurt you. I won't be able to stop myself." Images of the blood and torn flesh she'd reaped on Ghazi invaded her mind, but it only seemed to spur Jay on.

"You changed Drew, change me."

He was sucking the skin at her neck and moving up to her lips where he kissed and ran his tongue over the points of her teeth. "I have dormant genes. I need you to wake them," he said between blistering kisses that were leaving her breathless. The unmistakable, metallic tang of his blood was already in her mouth, swamping her senses. On some level she knew he was making sense and this was a calculated move on his part, but the fog was drifting over her mind. He was no longer just Jay, the weak human, he was prey and she ripped his jacket open with one tug.

Buttons pinged off against the walls and she leapt on him, felling him to the ground and latching onto his neck, hard.

She lost all reason and sense of time. Except this was no Ghazi, accepting her and offering himself as a sacrifice. Jay was hard beneath her and he rolled her off him in a fighting maneuver that whetted her appetite for him even more. He didn't take his advantage to run and escape, he used his weight to pin her arms to either side of her head and paused, out of breath, to study her face. He was noting her changes while her eyes went from his to the red rivulets staining the collar of his white shirt.

Phoebe went to lunge at him again, but he growled and slammed her back into the floor. "Do what you did with Drew. I know you didn't just drink from him."

She frowned at the real him, strong and demanding on top of her. Her thinking was clouded with blood lust, but his meaning filtered through. She *had* done something different in the beginning. Before she understood the Sirens' breath, she'd let some flow into Drew through her bite. She nodded. "I'm calmer now."

He relaxed and lowered himself down to her again, but didn't release her hands. This time she resisted the urge to savage his neck. She calmly pierced the skin, formed a seal around the wound and blew gently. The effect on Jay was immediate. He dropped on top of her like a dead weight. She rolled him over and knew the exchange was complete. His blood for her breath, but, just to make sure, for the kingdom she covered his lips with hers and gently streamed her essence into him. She felt the aching remorse that followed after she'd fed like that, but it made her strong and she would need that to help him rid them of Malleven.

After a few moments, his eyes flickered open. He would live. She helped him into a chair and held a wet flannel to his wound. "You will need a dressing on that."

Jay smiled a heart-wrenching smile. Tia was very lucky. He loved her beyond life itself. However that was what troubled her. He was wholeheartedly into this scheme without any thought for himself. To him, this was a mission from which he saw nothing the other side. "Thank you. I'm stronger. I can feel it already." His speech was labored; as if he'd been running.

She hoped that was true. The revelations she'd seen through their new bond troubled her deeply. She really hoped that her strength would help him not just win the kingdom for his best friend, but to live for himself.

CHAPTER 23

$\mathcal{A}$ntonio got up, threw on some old clothes, and, without so much as putting a comb through his hair, roamed the corridors. All he could think was to get above ground to breathe. He needed to think clearly. Malleven smothered everything. He permeated so much in his life that he had no sense of self anymore and it had felt that way for an endless number of days. His heart constantly raced and yet he felt desolate, unable to see a way out. Despite the fact Malleven came to him every night, everything felt lost. Malleven's demands were increasingly brutal, often making him lose consciousness for a time.

All the Sirens, except Lily, were rebelling, which should have made him rejoice, but all it did was send Malleven to him angrier than ever. Then the sight of his bruises made him angrier still. He wanted more than just his body; he wanted his love. Till then, he'd never stopped hoping.

He rounded a corner just as Isla came out of the room she now shared with Tia and Lacy. Even that decision enraged Malleven, because it was an act in direct defiance of him.

However, out of all the Sirens, this, the strongest, quietest one, the one Malleven hated with a passion, was the one he considered a friend. They'd spent many a lonely day in Malleven's New York residence together, battered and bruised, when she'd first been released after years of being held by the Americans.

Her eyes widened in shock when she took in the state of him: his disheveled appearance, his healing lip and his bruised cheekbone. He felt exposed to the one person who truly knew what was going on. Part of him wanted to hurry past, but she put out a hand to gently stop him. "Antonio. It's so long since I saw you. Where are you going?"

Her voice was so kind he nearly started blubbering there and then. "Just above ground to take a walk."

"May I accompany you?" Her smile was small. She showed her emotions very little. It was one of the things he admired about her. She was always in complete control. He almost said no, as the whole point was to clear his head, but there was something about her inner strength that he was always drawn to. Maybe she alone was the one person who could soothe him. "Very well, but please don't try to involve me in any of your sisters' schemes. I'm too tired today."

Her smile grew, making her incredibly beautiful. "I promise."

Isla was the most ethereal of all the Sirens. They were, of course, all beautiful and unique. She had alabaster skin, pale-blonde hair and eyes like an Arctic spring. He challenged any man not to be swept along by her.

She linked her arm through his and they walked through the Great Hall, up the marble staircase and into the lift before they were seen. They remained silent all the way up, breathing as if they'd been running, as if escaping was a great coup. They hurried through the dusty oak-lined hallway, that always smelled so ancient, and out through the double doors onto the shingle driveway.

Antonio stopped, closed his eyes and took a huge lungful of air. There was still strength in the late autumn sunshine and he let its healing power warm his face. The air smelled of earth and a hint that the season was changing. He slowly opened his eyes.

Isla had watched him the whole time. "Oh, Antonio. What has he done to you?"

Antonio sagged and went to walk off, but she quickly put her arm through his, refusing to let him flounce off without her. "I'm your friend. I'm not going to look the other way when you clearly need me."

He wheeled around on her angrily. She was insufferable. "What do you Sirens care? You play him up constantly and deny him so he can do nothing but be angry all the time." The ridiculousness of the statement was obvious even to him, but he couldn't help saying it. It felt good to blame someone other than the real culprit.

"So he takes it out on you," Isla said softly, laying a hand on his arm and giving it a squeeze. "How long are you going to put up with it? Until he kills you?"

Antonio let out an exasperated groan and began to walk again. She didn't truly understand. No one did. He wanted to rail at her, tell her she was wrong and that Malleven did have a softness hidden in him deep down, but all that came out was a cracked voice that whispered. "I love him, Isla, and he does love me in his way." And he did. In some weird and broken kind of way, Malleven did love him.

Isla was thankfully quiet for a moment, but then she ruined it. "He seems to care a lot for Lily and he doesn't beat her?"

He stopped walking abruptly. *Was she trying to drive him*

over the edge? "That's different and you know it. He's acting a part around her."

"So he *can* control how he behaves," she said, quickening her pace to keep up with him. It irked that she knew him so well and he couldn't fool her. "And you are fully aware how badly he treats you."

He stopped, infuriated with her. She was waiting with her eyebrows up in a question. He rolled his eyes and continued walking. "Why are you so insufferable today?" he threw back at her.

She ran to catch up. "All I'm saying is, what if Lily just brings out a softer side in him. She's never really challenged him."

Antonio bobbed his head. There could be something in that. "She is his favorite. It's true."

"She gets to keep her mate and everything," Isla said, kicking a stone.

She had certain concessions, but he knew it was mainly to keep her on side. "He's grown tired of Lance, believe me. He uses him in his hocus-pocus crap to see through his eyes, but he can't be of any real use to him by spying on Dante because he promised Lily she could keep him with her and she's here. Rest assured, he doesn't have long on this planet." He knew he sounded spiteful, but what the hell. He felt like it.

Isla whistled. "That'll kick the hornets' nest. How's he going to work that one so she still likes him at the end of it?"

Antonio looked across at her walking next to him to see what she was up to. She appeared to be just thinking aloud. "Not for much longer. He won't care after the big ceremony. Once you're all publicly pledged to him, there won't be anything any of us can do to contain him." It was a sobering thought.

They'd reached the cover of some trees and Isla swung him around and held his hands. "Listen to me carefully.

Malleven is not going to get a bloody pledging ceremony. Believe me, Antonio, Malleven's days as king are numbered. The rumor is spreading amongst the Magi that he killed their high priest. None of us will pledge willingly in front of Delissi, so, if you love him, you must be ready to catch him when he falls." With that, she held the sides of his face with her hands. "Or you can come with us and leave him?" But the look in her eye said she doubted that very much.

She pulled him to her and kissed his cheek tenderly. Then whispered, "Bye, Antonio." She released him and walked slowly back in the direction of the entrance. Her simple words echoed behind her like a grim portent and he watched her the whole way, until she was out of sight.

She had spoken the truth. In everything. He was in an abusive relationship. He wasn't stupid. He'd always known it. Malleven's hard-won kingdom was unravelling around his ears and he refused to see it. All he was interested in was rearing the little brat: Darkly Begotten, so he could control him and the Sirens with coercion.

If the kingdom fell apart, all he would have was him. He'd never been as happy as when it was just the two of them. Malleven would spout off about all his plans and wild schemes, and he'd just listen, praise and love him. He had been his most-trusted confidant in the world, and he wanted that again. *Was it wrong of him to want that?*

He suddenly became aware of another presence behind him. The strange Murr female went to walk by. She looked at him in that strange deadpan way all the Murrs had. She registered his bruises and then looked ahead of her. How he hated that. He bowed low. "Good day to you," was all he said, and he watched her walk away.

.   .   .

VIONNE NEEDED to check on his people's progress and hated that he needed Malleven's permission to leave. As he approached the ridiculous thrones, Malleven was leaning over a poor servant cowering on the floor. It was made worse as it was all in front of little JJ, who sat watching. It was an unhealthy environment for a child. Malleven's anger seemed dangerously close to the surface all the time, made all the more disturbing by the gold that continually washed over his eyes. "What do you want?" he hissed through clenched teeth. "Can't you see I'm issuing justice?" He looked a far cry from the crafty, mysterious magician he'd first met.

Vionne's eyes flicked to JJ, to gauge if he was scared. He appeared calm enough. "I have come to request permission to join my people. My sources tell me many are falling behind."

Malleven forgot the servant, who took the opportunity to scramble away, stood and stalked towards him. He pointed. "You will leave your Siren here. I want them all together."

Vionne balked at leaving anyone he cared about alone with him, the male appeared so erratic.

"You will return for the pledging ceremony in one week's time, where you will pledge fealty to me in front of witnesses and issue your challenge to Drew to win your Siren. Then you will kill Dante's pretend prince in front of the whole Atlantean world."

It enraged Vionne instantly, and Murrs were famously slow to anger. He was a leader of a proud people in his own right. Not some lacky that Malleven could order about and throw him a bone from his table. For a split second Vionne wanted to crush him, but too much was at stake. This wasn't the rant of a madman, despite the constant churning of his eyes. Everything he did had motive and was frighteningly clever. Phoebe would be collateral for his good behavior and

Drew would be eliminated by another's hand, freeing yet another Siren from the affections of her chosen mate.

He swiftly changed his mind and merely bowed his head. *I look forward to that,* he projected, which he wasn't sure was strictly true anymore. Phoebe's happiness meant his happiness and he knew if he destroyed Drew, they would be doomed to a marriage built on hatred. His eyes shot to Malleven's, swirling and feral. *Wouldn't that just suit him too.*

Nothing was said about Ashaya and he didn't bring her up, instead he asked for Malleven's leave and went to go.

"Hurry, Lord Advocate. I hear there is news of a rockslide just inside the trench of Oran. There have been casualties, I believe."

Vionne halted and stared at him blankly. His revelation was beyond belief. *And you didn't think to lead with that?* he said, eventually, flabbergasted. Malleven slowly smiled, reveling in the power he had over them all. Vionne didn't wait to hear any more. He strode purposefully towards the fountain, issuing a mental blast to all those Murrs in the area that would hear. Then he dove down into the depths of the tunnel, worry and despair gnawing at him as he went.

He reached the large waiting marine craft, captained by Axyl, with a sense of relief. Even without the news, everything had changed. The atmosphere at the castle was now oppressive and dark, a far cry from the cheery days of Dante's reign. Now all that was left was a desperation to salvage something out of this mess for his people—a family completely reliant on him. They had been fools to give Malleven the smallest chance to rule.

Ashaya joined him, demure as ever. She accepted the circumstances of their hasty departure without comment and observed quietly as they sped off at top speed. Her quiet support was a greater comfort than he would care to admit.

His eyes remained on the horizon, straining for a first glimpse of the tail end of his people.

The back of the line was still passing through the Strait of Gibraltar. Axyl slowed the craft and they surveyed the tired and rag-bag bunch who still had so far to go. He communicated to three more ships following behind to pick up the thirty or so stragglers at the very back. Then, at Vionne's order, they sped to the incident site to check on survivors and see what could be done for the injured. Another group of ships would be meeting them from the other direction.

The trench of Oran was a deep gulley that followed the shoreline of North Africa about a hundred miles north of the human city. The sight that greeted them was devastation on an epic scale. Thousands of people were gathered as far as the eye could see. Some were weeping, others comforting. Belongings lay in discarded piles and a great mountain of rock was being scaled by Murrs trying to pass down debris without causing any more damage to the already unstable mountainside.

Vionne, Axyl and eight of his closest officers prepared to aid in the search. He stopped and held Ashaya's shoulder as he went. *Go!* she said immediately. *Don't worry for me. I will clear space for the injured for when you get back.*

He merely nodded. A hard lump was already in his throat in anguish for his people, but it rose a little higher at her complete and undivided support. He didn't think he could appreciate a person any more than he did for her right then.

He and his men left the ship through the hatch in the floor and were immediately greeted by the travel-weary people. They wailed in gratitude at seeing them. Many pointed to the mountain of stones. *How many are missing?* Vionne said to an able male who seemed to have taken charge. He had organized the men into lines to pass the large stones between them and get to the trapped. Vionne and his men quickly formed another.

It was tempting to use mind control to shift the rocks, but they couldn't risk another rockfall. More joined the line, women and even children. They worked on.

Then, suddenly, a mental picture flashed into Vionne's mind. At first it was a white light that came with feelings of urgency and excitement. It cleared to an image of a white hand. Then flashed another. And another. Soon mental pictures were igniting through the people like photographer bulbs.

We've found them, one of his lieutenants blasted.

Vionne scrambled to the top of the pile and they were soon passing rocks between eager hands in all directions. The hand led to an arm, then the muddied face, tattered chest, body and legs of a male. He was moving, but held tightly to another. A woman and she was soon freed too.

It was hard to see the extent of their injuries, but they were alive and soon hoisted out and lifted above their heads. A great cheer of clicks went through the horde of people who had gathered around them; each anxious to follow Vionne's orders and help carry them to his ship.

Vionne turned his attention back to the rocks, conscious that the two pulled out were fairly close to the surface. Ones further down might not be so lucky. A heaviness weighed down on his chest. The more they dug, the less likely it was to find anyone else alive. They continued on tirelessly into the night until they came upon another two females. However, the flashes of excitement were soon doused by projections of gray and sorrow, as the onlookers understood that neither were moving. Their limp bodies were carried away to a great hum on a single note between them, that all would know of the great loss of life. Still there was no sign of the others. Three were unaccounted for, by all accounts.

Vionne dragged a weary arm across his brow. He was now shaking with the effort. It was no use, he had to take a break. He trudged down and surveyed the lines on the heap, now looking more like a collapsed hill than the mountain they'd started with. He was about to turn and go back the way he came, when he spotted a line of boys working as hard and as desperately as the adults. A female was with them, who appeared to be trying to pull them away. *Naomi.* He went a little closer to investigate and recognized the one at the front as the cheeky one, Loki, who'd approached him on his Bubble bike, right at the beginning of his journey. How full of hope and excitement he'd been then. Now he understood Naomi's concern. His bloodied hands were worn out from feverishly pulling at the stones.

Vionne looked into Naomi's sad eyes and she projected a bleak picture of death and devastation. Loki was digging for loved ones and his once-carefree friends were helping him. *You have done enough now, Naomi. You must come with us,* Vionne projected. He leaned down and put out his large hand to still Loki for a moment. He picked up the boy's hands to look at them. *You're injured,* he said. *Go to my ship and get them tended.*

The boy glared up at him, pulled back his hand, bent and scooped another boulder, which he threw and almost hit his friend. Vionne grabbed him and snatched him up to scold him. The boy squirmed and kicked. *No ... no ... let me go.* He felt flashes of pain straight to his head, along with pictures of a male and a female cradling a baby. Then he understood everything. The three still missing were the boy's parents and his small sister and he was desperately trying to find them.

One of his lieutenants whistled.

Vionne looked up hopefully and his lieutenant shook his head. The remaining ones had been found too late. The familiar hum of grief spread through the crowd. Rending the ache in his heart to shattered pieces. He issued a private order for them to be carefully buried, quickly, according to custom. There was no need to delay their passage into the ether any longer. Then he turned to the group of scruffy boys around him and said, *Come. You have worked hard and done what you can. You will pass the rest of the journey with me.*

The boy in his arms went limp. His expressionless eyes followed the group of people clustered around two bodies being carried between them. A collective wail of grief travelled like a wave through the people as they received the news. The boy already understood, without words, that he was now an orphan.

Vionne carried him all the way back to his craft while he silently cried in his arms. He saw Naomi and all the boys up into the craft where Ashaya immediately greeted them and made them comfortable. They were passed food and all except the boy in his arms, took it gratefully. He carried the boy to a seat where Ashaya tucked him in with a blanket and he stood back and observed the way she took care of him. She was a real gentlewoman, not afraid to get her hands dirty, managing only ever to go up in his estimations. Naomi's exhausted gaze met his and she smiled knowingly.

When the injured were settled and stabilized and Vionne was satisfied that the great body of his people were on their way again, he set a course east. The endless line still stretched for miles ahead of them, making the long and arduous journey and carrying with them what little belongings they could. He felt a mixture of anger, sadness and pride as he looked sullenly out at them through the membrane walls and his heart broke for the little boy in his care. Then his heart hardened at the indifference of Malleven. *Top speed to Filfla*, he finally said.

They are a strong and resilient people, Ashaya projected a while later, from next to him. He turned his head to look at her. He hadn't even felt her sit down. *We have done it many times through history and each time we become stronger than before.* She smiled with the words and he found himself searching the endless pools of her eyes. It hit him for the first time, that he wished she could have been his destined mate. It astounded him because he'd always believed that a compatible mate's pull could be surpassed by no one. Instead, he was thinking how he would like to kiss along the delicate markings of her jawline that disappeared down her neck. *You are right. Thank you for saving me from my self-pity. You were amazing today.*

Her head bowed. He should have realized she was modest as well. A blanket of warmth surrounded him, which he was sure she sent, unseen by onlookers, for his comfort. It was so purely Murr and something even the sirens were too human to do. It made him appreciate her even more, if that were possible.

They reached Filfla in a matter of hours and Vionne showed the refugees to the submerged catacombs where he handed them over to a health team. The boy was still in his arms and clung to him like a small bear. *You won't be here long,* he explained to them all. Then, to the boy, he said, *You would rather stay with me?*

The boy nodded into his shoulder. He was still in shock and despite a friendly female's arms reaching out to take him from him, Vionne smiled and explained he would take him with him.

He collected Ashaya with two of his lieutenants and sent the ship straight back to collect others. Together they swam the tunnel, with the boy still clinging around his neck, up through the fountain and into the center of Filfla's Great Hall.

He helped Ashaya up and showed the boy how to empty his lungs, which he'd never experienced before. Then they all sat on the fountain wall while their legs returned to shape. The place was eerily quiet. Dante's court was always so busy with people and laughter. Today there were just a few Santalini guards stationed at the fountain and at the lifts. *Where is everyone?* he mentally blasted, so any of the guards could hear.

The closest guard spoke into the mouthpiece of a headset he was wearing and held out his arm in the direction of the tunnels. "Your rooms have been made ready, Lord Advocate."

Vionne was really beginning to worry. *Where's the king?* he said, before even he realized that he still thought of him as that.

"I'm afraid His Highness is gravely ill," the guard said. "There is a meeting in the study as soon as you settle in."

He picked up the boy and helped Ashaya to her feet. She stood, a little wobbly but as graceful as ever. He signaled for them all to go to their rooms to wait for their leg bones to solidify so they could walk comfortably to the meeting.

What a contrast it was to the castle. The king was ill and the people worried for him, all eager to help. He looked down at Ashaya and he could tell she was feeling it too.

On their way to their rooms, they came to a door with two Santalini guards standing outside. *Dante's room,* he said to himself and came to a stop. It struck him how many guards had remained loyal even after Dante was deposed. There was no mandate for them to guard the old king, only the new one.

He looked down at Ashaya. *I'm going to check on him before I meet with the others.* He intended for her to go and take advantage of the rest. However, she warmed his heart again.

If it pleases you, I will stay. I don't really know him, but I feel an affinity to him and his people.

Ashaya projected what they all felt—made all the more pronounced as it came from her, a person who had been brought up far away. They felt a loyalty to this king. Again, he was struck by how well she carried herself.

Very well, he projected. *We won't stay long,* he said, shifting the boy in his arms. Loki was now sitting up, eyes open in bewilderment.

The guards immediately stood aside and they walked in cautiously, not knowing what they would find. What met him shocked him deeply. He couldn't believe it was the same man he'd left no more than a few days ago.

Dante was lying propped up on pillows. The Murr material that made up the drapes and linen on his bed had gone from cream to black. The living organism was dying, reflecting his illness. The room that was once monochrome and modern now seemed dark and ancient, to match the mood of its inhabitants. It would appeal to Dante's warped sense of humor, he knew, to think of himself as a resting vampire when he slept. Now he looked more like that than he could have imagined. His skin was pale and translucent, making his eyes dark and hollow, as if the life was slowly being sucked from him.

Real fear constricted Vionne's throat for a moment as he was transported back to his own father's death not that long ago, but a lifetime had passed since then. His father had led a long and happy life and Dante had barely begun in comparison.

He moved close to the bedside and felt Ashaya come with him in the shelter of his body, as if she too was afraid he'd rise up like a ghoul.

"Vionne?" Dante said, barely audible as his eyes opened to thin slits.

Vionne picked up his hand so he could project speech if that was easier. *What has brought you this low in such a short period of time? I will send for my most-skilled physicians.* He knew Atlanteans would weaken without their mates to replenish their bonds, but this was ridiculously fast.

Dante smiled wanly and tried to open eyes that were now sunken in his head.

It cannot be simply not breathing with your Sirens. You have declined too quickly. I am sure of it, Vionne projected vehemently. *There is more at play here.*

Dante let out a long, exhausted breath. "I have no idea. Cesaré seems unaffected as yet. But perhaps it is because I am joined to the four. No one seems to know. Nothing has been written. The point is ..." He coughed and tried to lean up on his elbows, but gave up and flopped back down. *How are Tia and the children?* he said, swapping to projected speech.

Vionne didn't want to pass on the news he knew he had to impart. He wasn't sure Dante was strong enough to take it. *They are well enough for now. Naomi is here safely, but I need to tell you ...*

Dante turned his head towards him and he was forced to continue. *Malleven becomes more and more unstable every day. His behavior is erratic and he deals with people in a violent and savage way. There are rumors he killed his own high priest. JJ is with him constantly and witnesses it all. He holds the children away from their mothers to control them and he has his damn public pledging coming up where they all have to behave. I am to fight Drew to slay him, legally, so he can eliminate another chosen mate and I have just come from a rockslide, that took ...* he looked down at the boy in his arms and quickly amended, *many casualties.* There. It was a gruesome catalog of events now he'd projected them out loud.

Dante's eyes dropped to the boy in his arms and understood what he omitted to say. He didn't reply, just closed his eyes as if the death knell had sounded for them all. When he finally opened them, his eyes looked clear. *You will do some-*

thing for me, Vionne. I know Malleven is behind my illness in some way, using my bond with the sisters against me. You must not fight Drew, but make an ally out of him. Him and all the Sirens' mates. Together you will be strong. Jay is hatching something as we speak to take the kingdom. I know it.

Vionne knew Jay's appearance at the castle had been suspicious. It hadn't made sense, the way he hadn't even contacted his best friend to see how he fared. Now he knew the reason and was shocked and appalled. He would never understand the relationship between the two of them. Jay's betrayal of Dante in his time of need was unforgivable. He should be here with his dying brother, not trying to fill his shoes.

Dante gripped his hand to get him to listen. *Trust him ... please, Vionne. Jay is strong and will do what is needed. He will protect the sisters and the children. Do that for me, Vionne. Give me your word you will support him in any way you can.*

Vionne resented that it reminded him of the oath he'd been forced to give his father. One that he hated even now. If he fought Drew and killed him, he could marry his Siren as promised—but he would live in misery. If he didn't fight, as the king now requested, he would betray his oath to his father and be damned. Phoebe would be happy and would marry Drew, and he would keep his oath to his king. It was an impossible situation.

Strangely, it was a squeeze on his arm by the woman who was becoming more important to him by the day that brought him back to his senses. *It is all very simple, really,* she said. *Just do what you think is right and not what others would pressure you to do.*

He looked into her eyes for a full minute when she'd finished speaking. Until embarrassment at being so obviously fascinated forced him to turn back to the king who'd witnessed the whole thing. *I vow to do what I can,* he said, eventually.

It seemed enough, and Dante relaxed back into his pillows. Vionne took Ashaya's hand and left him. He would help Jay, but, as soon as it was safe to do so, he would take his place. Nothing else would satisfy the vow he'd made to his father. Then he would marry all the Sirens and she could keep her mate, thus satisfying all the obligations bearing down on him. He had a plan.

However, glancing sideways at the thoughtful look of Ashaya, he couldn't help feeling that she saw it all.

Malleven discarded the empty glass of gold he'd just consumed with a loud clink and threw the crumpled piece of paper in Alfonzo's face. He hated that he'd been summoned to meet the human government heads before the pledging ceremony. "Who the fuck do they think they are?" he said to Alfonzo. He would have to speak to Delissi about this in future. An Atlantean king did not dance to anyone else's tune.

Alfonzo had the good sense not to answer in his current mood and they made the journey to the army base in Suffolk in silence. Little JJ was sitting quietly next to him. He'd managed to whisk him out early before anyone noticed him missing. He'd left it to Sebastian to smooth it over with his mother. He wanted to introduce him to the human world as his son and heir for stability. Plus, it was good for him to see the engines of government.

Delissi joined them and spoke hurriedly as they walked, "The US president and many of the European leaders have arrived. They haven't had time to notify everyone."

Malleven was still seething at being dragged there. "They

wanted the damn meeting, so they can bloody well do it when it suits me." It was bad enough he had to leave the safety of the castle. His Magi guard gathered tightly around him, at his orders, while he alone carried JJ into the building and straight into the boardroom to the waiting dignitaries.

Delissi looked troubled, no doubt noticing the lack of Santalini guards. This was something he wanted to do without alerting JJ's father. He was king and the quicker he got used to that, the better.

They swept into the windowless beige room that obviously doubled as a classroom, decorated with a whiteboard and a single potted palm in the corner. A chair was immediately pulled out for him around a huge oval table and another squeezed in for JJ on his left. Delissi shook Alfonzo's hand and sat next to him on his right.

ALFONZO EYED Delissi knowingly and sighed in relief that the two of them had finally gotten Malleven there. He raised his eyebrows to convey the weight of his task. This king would not be handled like Dante, or even advised. Delissi had no idea just how much Malleven was unravelling. He only prayed they got this meeting over with before he upset anyone.

Delissi pretended to pat his back in welcome to aid contact and spoke directly to his mind. *Why is the Magi here and Jay's son paraded like a fucking mini-me?* he projected. *We look like a circus.* Delissi's anger was a palpable cloak.

Alfonzo tried to keep his face blank while the US Secretary of State brought the meeting to order and welcomed the new king. *You don't know the half of it,* Alfonzo replied. *The court is falling apart in Ireland. The Sirens refuse to pledge and the Magi are about to revolt, despite what you see here today. Mates are withheld the Sirens' breath, putting lives in jeopardy. Santalinis desert Malleven for Dante every day and I have absolutely no idea how this meeting will go.*

Delissi sat back in his chair as if recovering from a blow. The secretary of state continued to convey congratulations from many of the countries who had sent their apologies, while interpreters interpreted, signers signed and a female clerk typed it all up. Alfonzo was only partly listening, until he came to the serious questions the world wanted to know. The room suddenly hushed.

"Do you declare that you have all five Sirens?"

Then, after a long pause for effect, Malleven said, "I do."

Everyone immediately looked at each other and the mood turned to one of unrest. No one was expecting Malleven to be so honest after so many years of honied words and skirting around the issue.

"I am here today purely for you to meet my son," Malleven said, indicating little JJ next to him. Then, astonishingly, he went to stand. "You will attend my public pledging ceremony and convey to your many governments that the greatest monarch of all times now sits on the Atlantean throne, ready to intercede for you when our ancestors return, any day now," Malleven finished with a satisfied grin.

The threat in those words was very real. Alfonzo died a thousand deaths at Malleven's total lack of diplomacy in a very delicate situation. He'd effectively told them to keep him sweet, or else. He half-rose, next to him, in a futile attempt to get Malleven to continue the meeting and allay some of the fears on the horrified faces, but he continued to pull JJ into his arms.

"Can you offer any explanation as to why the world is suffering so many natural disasters at the moment? They have gotten steadily worse over the last three years," the US president said over the din, looking at Delissi, exasperated.

Everyone seemed to quieten, interested in the answer.

"We have forest fires ripping through California, a tsunami in the South Seas killing thousands and an unprecedented number of hurricanes battering the Caribbean. And that's just in the last week. Doesn't that mean that the Orb is destabilized?"

Malleven didn't appear to hear or even acknowledge the president was speaking to him.

"Doesn't that mean things aren't being run as they should?" the president persisted, more loudly.

Malleven halted immediately. The president's Secret Service team took a step closer. The look Malleven gave him was black with warning, like an oppressive sky on a stormy night. Everyone felt it. "Not all things can be blamed on the Orb," Malleven said in a low, simmering voice. "Humans have been systematically destroying this planet for centuries."

"Atlanteans have always been the captains of industry," the president threw back in outrage.

Alfonzo had to hand it to him; the president had balls of steel when the gloves came off. Although he didn't fancy his chances if Malleven truly revealed himself, and he edged towards him to begin to herd him out.

Malleven narrowed his eyes at the president and then did a sweep of them all. "Know this. I am the greatest king for ten thousand years. And when my ancestors return it will be me they first meet. You would be wise to kneel before me because you face annihilation. You will exist only through me and my discretion. Think on that," he finished with a smirk.

The room erupted.

Alfonzo cringed with every syllable as he held out his arm to usher Malleven out of the door. "Smooth over this shitstorm," he hissed over his shoulder at Delissi, who was white with shock and embarrassment. Years of hard work and diplomacy had been wiped out in seconds.

"Get him out of here, fast," Delissi mouthed back. "You may address any questions directly to me," Delissi said, to calm things down. *Get a message to Dante to be ready,* he said as a parting comment in his head.

Dante is dying, Alfonzo projected back, desperately hoping Delissi could hear. There were several feet between them now and they could no longer touch.

They were soon bundled out into the corridor and into SUVs that took them at speed to their waiting plane.

Alfonzo was furious and bewildered. If it had been Dante, he would have asked immediately what the hell he'd been playing at, but, as they all took their seats in the plane he saw the volatile churning of Mallevens's eyes.

Little JJ's hand appeared on his arm and he projected straight to his head, *Don't say anything, Uncle Alfonzo. He won't do anything to hurt anyone all the while he's busy making his own noose.*

Alfonzo stared down at the boy, amazed. He was disturbingly right. All he could do was see to it that things were made ready for Malleven's fall and hope to god Dante lived to see it.

MALLEVEN SAT and fumed on his golden throne as he went through recent events in his head. He had replenished his bonds with Lily and Phoebe, but had met with a litany of excuses from the other three. It was no great victory to win what he already had; he needed all of them for the necessary link, or, more importantly, absolute control. He could never forget that Dante had the power of three of them by First Breath and he had only one. Lily had foolishly given hers to Cesaré. He must secure his throne.

He became aware of the boy swinging his legs next to him, watching him closely. He wasn't fooled by the childlike mannerisms. "And you do nothing for me," he said, as if the boy had followed his whole thought process.

The boy raised his eyebrows as if he had no idea where the sudden accusation came from.

"You are the Darkly Begotten one with the bracelets at your wrists to attest to it. I even made you my son. And all you do is look on. What do you wait for?" Malleven glared at him and dragged his eyes away in contempt.

"What would you have me do?" the boy said, eventually. "I told you I have nothing to do with politics here."

Malleven turned in his chair and scrutinized him. "Yes you did." His mind was churning on how he could find a loophole in that.

"Wouldn't any coercion on my part make the pledge void in the eyes of the law?"

Malleven nodded. He'd grown used to the child thinking way beyond his years. He began to smile as an idea formed in his mind. "Perhaps you could spend more time with the other children. I know you would like that. Persuade them to plead my case with their mothers … for their own good," he tacked on with a smile. He knew the exact moment his meaning turned on in the boy's brain.

"Then it wouldn't be my idea at all, but their own." JJ narrowed his eyes, knowing the proposed logic was skewed. Then he truly surprised him by asking, "How is my Dubonnetti father? I've had no news of him and neither has my mother."

The clever boy was bartering for information. He admired him greatly for that. The truth was, he'd hoped Dante would be dead by now but, still, he clung on. "Gravely ill, I fear."

"You fear," the boy repeated. "Why do you fear? Wouldn't his death be advantageous for you?"

Malleven watched his face take on a faraway look that he seemed to get a lot. He was never sure whether he was getting some sort of vision or lost in memories. "There will be two princes who fight for this kingdom. Both Dubonnetti. It won't be you and it won't be Dante. That is the true prophecy. You waste your time on such things."

Shock, terror, then rage took their place surging through him. The last made him almost strike the boy for daring to say such a thing. But he calmed himself down by remembering he had circumvented many prophecies to reach his goals. He always got what he wanted in the end. Instead, he stood and leaned over him. "And how would you know such things? You are a small boy."

There was no fear in him. He didn't even cower. He merely began to swing his legs again, just missing his shins. Then he jumped down and scooted around him. "I am Darkly Begotten. I know all things. Did you forget that, Father?" he said, sounding more childlike than ever.

Malleven had never dealt with children and certainly none as clever as this. His eyes washed over completely in gold and his body began to shake violently with the pain. It took him a couple of minutes to gain control. He was getting the spells more and more these days. He knew what it was. The gold took its toll on the body it inhabited. It was the price he paid for its properties.

When he opened his eyes, the strange boy was skipping off in the direction of the nursery. He hated that he needed him alive. "Who are the two princes?" he called after him.

JJ stopped and turned just before he reached the corridor in the rock. "Don't worry. They're too young yet." Then he skipped off out of sight.

Malleven fell back into his throne. The pain left him

exhausted. Working to control Lance and maintain Dante's illness was sapping his energy, too. The boy was unnerving. He was no nearer to controlling him than he was the Sirens. They were treating him like a fool.

He clicked his fingers to signal a guard. "Bring me Alfonzo and Sebastian Bonaci." It was time for the Sirens' uncle and father to earn their keep.

Ashaya thought what a splendidly happy place Filfla was, even though Dante was ill. It was full of lively debate and chatter by a number that grew every day. Dante insisted on being wheeled to the Great Hall to be among them on his better days. "To keep me alive," he often said. However, he soon tired and had to retire to his chambers. But still he came.

The boy they'd rescued she discovered was called Loki and was recovering and beginning to take an interest in his new surroundings. The young boys that had arrived with Drew were blossoming too. They swam, their skin tanned and they grew with abundant good food and Drew's tutelage. It was a joy to see. He trained them in the gym and created a structure of lessons to deprogram them from the indoctrination they'd received before. They were happy, it was plain to see to her and to Loki, who had been as sheltered from humans as she had been.

That morning, walking with Loki through the tunnels, they heard the joyful shouts of excited boys and squeaks of rubber shoes on a shiny floor. *Shall we peek?* she said conspiratorially to Loki, holding her hand. His eyes widened and an aura of excitement came to her. They went to the large doors and pushed one open to peer inside. It was a huge gymnasium with white walls and large wooden floor. Loki peeked in front of her. The boys were running this way and that.

Bouncing a ball, then shooting it through a hoop. There was one at each end. They were breathless and sweaty and their cheeks a charming red. They seemed happy. Everything about it was lively and joyful.

Drew blew a whistle and play stopped. Then they seemed to get in position to begin again. After a moment, Drew spotted them and she almost scurried away, but he waved her in with his hand. She looked down at Loki, who looked up at her expectantly. *What do you think?* she asked. He simply nodded and looked at the boys, who had stopped and were looking over with interest.

Ashaya walked slowly inside with Loki hugged into her body as if he'd be snatched away from her at any second. Drew jogged over. "Hey, welcome! Have you come to join in?"

The boys were looking at Loki, taking in his differences. He was blonde and his skin pale with mild stripes that never quite went. *He doesn't have the clothes,* Ashaya said, giving him the excuse to get out of it if he wanted. Loki looked up at her with huge round eyes. *Can I join in?* he asked, copying Drew's human phrasing, his excitement clear to see.

"It's OK. Stay as you are for today. If you like it, we'll get you the kit." Then he moved off, blowing his whistle and leaving it up to Loki. He was a born teacher, giving Loki the space to make up his mind. Loki wandered into the throng with a last turn of his head. His aura was pleasure as he started to mimic their jog. He was awkward at first. He was only around five Earth years, but his size and mental growth compared to around twelve or thirteen. He was unused to the gait out of water. However, it didn't take him long until he was covering twice as much ground as the other boys. They began shouting his name to catch the ball. Then, when he jumped almost as high as the basket and put the ball in the hole, like he'd seen the others do, everyone cheered and patted him on his back as if he'd always been one of them.

Ashaya became overcome with emotion, never having seen anything so humbling and so beautiful. She stepped back and receded into the background before anyone noticed.

Drew put up a hand to her, knowingly. "Don't worry, I'll bring him back to you when we're done. He's a natural."

Ashaya, haltingly, returned the gesture. Loki would be OK. She left the room and the game carried on behind her. She found herself wandering the tunnels wondering how letting Loki join in with the human children would be viewed from above, but he'd been so lonely and happy to be included that it seemed ridiculous to ever see it as wrong.

She couldn't help thinking it was much more like the center of the Atlantean world in Filfla than the castle. Even though Malleven held the title, people were arriving there in droves. It was clear that the only ones left were those forced to be there by design or deception.

Ashaya found an alcove and took advantage of the privacy to send a bulletin to her Watchers above. It took the form of mental pictures and feelings, to convey her findings and conclusions. The answer in their reply was clear: a clock ticking. They'd decided enough had come to pass and time was running out. She hoped her actions hadn't been the final straw.

The countdown had begun.

Ashaya turned and headed back to the Great Hall. It was still early and unusually quiet. She was surprised to come across the dark beauty she knew to be Ruby Santalini, staring out to sea. Spears of light were already appearing in front of the large window from the surface, spotlighting the many fish in a mesmerizing early morning dance. Although she seemed a thousand miles away.

Ruby's lustrous black hair was drawn back into a bun at her nape. Tendrils escaped it, hanging charmingly around her stunning face. It was still fascinating to see olive skin unblemished by stripes. She was also the most curvaceous woman Ashaya had ever seen. Today she was wearing a Human-style dress in scarlet that skimmed her knees. Her waist was usually cinched with a belt or a scarf and there was always a heel to her shoe to elongate her legs. Today they were shiny and black. *Hello,* Ashaya projected, to get her attention. *I don't believe we've been formally introduced. I am Ashaya.*

Ruby didn't turn around, just said, "Ruby," to the window. "You're the Murr from that far-off place."

Yes, Ashaya said, wistfully, thinking how true that was. Economy of words was safest here. *I've ordered some Human coffee. I'm getting quite addicted to the stuff. Would you care to join me?* She indicated to a couple of armchairs next to a low table nearby.

Ruby dragged her eyes to where she was pointing and she went and sat down, robotically, without speaking. Her eyes strayed back to the window, giving Ashaya the impression she saw nothing of its beauty.

The coffee came and the male servant poured the steaming liquid into two cups. Ashaya bowed her head and sent him a warm feeling of thanks. He disappeared to his duties and she was left studying Ruby. She took a few sips, and, with a loud *mmm,* put her cup down. *What brings you here to Filfla? Isn't your husband at the king's court?* Of course she was fully aware of Ruby's checkered past, but she'd always been an object of her fascination.

Ruby finally picked up her coffee and dropped in a lump of brown sugar. She stirred it several times before she said, "He's with his bitch."

Ashaya's eyes widened at the crude term for the Siren, Tia

Storm. However, the circumstances of the fascinating triangle between her, Jay and Dante had been constant viewing for the Twenty. Except, watching from above and seeing how it affected those around them at close hand seemed a very different story entirely. They were viewing dispassionately, to see how it affected the kingdom, but, down here, its effects on the lives around them were tragic and far-reaching. She found herself feeling sorry for Ruby, despite her conniving ways. *And you love him*, she said, in an effort to coax a conversation out of her.

Ruby stirred her cup and let out a small blast of derisive breath. "You know I dated a film star before that. Dante's brother, Marco," she said with a wry smile. "I became obsessed." She frowned as if she was becoming lost in her memories. "I never knew it was possible to love someone more than that."

And Dante?

Ruby's eyes shot to hers for the first time and she thought she'd blown it. Dante was her dirty little secret. "Oh, you know about that."

Gossip travels, she projected, simply relieved that she hadn't been called out on how she knew.

Ruby let out a breath and nodded.

Ashaya was also fully aware of Christian Dubonnetti's meddling with her in the background, all for politics and the furtherment of the Dubbonetti royal family. However, she found, now she was with her face to face, she was more interested in how her true feelings ran.

"I was angry at Jay. It was a mistake," Ruby said, looking down at her nails. "They can't keep their bloody hands off each other,' she added, flashing her eyes at Ashaya. "It was one silly day that I've regretted ever since."

Ashaya had formed opinions of these people before she ever came down among them. Now she found herself feeling sorry for this woman. She'd had very little love growing up a Santalini, in a household of soldiers. She was a princess in one of the most prominent families in the world, in an age where Sirens were on Earth. All the eligible princes wanted a Siren. That didn't leave much room for an ordinary princess, as ludicrous as that sounded. It was a recipe for unhappiness and made her vulnerable to manipulation. "So you want your husband back?" Ashaya said, projecting kindness.

Ruby looked at her oddly, as if she was only just receiving the warmth Ashaya had sent her. Then she frowned. "Yes. I'm hoping when he's done what he needs to do, he will come back to me."

Ashaya felt her anxiety acutely. Her deepest fear was that Tia would choose him. Ruby recognized he was only hers by default. It was a heart-breaking fact for a wife to come to terms with.

Ruby put her cup down suddenly. "If you'll excuse me," she said, and got up and walked away quickly in the direction of the tunnels.

Ashaya watched her walk away, a little bewildered, then sat back in her chair to drink her coffee. She alone was fully aware of what Jay was trying to do. It was troubling on many levels. Not only did she think Ruby had real grounds to be worried, but it was her job to find an argument to support his challenge as being legal. Her people would descend soon, and, she had to admit, now she was among them, she had real sympathy for their plight.

The water boiled beneath the surface of the fountain next to her and the blonde head of Naomi breached the surface. She was tall and beautiful, with long hair to her waist and large, kind eyes that rested on her immediately. She was the mother of all the Sirens and her mating with the Atlantean, Sebastian Bonaci, had been the single action that had fulfilled the prophecy that had sparked the last generation of Sirens.

Some might say Naomi was to blame for the world they found themselves in today, but it was hard to blame such a gentle woman, devoted to her husband and family and as much a victim of the Fates as the rest of them.

Naomi nimbly pulled herself up out of the water and sat gracefully on the wall. Then she regarded her for a long moment. Her look seemed so ancient and knowing, she could almost think she knew everything about her and not that it was the other way around.

Whatever Naomi was thinking, she kept to herself. Instead, she bowed her head demurely and said, *Good day to you, sister of the Five Moons.*

Good day, Ashaya replied cautiously. *You did a brave and selfless thing, staying with your people. It is a hard and arduous journey.*

Naomi inclined her head at the compliment. *It doesn't feel that way. I feel my place should have been with my husband at the castle.*

Ashaya thought of the kindly brothers and couldn't help thinking it was a weight off them to have her out of harm's way.

She was about to get up when the conversation took a far more personal direction. She was always afraid that Murrs would see through her cover. Naomi said, *I am not just mother to the Sirens, I am an aunt to Vionne too.*

Ashaya sank back into her chair. She hadn't thought about Naomi being part of the Borge family and therefore related to Vionne. *Of course,* she said, averting her eyes.

Naomi continued to regard her closely. *My nephew has always taken the weight of responsibility his father placed on him very seriously.*

Indeed, he is a most worthy male, Ashaya answered, not sure exactly what to say.

The woman he mates must forgo a life of her own and help

shoulder some of that weight. Naomi smiled and got up stiffy from the wall, leaving her hanging on what she meant.

Phoebe was her daughter and very definitely set on her own life. Naomi had spoken as if it was unclear who that mate might be.

CHAPTER 25

"*I* went to the nursery and a guard barred my way," Isla said, nonplussed.

"What? A Santalini refused you entry to see your own children?" Lacy said.

"No. It was a Magi. I hardly see our guards these days."

Jay was standing listening to the three sisters sitting on the bed in front of him. The strain was killing them. He wasn't sure how much longer they could cope with it. Even Isla's tough armor could be pierced with her children. And she was right. Malleven kept those few Santalinis that remained busy on inane tasks away from the Sirens. His stiffer restrictions on the mothers seeing their children was clearly a last push to make them pledge. They'd been summoned to the Great Hall and were all debating how they could possibly put it off any longer.

Another loud rap at the door and they all jumped and looked at each other, wide-eyed.

Jay put up his hand silently, for them to pause while he answered. He strode over, yanked it open and his whole body relaxed. Seven small faces, including Isla's two and his son, stared up at him. He immediately pushed the door open wide and they filed in.

The sisters gasped, jumping up off the bed. The kids threw themselves into eagerly waiting arms. Jay watched from the sidelines, not unaffected. He'd have to be made of stone to be that. Isla's eyes were wet when she put her forehead to Keefa and then Dannon's, breathing deeply and sighing in relief. Tia's children swarmed her and Lacy with hugs and loud kisses. Jay counted, they were all there: Zander, Roman, Xavier, Alexia and little JJ waiting his turn. He was ashamed to see the separation was as hard and scary for the kids as it was the adults.

Jay closed the door and waited for the greetings to pause. Tia spotted JJ. "You're not too big for kisses, little man," she said, scooping him up and kissing his cheeks loudly to giggles. It was heartwarming to see Alexia and Xavier join the cuddle. Just for a moment, Jay was struck that JJ was still an ordinary little boy who hadn't seen his mum. Then it went as quickly as it came as his serious demeanor returned.

Tia went to Xavier, the biggest. She held the sides of his face and scolded, "What are you doing here? You'll get in trouble. We have to go to the Great Hall now."

What she omitted was that the stalling was over and they'd run out of time. Alfonzo and Sebastian had been called to witness them pledging to Malleven.

Although it was Xavier she spoke to, and he would never say it out loud, it would be JJ who was the spokesperson. The youngest and smallest of all the royal children. They instinctively knew and stepped back, so the sisters had a clear view of him standing alone. It was eerie.

"You must still refuse him," JJ said.

Tia went to protest, but he put up his small hand and cut across her.

"He controls you with us so we must remove the threat.

You must send a message to Alfonzo that you are ill. He will know to stall proceedings. And in the confusion that follows …" He turned to Jay. "You will get a message to Vionne. Tell him to bring a craft to the sea gate and all the children will go with him." He looked like he was calculating something in his head. "Make it 3 a.m. That should give him enough time to get here."

Jay looked at his son, astonished. Not just because of the maturity of his plan, but that it could work. "But doesn't the law clearly say that royal children must stay with the king?" If it had been as simple as removing them, they would have done it right at the beginning.

"People desert the new king every day. Even his own men are turning against him. If the ambassador, Delissi, hears that the Sirens refuse to pledge, then he is not king. This has to be now. My father, Dante, is gravely ill." He turned to the fearful faces of the sisters. "If you make the link with Malleven, Dante will die."

It was enough. Tia looked at Jay, stricken. They had both felt what it was to be starved of the Breath. It had been for a few months and it had just been the two of them. Heaven knew what it was like to be joined to four of the five sisters and have one of them linked to Malleven. No wonder he was so ill. He would need all the sisters to survive.

"It is more than the Breath," JJ said, following his train of thought. "He uses something through his link with Phoebe to get to him. Only I can save him from that."

Part of him wanted to calm his son and tell him to leave it to the adults, but there was something in the boy's whole manner that told him to trust him. It was as though JJ was answering to something bigger than them all. "OK," Jay said, eventually. "Send the message to Alfonzo, so he keeps Malleven busy and I'll contact Vionne." He went to walk away, but paused. "What are you going to do?" he said to his son.

"I am going to put my mother and my two aunts into a sleep that only I can wake them up from."

Jay's eyes went straight to Tia's. It made total sense. They wouldn't be able to fool Malleven in any other way. Still, it was terrifying.

"Go!" JJ prompted. "They'll send someone for them any minute."

Jay left them quickly and found a service lift to the surface part of the house. He hurried along the wood-lined corridor to find the old study that Dante had carried out all his big meetings of state. Panic gripped his heart that he could actually lose his old friend. It robbed him of breath to imagine life without him. The pain was so great that it made him stagger. He swallowed, gritted his teeth and began to jog. He would not allow Dante to go before him. That had never been the plan.

Jay finally reached the study and went straight to the old bureau in the corner. It was, unsurprisingly, locked. He went through drawer after drawer in the large desk until he found what he was looking for: a small antique key. The lock opened and the table part pulled down easily. There, inside, was the technology used to contact the Murrs. He had no idea how it worked. All he knew was that it picked up thoughts and conveyed them to the person receiving the message on the other end. It was one of the many technical miracles that the Murrs had given them. He'd seen Dante use it, but he had no idea what he did. All he could do was press the button in the hope that, with no Murrtaine, someone would pick up the other end and understand his thoughts. Try as he might, he couldn't formulate any mental pictures that would make an ounce of sense. He was no Murr. In the end, he shouted, "For fuck's sake! Get the kids out now! I'll have them out of the tunnel at 3 a.m. Be there!"

With his heart still hammering, Jay shut the bureau and put back the key. Then, with shaking hands, he dialed Ruby as per his backup plan and hoped to god Vionne was somewhere with her.

"Jay?" she said, immediately. "Is everything OK? I've missed you."

"Listen carefully, Ruby. I don't have much time. You must speak to Vionne and tell him to bring a sub to collect the kids. I'm getting them out at 3 a.m. Did you get that, Ruby? 3 a.m."

"What's happened? Is everything alright? I've been so worried about you."

He softened a little. None of this was her fault. "Can you do that for me, babe?" He knew his soft tone would reduce her to putty and guilt pricked him, briefly. But it worked.

"Of course," she said immediately.

Then he clicked off his phone and turned straight into the chest of the Magi.

It took Jay a moment to recognize that it was the one who protected Phoebe. It gave him a certain amount of relief, but there was nothing pally about him today. His face was hard and he was not moving out of his path. "You heard my message?"

"I did," Ghazi said.

He expected some further questioning, but he surprised him by stepping aside.

Jay immediately sidestepped him and went to the door. "Will you say anything?" he asked, before he left. Ghazi's face was impossible to read.

"There will be no Magi in the Great Hall at three."

It was enough and Jay gave him a single nod. The plan

was on. As he walked briskly back through the corridors to find the girls, he prayed it would all come together.

ASHAYA WAS SITTING on the fountain wall of the huge hall of Filfla, with Vionne, surveying the huddles of people as she often did, when excitement rippled through them like a fast tide. Suddenly, the whole of Filfla came alive and turned, wide-eyed, to their neighbor, speaking in loud whispers, far more animated than before. She and Vionne both noticed it at the same time and watched curiously, on high alert for what it could be.

One of Vionne's lieutenants came purposely towards them, bowed and projected a message, followed by Ruby, who streaked across the black marbled floor, barefoot, to reach them. "Jay just phoned," she said breathlessly. You must get the kids … at 3 a.m.," she panted.

Vionne had already got to his feet and Ashaya slowly rose with him. This was huge. He put out a steadying hand to Ruby's arm. *Be at ease,* he projected. *I have the message. We will leave right away.* He was already pulling his black shirt over his head to reveal his striped muscled torso.

Ashaya swallowed. *What do you need me to do?*

Can you go to the king? It will save me time. Tell him Axyl is in the vicinity so we will travel in the Needle.

Vionne's brother Darres was striding over to his brother's call. His own children would be in that party. Ashaya rested, slightly relieved, knowing he had his strong brothers around him.

Ruby was still chattering on as they stepped into the fountain. "I don't know what's happened."

It is still unclear. Be at ease, Vionne repeated and disappeared into the depths.

Ashaya wasted no more time and headed straight for the

king's bedchamber, leaving Ruby sitting nervously on the fountain wall. She'd finally done the honorable thing by delivering the message and proved she loved Jay more than ambition. Ruby had gone up a notch in her estimation.

Ashaya concentrated on navigating the maze of tunnels, remembering that the line of blue lights in the ceiling was the main way through. She remembered the king's bedchamber was a little way down in an avenue of red. It occurred to her as she came to a standstill in front of it, that even she thought of him as the king. It made what she had to say all the more important. She prayed quickly to the Moon Goddesses that she would be allowed in and Dante was awake and lucid inside. The time had finally come. This latest emergency had only brought forward her revelation by few hours. Time had run out for the inhabitants of Earth. The rest of her Twenty were coming. *Please, I have something of grave import to say to the king,* she said to the two Santalini guardsmen stationed outside. The fact there were two made her more fearful, as a sign of the dangerous times. Dante wasn't given to shows of his rank.

One nodded to the other and he disappeared inside. The one left smiled, nodded once and remained aloof, staring out in front of him.

Ashaya looked up and down the corridor in the hope of seeing someone to intervene. This was taking forever. As a last-ditch attempt, she flashed him an image of a large clock and a wave of her anxiety, hoping her Murr language would get through better than words. His look was one of puzzle-ment, as if he didn't fully understand. *How could he?* He wasn't Murr. It brought it home to her that they were a people apart.

She took a step back, and, with fingers to temples, sent out a blast, *Dante! Please! Wake and let me in! I need you urgently. Please!*

The guard was frowning as if he didn't trust what she was doing. He went to take a step towards her when one of the doors opened and the other guard peered out. "Five minutes," he said, ushering her in with his hand.

She looked wanly at the other guard, who still wasn't sure.

Inside, Dante looked pale and listless but, thankfully, awake.

Greetings, lord, she projected with a deep curtsey at the foot of his huge bed. The room was large but simple, with no pretentions of being anything other than functional. She admired that about him. For an Atlantean and a royal, he was very unmaterialistic.

"Come closer," Dante said in a husky whisper. "Tell me what it is you want?"

There was no edge to his words, but it made her feel shame that she'd been so transparent. She guessed her emotions weren't as hidden as they once were. It was impossible to hide them amongst these people.

She went to the side of his bed and bobbed a curtsey again. *Forgive me, Lord.* Then she set out the message delivered by Vionne's lieutenant and Ruby.

Dante struggled to sit up. A nurse was straight there, adding pillows behind him and easing him back against them. "You can't get up, sire," she said.

He looked exasperated and rested, eyes back on Ashaya, now resigned. He knew the nurse was right; he was useless. "Thank you, Ashaya. You have been a great comfort to many of the people here. We can only wait and trust that Jay and *Vionne* will come through for us." His eye held a twinkle when he emphasized Vionne's name.

She did not want to think too deeply on what he was hinting at; what, even in his illness, he found so amusing.

You still trust Jay? she projected quickly, to change the

subject. She'd heard the mutterings between the guards of betrayal. Dante had never commented on the subject.

"Jay is and will always be, my man," he said, visibly stiffening, in his thick Irish accent. He smiled a little. "But that's not entirely why you are here, is it, Moon Goddess?"

His choice of words and demeanor disarmed her completely for a moment. Could it be that he had known all along who she was? *He couldn't, possibly.*

She gathered herself to deliver the blow that she now felt he'd somehow softened. It was very unsettling. *I have come here to request that you summon the Lord Duke Delissi, the ambassador, and have him meet me at the castle prior to the current king's public pledging ceremony.* She paused before she delivered her next words. It would reveal who she truly was. After a breath, she put up her chin and projected, *I need to debrief him before the ceremony goes ahead.*

Despite his fatigue, Dante narrowed his eyes curiously and studied her. It made her convinced he absolutely knew. *You know,* she stated, flatly.

He bobbed his head a little. "I suspected. I knew you were not from Murrla."

She swallowed. *No, I'm not ... It was never my wish to deceive you.*

He didn't appear to be angry. Just thoughtful. "Then where are you from?" He wasn't looking at her as if he was waiting for her to confirm his thoughts out loud. She could see the rise and fall of his chest in anticipation.

Finally, she delivered the sentence she'd practiced a hundred times in her head. *I am part of a federal delegation of twenty judges sent to observe the Earth. We have been here for some time, gathering data in order to form a judgement. I was chosen to come and live among you to make final observations, to enhance what we have gathered using our technology from above.*

It was hard for her to explain in words what that actually was.

"Human emotions," Dante filled in for her. "It's a fine feeling when you get them, isn't it?" he said, smiling.

He seemed nostalgic and not at all scared of her and the power she held. He was a remarkable male.

"So the day has finally come," he said, more to himself. "You know there was a time I never even believed in Atlantis or who I was?" He let out a single blast of air. "I was younger then."

I know, she said. She'd seen it all.

He frowned in awe when the realization of just how long they'd been there watching came over him. "Shit … I'm so busted, aren't I?"

She burst into laughter. She couldn't help herself. Heaven knew what her fellow Twenty members would make of that. That she'd lost her mind and been corrupted over to the dark side, probably. The sound was strange even in her own mind. *You're all busted, as you put it. The jig is up*, she projected, arching a brow. Another expressive facial movement she'd learned from Vionne, she realized.

Dante was looking at her in amazement. "You're a great actor. No one would have known."

Except for you, she said, bowing her head demurely. *If it's any consolation, not all of it was an act. I am indeed a priestess of the Five Moons. Just not of Murrla*, she added. *I never actually said I was from there, people just assumed.*

Dante inclined his head as if he understood completely. He waved over the nurse with his hand. "Have Cesaré contact Delissi immediately and patch him through to here," he said, gesturing to the phone by his bed.

She nodded quickly and left them.

He smiled at her, still nodding, as if she'd got him in a good prank. "You know, everyone has wittered on about it for so long that I don't think anyone actually believed the end would come." He let out a single blast of air in amusement. "Shit's about to get very real here, girl. Are you ready?"

She couldn't help but find him enchanting. She bowed her head. Atlanteans were nothing like the tales they'd been told by their ancestors. They were not Murr, but not human either. They were something other. "Yes, I'm ready."

"Guard!" Dante called.

The guard put his head just inside the room. "Sire?"

"Call Keenan and Cesaré. We're going back to the castle."

JJ couldn't stay the whole time in his mother's bedchamber, he'd be missed. Instead, he went back to Malleven as if he'd just been visiting his siblings in the nursery. Something Malleven would never check as he had no interest in them other than their value to his mother and aunts.

JJ came upon Malleven in his underground cave. As he entered, he was nearly knocked off his feet by a servant sprinting out with his nose broken and bloodied. Malleven was hunched over on the edge of his bed. JJ moved closer and pulled himself up on his own bed nearby. He said nothing, just looked out to the luminous green lagoon. He was a little curious as to why Malleven hadn't questioned where he'd been. Malleven's eyes were closed and he was breathing hard, his face covered in a light sheen. Pain. *The gold.* The substance he worshipped as his savior but had turned into his curse. Even as young as he was, JJ recognized the signs of a destructive addiction. The thing he wielded, now wielded him. It governed his decisions and clouded his thoughts, turning an already cold, calculating man into a sociopath. It seemed pathetic to allow something he'd worked so tirelessly to achieve to be robbed from him at the eleventh hour by mere particles on the wind.

He thought about it for a moment, deciding whether it was best not to approach. Instead, he waited quietly, knowing his presence there would calm him. He was eventually rewarded. Malleven slumped back against his pillows, his eyes slowly closed and he drifted into a heavy, stupor-like sleep.

JJ slid down, approached his bed and waved a hand in front of his face. There was nothing. When he hadn't stirred for a full minute, he ran as fast as he could out of the cave.

JAY SLEPT in the same room as the girls, in a chair. Well that was the idea. There was no sleep for him.

JJ had returned and joined all the kids camped in the room too. They were squashed in the beds between the sisters, who slept on their backs as if they were dead. They looked like statues of knights on their tombs with their hands resting gently on their abdomens. Their skin was deathly white, their eyes tightly shut and their chests barely even moved to breathe.

Jay looked over at his son, who sat up in his sleeping bag watching them too. He'd be a liar if he said his son's power didn't freak him out. The whole thing was staggering. "How will you bring them around?" he said.

JJ shrugged. "It's just a simple switch in their brain. I'll just enter their minds and turn it back on." The little boy smiled as something had just occurred to him. "Malleven could even do it, eventually, if he thought calmly enough about it."

Jay understood what his son meant. When the girls hadn't turned up after Malleven's summons, he came in and blustered at everyone, shouting and demanding like he was deranged. He'd sworn and ranted and tried several spells, while his eyes washed over with the gold that was clearly sending him mad. Then he'd stomped off and shut himself away.

"He thinks it's complicated magic when all it involves is a simple mind walk. He can't see what's in front of his face. Even if he does guess, it would take him a long time as he's never navigated their minds and Isla's is completely closed to him, even in sleep.

Jay let out a deep breath of relief. He was impressed. His son appeared to have thought of everything. Then his eyes rested on the thick bands of gold circling his son's wrists. "Were you always this clever or are you helped by those?" he asked, pointing at them.

JJ smiled his weird, enigmatic smile. "The bands help me to know certain things I wouldn't otherwise know, but the cleverness is all me, Dad."

Jay couldn't help bursting into laughter and one of the kids stirred in the bed. He shook his head in awe of his son. "Whatever happens, I'm proud of you, Son."

JJ got out of his sleeping bag, wandered over and reached up his arms to be pulled up into his lap. Jay drew him into the heat of his body and hugged him tightly. It was such a wonderfully childlike thing to do from someone who was always so grown up. Jay dwelt in the moment, enjoying the smell of kids' shampoo when he kissed the top of his head. "Are you scared?" he whispered, mouth still buried in his hair.

JJ nodded into his chest.

"So am I," he whispered. "We'll keep it to ourselves, OK?"

JJ broke away to look up into his face, amazed. "OK, Dad," he repeated. "But it means you're braver if you're scared."

"Who told you that?" Jay said, smiling at his son, intrigued.

"Dante always says it to me when I don't want to do something. He says, 'If you're scared and do it anyway, you can't get braver than that.'" Then he added, "'A true nutter, like your Dad, never feels the danger. They're the ones you really have to watch.'"

Jay burst out laughing at JJ's comical impression. He could hear Dante saying it so clearly. *Cheeky bastard, saying that to his son.*

JJ was watching him closely, captivated by his reaction.

"Dante says a lot of things," was all he said and then he hugged his son to him again.

The boy fell sleep and Jay contented himself with the warm glow he felt sheltering him in his arms; a gift so rare.

At long last he heard the quiet knock at their door. He checked his watch. It was 2.45 a.m. He got up and gently shook the shoulders of the other six children, quietly telling them to leave everything behind.

Before he left, he bent over Tia's sleeping form and kissed her cold lips. Part of him wanted her to stir and groan and welcome him into her bed, but she seemed dead. A stab of fear hit him square in the chest. He ignored it, kissed her head and whispered, "I'll never leave you." Then he ushered the kids out of the door with a, "Don't make a sound."

They went through the dim corridors, eyes wide with fear and excitement. The youngest, Roman and Zander, thought it a great adventure to be woken out of bed in the middle of the night, without any comprehension of the danger they were in. Xavier, more serious and knowing, hugged his sister, Alexia, into his side as they walked. When they reached the dim light of the edge of the Great Hall, Jay whispered, "Wait!" and went to the front of the line. He peered around and saw Ghazi had kept his word. The creepy

Magi often skulked in the shadows, but there were none in the Great Hall tonight. Just a lone Santalini guard who signed it was OK and patted Jay's back as he passed.

Jay motioned with his arm for them all to follow. "Go straight to the fountain," he said.

The kids ran in their slippers through the cavernous room, as Jay ticked them off in his head, one by one, to make sure he had them all. They came to an abrupt stop at the fountain wall and Jay checked his watch. It was 2.53. Seven minutes was a lifetime to wait. He barely breathed, his senses prickling, feeling completely exposed. The kids' caught on to his nerves, their eyes darting to the fountain and holding their breath at the smallest lap of water. There was no time to hide and they couldn't go in alone. They just had to wait out the last agonizing minutes.

At last, the center of the fountain, where the water was darkest, began to bubble. Jay stepped over into the shallows to get a closer look. He would pounce on any unwanted guests as soon as they came up. However, with perfect timing, black soulless eyes appeared and hovered just beneath the surface, waiting for the signal that the way was clear. Jay nodded the OK and Darres' dark head breached the water first. He pulled himself out and dragged himself to his full height in the shallows. His boys, Keefa and Dannon, immediately went to him and hugged his legs. It was good to see, as they'd been kept from each other since Malleven took the crown, but they were short on time. Magi could come back at any minute. He wasn't sure exactly what Ghazi had done to detain them. The last few Santalini guards were at the castle doing their duty, but they were on side. They were a close family, something Malleven wouldn't understand. Nevertheless, he would avoid a fight at all costs. The kids needed to be away before Malleven even knew they were gone.

Vionne came up next. Jay clasped his arm and helped him up. "No time to explain, just take 'em. I've got things covered here."

Xavier, Alexia, Roman and Zander stepped over the fountain wall ready to go. They were all skilled water breathers. JJ was the only one who held back. Then a dark suit loomed behind him and came into focus.

Jay's heart dropped. The last thing he needed was a fight when they were almost home and clear. He followed the excellent tailoring up to the bruised face and sagged in relief. *Antonio.* He sloshed through the water to face him and put his hands up to wait. "It's not what it looks like."

"It's exactly what it looks like," Antonio said, taking in who was there while his hands rested on JJ's shoulders.

"Let him go," Jay said, adrenalin already pumping, ready to fight. Despite Antonio's choir boy looks, he'd grown up in the same family of boys and sadistic father, so he knew how to defend himself. "Listen to me," he said, trying to calm him. "It's all gone to shit here. No place for children. Let me get them out, safe … please? …Can't you turn a blind eye just this once?" Jay said, appealing to the small shred of decency he'd known since he was a kid.

Antonio was already shaking his head. "This will finish him. He'll go over the edge." Then he looked Jay dead in the eye as if to say, "look at me". "He'll kill me."

Jay knew he spoke the truth by the constant bruising on his face, but, kingdom aside, this was about the children's safety and the leverage Malleven used without a care for their wellbeing.

It's time, Vionne projected from behind him.

Jay closed the gap and put a hand on Antonio's shoulder. "I know I'm asking you to go against someone you care about, but we don't always agree with the people we love. Doesn't mean we don't love them. Sometimes what they want is wrong … for them and everyone else around them," he said desperately. "No one would blame you for trying to stop him going over a cliff."

Time, Jay, Vionne prompted again. This time, Darres loomed next to him and Antonio looked up at him warily. He would read the threat and understand that Darres would kill him in a heartbeat.

Jay used the lapse to call JJ. "Come on," he said, with his hands. But, to his horror, JJ shook his head and stepped back into Antonio's legs. "No, I've got to stay."

Jay's heart thumped, anxiously, and he dropped down to his height. "There's no time for this, JJ. I need to get you out of here."

"Someone's coming," the Santalini guard said, stationed at the mouth of the corridor.

Panic surged through Jay and he went to pick up his son and force him to go.

"I'm staying, Dad," JJ said again, pushing him away. "I need to be here to bring Mum around and I haven't finished with Malleven … It might keep him alive a bit longer," he said, pointing a thumb over his shoulder at Antonio, standing behind him.

Jay peered up at Antonio. What he said was true, but he was still just a child. He went to reach out his hand again when Darres touched his shoulder. *I am staying too. Isla needs me.*

Jay understood that there was no separating him any longer from his mate. He would be added protection for the sisters and his son, as probably the strongest of all the Murrs. The deadly lone wolf, who'd been trained at the same American base as Isla.

"OK," he said to Antonio. "Get him out of here."

He immediately turned his attention back to the other kids and began handing them down to Vionne, already submerged in the tunnel, while everything in him screamed to turn back around and get JJ out as well. He glanced over his shoulder and saw Antonio briskly walking JJ out of the room. At least with JJ in the bed next to him, Malleven wouldn't suspect anything right away. Maybe Antonio would salvage something and live a bit longer. He felt bad for the boy he once knew. It proved that his loyalties were torn. Anyone in their right mind would think of the children.

They came to the last one: *Xavier.* "When you see your father, tell him whatever happens, we're back to back, OK? It's important. He'll know what that means." Xavier nodded and disappeared down into the arms of Vionne in the dark water.

Vionne gave him one final look and disappeared with a *Be careful* drifting through his mind.

He wished they had more time for Darres' legs to harden, but they didn't. He wasn't sure how long Ghazi's window was, so he pointed at the tradesmen's entrance at the far side of the hall by the dais. Tia's record decks were still there, unused since the fall of the kingdom. No time to dwell on happier times. Jay got under Darres' arm and the Santalini guard grabbed the other and together they walked him towards the exit.

"You there!" someone shouted from behind them.

The three of them whirled around to see who it was. A Magi was walking quickly towards them when no one must know Darres was there.

Go! Darres projected, pointing to the door. *Go and cover your ears.*

Jay didn't wait for explanations and he and the Santalini guard ran flat out to the door. "Check on the girls," he ordered as soon as they were on the other side. The guard nodded and disappeared quickly down the corridor. He couldn't resist looking back through the glass to see what happened next.

Darres was standing still, towering above the Magi. His black hair clinging to his back in wet clumps to his waist. With his stripes he looked a fearsome warrior.

The Magi readied his stance, expecting a fight, but it didn't come. Something blasted from Darres, sending blood shooting from the guy's ears, nose and mouth. It happened frighteningly quickly and felled him like a lump of timber in a single second. It hit Jay's ears so hard he had to cover them, even with the door between. Without a single movement, Darres had destroyed him. His strength was astonishing.

When Darres hadn't moved, he peered back in. "Come on. You need to get out of there." The sonic force would have been felt for miles.

Darres turned his head calmly, unaffected by what he'd just done. *I must get rid of the body first. I will join you soon.*

Jay nodded and walked back out, checking over his shoulder just in time to see Darres dragging the body by the feet over the fountain wall where he pulled it down like an animal taking prey to its lair.

SOMETHING WOKE MALLEVEN FROM A NIGHTMARE. He gulped huge lungsful of air in relief. It was the one where he couldn't breathe underwater and he hadn't had that since Lily had freed him by opening his gills. Just lately, they'd begun to rob him of sleep again.

He sat up and checked JJ's bed. He was sleeping soundly. He leaned over and checked his gold timepiece that hung over the wrought-iron bed. 5.15 a.m. He needed Antonio. His instincts were screaming something was wrong.

Conspiracies were everywhere. Everyone was out to get him or waiting for him to fall. They lurked in the darkness to kill him and take his crown. For an insane moment, he actually considered that Antonio was as royal as he was. The deposed king was his brother, but even he, in his neurotic state, saw the ridiculousness of that.

Panic seized him suddenly. *What if Antonio was dead?* His own sweet, faithful Antonio to walk this Earth no more? To touch and whisper encouragement never again. He could barely breathe, his throat contracted so much.

He'd treated him abysmally of late. He needed to find him to say he was sorry. He kicked the crumpled sheets off his legs, threw them over the side and slid off the bed into his slippers. He strode past JJ, uttering "Sleep" as he went past as the boy's eyes flickered open.

The dim corridors offered little light, but he navigated them easily. Despite the early hour they were surprisingly quiet. It felt as through the whole castle was deserted. There were no Santalini guards nor Magi anywhere to be seen.

His heart thumped in his chest and his mouth suddenly went dry. He came to Lily's room first. He composed himself, resisting the urge to burst in and tried the doorknob. It was locked.

It made him frown. They all knew not to lock their doors, on his orders, as guards were always stationed outside. He strained to see down the corridor but there were none. The lock was easy to click open. He simply entered the mechanism with his mind. Then he peered inside. Lily's mop of black curls was sprawled across Lance's body. The tanned surfer's chest was rising and falling peacefully. His arm draped over *his* wife's hip and his head was to the side. They hadn't moved for hours.

Malleven's eyes washed over in gold as his rage gripped him. Illogical, because Lily was exactly where she should be. It was more to do with the fact that she, along with Antonio, had become very dear to him. And this human, linked to the race though he may be, dared to come between them. He told himself for the umpteenth time that he could wait. Although this time, he added, not for long.

He left them undisturbed and went further along the corridor. Passing several rooms, he came to the one he knew was occupied by Phoebe.

He stopped abruptly. He almost didn't see him; he was so well hidden. In his Magi garb that absorbed the light, a lone dark figure guarded her room. *Ghazi.*

Malleven went up to him, narrowing his eyes. Ghazi remained staring ahead of him in the semi-awake state the Magi had perfected to sleep and remain alert at the same time. "Why are you here?" Malleven asked. "This is not your duty."

Ghazi's gaze moved to his and there was no surprise or fear. "I found no one here and decided to guard your most precious subjects, Your Highness."

He said his final title as if he was far from it, confirming for him why he hated this brother most out of all his brotherhood. He dared to be fond of Phoebe and that he wouldn't abide. It undermined anything she might feel for him, her master. "And yet it is outside Phoebe's door you stand."

Ghazi said nothing, but the contempt was easy to read in his eyes. It quite shocked him. Then eventually he answered, "She is the only one of the Sirens that has no Protector this night."

It was reasonable, he supposed, and he nodded begrudgingly. He put his head in the room nonetheless and saw she slept peacefully. He pulled the door closed, silently. "Where then are our brothers?" The increasing amount of gold in his system was making it harder and harder to think straight to commune with them.

"I don't know," Ghazi said with a shake of his head. "I found this floor empty and remained here."

Malleven scrutinized his face for lies and found none. Still, the male annoyed the hell out of him and he marked him again as not long for this world. He moved off without even a thank you.

A little further along and he came to the room the three sisters openly defied him by occupying together. Again, he found the door locked. He opened it as easily as he did before and stepped inside this time.

Jay was in an armchair in the corner, blinking awake. However, Malleven's eyes were drawn to the makeshift giant bed containing the sisters, laid out side by side, as if lying in state. He wanted to be angry with them, but the sight paralyzed his heart at what it could mean for his kingdom. Seeing them like this was the first recognition of what he'd come to. After all these years of plotting and planning, when he'd had it all, he'd managed to alienate almost everyone. The world, both Atlantean and human, had become chaotic. His subjects, fearfully retreating to the safety of their strongholds. And here, three of the most important creatures ever born, would rather do this to themselves than support him in his reign. *How could they?* He wanted to scream with impotent rage at what they'd done to him. He should have crushed their spirits from the start.

Malleven's spine tingled as he felt the presence unfurling behind him. He turned to see the huge frame of Darres, standing up from a chair he'd been sitting in behind the door. "You!" he seethed. Out of all the sisters' mates, this was the one he hated most of all. "You do not have permission to be here." White spittle flecked from his mouth and his eyes bulged with anger. His mind raced at what it could mean, him sneaking in there. Perhaps he was responsible for the lack of guards. Maybe he'd killed them all. His mind rambled on and on with theories and implications.

If my mate is sick and under your care, I have every right to be here to see that she is cared for.

Seeing the control ripple through the male who would snap his neck in a heartbeat made Malleven's eyes wash completely in gold. His anger was molten; that he had no guards to seize Darres and take him away in that moment, so he gathered himself and switched his attention to Jay. "And you! You're supposed to be a Santalini guard, which is the only reason you are tolerated in this castle. Take him to the cells."

Jay rolled his eyes, infuriatingly. "As handy as my fighting skills are, I doubt there is anyone who could make Darres do what he doesn't want to do."

Jay got up and steadily approached Malleven. Malleven jumped to put his fists up to defend himself.

"Your Highness," Jay said calmly, holding his hands up in surrender. "He's doing no harm here. There's no one around. He'll be a good guard for them," he said, bobbing his head towards the bed. "And do you really want to initiate a fight where they might get hurt?"

Jay's reasonableness made Malleven's hatred for him simmer even more. The prettiness of his face just compounded it, because, despite it, he was a strong and able male and wasn't, nor ever would be, his man.

However, he was right. A Human would not stand a chance against a Murr. His eyes went back to the almost seven feet of Darres. The honed killer. His time would come, he himself would see to it. Just as soon as he got to the bottom of what was going on here. It had been a long time coming.

Without another word, he left the room.

His mind churned all the way to the Great Hall. *Why had Darres come? Who had got word to him?*

The huge cave was empty and filled with absolute silence.

Only the sharp tinkle of the fountain cut through it. With no guards there either, he became filled with absolute terror. He broke into a run, heading down the corridor behind the stairs that led to the nursery. Not a single guard was there to stand in his way.

There was no caution this time. He flung open the unlocked door to the children's room and it smacked loudly against the wall with the force. He instinctively knew what he would find—his worst fear realized—six, empty, rumpled beds. He marched into the room, looked under each bed and yanked open their closet. Their bathroom was empty too. They'd vanished without a trace, without taking a single thing with them.

His brain raced. *Vionne.*

It was a plot against him. Vionne must have taken them when he'd brought Darres there.

JJ. He let out a breath and thanked the stars he'd had the foresight to put him in his chamber with him, because he was in no doubt that he would have gone too.

He roared like an injured lion at his own stupidity.

The noise of his grief travelled. Alfonzo and Sebastian looked disheveled from bed as they rushed into the room

"Where are they?" Malleven shouted.

Both men looked around them, flabbergasted. "The children? I have no idea," said Sebastian.

Despite knowing they weren't lying, someone at the castle was acting as a spy and getting information out. He went nose to nose with Alfonzo. He was a greying man in his sixties with enormous strength and vivaciousness for a male of his age, but he was no match for Malleven.

Alfonzo appeared remarkably unaffected by his aggressive stance and looked into his eyes defiantly. "Have you checked with their mothers?"

Malleven almost combusted. "Don't fuck with me!

They're unconscious!" he shouted in his face, frothing spittle making him blink. "Get out! … Get out!" he screamed, walking away. "You all conspire against me."

Then, the one person who would never do such a thing came to his mind. He loved him more than any other. *Antonio.*

He pushed between the brothers, marched out and unceremoniously barged into Antonio's room. He was sleeping on his side; his pale, bare shoulder uncovered revealing the purple bite marks he'd given him earlier.

Malleven calmed down and closed the door a little more quietly when he saw him exactly where he should be. He sat down on the bed next to him and put a gentle hand on his hip. Antonio stirred and instinctively turned towards him. That alone brought a pain to his chest.

There was a vivid, fresh bruise on his cheekbone and his lip was healing. With everything that had happened, seeing him like this was too much to bear and a single sob escaped him.

Antonio was awake and sitting up in a second. His arms circled him to comfort, making him turn his cries into the familiar-smelling shoulder. "I'm sorry, Antonio. I'm sorry."

Antonio, bewildered, said nothing. He simply rocked him in his arms for quite a few minutes. "It is slipping away, Antonio. I can't hold it. This kingdom is designed to send its princes mad. It's like holding eels … The Sirens won't wake up, preferring death than to follow me. And now the children, my only leverage, have gone."

He was thankful that Antonio made no comment. He didn't have an ounce of political interest in him. It was why they worked so well. "Shh." Antonio kissed the top of his head. "Don't cry." He stroked the hair away from his face and whispered, "We'll come out of it. We'll go away. Regroup and you can plan again. You have JJ. He will help you. He is the Darkly Begotten, after all. That has to count for something."

Malleven nodded, stopped crying and blinked. His upset was suddenly dissipating, along with the fog in his brain. He frowned as his grief was replaced with curiosity and then anger. A white rage, such as he'd never felt before, entered his blood and filled every cell one by one, taking over his body so there was nothing of him left.

He pulled apart from Antonio just in time to see his face pale to ash. His doe eyes widened, understanding his mistake and then lowered in resignation.

"I said the children had gone," Malleven said in a voice that was calm and quite unlike himself. "I didn't mention JJ."

Antonio began to shake his head as Malleven bore down on him. "He sleeps with you … he sleeps with you," Antonio kept repeating desperately, like a madman.

Sane thought disappeared as Malleven seized Antonio's throat. Gold particles took hold of his whole body as they wrapped themselves around his hands, squeezing the life out of Antonio.

Antonio couldn't even plead. He just made an awful clucking sound as he tried to draw in air and his eyes clouded with blood.

"I warned you, Antonio. Never betray me. You were the only person in this godforsaken planet I trusted." Each word was ground out with the effort Malleven was using as he literally crushed Antonio's throat in his hands. "You betrayed me. You fucking betrayed me."

Antonio was long dead by the time Malleven finally let go. He threw him away, disgusted, and attempted to get a hold on himself. Breathe. In. Out. His whole body was shaking. He pushed a trembling hand up through his hair, sprang off the bed and looked down at Antonio's lifeless body. "Wake up," he demanded, kicking his foot as if he were faking. Terror was creeping up his spine at the little voice that whispered he wasn't. A reddened, misshapen throat attested to that. He looked down at his own hands. His gold-fueled rage had taken over and reduced him to this.

All he could do was run. He screamed through the corridors in his grief, smashing glass with his power. For the light in his life was snuffed out and not one person in the whole castle stopped him.

CHAPTER 27

*L*ily collapsed against Lance's chest and let the shower water cool down her burning face. His breathing was labored and his heart was beating hard against her cheek. The water drove her wild, glistening on his human skin every bit as much as if he were Atlantean. The surfer boy was at home there just as much as she was.

Lovemaking with him was always as feverish and exciting as the first time. Except, since being there with Malleven, a subtle wedge had been driven between them. It was taking her longer each day to allay his doubts about how much she cared for him. So she would do the only thing he would understand: Worship his body and breathe for him. Then he could feel the soul of her within him. How could she not? She ran her fingers through the water on his ribbed abs. His laidback California accent, messy sun-tipped hair and the cutest face never failed to seduce her. He was like warm honey; seeping into every pore, loving her, holding her to him. She sighed at the heavenly athlete's body that never kept hold of an ounce of fat because of all the surfing. His chuckle reverberated through the tight drum of his chest. "Is that better, Tiger?"

She grinned up at him and nodded, always loving the nickname he'd given her right at the beginning because of her stripes. She was met with half-closed bloodshot eyes, as always, when she'd filled him with her essence.

Surely Lance must know that she loved him now more than anything in this world. The Fates had even seen to it that he was reincarnated for her over and over, so they could continue their great love in every generation and the race could have a compatible mate from the human gene pool. It had to count for something, despite her liking and respect for Malleven.

Yet every time Lily had any interaction with him, she felt Lance withdraw from her a little more. It terrified her that, one day, he would never come back.

Today she would have to risk it again, because she had to speak to Malleven about her sisters. She was worried about them and knew that he would be too. As king he needed them. Without them, the kingdom would die as it had done in every other generation. Except in this one, they'd run out of time, as all the elder statesmen agreed it was the end of days.

Suddenly, without warning, Lance staggered and almost fell.

She just caught him and rested him back against the wall. He held his head and slid slowly to the tiled floor in obvious pain.

Lily crouched down with him. *What is it? Look at me. Lance? Look at me,* she projected.

His eyes flashed open and what she saw there shocked her to the core. His eyes were completely gold. Only one other person's eyes did that: Malleven. It froze her in terror.

Malleven had once given her a drink that had almost

killed her and it looked just like that. Gold, but alive. Moving and churning like a living organism. Now Lance's eyes were exactly the same.

Lance. Lance. After a couple of minutes, the gold dispersed and he returned to normal. She straddled his legs and held him to her. It felt like he'd been gripped by something and then suddenly let go to breathe. She reached up, turned the shower off and pulled down a towel. She held the sides of his face. *Lance. Are you OK? You scared me half to death. What happened?*

He blinked and shook his head as if he was coming round after a fall. He tried to get up. "I'm not sure. It's happened a couple of times."

He looked embarrassed, so she didn't push it. She helped him scramble to his feet and wrapped another towel around him. Then she led him to the bed where he sat down. *Look at me,* she said, checking out his eyes closely. They were back to warm hazel and completely clear.

"What is it?" he asked.

Nothing, they look fine. It's just when you were in there. Just then, when you collapsed, they went really weird. The more she voiced it, the more the fear crept up her spine, so she didn't say any more. She didn't want him to feel it through the bond. He'd be more concerned for her. She needed to look into this on her own first.

She got a glass and tipped in some water from a pitcher by the bed. *Did Malleven ever give you anything to drink—something strange, medicinal or anything?*

Lance took the water and frowned like it was the weirdest question to ask. "What? No. I wouldn't take a beer from that guy."

She sighed and looked at him drily. She didn't want to get into the Malleven argument again. She got it that it was hard for a man to watch as his partner spent time with someone else, but it bothered her that no one even gave Malleven a chance. He had given her everything and yet people seemed to hate him no matter what he did. *I have to go and see him today,* she projected, getting it out quickly without looking him in the eye. She got up and began picking things up off the floor and putting them in the washing hamper. Her body tensed, waiting for the argument, but it never came. *Yeah,* she continued, as if he'd asked for details. *I want to ask what is being done about my sisters. I'm worried about them.*

"OK," he said, getting up from the bed. He went to the dresser and pulled out his trademark battered, loose-fitting jeans and worn t-shirt that looked effortlessly fabulous on him.

After a pause and realizing he wasn't going to say anything else, she did the same. She opted for jeans, boots and a vest. *I'll go now then,* she said, hating how weird things had quickly gotten between them. He pulled sneakers on his bare feet and steered her towards the door. For a horrifying moment she thought he was attempting to come with her, which she would have had to close down.

"I'll walk part of the way with you. I want to see Jay."

Guilt prickled with her sense of relief and she didn't look him in the eye. They came out into the corridor and were met by silence. Nobody was around. There would usually be guards or at least a servant hurrying around at this time in the morning. Today it felt like the castle was deserted.

Lance felt it too. He reached for her hand and they walked cautiously along the corridor to Phoebe's room. There was no guard stationed outside. They looked at each other, alarmed, and Lance knocked on the door. When there was no answer, he put his head inside. "There's no one there."

Lily's sixth sense plucked at the taut wires of her nerves. *Be careful,* she projected.

Lance gave her hand a reassuring squeeze and they

continued on to Tia's room. A Magi was standing on guard outside and she breathed with relief. It meant they weren't completely alone. This one nodded and actually spoke, which was strange for one of Malleven's men. "Your sisters are inside, together."

Satisfied that all seemed OK, Lily turned and kissed Lance quickly on the cheek. *I'll be back. I just want to check what's going on.*

"I'll come."

No, it's fine. You go in. Then, without looking back or engaging in any further argument, she went back the way they came. She broke into a jog and headed for Malleven's bedchamber.

LANCE KNOCKED and put his head inside. The room seemed full of people in animated conversation, so he quietly slipped in and closed the door behind him. It buzzed with excitement of something big having gone down. All the main players were present—well, all except one: Malleven.

The big Murr was dwarfing an armchair just inside the door, even though he shouldn't be there. The three sisters lay still on the bed, sleeping, with Phoebe perched on the edge and Jay and several of the guards in deep conversation with Alfonzo and Sebastian. "What's going on?" Lance said, loudly.

The group of men looked over at him.

"It's deserted out there, except for one guy."

"It's OK, he's ours."

Lance raised his eyebrows and looked for somewhere to sit. His instincts had been right. This had all the signs of a coup.

His eyes rested on the sisters, who hadn't even stirred. "Are they OK?" he asked, a little disturbed.

Jay pulled out a wooden chair for him and indicated for him to sit. "Don't worry. They're just in suspended sleep so that Malleven can't use them."

Lance went over, warily, sat and waited. "Someone gonna tell me what's going on?"

"Now!" Jay shouted.

All Lance had time to do was flinch, he was taken so off guard. His hands and feet were bound and a guard stood behind him, holding him down in the chair by the shoulders. "What the fuck?" Lance shouted, struggling. His head pounded with adrenalin and his heart thrashed. These guys were meant to be his friends. "I haven't done anything!" he shouted.

They stepped back from him when they were satisfied he was tied and couldn't escape.

Jay just pointed at him. "There! Do you see it?"

Alfonzo and Sebastian stood next to him and nodded. A couple of guards joined them in curiosity.

Lance struggled and swore, thinking everyone had surely lost their minds.

"Call Ghazi and take his place," Alfonzo said to one of the Santalini guards.

A moment later, the Magi guy from outside came into the room.

Lance began to struggle again. "Fuck! Let me go. I swear to god—" he roared in his temper.

The guards around him just tightened their grip.

"You see," Jay said, pointing for Ghazi to see this time.

The Magi nodded, sagely. "Malleven has always worshiped gold in its purest form. We all do. But too much and its addictive qualities can take hold of a man." Ghazi came closer to look more deeply into Lance eyes, as if searching for something. "It has entered him in some way."

Lance wanted to headbutt him, but there was something

very calming about the guy and, instead of becoming angrier, he found his anger ebbing away. "Please, what's going on?" he said.

Jay stooped down to see what the Magi saw. "Malleven is using you, Lance. He's got inside you. Probably through the bond you both have with Lily. We're gonna try to get it out before Malleven has time to regroup and come for us."

Lance looked around anxiously and got nods and sympathetic smiles. "I don't understand?" But he was already thinking of the blackout and collapse of that morning.

"You do," Jay said. "You must have felt weird and not like yourself?"

He had, for a while now. It had been worse since being there at the castle. The thought that the guy had invaded him in some way made him sick to his stomach. He gripped the edge of the chair, making his knuckles go white as he seethed in anger. "What do I need to do?" he said through gritted teeth.

Jay stood up so Ghazi could position himself directly in front of him. He opened his hand in front of his eyes and said simply, "There will be pain."

Lance's eyes felt like they were being sucked up inside his head as he fought to keep them in place to see what the Magi was doing to him. A stream of gold-sparkled light appeared to be coming out of his head and into Ghazi's fingers. Then nothing registered after that because lightning scalded his insides.

LILY WALKED TENTATIVELY into Malleven's subterranean bedchamber. She'd never liked it; she found it too big and creepy, never knowing if something would come out of the sea while you slept. Plus, it was Dante's bedchamber. Even she recognized that. Malleven was used to the finer things in life and, in here, he just didn't seem to fit.

That said, it had been a morning of weirdness. She still hadn't met a single soul on her way there. Something was gravely wrong.

Malleven was sitting up against his pillows, staring out across the green water. He didn't turn his head, even though he would know she was there. She shuddered. The room felt like death with the flatline of emotions coming from him.

Her attention was drawn to the child's bed next to him. JJ was awake and playing with his cars; broom-brooming them across the bumps in his quilt.

Hello! She projected out so as not to startle anyone.

"Hello, Auntie," JJ said with a big smile. "I'm playing cars."

That's nice. I'm just here to speak to your Uncle Malleven.

"Father now, Auntie. Father."

Lily frowned at that and wondered what else had changed without her realizing. She slowly approached Malleven's bed. He hadn't looked at her once, he was so lost in thought. Grief hit her through the bond in a sudden punch that took her breath away.

Something terrible had happened. *What is it?* she projected, sitting on the edge of the bed. She reached for his hand, making him turn his head and look at her for the first time.

There in front of her, she was sure, was the Malleven no one had ever seen. Disheveled, unkempt, hair messy and the collar of his shirt askew. He'd slept in his clothes or not slept at all. His eyes were bloodshot and his face still wet with tears.

Her heart went out to him. *What's happened?* she asked. *Please tell me, Malleven. I can feel your pain.*

He didn't speak at first. His mouth went to move and no sound came out. His eyes raked over her face like he was reacquainting himself with it. Maybe even making sure which one of her sisters she was. "He's gone," he said eventually. "My best friend … my love has g—" He buried his face in his hands. Devastation washed over her through the bond.

She took a moment to catch up with who he meant. *Who?* She struggled to think because Malleven was always so strong and composed, even with Antonio. Then it came to her. *What, Antonio has left you?*

Tears fell down his inexpressive face without him even crying. As if they fell from a dripping tap that couldn't be turned off. In the end, he rested his head back against the pillows and closed his eyes. "Yes, he left me. He left me all alone."

Lily was astonished. Not that they'd argued, but at the depth of feeling Malleven had for Antonio. She'd had no idea. She shuffled closer and took the edge of his sheet to dab away some of the tears. *Oh, he'll come back. He loves you. I know he does.*

Malleven turned away from her and shrugged off her hand. *No, he will not. Now leave me.*

His back was shuddering with his emotion again. It was useless. There was nothing she could do but give him space.

JJ was still playing all on his own. She got up and held out her hand to him. *Come on, JJ, let's go and find Daddy for a while.* This was no place for a child.

JJ slid down off the bed with a shiny red truck in his hand and together they trudged across the sand, leaving Malleven alone.

LILY COULDN'T BELIEVE the guard didn't want to let her into her own sister's room at first. In the end she had to scoot around him and barge in. What she was met with rendered her speechless.

She dropped JJ's hand and went to run to Lance, but Darres caught her around the waist. All she could do was struggle helplessly while a Magi held a blinding light to Lance's eyes and he sat alarmingly still. *What are you putting into him?* she shouted, struggling and scowling at Jay, who seemed to be the ringleader in everything these days.

He was as calm and unapologetic as ever. "We aren't putting anything into him, Lily, we're taking it out. Malleven's power, to be exact."

She went to struggle again and call bullshit, when Jay came over and nodded for Darres to let her go. "It's true, Lily. I have no reason to lie to you."

She glared up into Jay's astonishingly clear blue eyes and shook her head. He may be all calm assertion, but he hadn't just come from Malleven's bedchamber. *Then you have got it wrong. Malleven is in pieces after his boyfriend just left him. He hasn't got the energy to do something like that. He's devasted. You didn't see him. Now let Lance go.*

"We're almost done," Jay said, in the same level tone.

He put his head to the side a little to study her, which she found as annoying as hell. He'd always had it in for Malleven.

"Surely you've noticed something odd about Lance—in his eyes, perhaps? Blackouts? Zoning out for a while. Strange behavior, maybe?"

She went to deny it, but the words died immediately. She had. Only that morning. She shook her head, not willing to entertain it. *What had any of that got to do with Malleven?*

"The bond is a great thing in a lot of ways, Lily. It allows the king to link and protect the Sirens, but it also links him to all the mates on the bond too. Some are stronger to resist it than others." He paused while she caught up with what he was saying.

She couldn't believe it. *Not Lance.*

He nodded when he knew that she got it. "We believe he got to Lance very early on."

Something was happening. The light stopped and the men around Lance appeared to catch him as he slumped. Ghazi stood and stretched out his back. He was sweating as if he'd exerted great effort in what he'd just done.

Jay went over and put his hand on his shoulder. "You OK?"

"The gold is volatile and resists. It brings with it pain," Ghazi explained. He looked exhausted.

"Thank you," Jay said, patting him on his back.

Lily couldn't believe one of Malleven's own men was working with them like that. She refused to look him in the eyes as he walked wearily past and went to the door. Lance was coming to. She hurried over and crouched down in front of him while they released his bindings. She stroked her thumb across his cheek. He looked spaced-out and drowsy.

"He'll probably want to sleep a while," Jay said, pulling the chair over that Ghazi had vacated for her to sit on. "I just want to talk to you first."

Still holding Lance's hand, she sat down and looked at Jay doubtfully. She'd listen, figuring it would take less time than arguing.

"Antonio didn't leave Malleven last night, Lily. He killed him," he said, softly.

Lily sat, motionless, stunned. It was the last thing she expected him to say. Then she tutted and waved the comment away with her hand. *He wouldn't do that. He loves him. I feel what he feels. I feel his grief, remember?* she said, thinking what parasites they all were, feeding off Malleven's misfortune to forward their plans. Her temper was rising and she fought to keep it down so that she and Lance could get out of there more quickly.

Thankfully, Alfonzo stepped forward. He at least was

someone she could trust. "It is true, I'm afraid, Lily. My brother and I got there minutes after it happened. He strangled him for helping the children to escape. The body is being prepared for the funeral as we speak and the Duke Delissi has been informed."

Lily looked at each of their faces in disbelief.

"Please believe that despite where my loyalties lie, politically, Antonio was my brother and cousin to us all," Jay said.

Lily shook her head. *He wouldn't.* The man she knew was thoughtful and caring. He would *never* do anything like that.

"Malleven isn't what he seems … to you," Jay said. He half turned and pointed at her sisters who, she just realized, hadn't moved throughout this whole thing. "They would risk their lives by being put in an induced coma rather than pledge publicly to him."

Lily felt dazed. Nothing they were saying fitted with the Malleven she knew. Jay walked off and flicked his hand at Phoebe, who'd been quiet the whole time. "You tell her."

Phoebe sagged as if she was exhausted. "Look, he had me kidnapped, Lily. He kept me for a whole month against my will. He forced me to give him my First Breath without my knowledge, all to get the kingdom. Then wiped my memory. It only came back when I saw him again, here. Please believe me because Lance and Drew's lives depend on it."

Lily knew this sister the most out of them all. They'd even shared breath in the past. She knew she wasn't lying. But none of them understood what she and Malleven shared. She was literally the only person he had now. She couldn't hurt him.

Lance was looking at her, wide awake now, waiting for her to say something. *I won't hurt him, but I won't give you away either,* was the best she could do. She needed time to process all this.

She got up and helped Lance to his feet.

"You'll have to make a choice in the end," Phoebe said.

Lily moved slowly with Lance towards the door.

"Pretty soon it's going to have to be Lance or Malleven," Phoebe called after her.

Jay motioned to Darres to follow. "In the meantime, Darres will help Lance improve his mental blocks so Malleven can't get into him again."

Lily was reminded of the searing pain when Malleven had first entered her mind and felt the first tentacles of doubt. She left the room with the huge, quiet presence of Darres behind her.

The castle was deathly quiet and the corridors empty. No one had heard from Malleven for a full twenty-four hours so everyone used the opportunity to regroup and prepare. The Sirens' bedroom became center of operations with everyone huddled into the small space to be the first to hear any news.

'Has anyone heard from Delissi yet?' Jay asked, perched on the corner of Tia's bed.

"I called him immediately. Delissi should be here any moment," Alfonso said. "I think the sirens should be woken to speak for themselves. He looked down at the three sisters, troubled. "I want nothing left to chance."

Jay nodded. The last thing he wanted was foul play judged on their part. "Are the Magi ready?" he said to Ghazi, standing guard next to the door.

"Santalini guards are flooding back into the castle as we speak. My brothers wait in the shadows for my signal to move on Malleven. They know it is almost time."

Jay let out a ragged breath and nodded. It was the most nervous he had felt in his life. He'd pulled off huge deals and dealt with the biggest moguls of industry, but never had so much rested on him to save so many of those he loved. "Come on, mate," he said, helping JJ climb up onto the sisters' bed. Then he stood back with Alfonzo and Sebastian to watch.

Jay wasn't religious, but he prayed the sirens came out of this OK. He watched in awe as JJ simply touched his forehead to his mother's and she stirred, filling Jay with relief. Tia stretched and smiled as if she was merely waking up from a long nap.

JJ crawled across Tia to repeat the process with Lacy and then again with Isla. They groaned and stretched with an "Ow!" and "Move over" when elbowed or kicked.

Tia, now fully awake, quickly remembered where she was and what had happened. She pulled JJ to her and hugged him fiercely. "Clever boy," she said between loud kisses. He squeaked at being squeezed so tightly and she let him go.

Every muscle that Jay hadn't realized he'd been holding, relaxed. They'd come out the other side. He passed each of them a glass of water from a jug on the nightstand.

"Is it over?" Tia asked, then glugged hers down.

"Almost. Delissi will be here soon," Jay said, watching JJ slide down from the bed and head for the door. "Where are you going?" he asked when he reached for the handle. "We'll need you when the ambassador arrives."

"I'm just going to see Auntie Lily," the boy said, looking wide-eyed and innocent.

Jay couldn't see the harm; it was only at the end of the corridor and nodded. "Five minutes though."

Tia was now sitting up and his attention went to her. As if no one else was there, he pulled her into his arms.

. . .

LANCE WAS ARGUING SO INTENSELY with Lily that he didn't notice JJ slip into the room. "I can't believe you let the fucker in my head, the whole time, spying on my thoughts, making me his bitch!" he shouted in Lily's face.

She glared at him. *I had no idea ... I swear.*

Come to think about it, he'd felt Malleven reach out a few times in the minutes he'd been free, but he'd managed to slam him down. Darres had taught him some simple avoidance tricks and promised more later.

I swear to you I had no idea. I thought we were happy, Lily projected.

"Happy?" Lance mimicked. "I have to come here and share you with another dude and you think I'm happy?"

It was only then he noticed JJ, seemingly unaffected by their tempers, wander across the room and climb up onto the bed. He nodded in JJ's direction so Lily would know he was there. "Hey, dude. What are you doing here?"

"You need to stop arguing and get ready because he's coming."

Lance took a moment to process what the little guy was saying. Then he began to hear what he'd come to realize was a familiar glass, ringing sound. "Hide!" he hissed to JJ and instinctively stepped in front of Lily.

Gold particles were coming into the room from the tiny gap around the door and the keyhole and coming together to form the shape of a man in front of it. "Now, JJ!" he shouted, stamping his foot, when JJ hadn't moved and the only way out was blocked.

The boy remained frozen, eyes wide with wonder as he watched the shape forming, but still he didn't move.

Cursing, Lance lunged for the bed, slicing his hand between the mattress and the bed base, moving it hurriedly in an arc until it bumped the hard object. He clumsily grasped the hilt of the huge hunting knife, stashed there when he first came to the castle. Then he scrambled to his feet, quickly putting himself in front of Lily and JJ again, holding it shakily out in front of him.

Malleven casually flexed the stiff arms of his newly solidified body. "I had you down as a lover not a fighter," Malleven said with a grin. "It's time to go, faithful one." There wasn't a trace of anger or grief in his voice as he held out his hand and spoke through Lance to Lily, as if he wasn't there.

Lance pulled her back by the arm as she went to pass him. "Stay with me!" he pleaded, and, for a moment, she paused and looked back into his eyes.

Malleven held out his other hand to JJ, who slipped off the bed to go to him. To his horror, Lily used the distraction to slip out of his grip and go to him too. *They're saying you murdered Antonio.* Lily projected.

Malleven's composure slipped for the first time. For a single moment grief contorted his face, but he quickly brought it back, composed himself and raised his chin. "Antonio betrayed me … We fought as we often did." He held out his arms dramatically and looked to the heavens. Then dropped them down to his sides, exhausted. "I lost my temper, Lily. I regretted it instantly," he said, shaking his head.

Lance could only look on in exasperation as Lily absorbed and bought the explanation as if it was reasonable.

What shall we do?

Fucking we? Lance couldn't believe what he was hearing.

"I'm leaving this place and I want my wife and son to come with me," Malleven said, holding his hand out to her.

Lance found his motor skills and reached for Lily's arm. "No, you can't go with him."

She turned to look into his panic-stricken eyes and in that single moment he knew she was going to go with

Malleven, no matter what. When she didn't say a word to say otherwise, he turned to Malleven. "Where?"

"To safety … Syria. It is no longer a safe place for us here. My brotherhood can protect us. I have already made the necessary arrangements."

What about Lance? Lily projected, looking over her shoulder as she walked away from him.

It was a nightmare come to life.

Lance couldn't believe Lily would do this to him. Except this time, when he went to move to stop her, an invisible force held his feet to the ground.

"Lance knows what to do. He will cover for us here to buy us some time to get away." Malleven said, calmly. All the while looking at Lance in the eye, maliciously. A look that said it all and was, of course, completely unseen by Lily. "You will see him soon." He smiled at Lily and lovingly squeezed her shoulder. Lance couldn't move or form a single word to stop her. "Make your way to the Great Hall, I'll meet you there."

Lance watched helplessly as Lily cautiously walked away from him, waiting for Lance to stop her, checking over her shoulder several times, until she finally left the room. Malleven held out his hand to JJ and, for a moment, Lance thought Malleven was just going to follow her out. Lance's mind had already switched to how best to alert everyone when Malleven turned back at the doorway and slipped back into the room. The knife Lance still held was prised out of his hand and a hot spur of pain penetrated just under his ribs and took over everything. Lance's eyes widened with the realization of what was happening to him and the blood drained from his face as Malleven whispered close to his ear; "I reclaim my wife."

He was so close Lance could feel his breath, hot and sickly with the smell of brandy. Then, with one last heft, he twisted the knife. Lance could do nothing. He couldn't even cry a word of warning to JJ, who he knew hovered somewhere outside the doorway.

Malleven casually released his hold. Lance's last sight of him was his expensive Italian shoes walking away from him as his cheek hit the floor.

JAY STOOD SOLEMNLY with Alfonzo and Sebastian, shook hands and received the Duke Ormond Delissi and his huge entourage of guardsmen in Dante's old above ground study. Christian Dubonnetti and his remaining three sons arrived soon after and stood dazed in front of him. Jay was surprised at how gray and shrunken the old goat was. All the bravado looked sucked out of him. He guessed even he had a heart somewhere and grieved the loss of his son.

Jay quickly signed to a servant to take them to their rooms. He wanted Christian nowhere near the meeting to follow. Christian made no argument and simply nodded. Marco and Paulo followed him out, sullenly, with their heads down and hands in their pockets.

"Welcome. Thanks for getting here so quickly. As you're no doubt aware, we need to move fast," Jay said, quickly taking charge.

"And you're sure it was Malleven, himself, who killed Antonio?" Delissi said, getting straight to the point, clearly finding it hard to believe.

"My brother and I arrived moments after it happened. It is not the first time he has demonstrated somewhat erratic, aggressive behavior," Alfonzo said.

Delissi still looked unconvinced. "You are laying a serious charge at a prince with five pledges," he reminded them. "This will have serious and far-reaching consequences."

Jay was already shaking his head. "He had Lily conned

and Phoebe admitted that he took her First Breath by force. She only went to him that day because she thought Dante was responsible for the Drew's death. Lacy was brainwashed and the other two just went to protect them."

Delissi's eyes widened at the implications of what he was saying and looked to Alfonzo and Sebastian for confirmation. They both nodded.

Jay explained Malleven's increasingly bizarre behavior, his escalating and obvious abuse of Antonio and appalling mistreatment of staff. "He continually threatened the sisters by holding the royal children. They went as far as being put into an induced sleep to escape the public pledging and we evacuated the children for their safety."

Delissi put his hand to his forehead and looked visibly shaken. "You know what this means? Murder of a royal, even by a king, cannot be overlooked." He walked slowly up and down. "This will rock the kingdom."

"You saw yourself what a liability he was at the meeting with the Humans," Alfonzo reminded him.

Delissi stopped pacing, let out a long breath and nodded wearily as if he'd made up his mind. "You did the right thing," he said directly to Jay.

The room seemed to collectively relax. It was always going to be a flashpoint as to how Jay taking over was going to be received.

Jay passed Delissi a drink and he sank heavily into a chair. "Has someone sent for him?"

Jay nodded. "I think he needs to be held in a reinforced cell until the trial." As he watched it register on Delissi's face, Jay thought again how ridiculous Atlantean law was. Princes could hunt each other to extinction when it came to Sirens, but, as soon as you took a Siren out of the equation, it was murder.

"Agreed," Delissi said, clearly in shock, downing his whisky in a single gulp.

"How is Dante?" It had been the first opportunity he'd had to find out. Delissi knew everything about everyone and now Malleven was finished, there was no need for silence between them.

"He is ill. Although I think he is still traveling here, with everyone else." He looked at his watch. "They will get here any time now."

Jay only had a moment to register how quickly everything appeared to be moving when there was a light knock at the door and Tia slipped into the room. He immediately felt her worry. Christian followed shortly behind her, and, despite his haggard appearance, any sign of his previous grief appeared to have disappeared. "Good!" he said. "I think it's time to reveal our plan," he announced, flashing his eyes at Jay.

Jay sagged, wearily. He wanted Christian safely away from these proceedings grieving, but here he was, determined to grab the opportunity. Christian stalked across the room and slapped a piece of paper down on the desk next to Delissi.

"What is this?" he said.

"Paternity results," Christian said. "Proving Jay is my son … making him one of five," he said, when he got no immediate reaction. He smirked at Jay and wandered back to his previous position next to the door.

Jay's eyes went straight to Tia's. *What are you going to do?* she projected.

He knew exactly what he was going to do, but there was no way he wanted to show his true hand yet. He wouldn't be bullied or rushed by Christian Dubonnetti—or anyone else for that matter. He wanted Dante safe first and he didn't trust his old goat of a so-called father.

Jay cleared his throat and looked Delissi in the eye. "I have breathed with four out of the five sisters. The only one I haven't is Lily, who is the only one loyal to Malleven.

Everyone in the room, except Tia, looked deeply shocked. Jay held his nerve while they all looked at each other trying to gauge who knew.

Another knock at the door paused the tension. "Come in!" Delissi said, breaking his glare with exasperation.

A nervous-looking guard came into the room.

"What is it?" Jay demanded, bracing himself for the bad news he knew was coming.

The guard's eyes flicked guiltily to Delissi before he delivered the blow. "Malleven has gone. Lance has been stabbed and we think he's taken Lily and JJ with him."

Jay sank back into his chair. His brain raced, fraught with fear. "Are you sure JJ is missing? Has a doctor been called?"

The guard nodded.

"Call for a team of Murrs." Jay hadn't seen this coming. He'd assumed Malleven was still incapacitated with grief and the Magi were supposed to have deserted him. The plan was for the brotherhood to stand aside so they could seize him, with the promise they could try him for the murder of their high priest afterwards. However, it looked like they'd decided not to wait. Nothing had been said about Lily and certainly not taking his son. "Where's Ghazi?" he asked, furious, but he knew the answer already.

"Gone!"

Jay's mind raced to see if there was another play he hadn't seen, but all he could come up with was a mess. The Magi had worked to their own agenda. Then, with impeccable timing, Delissi stood up to deliver the final blow. "I'm afraid that's not all. This chaos with the kingdom," he said, gesturing with his hand and then putting it to his forehead. "It could not have come at a worse time."

Jay couldn't give a shit about the kingdom. All he could think about was getting a crack squad together to get back his son. He slowly rose from his chair. "My son!" he reminded him. "You think I care about politics right now?" he shouted, banging his hands on the table in a rare display of anger.

Delissi didn't miss a beat or raise his voice. "Then you should." He fixed Jay with a hard glare that said it all. Dante would have dealt with this without breaking a sweat. Dante was single-minded with anything connected with the kingdom. Delissi knew it right then and so did Jay.

Delissi made a slow turn and looked at every face in the room. "I have been secretly informed that tomorrow, when every delegation arrives from around the world for what was meant to be the public pledging of the Sirens to their king—when we don't even know who the fucking king is—twenty representatives from Atlas will attend to judge the whole inhabited Earth." He laughed mirthlessly. "They are here, ladies and gentlemen. Atlas has returned."

CHAPTER 29

*J*ay squeezed Tia's hand to reassure her. She was shaking; scared like they all were, but worried to death for her son. *Shit, Jay,* she projected. *Is this really happening?* Lacy stood at her shoulder with Isla and Darres, next to the fountain and the Dubonnetti clan.

Groups of every royal family, dignitaries and their affiliates, assembled, standing room only, in the Great Hall of Ballygowan Castle.

Jay waited with the Dubonnettis like a prize fighter in his corner. He could have chosen any one of the three Atlantean families that had adopted him, but because of Christian now being his father, his seemed the logical choice. It felt kind of weird, Dante being a Dubonnetti too and now having no family.

The underlying atmosphere in the room was a feverish level of excitement. Gossip ran wild. No one really knew how any of this would play out. They didn't know who the king was or even if there was a kingdom at all. Any way you looked at it, it didn't seem good. They'd been told that Atlas had returned and all anyone could do was wait to hear their fate from their faceless judges. Everyone had their opinion on what the sentence would be. Then, when they heard the human president himself would attend, the weight of the occasion truly began to sink in. It had never happened in living memory. It meant this was a world issue if the human leaders were involved. Weirdly, everyone seemed to agree that apart from being scared half to death, they were privileged to be there to see it.

Jay's eyes stayed glued to the lift. It opened continually, bringing more and more people into the hall. This time Secret Service men in black suits poured out, wearing headsets. They lined the staircase and the President of the United States emerged, with the Duke Ormond Delissi accompanying him.

The president surveyed the room in wonder as everybody did when they first saw the massive cave. The huge window, the fountain, the sheer size of the place, viewed from the vantage point of the great staircase, was an unparalleled sight.

Jay watched Alfonzo and Sebastian greet him from the bottom of the steps. They knew the president well from being their Atlantean spokesmen for years. The greeting looked warm despite the circumstances. He guessed they were all affected by the outcome today, human or Atlantean.

"Remember who you are," Christian whispered in Jay's ear. "You are a Dubonnetti first and foremost."

Jay nodded at the advice. He knew what he had to do; he'd known right from the beginning.

Ironically, after shaking his and Christian's hand, Delissi led the president to the dais with the chair that Malleven had called his throne. Jay looked sideways at Christian's outrage and smiled. The world had truly gone mad.

The lifts opened again and Jay's heart quickened and then leapt. Keenan and a very tired-looking Cesaré stepped out, followed by Drew pushing someone in a wheelchair. Jay couldn't make out who the old man was until his heart stopped. "My god," he whispered and gripped Tia's hand.

Tia followed Jay's line of vision and a hand went to her mouth. *Dante!* The two of them pushed through the crowd. Four Santalini guards carried his chair down the steps and gently put it down on the floor, just as Jay and Tia finally reached him. His once-black lustrous hair was dull and wiry, his skin sallow and his eyes sunken. Being cut off from the Sirens had ravaged him completely. Dante blinked with the effort of trying to focus on Jay. "Make way!" Jay said, snapping himself out of his shock.

Tia bent down to kiss Dante. "Come with me."

Drew kicked the brake off on the chair and the crowd parted immediately as they made their way across the room. They were heading to the privacy of the bedroom corridor and Tia's room. Jay eyed Cesaré and thought that although he was walking, he wasn't faring much better than Dante. It was a shock as he was always so vital and alive. The Sirens' breath, that brought so much pleasure and joy, could reduce a man to this when he didn't get it. "Lily's not here," he was forced to say when he saw Cesaré scanning the room for her. The disappointment killed what little glimmer of light there was left in his dead-looking eyes. "I understand," he said.

They had to win this situation. They just had to.

Once safely settled in Tia's room, Jay needed to return to the Great Hall. "See to him." Now that he was in the light, Dante looked worse than ever. He was holding Tia's hand and completely focused on her. Jay signed for Keenan and Drew to leave with him. "I'll send the other sisters," he said, walking towards the door. "I want him at full strength before the visitors arrive."

Jay took one last look at his old friend as he was about to leave when Dante looked straight at him. *What happened to yer,* Dante projected, smiling lazily. It reminded Jay of when Dante used to get drunk when they were kids—a lifetime ago. Except this was different. If the sisters didn't breathe for him soon, Dante would die. He was far too weak already. There was so much Jay wanted to say and no time to say it. All he could say was, "Do you trust me?"

Dante bowed his head. *Never doubted yer.*

Jay nodded once, never given to outward displays of emotion. It was too much. His voice was strangled when he said to Tia, "Breathe for him. I'll be out by the fountain." He left them to it. He had to. While he strode briskly down the corridor, he tried to imagine life without him—without Dante or Tia and it was impossible. The mere thought robbed him of breath. Together with the children, they were the only family that mattered. Jay vowed then that, while he had life in his bones, he would never desert them.

CHAPTER 30

At the close of the door, Tia leaned down and put her lips to Dante's. No, hello, how are you, or anything. She knew what she had to do to make him feel better. Worry for JJ was still a burning presence in the back of her mind and a fierce pain in her heart, but she had to help Dante first.

His lips were dry and cracked as if he'd been parched in the desert. She hadn't felt the effects nearly as much, probably because he was starved of four sisters and not just her. She tried to imagine not being able to breathe with either Dante or Jay and shuddered at how terrible that would feel.

Tia strongly suspected that the spell Malleven had used to cut off their mental links had added to that too; sending the mind into withdrawal. Malleven's plan had been for Dante to shrivel up and die, therefore removing him as a threat, and all without laying a single hand on him.

Her essence flowed into Dante in a slow, steady stream. He warmed up immediately and stopped shaking enough for her to perch on his lap. His arms eventually came around her and she could relax properly with her full weight. After several minutes it turned into the languid kiss of lovers.

Dante sighed softly and rested his forehead against hers. Tia pulled apart to look at him. His color was better, his eyes brighter and the darkness under them was disappearing. She ran her fingers through his once-lustrous black hair, now peppered with grey, and saw the twinkle enter his eye. "Do you mind being stuck with an old man?" he said, amusement playing on his lips.

"Meh," she said with a shrug. "You might have to take some afternoon naps to keep up with me."

He chuckled and hugged her to him, tightly. "I've missed you so much," he whispered into her hair, emotion catching in his voice.

Tia clung to him, feeling his fierce terror mixed with love through the bond. "I'll never leave you again," she promised. Sadly, there wasn't time for a lengthy reunion. "He has JJ and Lily, Dante, and he'll hurt them." She collapsed into sobs, unable to hold herself together any longer. The idea that she could have lost him was too much and she couldn't bear to lose anyone else.

Dante tightened his grip around her while she cried into his shoulder. He whispered, "It's OK, we'll find him," into her hair. "Listen to me." He pulled her chin up to look at him. "Malleven knows he's lost. He won't harm them. He'd lose his collateral for safety if he did that."

Tia studied his face and her tears stopped. His expression seemed so honest and sure. "He's a madman though, Dante. He killed Antonio." She wasn't sure how much he knew.

Dante pushed the hair back from her face and looked so sad. "Antonio was my brother, but he loved Malleven and made his own choices." He held her gaze until she eventually nodded. "We have to save ourselves now."

A hard rap at the door made Tia jump, but she didn't take her eyes from his face. It was a startling reminder of the danger they all faced.

"Come in," Dante said.

Isla, Lacy and Phoebe traipsed in, knowing straight away what they were there to do. "We don't have much time. Just give him a little to get him up and walking. We can do it properly later," Tia said, getting up off Dante's lap.

There'd be no cooling off in water today, so each of them leaned in, one by one, as if to kiss him on the cheek and breathed into his mouth for no more than about five seconds. Dante's face was flushed, as if he'd sat next to a fire, by the time they'd finished. Tia only hoped he was strong enough to take it.

Lacy immediately nipped to the bathroom and came back with some cooling flannels, which she dabbed against his face and neck as he rode out the last ripples of euphoria. He was already looking better. "Do you think you can stand?" Tia asked.

"I think so."

Tia and Isla got either side of him to help Dante to his feet and he shuffled slowly to the door. Tia guessed his legs were stiff from lack of use. However, as soon as Lacy opened the door and his men straightened to attention outside, his shoulders went back and his tremors disappeared. He seemed to grow in height and presence before their eyes and he became the strong king she remembered. Her heart swelled at the effort she knew it was taking.

The room hushed at the sight of Dante when they entered the Great Hall. For a second, Tia was unsure of his reception. Then someone clapped. And then another. Until cheers and applause went through the vast room. The crowd parted and the four of them walked easily through, while Dante shook hands and got pats on the back. Tears welled in Tia's eyes, that people were finally seeing him in the way she always had.

Jay was waiting for them at the fountain, clapping along

with everyone else. He seemed relieved to see them. Whatever the outcome of today, Dante was acknowledged as a king who had earned their respect over time and she couldn't be happier. If only little JJ and Lily were safe, her happiness would be complete.

Thankfully, a chair was brought for him when he reached the president. "Your entrance was bigger than mine," the president said, shaking his hand, warmly.

No one seemed to notice his tremors returning from the effort.

Alfonzo tapped Dante's shoulder gently and Tia turned to see the Murr delegation coming up through the fountain. She couldn't help checking out the reaction of the president. Vionne, Axyl, Dax and Caan were pretty magnificent; each one striped and muscled, a full seven feet in height. She grinned; the president couldn't conceal his awe.

Darres, who was already at the castle with Isla, went and stood with them, making the five sons of Borge complete. Tia felt proud that she knew them all personally. She could hear the duke explaining who each of them was in the president's ear.

All except Vionne took seats on the fountain's edge for their legs to harden, when the water began to bubble again. A nervous ripple went through the crowd as they anticipated who it might be. Only one party was yet to arrive.

Vionne reached down and helped up a female that Tia recognized: *the girl, Ashaya.* She nudged Dante, to make sure he was seeing what she was seeing. Even from this distance it was clear the regard Vionne had for her. She thought he was supposed to be lovesick for Phoebe. *Men were such shits.*

Ashaya was dressed weirdly and she wasn't alone. Murr after Murr appeared to be following her. Each stood in the shallows until they were helped out of the fountain and given a towel. There were ten males and another nine females of varying ages. All were dressed in the same steel-grey, figure-hugging wetsuits that seemed to complement their pale complexion and pure white or coal-black hair.

The room fell silent as everyone came to the same conclusion. These weren't Murrs; they were Atlasians. The prophecy was finally fulfilled; they'd come back at last. And Ashaya was one of them. Tia swallowed at what that meant. She'd been living among them the whole time.

It took a grueling five and a half hours on the Florianna jet and a further two in the motorcade of armored SUVs, but Malleven finally reached the palace of the Magi brotherhood in Syria. He thanked the stars and the planets for giving him this sanctuary to go to. He breathed in the marzipan-scented air. He was home. How stupid he'd been to try to fit into the world built by Dante and the outmoded Bonacis. He would make his own court here among the shady almond and fig trees and carve out a center of culture that the world would flock to. He walked briskly, carrying JJ, through the long open-sided corridors that overlooked the splendid gardens and many fountains, issuing orders and forming plans as he went. Lily had to run next to him to keep up.

He would execute Ghazi at the first opportunity and elevate himself to high priest. It was only fitting, as he was already king of the Atlantean world. Then he would plan his return to power from there. The castle would fall into chaos with the infighting the power vacuum would create, then he would swoop in and regain his place after they were weakened and their numbers diminished.

What's happening? Lily asked for the umpteenth time.

"Must you perpetually plague me?" he snapped. Then he

calmed himself and counted. "Forgive me. It has been a trying day."

At long last, they reached his large, familiar suite of rooms and he put JJ down. Then he sat heavily on the bed. Servants immediately started arriving, bringing food and drink and laying a table in record time. Malleven loved the sense of order in this place.

Then the room began to fill with every brother of the Magi, dressed in ceremonial black robes, their spirit name daubed into their cheeks in paint.

Lily instinctively went to JJ to protect him. Malleven looked more curious than perturbed. Around thirty men assembled in front of him. "What an honor to have my whole brotherhood here to greet me," Malleven said.

Lily felt something was off. A seriousness hung in the air around them and her street senses were screaming for her to get out. She slowly pulled JJ off the chair to stand closer to her when the Magi, Ghazi, she remembered from the castle, came forward and bowed his head to speak.

Lily looked between them. This wasn't good. Malleven was angry. "You should prostrate yourself in front of your high priest, Ghazi."

"And we shall, when we know where he is." There were gasps of horror from the other brothers and Ghazi's eyes came up defiantly to look directly at Malleven. Lily saw the wash of gold sweep though him and then she caught up with what must have happened. If Malleven had assumed the title, then he must know the high priest was dead. "You must first answer the charges brought against you," Ghazi said.

Malleven sneered and rose dangerously, like a cobra. "I am king of the whole Atlantean world. I bring the Magi greatness. You should all be kneeling in front of me."

Lily had never seen him like this; like he'd kill a man as soon as look at him. He was terrifying. However, the man,

Ghazi, didn't shrink away. Instead, he shocked her by turning and walking towards them and kneeling in front of JJ. She looked across at Malleven who was lost for words. "You are the prince who was foretold to us. The Darkly Begotten. The manifestation of your books and ours. I ask you … do you see this man as your king?" Ghazi asked softly, turning and pointing at Malleven.

Malleven straightened, indignant.

Lily wanted to intervene and remind them that JJ was just a little boy, but Ghazi put up his hand to stop her and JJ didn't appear to be afraid. Instead, he surprised her by putting out his small hand and touching it to Ghazi's forehead. "Thank you for the protection you gave to my Aunt Phoebe. You have been a true and loyal servant to the Atlantean race." Then the boy's eyes tracked across to Malleven, looking on in astonishment. "This prince adopted me and I became a Florianna: the last piece of the prophecy —a part of each royal family. For that I call him father. But I do not call him king. Just two of my aunts pledged to him, he wears no ring and flouts the laws of nature. He must answer for his crimes, here, or at the Atlantean court. He is one of you, so I defer to you and act as witness."

Malleven erupted with rage and Lily went to go and calm him, but she had no time to move. He ignited and threw some sort of energy ball directly at them. A bubble immediately appeared around them. Lily wasn't sure if JJ or Ghazi had caused it, but the Magi murmured in wonder, proving it was the former. Then they quickly recovered and moved in and seized Malleven. He fought and swore and gabbled what sounded like incantations, but nothing worked against men who were as strong as him.

Lily didn't know what to do. Part of her wanted to protect him, but she was sure he would hurt JJ if he could. So, as much as it pained her, she remained where she was, as he was dragged from the room. "Lily! Lily!" he screamed, making her panic and want to run after him. "I made you … I'll give you riches… anything you want." His shouting went off into the distance and then out of earshot completely. "Where are you taking him?" she said to Ghazi.

"He will be tried by fire for the murder of our high priest, Nasr."

She could feel Malleven in her head. Over and over. *Help me, Lily. You are the only sister I loved.*

Ghazi held her shoulders to bring her attention back to the room. "Malleven has killed many people, Lily. He disregards his oaths to our traditions. He is first and foremost a Magi and merely used it to his ends. The kingdom was all he ever truly wanted." He was stooping to look at her at eye level and his eyes were earnest; she knew he was telling her the truth. She went to struggle, but all she could do was crumple into tears. "Listen to me, Lily. Lance has been mortally wounded and your ancestors are here. As soon as Malleven has been dealt with, we need to get you back."

Lily's mind fell away at hearing Lance was wounded and she was already moving towards the door. Ghazi stooped to pick up JJ and followed. *How? What happened?* But it was already making sense. Malleven remaining in the room and Lance not coming. *Malleven.* Her heart went cold.

Ghazi caught up with her, sensing the change in her. "Do not worry. Come with me. I'm to go to the temple. Malleven must first be tried by the whole brotherhood. He will die by fire and his spirit will not commune with his brothers, nor will he rise to the Ether. His ashes will be consumed by the gold he loved most and there will be not a single particle of him left."

Lily began to run, hands over her ears, not wanting to hear any more.

"There is no hiding from the truth any longer," Ghazi called after her.

She slowed to a walk, wretched in misery, and allowed Ghazi catch up and lead her down avenue after avenue, not caring which way she went. All she could think was the trust she'd put in a man who had tricked and betrayed her to hurt the one person she loved. *Lance.* Who'd gone along with everything to protect her because he loved her, no matter what. Even when she put another man, who didn't deserve it, ahead of him.

They came to a stop inside a huge, circular building, built from the familiar yellow sandstone. Glassless windows were filled with an intricate wooden latticework that made the inside dark with speckled light that danced everywhere, like stars. *The temple.* Ghazi steered her towards a carved stone seat to sit with JJ. "Wait here. This will take only a matter of minutes."

She watched, dazed, as Ghazi, ceremonial silk robes swirling behind him, walked away, through an arch and into the center of the building. Then she heard loud voices in heated discussion, echoing in what must be a large space.

JJ pointed to the bank of large latticework windows that formed an internal wall in front of them. "We can probably see from there."

Lily wasn't sure. She was torn between getting away and being reliant on Ghazi. Needing to find out what was happening, but unsure it was something JJ should see.

"I'm more grown up than I look, Auntie Lily," JJ said as if he'd read her mind. "You'll never be sure what happened to him unless you look."

She took in a deep breath, then shouts from the direction he'd pointed in made up her mind. *Come on then, but be quiet.*

JJ conspiratorially put his finger to his lips and slid down off the seat. Together they went the fifteen or so feet to the latticed window to see what they could see.

They were a long way off. The brothers were in a circle around Malleven, hands tied behind his back. Despite what he was supposed to have done, tears welled up in her eyes to see him like that. "Where is the high priest, Nasr? He came to the castle and no one has been able to sense him since."

Malleven seemed unrepentant and Lily remembered poor Antonio. If he'd murdered his high priest as well, that was two people he'd killed. It was no stretch then to think he could have hurt Lance. A sob escaped her that she could have got it all so wrong.

JJ's hand came around her legs at exactly the right moment to comfort her. When she looked down, he could only just see over the lip of carved wood. "Watch, Auntie. This will be your justice."

She was amazed at the fascinated expression on the tiny boy's face. He was like a scientist about to see the outcome of an experiment. Until Malleven's booming voice pulled her attention away to look at him: "You have no proof."

Even from around seventy or eighty feet away, his eyes found hers, as if he was speaking to her directly. *That's it, little flower. Join with me and we will battle these insects and rule the world.*

In that moment, everything became clear. There was no sorrow or begging for forgiveness. She would have latched onto any feasible excuse, like, they'd fought and Lance had fallen on the blade. Anything. But there was none. Only defiance and the need for power right up to the end. She hardened and he knew. Then she got the satisfaction she was looking for: fear.

"You have been found guilty of the most heinous crime recorded in the long history of our brotherhood. Vaticide—the killing of a great prophet and the betrayal of your brothers who are your flesh. The element that binds us together and the one you so revere can no longer be joined. Your flesh must be ripped from it and released. And so your sentence is a thousand deaths by fire."

Lily pulled JJ closer as Malleven began to shake his head. "No … No," over and over. There was a loud, grinding sound of stone against stone as a great circular rock was rotated and dragged across the floor revealing a circular pit. Strange blue flames licked upwards fiercely, like no ordinary fire. She could feel the heat from there.

Malleven began to fight and struggle, but it was as though a force held him and pushed him slowly towards the pit. His threats to punish them, to peel their skin from their charred bones, were lost to screams as he realized no one was listening to him. There was one last micro-second where his distraught eyes met hers in one final plea and she closed her eyes. Then the air was torn with a final stomach-curdling scream, followed by silence.

Lily opened her eyes slowly to cheers as the great stone was rolled back over him. Somehow, that felt worse than the flames themselves. To be trapped like that. His fear of drowning to be replaced by a consuming fire. The brothers all knelt saying incantations around it, but Ghazi was already heading back towards her. He came out to where they were standing, phone to his ear. "Yes, it's done … we're on our way back now."

Lily went along with him in misery. JJ touched her leg in concern a few times, but she looked at him unseeing. She was vaguely aware she was in a car, then a plane. All she could think of was: Malleven was gone. Lance might die and everything was her fault. She'd left without speaking to him, assuming he was just angry with her and would get over it, as he always did. Maybe he wouldn't get over this.

Distraught, she reached out telepathically to him over and

over, hoping he could hear her. With every moment her heart died a little more when she felt absolutely nothing on the bond. Just a small glimmer of Cesaré, so small it was barely there. *I'm coming,* she said to him over and over. Cesaré should have replied but he didn't. Maybe he hated her too. There was no Malleven and, terrifyingly, no Lance. It was as if he was gone already.

Murrs stood unnaturally still, without the need for constantly moving like humans, and so, it would seem, did their ancestors. Vionne couldn't take his eyes from Ashaya, standing with the strangers, while the watching crowd shuffled feet, coughed and nudged each other in an awkward silence. Terrified whispers went behind secretive hands, as heart-dropping understanding came to them of who they were.

You lied to me, Vionne projected to Ashaya so only she could hear.

She flashed him a feeling of anxiety and a sharp, *No, you assumed. If anyone had known who I was, I would have been recalled straight away and replaced with another.*

There was no apology, no stroke to his damaged ego. He felt madder than ever. She had been the balm that had made Phoebe's love for another man bearable. His eyes went to Phoebe, as they invariably did. She was standing openly, her lover's arms around her. Ashaya followed his eyes and sent him an unmistakable feeling of sadness. *What point would there have been, anyway? Your heart is set on another,* she said.

One of the males introduced himself to the room as Seti, leader of the delegation. The solemness of the occasion should have hit Vionne, like it did everyone else in the room, but instead he felt foolish and desolate. It wasn't until that exact moment that he realized that Phoebe had been a dream he'd cherished to keep something of his father alive. His heart was not set on her as Ashaya believed, it clung to her. Now, with all these people here and knowing Ashaya's true identity, it was too late to tell her. All he could do was flash Ashaya feelings of apology and shame in the hope it was enough for her to forgive him.

Seti began his mental broadcast and Vionne was forced to leave his link with Ashaya's mind and listen. *You know why we are here,* his experienced psychic orator's voice boomed. He was clearly a leader and immediately captured everyone's attention and respect. He stepped out into the open space in front of them. *We set off from our home planet two hundred and fifty-eight years ago and have been here observing you for three. We greet all representatives—including our hosts,* he said, turning and bowing at the waist towards the president.

JAY FELT weird being addressed by what were, effectively, aliens. Then he looked down at his hand, holding Tia's, and saw that she also held Dante's, on her other side. Something sighed and resigned itself inside him. It seemed a small thing in the light of the things happening in front of them. To his right was the President of the United States of America, surrounded by six of his Secret Service agents. He guessed he was maxed out on weirdness.

We are not here to harm you, Seti was saying. *Merely to pass judgement over the next few days.* Then he looked straight at their little group. *Today we will sort through the sorry mess of this kingdom. We will then conclude in New Murrtaine for final judgement.* He circled, picking out a few faces in the crowd. *I hope that is clear.*

It was. In perfect newsreaders' English, he had given them a timetable to their doom. Jay received it loud and clear. Only true Water Breathers would be attending the last part. The likes of him and many of the royal families would not be included. It felt like a pronouncement on his bid for the kingdom, already.

Tia looked up at him. She was, no doubt, thinking of the time she and Phoebe had been taken to the old city and how it had been Dante who had come to rescue her. He smiled at her weakly. The apology was in her eyes. It meant the building work of the new city was finished. Maybe they'd been foolish all along to have ever fallen into this plan of winning the kingdom back for Dante.

He had to hand it to them. The choice of venue was clever and deliberate. The Murrs were all about purity and preserving traditions. He guessed those from Atlas were the same. It didn't bode well for the mess they found all around them.

You! Seti said, pointing directly at Alfonzo. *Elder Bonaci! You will scribe for those above the water.*

Alfonzo nodded, a little uncomfortably. He had never been spoken to like that before. Everyone had always respected the brothers who had steered the nation for years before there was a kingdom. It bristled to have to watch. A real scribe came forward with a leather-bound book and pen and servants with a small table and chair.

Then Seti pointed to Axyl, one of Vionne's brothers—another leader of his own city. *You will mentally log for those below.*

Dante Dubonnetti and Jay Gardiner! Seti boomed, snatching him from his thoughts. Jay followed when Dante immediately stepped forward.

There you are, Seti said, turning his full attention to them. *The reprobate ex-king who never believed in his heritage until it was thrust upon him and the best friend who can't make up his mind which family he belongs to or where his loyalties lie.*

Jay remained calm, but he felt an instant dislike for this guy. He couldn't make up his mind whether he was deliberately goading them or had already made up his mind.

Christian Dubonnetti stepped out from the crowd waving a piece of paper. Jay rolled his eyes and shook his head. This was not the time for it. "I have the proof right here that Jay is my son. He is Dubonnetti. One of five!" he said loudly, holding it up so everyone in the room could see it as well as the visitors.

All Jay could do was look sideways at Dante. His eyebrows rose, but he remained facing front. It was unlike him to give nothing away. *Had they really drifted that far apart?* "Go with it," Jay whispered, hoping he heard.

Dante let out a long breath and looked on. It was driving Jay mad. He wanted to shake him and explain, but was forced to endure this ridiculous show.

Someone shouted from the crowd. "You already have five sons. The prophecy doesn't say six."

Christian turned and pointed to Dante. "He is not my son, he is Delissi's brat."

It sounded like the whole room took in a collective breath of shock and whispered to their neighbor, asking if they'd heard right. Jay had forgotten that very few people knew Delissi was Dante's real father. It was typical of Christian to out him like this, without a care for anyone concerned. It also compromised Delissi's position in Washington, if they thought he was father to the king. He could strangle him. All he could do was shuffle his feet and grit his teeth. This wasn't at all how it was meant to go down.

Tia stepped forward and held both their hands again. It

wasn't until then that he fully appreciated what an anchor she was to them both. Had always been.

So you are saying the former king's claim is illegal, Seti said loudly, for the scribes to log and write it down.

That's right! The pompous old goat said, triumphantly. Then he stepped back as he became conscious of the quiet room and all eyes on him.

Jay looked across at Dante; he hadn't said a word. Jay was proud of the man Dante had become. It wasn't that long ago he'd have told the old gobshite to sit down. Today he carried himself with real bearing. He hoped everyone else thought so too.

"He is still one of five on his mother's side," Alfonzo said, sitting at the little desk, holding up his pen for Seti to notice him.

Seti nodded and pointed to his book. *Write that down.* He faced the crowd again. *I call the Sirens known as Tia Storm, Lacy Rain, Isla Snow, Lillian Gale and Phoebe Ray—you can fill in their legal names after,* he said to Alfonzo. *Step forward,* Seti said.

Alfonzo put up his hand again, making Seti pause. "Lily is not here. She is on her way back from Syria at this moment. She will arrive soon."

Seti appeared to think about that for a moment. *Very well. We will proceed without her for the time being.*

The four girls assembled in front of the delegation and Jay wanted to rush out to hold Tia's hand. She was hopeless in situations like this. Then the sad fact dawned on him that it wasn't even his place to do that anymore. Ruby was a little way off with the Santalinis and he smiled at her sadly. Her eyes were only ever on him. "You OK?" he mouthed.

She nodded and he shelved his guilt for another time. It was something to face, but not now.

He looked at Dante, as anxious to protect Tia as he was.

Husband, Partner, Destined Mate. There, watching keenly, looking a lot better than he did before—the one who had every right to love and worry for her.

Tia Storm, Seti projected loudly. *Queen and bonded mate by First Breath to Dante Dubonnetti. Is that correct?*

She nodded. "Yes, sir."

Speak up!

"Yes, sir," she said more loudly.

You are also bonded by breath to Jay Gardiner, friend and would-be brother to Dante Dubonnetti. Is that correct?

"Yes, but it's complicated."

Simply state yes or no.

Jay gritted his teeth and clenched his fists. It was feeling more and more like a court.

"Yes!" she shouted.

Please state for the room whether or not you have a blood bond with the former king, Dante Dubonnetti.

Jay's heart began to sink as he knew where this line of questioning was going.

"No, I do not," she said.

Please don't lose your temper, baby, Jay thought, hoping she could tune into his thoughts as he couldn't project them. He could see her hackles rising and she was doing so well.

Please state for the room whether or not you have a blood bond with Jay Gardiner.

Jay swallowed and looked across at Dante. His eyes were riveted to the scene like a slow-motion car crash.

"Yes, I do, but you know that already, don't you? Otherwise you wouldn't be asking me!" Tia shouted.

Jay shifted uncomfortably. The room became filled with chatter and unrest, like it could get ugly any minute. Tia was looking around her, not sure what to do.

Dante was concentrating. Jay guessed he was talking her

down in her head. It was something he'd always jealously resented. Today, he was simply grateful.

"Silence … silence," a guard shouted to regain control of the crowd.

Write it! Seti demanded, pointing at Alfonzo.

The whole proceedings started to feel like it was only going to go one way. Jay was already thinking of affairs that he needed to get in order before it was over.

Ruby Santalini!

What the hell did he need her for? Jay was forced to watch in horror as a very scared- looking Ruby stepped out from the shelter of her family.

"I do," she said, before he had the chance to ask the question again.

Seti inclined his head in thanks for her answering so quickly. *And do you share a bond with anyone else?*

Ruby looked so nervous. Jay felt sorry for her because he knew what she had to say. She'd been dragged into politics when, in reality, she was innocent in all this. She pointed a shaky hand to Dante. "I drank from him. But I swear he did not return it."

Jay moved closer to Dante. He swayed, either from weakness or the public airing of all his sins. The bastard was determined to make him look bad. The situation between them had always been fucked up, but this was unfair.

Write it down! Seti shouted as Alfonzo paused to take it all in.

Jay couldn't stay silent any longer and stepped forward with his hand up. He wanted to punch Seti; he was acting like such a prick. An invisible force halted his progress and his blood surged in anger. "It wasn't his fault," he said, barely keeping a lid on his temper.

Seti studied him with interest. He swore he smiled even though Jay knew his face never moved. He cocked his head to the side. *Strange ... you attempt to protect your friend's honor and yet you would take his wife and his crown.* Then he looked accusingly at Christian Dubonnetti as if he knew he was the instigator. Maybe he did.

Jay just looked to the heavens at the oversimplification of their situation. "You don't understand," he said, shaking his head. *How could he?*

You will have your turn to speak. Seti turned to Alfonzo. *Please state clearly the law on the sharing of blood outside of the Santalini royal family.*

Alfonzo took a fortifying breath and launched into the sentence they all knew by heart: "There shall be no ingesting of blood for any purpose."

For the punishment shall be?

"Death."

Louder!

"Death!" Alfonzo shouted, so his voice reached the roof of the vast room.

Who here has ingested blood outside of the Santalini family, mmm? Seti began a slow pace of the clearing with his hands behind his back. *Tia, Isla, Lance, maybe ... Drew, Phoebe ... the king?*

When Seti finished his list, he stopped directly in front of Jay, looking him dead in the eye. Jay was mortified that he was the worst offender of all and did it for no other reason than to feed his addiction. And, laughably, he was the only one covered for his sins by a piece of paper that said he was adopted into the Santalini family. He was also married to Ruby. The bloke was good; he had to give him that. He'd made him the schoolboy who got the whole class detention because of his bad behavior.

It was enough; he'd made his point. Seti moved on, and Jay was forced to watch as hands slowly began to go up: Phoebe, Drew and Dante.

No, no, no. Jay wanted to shout at Dante not to admit to it. Jay had forced Tia into a blood bond that Dante was forced to ruin with his own. That wasn't his fault, it was his.

Ah, Lord King, Seti said, when he came to him. *And which female did you bond with illegally?*

For the first time, Jay longed for the rash Dante of old, who would have swung and knocked him clean out with a succinct, "Fuck you!". Instead, Dante looked down and said, "Not a woman."

Louder!

"No woman!"

Please tell the room with whom you share this bond?

"My best friend," Dante said, looking Jay sadly in the eye.

Jay wanted to shout at him not to be so stupid. It wasn't his fault. He was out of control and had forced his hand. He'd always tried so hard to be a good king. Instead, Jay seethed at Seti for knowing full well what he was doing. Nothing he could say would change a thing, because he was a Santalini and Seti had made up his mind. He was showing him quite maliciously that what had saved his life many times over would not save his friend.

The crowd was also getting angry and had started shouting and calling out. It was hard to tell if they were angry at Dante, him or at the newcomers for stirring all this trouble. Either way, the mood was getting ugly.

Without breaking his stride, Seti shouted at Alfonzo, *Write it down!*

Santalini guards came forward and formed a line, pushing the crowd back and attempting to quieten them down.

Jay looked behind him to check on the president, who he'd forgotten was there. His Secret Servicemen looked nervous and had formed a human shield around him.

Let us start to make a royal blood offenders' list, shall we? Seti was saying. *Top of the list is the former king, Dante Dubonnetti. Best friend can't be counted. Ah, yes. Chief wife and queen, Tia Storm.* He began checking off his fingers, mimicking Human behavior purely for the benefit of the room. This was all some elaborate show and Jay hated him all the more for it. *Lacy Rain is Santalini. Isla?*

Darres automatically put a protective arm across her when she went to step forward. She looked guiltily across at Drew. "No, sir, *I* haven't," she said. It was clear what she was omitting to say.

That brings us nicely to the Human/turned Bonaci prince. Who's very coming into being has been determined from a blood bond. You bonded Isla to you, did you not?

Drew stepped forward and Phoebe went with him, ignoring his request to stay back.

This was descending into carnage. Never in all Jay's imaginings of the return, did he think it would be reduced to this.

"I did, sir, and I'm sorry," Drew said, looking across at Phoebe, sadly. "It's not an excuse, but she had just opened my gills. I didn't know what I was doing. I needed to breathe the water to save Phoebe."

Jay remembered Drew's desperation to go and get Phoebe from Murrtaine. This was awful. Everything was getting twisted and taken out of context, so it looked worse than ever.

You also share a blood bond with the Santalini prince: Keenan.

Keenan scowled. "That was a fight."

Several people in the assembly laughed.

Seti looked up to the ceiling for strength. *Write it down,* he said, wearily.

Phoebe stepped forward and put a hand up to Drew to let her speak. "It's my fault." She turned to address the assembly and not Seti, which Jay applauded. No one gave a shit what these guys thought. It was their people that mattered. "I am a Soul Breather, but I'm also a Nix. In case you don't know what that is, I can change. I have teeth like a Santalini and I can alter the makeup of things around me. I chose Drew and I made him into what I wanted him to be." She finished by flashing the universal look of fuck you to Vionne.

Jay registered the ouch on the poor guy's face, but he admired her for it.

So you admit you ingested each other's blood? Seti persisted.

"Frequently!" she said brightly, making Jay smile.

She must have made a good case because Seti changed tack. *He is not your most compatible mate.*

Jay started to see where he was going and realized what a clever interrogator he was. He had neatly steered her in the direction he wanted her to go. He was doing it over and over. Setting up explosive lines of questioning for each of them to fall into and having the worst possible things recorded.

"No, he is not." Phoebe looked down into her hands.

Drew came up and put a comforting arm around her shoulders. Then she looked up accusingly. "It's not my fault, it's not Drew's or Vionne's either. It's another long story, of which you probably know."

Jay wanted to kiss her as he knew what she was doing, too. She hadn't finished, and Jay happily watched while she gave him both barrels. It was good to watch, like a bully getting his comeuppance.

"You made this awful system that has done nothing but encourage corruption and infighting."

Isla stepped forward. "She's right! … Cesaré?" she called.

Jay turned his head as Cesaré put up a hand. He looked awful, scruffy, like a drunk who hadn't slept for a week. The poor guy hadn't had the chance to breathe with Lily yet.

Isla pointed at him while she shouted at Seti. "His own cousin—the so-called king, Malleven, tampered with his ring to win me and the crown. Everyone bloody knows he is the worst possible choice as king for this nation."

And yet, one of the few without an illegal blood bond, Seti said like the smug bastard he was.

"He is dead!" a loud voice said from the top of the staircase.

CHAPTER 32

The whole assembly turned towards the voice.

Ghazi was standing at the top of the staircase, carrying JJ, and Lily was there next to him.

Jay pushed through the crowd to get to his son.

Take me to Lance, Lily projected immediately, without a single question about the circus below.

"I'll take you." Jay was done with the farce anyway. He scooped JJ up and kissed his cheek in one fluid move, nodded a thanks to Ghazi and pulled Lily by the hand through the packed room. However, before he reached the corridor, the crowd parted to reveal Seti staring straight at them. "This is my son, Lily Bonaci and Ghazi, one of the Magi brotherhood," Jay explained.

Ghazi had descended the stairs to join them.

"You say King Malleven is dead?" Seti asked.

"He is, sire." Ghazi bowed his head as he spoke. "He fled to Syria after he killed the prince, Antonio Dubonnetti, and wounded the Siren's mate, Lance McCabe. He was tried and found guilty by my brotherhood for the murder of our high priest, Nasr."

Lily butted in. *Look, I know who you are and how important all this is, but I don't care. I need to go to him,* she projected, imploring Jay to keep walking.

When Seti said nothing further, Jay nodded and walked on briskly with Lily and a guard following closely behind.

VIONNE USED the diversion of Ghazi's arrival to edge closer to Ashaya. After a brief, impatient glance, she returned her gaze to Seti, who now looked troubled as he paced the large circle he'd made. *So we have returned after ten thousand years only to find you without a king, blood abuse rife, a blatant disregard for the Fates and ignoring of the destined mate system. Sirens are choosing mates for themselves and watering down our race to the point of near extinction. If the Orb is not reset, your weather system will destroy your planet even without our intervention,* he said, looking around him angrily.

Vionne guessed it did look bad to an outsider. He stepped forward and spoke up for the first time. *That isn't strictly true. Until recently, Murrtaine was completely cut off. We are a pure race and remain loyal to the old ways.*

Seti tipped his head in deference. *Forgive me. But isn't it true that you, the Borge, have the Florianna and not the Borge Siren through a brother who has no loyalty to anyone other than his mate and his children?* He cast a dark look at Phoebe. *Your own does not choose you, nor will she.* Then Seti looked Vionne dead in the eye. *Your obvious option is to challenge your competitor, making her revert to you on his death and leaving you the strongest contender to be king.* He was right and he'd be a liar if he hadn't thought about it himself. His eyes went to Ashaya, who remained unreadable but was watching him closely.

Tia saved him by stepping forward. "I won't pledge to him … sorry, no offence," she said, glancing at him as she spoke. "But I won't."

Seti went and stood right in front of her. He was a formidable man who completely dwarfed her. *Not even if life on this planet depended on it?*

For once, Tia had the sense to keep her mouth shut, making Vionne inwardly smile. Jay came up behind her and JJ ran and hugged his mother's legs. Seti's eyes dropped to the little boy. *Ah, the fruit of an unholy union.*

Tia put a protective arm around JJ. "He's a miracle."

Vionne could see Jay tense, ready to jump in should she lose that famous temper of hers. Seti seemed to be considering what she'd said. *And yet he wears the bands of the Darkly Begotten.*

He was looking her in the eye, oblivious to the sharp intakes of breath in the crowd.

"It's not his fault that his mum was hidden in this unholy world under your instruction," she said, mimicking his tone. "You can't have it both ways. Chucking us out there and complaining when we make the best of it." Then she threw up her hands in exasperation. "And I ended up with the right prince anyway."

The Darkly Begotten appears for a reason, Seti said, stepping into her again, menacingly. Jay had heard enough this time and put himself between them. Seti seemed unperturbed and stepped away.

Jay would be lying if he said it didn't hurt hearing Tia say she'd found the right prince in the end. She'd chosen a long time ago and he'd messed it up himself, but it still hurt like a bitch.

"The Fates won in the end, didn't they? They always do," Tia said.

Seti didn't answer right away and looked into the crowd in that unnaturally frozen way they all did. Then, as if someone had switched his On switch, he moved again. *I have heard enough. We will leave for New Murrtaine with those able to make the journey.* Seti turned, looked Jay directly in the eye and he knew. In that moment. It didn't matter how many pieces of paper Christian produced about his Atlantean genes, or how many Sirens bonded to him or even sons he fathered. Only Water Breathers would be going on this trip. That meant there would be no outsiders to witness it, like the president, or anyone with watered-down genes. In one fell swoop he'd been disregarded as king.

Dante roused Jay from his musings by pulling him into an embrace. The crowd had already begun to disperse and, of course, he understood what had just happened. "Get Cesaré," he said. "Lily needs to breathe for him so he can make the trip."

There was no reproach in his voice, no condemnation or even a question. Jay wanted to explain so much, but there was no time to say it. In the end he just patted his friend's back and nodded. "Welcome back," he said with a wry smile.

Lily went straight to Lance. It was strange that it should occur to her then that she'd run away from every single situation in her life, but Lance was the only person in her whole miserable existence that she ever ran to. He was her safe haven; trusted and picked by the Fates themselves.

The guard stepped out of the way when he saw her. She threw open the door and stopped dead on the threshold. Their old bed had gone and Lance lay asleep in a hospital bed, surrounded by charts, drips and life-support machines. A human nurse looked up from writing in her notes with a smile.

How is he? Lily projected.

The nurse only looked mildly surprised to be spoken to in her head, proving she was used to weird. "Stable," the nurse said. "The knife ruptured his liver, narrowly missing his spine and lung."

Tears were already falling onto Lily's cheeks. *Will he be alright?*

The nurse did that thing all health professionals did when they didn't want to give a person false hope; she skirted. "He's a strong young man to have got this far." She touched Lily's shoulder as she walked towards the door. "I believe a new team has been called … I'll give you a minute with him. I'll be just outside."

Lily nodded. They'd called the Murrs. They were supposed to have medical practices far superior to Human ones. She only prayed they got there in time.

She sobbed when she picked up one of his hands, now yellow instead of the beautiful honey tan. A cannula was taped flat to the back of his hand. "Oh, Lance, what have you done? You knew it was always going to be you."

Lily remembered then the recurring nightmares he'd had since he was a child. They were memories of his past lives that always ended in bloodshed. He'd been terrified the blood was hers and that it was a premonition that he'd failed in his task, but they'd learned recently that in every lifetime, he always died saving her. This was his nightmare come true and it was her fault. She bent over his arm and cried broken-heartedly.

She should have listened more and not put her misguided gratitude to Malleven above his needs. He was the little boy, taken from his mother, adopted into an Atlantean family, purely to meet her by fate, destined to die for her again and again. She couldn't bear it; she loved him so much. *Never again,* she vowed. If by some miracle he survived, she would never allow him to suffer this again.

She cried herself dry, face down into the sheets. Eventually she twisted to look at the door, remembering what was happening in the Great Hall. This was the last generation. It was a relief to think that at least none of this could happen again. Lance had to live. *Please,* she begged.

The middle finger of his left hand was bare. For a moment she panicked, afraid someone had stolen the divining ring that was the symbol of everything they were to each other. Then she saw it, sitting on the nightstand in its resting pearl white. They'd probably taken it off for his operation. She slipped it back on his finger and watched it swirl to its comforting purple. All the while he was alive it would stay that color and she would guard him like a lioness or tiger, she thought, sadly, tears welling again.

His hair was its usual mess on the pillow, but it seemed darker, without the shine that it always captured from the sun. She moved it gently off his face with her finger. *Hey, do you remember teaching me to surf? How hopeless I was, crashing in on everyone's waves and getting on their nerves. No one ever spent the time teaching me anything like you.*

She sniffed and battled with her tears, only just holding it together. *You named me Tiger and everyone called me it after that. You gave me a new life—a new identity. I loved that name and how it sounded when you said it.*

It was no use. She buried her head in his sheets and sobbed out her broken heart into them. *I'm sorry, so sorry. Please live, Lance ... please live.* Her whole body shook as sobs racked her, rocking the bed.

Lily didn't hear the door open. She only saw the smart shoes and tailored legs as she rested her forehead on the edge of the bed when she'd cried herself out. She pulled up her head and blinked at the light. It was Jay.

He passed her a wad of tissue, which she took and sunk back into the chair. *Thanks.* Then her misery engulfed her again. *I don't understand. What happened?*

"Malleven."

She was already shaking her head. *He was with me.* As she projected it, she was working through who else could have done it on his behalf. Still, she came up with nothing.

"Before he left. An inch or so higher and he would have bled out before anyone found him."

He stabbed him? She remembered the knife Lance grabbed from under the bed and Malleven catching up to her, wiping blood off his hands. It was on the front of his shirt and he'd said he'd had a scuffle with a guard. She'd stupidly believed blindly when Malleven said Lance was creating a distraction. Then again, when they left without him for the airport, that he would meet them there. Everything was so hurried, she hadn't questioned Malleven and had taken him entirely at his word. If only she'd known Lance *was* the distraction.

Jay sat in a chair on the other side. He didn't seem angry; in fact, he looked the most sympathetic she'd ever seen him. Tears threatened to well up in her again. *Why didn't I see it?*

Jay sighed and sat back in his chair. "He was very convincing … When a guy says all the right things and spends time with you, it's hard not to believe him." His eyes bore into her as if he saw right through her. Like he'd seen it all a million times. His appraisal of her made her uncomfortably exposed and she pulled a blanket around herself.

"I wondered whether you would do something for me?"

Lily was completely left-fielded and stared back at him, at what he could possibly want. "Cesaré is here and he's in a bad way. He needs you to replenish the bond."

She sagged and rolled her eyes.

"Will you do it?"

Cesaré had always been a mistake. Lily had breathed for him after a surfing accident and saved his life. She had no idea what she'd done at the time. She shrugged wearily. *I suppose so,* she said getting up. *I'll do it now in case Lance wakes up.*

Jay stood and followed her to the door. He stopped right in front of her and looked down at her curiously. His blue eyes looked angelic. So different from the warm hazel of Lance's or the scary midnight blue of Malleven's.

She found herself having to clear her throat at how close he was standing. His presence was an undeniable force around her.

"I wondered if you'd do the same for me?"

At first she thought she hadn't heard correctly and took a step back. Jay put up his hands defensively. "Don't be scared. It's just that all your sisters have done it in case there's a problem with Dante's claim for the kingdom. Now that Malleven ..." He didn't finish. He just bobbed his head for her to fill in the blanks, not wanting to set her off again.

She hadn't really processed Malleven dying. She hadn't had time. *So that's it—why you're here? You want me to breathe for you like all the others.* She narrowed her eyes at him while she tried to make any kind of sense out of it. *Lance might die and I thought Dante was your best friend.*

Jay shifted his weight and huffed in impatience. His face hardened and she saw the anger he held tightly in the stiffness of his jaw. "He is." He took another breath as if he was trying to remain calm. "If that lot get their way, Lily, it doesn't matter if Lance wakes up or not because it'll be the end of us all. Please trust me. You're the last one."

All she could think of was what a poxy world it was for them all, anyway. The lying, fighting and everyone stabbing each other in the back. In the end she just swore and pulled his head down to her mouth.

However, before she covered his with hers, he held back. "And you'll give me your pledge if they ask?"

She rolled her eyes. *I suppose so, for what it's worth. Now can you hurry up because I've got to do Cesaré as well and I want to get back here.*

A single blast of laugher escaped him and he grinned into the kiss. The wonderful smell of his cologne wrapped itself around her. She blew for no more than a few seconds and pulled apart. It was cold and clinical and felt nothing like Lance. She was surprised she was able to give him anything at all.

It did affect him, however, and she helped him back to his seat. She waited a minute while he rode out the euphoria and then slipped out of the room to find Cesaré. *These fucking princes,* she muttered to herself. Power was all they thought about. Lance was the only one who didn't.

CHAPTER 33

*D*ante held Tia's hand. The onlookers in the crowd behind them became restless. When nothing further appeared to be happening, they began to talk between themselves and then gradually filtered up the steps to the lifts, or, if they were staying, out to the bedroom corridor. He guessed they would want to process, prepare and spend time with their families in case the world ended. However, the necessary representatives from the five families, the president with his Secret Servicemen and the Twenty remained. He gave Tia's hand a squeeze. "Are you OK?"

Her arm snaked around his waist and she leaned into him. "I am now."

He kissed the top of her head, so grateful for having her there, real and in his arms. He couldn't help the spike of worry he felt for the time she'd spent alone with Jay. He knew how she felt about him. Nevertheless, it was Jay he'd always want to look after her and the children if he wasn't there. Still, it hurt that they could never help themselves.

She must have sensed it as she gazed up at him with those luminous-green eyes. "I didn't," she said simply.

He smiled sadly, taking in the beautiful face. He was glad and grateful for her sacrifice, because that's what it was: a conscious sacrifice instead of an easy choice. Jay had joined with all the sisters, except Lily, and looking around and noting that neither were there, it wasn't a huge stretch of the imagination to guess what was happening. He knew his devious friend.

His musings were immediately shelved with the sound of a crash as a scuffle broke out. It was right in front of the Twenty. "Stay there," he ordered. Then he rushed into the fray to see what was happening.

Darres was struggling to get between Vionne and Drew and Keenan and Reeve were trying to pull Drew back by the arms.

"She's never going with you," Drew was shouting, trying to move beyond Darres to get to Vionne.

Darres' granite body remained in the way. *She is my brother's Siren.*

"And yours belonged to Malleven," Drew threw back at him as they went nose to nose.

Dante knew this was more than Darres sticking up for his brother's honor. This was to do with Isla. He put his forehead down to Drew's but there was no friendship in it. There was an internal conversation going on that no one else could hear.

"She helped me, that's all. The blood was an accident," Drew said, proving he was right.

Dante was forced to intervene, even though it was like stepping between two rutting stags. Murrs were not naturally aggressive but Darres was no ordinary Murr and when a bonded female came into it, Murr or Atlantean, they would revert to instinct to protect what was theirs. Darres was always going to be a problem over this. "Listen, Darres. It was necessary for him to breathe the water to save Phoebe, that was all," Dante said.

He used his teeth and drank from her.

It did sound bad when put like that. Dante felt the power radiating from the male. He could level everyone in the room if he wanted to. "An involuntary action, I swear. I was there." Dante looked behind him to Vionne, who seemed much calmer. "Isn't the real issue to do with her?"

Vionne looked sideways, not to Phoebe but to Ashaya. The one who'd spent a whole lot of time with them—him particularly. Then one of his hunches began to take root and grow. It was an idea that the more he thought about it, the more he believed could save them all.

He turned and looked for Phoebe who was behind the wall of testosterone holding Drew. "Let him go," Dante said. Phoebe quickly pushed between him and Keenan and held Drew's hand. It left no doubt in his mind who she would choose in a test. "You have bonded with him?"

She frantically nodded back, as if she sensed he was making up his mind about something.

"But you haven't with her?" he said to Drew, who shook his head.

"Only because we haven't had the chance to try it yet," Drew said.

Dante turned back to Vionne. "And you've bonded with Phoebe, but she refuses to return it?"

Vionne reluctantly nodded, knowing full well where he was going. *That is correct.*

Dante flicked his gaze to Ashaya and, as he suspected, it was Vionne she had her eyes on the whole time.

He returned his attention to Vionne. "You know his ring was purple before the explosion."

Vionne was already shaking his head, getting angry at the

direction Dante was taking. "Only because the Scythians had given him my blood. I am her true mate."

"But just as in the case of your brother, Darres, and Isla, true mates don't necessarily gain the love of their Siren. If that were true, she would have remained with Malleven and we would have lived a very different day today."

It blew Dante's mind for a moment when he thought about it. Malleven would have held the kingdom irrefutably then. But then he remembered that Malleven had brought about his own downfall with his ego and his determination to circumvent the Fates. He pointed at Phoebe and Drew. "Look at them … take a long, hard look. If it were down to a case of a simple water test, she would let you drown."

Vionne's face hardened. *But it is not down to a water test. I am a Murr, pureblooded and have no need of such tests. She is mine by right. I am lord advocate and I swore to my father that I would secure my Siren for the security of my people.*

And there it was: the real reason Vionne was being so pig-headed over this. It had evaded him until then. Vionne didn't really love Phoebe; not like Drew did. He probably hadn't even faced the fact himself.

He didn't call him out on it. Instead, he turned to Seti who was standing with the other visitors in silent conversation. "Can I ask that the matter of Phoebe's mate be deferred until after your verdict? It's causing a lot of trouble and might be academic anyway?"

The male Atlasian looked him intently in the eye. They both knew he was right. Seti had no love for the people he found here. He'd already made up his mind. His shrewd look showed he knew he couldn't appear biased and he inclined his head, no doubt logging the crafty maneuver he'd just pulled by heading off a fight. *Until after,* he said, so they could all hear.

They all seemed relieved. Vionne looked more troubled at

what the hell he was playing at. Dante didn't want to admit that Drew didn't stand a chance against the leader of the Murrs, even with his Scythian training and Phoebe's bestowed abilities. Instead, he hoped the Five Moons would interject through the Orb and she would make a decision the visitors would have to accept.

He let out a slow, ragged breath at the reprieve he'd just secured. No blood would be spilt today, at least. Surely they all understood there would be no kingdom if one of the Sirens died of a broken heart.

Tia hugged into his arm and he kept his thoughts to himself, satisfied with the small nod of respect Seti gave him.

The president paused in front of him, as Delissi ushered him to the lift and his waiting helicopter. He looked aged by ten years since he'd last seen him. The weight of office and what he'd witnessed today was taking a visible toll. He knew the feeling. He didn't ask anything or engage him in conversation in anyway. He just held out his hand for him to shake. "Win this thing for all of us," the president said, holding his gaze and his hand a moment longer than was necessary.

"I'll do all in my power," Dante said, emotion suddenly high in his throat.

Delissi came next. Usually business-like and completely undemonstrative of any relationship between them, he pulled him into his body and spoke next to his ear. "I will be at Filfla, waiting. May the Moons be with you, my son."

Delissi moved away without looking at him and Dante was forced to watch him, stunned at the first open acknowledgement of him.

Come! Seti announced loudly. *We leave for New Murrtaine.*

To Dante, the Atlasian marine craft they travelled in was high-tech even by Murr standards. It was like nothing they'd ever seen. He guessed it had come with them from space. Of course the Murrs were all over it, fascinated by any technical advances, comparing them to their own.

It was barely visible until you got up close. It wasn't transparent like Murr craft, it simply wasn't there—like a hologram you could only see at a certain angle and then it was gone. When seen, it was a deep blue, perfectly smooth, rocket on its side, that seemed to have no solid form when you touched it. There were no windows, no door or blemish on the outside in any way. Just a cylinder that went to a point that would cut through the water efficiently and no doubt be undetectable to human sonar.

They entered one by one through the wall that was there one minute and gone the next, to an interior that was filled with water—as Dante had expected. It was fairly dark. The walls and furniture of small tables and seats were all in the same indigo as the craft.

The business end was at the point. Dante slowly made his way there, examining the lights embedded in the walls and the control panels that came up in the air at will, when one of the Twenty moved it with their hands like the conductor of an orchestra. It was utterly fascinating.

All the Water Breathers making the journey, fitted into the craft easily, plus their Twenty and his and Jay's children, Xavier and JJ.

Dante thought then of his last awkward embrace with Jay. As always, he was up to something. He wished he wasn't so close-mouthed. If they'd had the time, he was sure he could have got it out of him. Jay would have to go by air to meet them on Filfla. He would hate it, but most of the land-dwelling families and the rest of the children would wait it out with him. He guessed Xavier and JJ were chosen to come along as the eldest males.

He sat down in one of the seats with Tia. She hugged into

him to rest while the boys explored a little way off. One of the Twenty began to show them a holographic chart of their journey from space. They were mesmerized by it—particularly JJ. Xavier's head came up and he looked over and spotted them alone. He smiled at the guy teaching them and wandered towards them.

Everything OK? Dante projected to his son, curious at what had pulled him away from the demonstration.

Yes, Xavier said with a shrug. *I wanted to give you a message from Jay ... Sorry, he told me to tell you when we escaped the castle, but it's the first chance I've had to speak to you alone.*

Dante smiled sadly. It had been so hard on them all. *What is it?* he said, touching the side of his son's face.

He looked thoughtful, as if he wanted to make sure he got it exactly right. *He said to tell you, we're back to back.* Xavier looked mildly puzzled, as if he had no idea what it meant. *Yeah, back to back. That was it.* Then he waited for Dante, as if he would explain.

Dante could only smile sadly and thank his son as a wave of nostalgia hit him hard. Xavier moved off back to his brother, puzzled but satisfied that he'd been able to deliver the message.

What is it? Tia asked, intrigued.

Dante forced himself out of the memories that threatened to engulf him. The pact they'd made since they were just two small boys fighting back to back against the village children, bent on singling out Jay for being an outsider. Jay was reminding him of it. It was a plea to remember they were together against the world. Instead of lifting him, it filled him with sadness. He couldn't help wondering if it was too late, too long ago, or if all this was just too big for two small boys to sort out, whether they stuck together or not.

Nothing, was all he said.

Dante kissed the top of Tia's head. The craft moved off

effortlessly, until he forgot they were moving. It wasn't a bad journey. Everyone seemed happy enough, although a weird kind of anticipation crackled between them at what was going to happen when they got there.

As much as he tried to rest, Jay still troubled him. *Were they together? Were they back to back?* Jay's signature was all over the bonds he had with the sisters. Cesaré came and sat opposite him, reading his disquiet immediately. He followed his line of vision. Lily was a little way off, staring into the distance. A wave of the hand revealed an area of transparency to view the outside whizzing past at frightening speed. She'd been pulled away from Lance against her will, with the promise that the Murrs would put him in their healing chamber and he would be well enough to meet her at Filfla. *You should speak with her,* Cesaré said.

Dante nodded, knowing instantly what he was driving at. *You feel him?*

Cesaré nodded, confirming his suspicions. He would feel Jay on the bond as surely as he did with the others. He gave Tia's hand a squeeze to indicate he needed to get up and made his way to the seat next to Lily. The water molecules around him were unseen and behaved like air, so he could easily forget he was submerged in water.

Hey, he projected, sitting down next to her. *How you doing?*

When Lily looked at him, her eyes were desolate. She was the one he knew the least out of all the sisters and perhaps had the hardest upbringing of them all. He'd never blamed her for her loyalty to Malleven. Being the only one had showed an inner strength and goodness he admired.

Why didn't I see it? she said, searching his eyes. *Everyone else could, but not me. I wouldn't listen.*

He didn't have the relationship with her to hug her, but he did pick up her hand. *Because he wanted you to,* he said, simply. *Never forget that, Lily. He based his whole campaign for the kingdom on your trust in him and worked tirelessly at it.* The bastard had homed in on her vulnerability right from the start.

However, his soft words didn't help and she pulled her hand out of his and cried into it. He didn't think he'd ever seen her break and cry; she was such a tough cookie. It was no good, he had to pull her to him. She didn't fight him and he felt the sobs shake her whole body.

I put him before Lance. He could have died and he'll never forgive me.

He will, he said, kissing the tight curls of her hair. It was heartbreaking to see her come apart like this. *You couldn't do anything else. He would have simply got rid of Lance earlier. You probably kept him alive.* She seemed to listen to that.

Dante rocked her and stroked her hair. Tia was watching, sleepily, from their seat. She was curious, but there was no judgement in her eyes. *There is something I need to ask you, Lily?*

She sat up uneasily and dragged the back of her hand across her eyes. A pointless act in the water. *What is it?*

Jay ... when you were back at the castle, did Jay ask you to breathe for him?

Lily shifted awkwardly, as if she was only just realizing the implications of the question and not sure how to answer.

It's OK, Dante said, watching her intently. *I just need to know.*

She nodded.

And did you?

She nodded again, a little more anxiously this time. *He said it was the only way to save the kingdom.*

Dante nodded absently as he looked out at the seascape flying past. Then, for the first time in his life, he prayed to the Five Moons that he could still trust him.

CHAPTER 34

The dome protecting New Murrtaine astounded Dante every bit as much as the original, except this one was on a much larger, grander scale.

The dome was a permeable bubble that regulated temperature, shielded its inhabitants from predators—Human or animal—and made the city it covered invisible and undetectable to the outside world.

They passed through slowly. Once inside, it was a place of wonder. The strange and amazing architecture was in the hues of green and blue that he remembered, with rounded edges and domes that aided the undetectability of the place. Gardens had been planted with colored sea plants he never knew existed. Kelps and treelike seaweeds lined the streets and led to a huge citadel in the middle. It was a remarkable feat of engineering to be accomplished at all, let alone in just a few weeks.

It is almost complete, Vionne said, coming up next to him as the ship softly docked next to the palace. *Just a few final touches. My people move back tomorrow—if all goes well,* he added, dryly.

Dante raised his eyebrows and smiled weakly at the stark reminder. All this could have been for nothing. They made their way with the queue of people, all eager to get off at once, like holidaymakers. The journey had certainly taken no longer than a plane. Shorter, if you cut out the red tape.

I wanted to thank you, Vionne said, as he stepped out to tread water behind him on the dock.

Dante turned to face him, a little surprised.

For not holding my neutrality with Malleven's reign against me during all this. And for stopping the combat.

"Don't mention it." Dante grinned. It proved he was right. He wanted to tease him and act surprised that he no longer wanted to tear the boy apart. Instead, he moved over to make more room for people alighting the ship. *There is no need to thank me,* he projected. *You were a good and loyal friend and a valuable spy.*

Vionne smiled his awkward smile that he was sure he'd been working on.

With regards to Drew, I got the feeling that your heart wasn't in it. He flicked his eyes to Ashaya, in her very becoming uniform, in conversation nearby. *You should tell her how you feel.*

For a Murr, Vionne moved a lot and he certainly gave away how uncomfortable he felt at that. Murrs instinctively distrusted Atlanteans, and humans even more so, and yet he was becoming more like them every day. It was a constant source of amusement to Dante. *Think about it. You might not have much time.*

Seti signaled for them all to follow him towards the grand palace and they became quiet as they took in its splendor. The architectural design wasn't dissimilar to old Murrtaine, with its soft edges and many domes. Inside the familiar atrium were burrowlike tunnels that led off in various directions and hidden technology that revealed itself with a wave of a hand. The differences seemed small, mainly aesthetic; such as the statues, not so much classical as huge installations that looked transported from a future time.

Dante could sense the excitement building in Tia and grinned to himself. He glanced over his shoulder to check where she was. She was walking with JJ in her arms and Xavier right beside her, wide-eyed with wonder. He was waiting for her to do it.

Hey, Vionne. Have you had one of those swirly clubs built yet with the super cool gas pipes in it?

And there it was.

Seti looked across at Tia with obvious distaste.

Vionne tried to hide his smile and replied innocently, *Of course.*

Yes! I'm so getting breathfaced.

Dante faced front and tried not to laugh. Tia's natural response to any awkward situation was to act out. Everyone knew. Except, of course, the Twenty, who looked puzzled.

VIONNE WENT ALONG with everyone else to the conical-shaped room that held the Orb. He knew it because it was identical to the one they'd built for her in the old city. They were wasting no time by going to their rooms. It didn't bode well if they thought there was no point.

As Vionne went to go in, a hand roughly pulled him back. *Ashaya.* She nodded at the last of the people filtering in and looked nervously into his eyes. He was inquisitive as to what she would say. It was rash behavior for a pureblood.

They were now alone so he allowed himself to smile. *There are many sides to you I never knew,* he projected. He tried to keep the disappointment out of his mental aura.

I couldn't tell you, otherwise I would have failed in my task.

It explained a lot, but didn't make him feel any better. It felt like a betrayal from the one person he thought he could trust. *Was any of it real? Or was it to gain insider information?*

An Atlantean or a human would have balked with indignation, but not her. She paused in that unnatural, still way and processed the barb in the comment. He felt a pang of shame.

It is true, I was here to observe, but with you I became ...

She paused to find the words, but he was losing patience. He was conscious of everyone waiting for them in the room behind him and was angry and hurt. *What is this, Ashaya? What are we doing here?* he said, gesturing his arm between them, knowing she took what he said so literally.

I ...

She didn't seem able to say anything in her defense, so he went to turn.

I wanted to know ...

He paused and waited for her to continue, without looking at her. He knew he shouldn't feed the small glimmer that lit in his chest.

I wanted to know, if I was here as an ordinary Murr, whether you would have given up your Siren—

He turned back to face her squarely in surprise.

For me? she continued.

Vionne was speechless for a moment. It was the perfect question that got to the absolute crux of the matter. In all this, he'd focused on her withholding the truth, when the reality of it was obvious. His vow to his father, his one-sided bond with Phoebe; there had never once been an offer made to her because of one very real reason. That he'd never once in his life ever been able to be him.

He was wildly attracted to Ashaya. She was beautiful, accomplished and intelligent and he wanted desperately to tell her what was in his heart, but it petered out before it formed a sentence. She deserved the truth: that, in reality, he just didn't know how. His vow to his father was everything about who he was and there would never be an opportunity to really know whether it was stronger than the possibility of his own happiness. Instead, he answered weakly with: *Life seldom gives us what we want.* He turned and went to continue walking.

In an ideal world, all else aside, she threw after him, not willing to give up.

He stopped in his tracks, reminded of her tenacity. Everything she said made him love her all the more for it. *Love.* It was the first time the word had ever come to him in connection with a woman. In an ideal world he did know the answer. *In a heartbeat,* he said.

Vionne! his brother, Dax called, dragging him from his thoughts.

Without giving her another look, Vionne walked into the room under a blanket of self-loathing. The door shut behind them and a female voice he recognized welcomed them.

"Please wait while I generate power," she said.

Everyone moved back against the walls of the circular room, looking around them for where the voice came from.

He was acutely aware of Ashaya's presence moving behind the assembled people, to stand with the rest of the Twenty on the other side of the room. He wished he'd chosen somewhere better to stand because they were directly opposite each other. The conversation troubled him, knowing he'd let her down with so little to offer.

Dante's knowing eyes watched him with a hint of a smile.

DREW HELD Phoebe's hand the whole time. The place reminded him of the day he was meant to die and he refused let go of her.

He watched the familiar white pedestal rise in the center of the room and the beautiful hologram of the woman appear. She was exactly the same as he remembered her. *The Orb.*

"Welcome, Atlanteans, Murrs and delegates from Atlas, to this long-awaited, auspicious occasion. It has been a long time since we have congregated together."

Just like before, she totally blew Drew's mind as he tried to work out exactly what she was; a supercomputer or an entity of her own? He just couldn't decide, exactly.

"You have been brought here for the final judgement of your time on this planet. Prophecy has been fulfilled and you will find out your fate. The delegation is simply here as your jurors. I am the judge that will pass sentence." The hologram slowly rotated so they could all see her. It really felt like she was looking them each in the eye.

Drew's hand tightened around Phoebe's when she stopped and looked directly at him.

"You survived and you did well, new son of Bonaci," she said and smiled. "You have served the race in the short time you've been among us."

He didn't know what to say, just bowed his head slightly.

She turned to Phoebe. "The Nix, the dark one, who turns all things from the light. Do you choose the Bonaci prince over the Borge?"

Phoebe nodded immediately. *I do!* she projected, loudly.

Drew realized he was already crushing her hand, so he released his hold and gave it a gentler squeeze.

The Orb rotated again to face Vionne. Then again to Seti. "Have it noted that the Bonaci Siren has chosen."

Seti bowed his head and flashed his eyes to Axyl, who bowed back. He was doing the whole mental record thing.

Then something began to happen to the pedestal below the Orb's hologram. It rose and widened out into a high, circular table with indentations in the top. He couldn't make out exactly what they were from his vantage point.

"Come closer with your mate," the Orb said, beckoning him with a holographic hand. "As I call you, each Siren and their mate will approach and place their hand on the tabernacle to bind their contract to me, with Atlas and to the sacred Earth that is their home," she said, addressing them all.

Drew looked at Phoebe, who nervously smiled back at him, and, together, hands gripped, they went towards the Orb. They stopped in front of it and he could see it was divided into five sections. Each had a depression in the shape of a left hand and one of a right. The one closest to them had a depiction of the sun and the moon above it.

"Light and darkness. Fits Phoebe Ray, does it not?" the Orb said, her hologram smiling kindly. "Phoebe, place your left hand and, Drew, place your right, please."

They looked at each other again for reassurance and did as she asked. It felt surprisingly warm and soft, like skin, but he didn't look at it. His eyes remained on Phoebe the whole time. He should have been scared or anxious, but it felt like the happiest day of his life. Like a marriage, or something. He was together and accepted by the woman he loved. He knew this ceremony, or whatever it was, was permanent and binding, and no one—not even the big Murr—would be able to pull them apart.

A warm buzz went through him, starting at the top of his head and going down to his feet.

"From this moment, all other bonds cease." The table compressed slightly, went hard to the touch and then black. Then, before he could rejoice, there was a, "However, it cannot be ignored that blood corruption exists with the Prince, Keenan Santalini and the Siren, Isla Snow—all the more serious because of their connection to the former king."

Drew knew exactly what she was referring to: Keenan, when they'd got into a fight, and Isla when she'd mind walked and breathed with him. *Shit.* He'd hoped it had been overlooked because of his newness to the race.

CHAPTER 35

Those two things struck Dante, as he was sure it did every person in the room. Blood corruption still counted and all other bonds died. For him that meant Jay. Always Jay.

It meant that they'd been chasing their tails for nothing. A king was not determined by the bonds that he made. It should have made him feel better after Jay managing to get one more Siren than him, but it didn't, because that only left blood and Jay was immune to prosecution for that.

He caught Tia's eye and she looked as baffled as he was.

"Lacy Rain and Keenan Santalini!" the Orb called out.

Drew and Phoebe kissed, clearly elated, like a newly married couple and moved back out of the way. Keenan and Lacy took their place. The pedestal rotated a few degrees and a fresh pair of handprints was in front of them. Lacy put in her left and Keenan his right, just as Drew and Phoebe had done before them.

"As would be expected, the Santalini priestess of water and rain is with her destined mate and bound by breath and blood." Their table compressed and their section went black.

"Blood bond is noted between Keenan Santalini and the Bonaci Prince, Drew Stone, but can be voided under the Santalini exemption contract. Further breath bonds between the Siren, Lacy Rain with the former king, Dante Dubonnetti and Jay Gardiner are also voided and no longer need replenishment."

Dante watched, fascinated, as the weird ring of light buzzed in a hoop around their bodies, from head to feet, making him wonder what it was actually doing to them. It could only be some sort of scan that changed their DNA to cancel all other bonds.

He thought about that for a moment. The very thing that had enslaved him, Tia and Jay for years would be eradicated in seconds. The whole bunch of them had got themselves in a mess, and the Orb, with a sweep of her sensors, could take it all away. It made him wonder why they'd been left to do it in the first place, only to be pulled apart like naughty little school kids, summoned to the office by the principal who had to sort it all out.

Keenan stooped and picked Lacy up, kissing her. Then he put her down and led her back to the edge of the room.

Lily jumped when her name was called. "And Cesaré Florianna," the Orb said. With Lance not there, Lily wasn't expecting to be called.

A little stunned, she allowed Cesaré to pick up her hand and lead her to the pedestal. He looked much better after she'd renewed her bond with him. His handsome, sad smile apologized for being a poor substitute for the man he knew she'd rather stood there. It made her feel guilty.

"Mutual bond accepted by First Breath and high standing of the Florianna house," the Orb was saying. She almost snatched her hand out of Cesaré's, but she stopped at the Orb's, "However … he is not your fated mate."

Lily waited, heart pounding, and shook her head in case it was a question that required an answer. She no longer felt any animosity towards Cesaré. He was the one other person duped as much as she was by Malleven. *I was married to another Florianna prince, the former king, but he's now dead,* she explained.

"He was not your destined mate either, was he?" the Orb stated.

It wasn't a question, it sounded more like an accusation. She was starting to feel angry. *No,* was all she said, balling her fist on the table and clenching her jaw. *He's been fighting for his life.*

"Please state for the record who he is."

Lily couldn't believe she was doing all this; she should be there with him, by his bedside, praying for him to get better.

Cesaré gave her hand a squeeze. *Be patient. It's OK,* he projected, holding her in his intense blue gaze.

She stayed there, grounding herself in him. After taking a moment, she turned back to the hologram. *His name is Lance McCabe. He has the purple ring. He is an incarnate and a human,* she projected loudly.

"The Siren is accepted as the Florianna priestess for the wind," the Orb said, immediately. The handprint she was leaning on compressed and that section of the table went black. It happened so fast Lily couldn't process what it meant.

"There is blood corruption with the human, Lance McCabe," the Orb said.

He is born from the wind priestess, but he can't be here, Lily gabbled anxiously, but her words were ignored. It felt like Lance had been overlooked. She wanted it clarified who the

Orb thought she was actually with, but it was as though she'd already moved on.

The weird light went right through her in a red hoop in a couple of seconds.

Don't worry. It's OK, Cesaré said, pulling her away from the podium.

DANTE'S HEART felt pierced through again when the Orb said, "A further breath bond with Jay Gardiner has been voided." He wasn't as relieved as he should have been. It only compounded his disappointment that Jay had achieved all five Sirens in such a short period of time. In all honesty, he had lost all idea of where that left him as king if other bonds were null and void.

He hoped Lily took hope from the fact that the Orb had not voided her bond with Lance. It seemed that she'd been allowed to keep two, probably because Lance was Human, and he was expected to die long before her. It was clever, really. This way, she would always be the Florianna Siren.

When the Orb called, "Isla Snow and Darres Borge," Dante knew he and Tia were deliberately being left till last. It made him uneasy. It proved they were the most complicated, or the most damned.

Darres led Isla over. They looked the perfect couple and Dante was pleased for her. Darres' ring was now purple on the death of Malleven. Fate had realigned itself, making him her most compatible mate. The tough girl, who'd made her way into his affections with a strong determination, was getting what she'd always wanted. She was his bias; he couldn't help it.

He glowed like a proud parent as they placed their hands on the round pedestal and smiled into each other's eyes like there was no one else in the room.

"The Borge has its priestess of ice," the Orb said simply. "Blood corruption with the previously noted Drew Stone was not reciprocated and can be struck from Isla's record. She is bonded to the former king, Dante Dubonnetti, and Jay Gardiner and has two children with Darres Borge."

The details were not important. Isla and Darres were accepted without issue and Dante was glad.

However, now it was his turn. "Please come forward, Tia Storm and former king, Dante Dubonnetti." Holding Tia's hand in his, Dante stepped forward.

"The priestess of electricity and power is destined mate to Dante Dubonnetti, bonded, with a legacy of four children and one to Jay Gardiner: Human Prince of Dubonnetti, Santalini and Bonaci, with whom there is a bond in both breath and blood."

They were always going to sound the messiest of all the couples. It wasn't so bad.

The Orb rotated above her pedestal to take in the whole assembly. "While all accept the extenuating circumstances that brought these bonds about, blood corruption exists with all parties. Bearing in mind that Jay Gardiner cannot be tried as part of the Santalini royal family, both here stand accused."

It was damning. Dante looked down into Tia's eyes and projected, *Whatever happens, I love you.*

Tia smiled so beautifully back that it stopped his heart, just like the very first time he saw her DJing in that club in the West End. Neither of them argued. They were guilty as charged. It rankled a little that the worst offender was Jay and he was immune, but part of him laughed, as Jay would have done, with some smart-assed apology, had he been there.

"Place your hands down, please," the Orb said.

Dante obeyed mechanically, still working on the ramifications of everything he'd heard. The table compressed and went black before he could register the enormity of what had just happened. All other bonds were cancelled and he was joined and accepted permanently as Tia's mate. He should have shouted for joy from the rooftops. Instead, he faced the Orb. *Can I ask for the room to speak to you privately, Your Excellency?*

The Orb's hologram appeared to freeze, no doubt running the question through her memory banks, or whatever, to see if she could allow it. "The Twenty must stay," she said, eventually. Then she turned to those assembled and boomed, "Please clear the room."

It's OK, he said to Tia, when she didn't want to let go of his hand. She searched his eyes to work out if she could trust him, then reluctantly walked out with the others.

At last, the door was closed and the Orb faced him once again. Dante was aware of the Twenty, off to the side. *I just wanted to ask a personal question.*

"Go ahead," the Orb said.

If you know of the blood corruption in all of us, then you know of the genetic makeup of us too. He waited for the Orb to catch up with what he was saying.

She eventually nodded.

Can you tell me if Jay's blood is Human or Atlantean, as my stepfather would have us believe?

The Orb did the weird pausing thing again while it ran over what he'd said. It was a very machine-like thing to do, but then she surprised him. "You didn't need to clear the room for that. Surely it would benefit you greatly for all to know the outcome?"

Not him. Despite his misgivings with what Jay had been up to and god knew he was a law unto himself, but he'd been born into a life with a mother who sold herself for money. There had always been a question mark over his paternity. It made sense that he'd been brought into the Dubonnetti household as a child because Christian believed he was his son. *I want to know if we're blood. There is no need for anyone else to know.*

"If it is positive, he will not be your brother," the Orb reminded him. They would still have a different father and mother, even if Christian was telling the truth.

Jay has always been my brother, long before all this.

The Orb went quiet and her lights flickered all the way up the conical shell to the ceiling. He came to think it was her brain working. "Negative," she said, eventually. "There are no Atlantean markers in the blood ingested by you or your Siren from Jay Gardiner."

Dante was genuinely surprised. He wasn't sure what he expected but hearing it like that was still a shock. The door opened and the Orb called the others. He quickly projected, *Don't say anything ... please?*

"Will you?" she countered, as the people filtered back in the room.

He shook his head, *No*. There was no point. It was something only he needed to know. Jay was tied permanently to the race, adopted by Dubonnetti, Santalini and the Bonaci families. Then his mind tumbled to JJ, who, by his father, was all of the above, but Borge because of the other half of Tia and Florianna because of his adoption by Malleven. The Darkly Begotten prophecy was realized right there: offspring of all five families. *What of Jay's son?* He was genuinely frightened for the little guy, who he saw as one of his own. If he knew JJ was Darkly Begotten, then so did she. *What will happen to him?* Jay being Human only proved him more so where the Atlasians were concerned.

Dante turned his head to the Twenty, who remained unmoving and unemotional as ever. They had been the same throughout. He wanted to shake them to see some humanity in this whole sorry mess. *He's just a little boy,* he found himself saying directly to them.

Tia's arm snaked around his waist and grounded him when he would have lost his temper, while the Orb grew in size to address them all.

"The Twenty have returned to no organized kingdom. There has been misappropriation of wealth and power ... blood corruption. Unnatural bonds—the Darkly Begotten is living proof of that. When The Way is not followed, ideals become homogenized and debauched. We are left with nothing as intended. Know this: the child himself is not the Darkly Begotten but a symbol of it—a product. One that will remain a problem even if the world survives."

She turned to address the Twenty directly. "I leave you to think on that with your deliberations. Think deeply, not just what has been lost, but on what has been gained, for there may be more than you think."

It seemed an odd thing to say after all the wrongs she'd just listed. It seemed pretty bleak. Dante shivered and pulled Tia into his body. The cold was seeping in.

The Orb turned to them again. "You will return to Filfla. The Twenty will deliver a verdict in twenty-four hours. These are difficult times and I wish you all the blessings of the Five Moons." Then the hologram flickered and disappeared.

Dante wasted no time, picked up Tia's hand and walked quickly out of the room.

What is it? she projected, swimming next to him.

Nothing ... I just need to speak to Jay.

It silenced her. Except he felt her anxiety through the bond, the one only he and she shared.

CHAPTER 36

*J*ay couldn't relax and readied himself for the worst. A message had been sent that they were on their way back and, more worryingly still, the constant ache for Tia in the center of his chest had gone, meaning just one thing: bonds had been severed. And not just theirs. The new ones he'd managed to get with the others had disappeared too. Dante would have felt it. If not right away, then when Tia breathed with him, as surely as if she'd whispered in his ear. There would be trouble. There always was when it came to the three of them.

His old friends, Tia's Protectors, Cash and Sean could sense it in him. They were quiet and restless, walking the room in front of the window. Sean had been tetchy when Sarah and Ronnie, his wife and child, had arrived and were quickly shown to their rooms, out of the way. They wanted no distraction from the tension and were on high alert for the slightest news.

Looking around him, no one else was faring any better. Keenan's close-knit boys, the rest of the guards, Alfonzo and

Sebastian, were subdued, drinking more than usual, fidgeting and tapping their feet. Lance had been declared fit enough to travel and would touch down on the helipad in a few hours. All the world's most important people would be here when Dante, Tia and the others got back.

The three of them had gone through so much, but this was the most nervous he'd ever felt about their friendship. They had shared some difficult times along the way, but always managed to stay friends because of their underlying love and respect for each other—even if it was strained. However, something else was in the air today. With his bid for the kingdom, if Dante didn't fully understand his motive in what he'd been trying to do, he didn't have a clue what would happen. There were simply too many variables out of his control and he hated that.

At last, the center of the fountain began to bubble as if it was boiling over and people began to pour into the room. They all appeared to be there, except for the Twenty.

We've got twenty-four hours, Keenan projected as he walked past, dripping, with Lacy.

Jay nodded. They were all somber and no one seemed in the mood for talking. His heart thudded when his eyes inevitably found Tia and Dante. They expelled their lungs, stepped over the wall of the fountain and helped Xavier and JJ do the same. Then they took towels being distributed by an army of servants and wrapped them tightly around them.

Jay took a ragged breath and walked over.

He kissed his son and ruffled Xavier's hair—all the while his eyes remained on Tia, who seemed anxious. Dante seemed hard and determined and went to walk past him. "What happened?" Jay said, barring him with his arm. *Be in my study in one hour,* Dante projected.

It was exactly the time it took for his voice to come back

after breathing underwater. That wasn't a good sign. It meant he needed to be at one hundred percent when he faced him. "You OK?" he said, stepping in front of Tia, who went to follow him. She just stared up at him as if she was lost for words.

He'd be lying if he said it didn't hurt after all the time they'd spent together over the last weeks. But he kind of understood. Dante had almost died, she hadn't seen him and then all this. He nodded and stepped out of the way to let her go. She paused before she walked off. *It turned to shit, Jay. Almost everyone, including the two of us, has been accused of illegal blood corruption.* And, without any more explanation, she caught up with Dante. The words "what about me?" died on his lips.

His eyes followed her. She rounded the stairs and disappeared into the tunnels. Then it came to him. He was Santalini. It would have been funny under different circumstances. He, the one who had flouted the blood rule more than anyone, was the one who was immune.

VIONNE FLOPPED down onto the fountain wall to rest his legs with his four brothers. He felt weary with so much swirling around in his head, always ending up with Ashaya, but he didn't have the luxury to wallow. New Murrtaine was completed and he needed to prepare his people to leave for their new home, praying that they, at least, would come out of the Twenty's decision positively.

It really was a momentous occasion after an enormous undertaking. One his father would have been proud of. And yet it felt hollow, like he'd failed in his vow to him today. Darres held the Siren for the Borge.

There was no use fighting Drew Stone for Phoebe,

because he had already won. The Orb had accepted him. Phoebe loved him. Isla was living proof that it was possible. She had chosen Darres, despite being most compatible with another. The Fates obviously weren't always right. It would be futile to force the issue.

The source of his exhaustion forced herself into his conscious mind, as she always did. There was no use fighting what everyone else had seen. He had fallen in love with Ashaya, probably from their first meeting. Which was even more futile than Phoebe, because she was part of the Twenty, responsible for condemning the Earth. And even if by some miracle they got some sort of reprieve, she would get on their spaceship and he would never see her again.

Everything was hopeless in the end.

Keefa and Dannon came running up to their parents, Isla and Darres, to greet them. Envy stirred in his chest, but he didn't begrudge them their happiness. It was warming to see. They'd both been robbed of their own childhoods in a warm, loving family. Together they had thawed each other's hearts and created a close-knit family of their own. He could never deny them that. If this was the result of the Darkly Begotten generation, then he was proud to be counted among them.

Darres looked at him curiously. Then read him with his uncannily accurate intuition. *I have the Borge Siren, but I have no interest in the Lord Advocacy of Murrtaine.*

Vionne nodded a thanks. He took it in the spirit it was given: a gift. However, Darres had no way of knowing he would forgo it in a heartbeat for what he had. Then he surprised him by flashing an image to his mind of Ashaya in her full high priestess regalia. *Even he'd known*, before he did.

Be honest with her, Darres said, with a very Human-like shrug. *What do you have to lose?* Then his eyes rested on the awkward looking Murr boy, Loki, hovering nearby, unsure of whether to approach or stay back. He'd obviously been playing with Darres' boys.

Darres nodded back at him with amusement. *You're not just the father to our people ... if only you would allow them into your heart.*

The possibility of already being a father to Loki or anyone else deeply shocked him, it had never occurred to him before. Vionne continued to sit with his brothers who, one by one, rose and touched him on the shoulder before they left for the comfort of their rooms. He continued to sit a while with no real place to go. Loki came and quietly sat with him.

DREW DIDN'T GO inside the tunnel to the fountain right away. Instead, he pulled Phoebe to swim far enough away that they were hidden from view by some rocks. Then he pulled her into his arms. It was the first chance he'd had to get her on her own in the water.

The sea was rough on the surface, but a gentle sway where they were. Unseasonal winds were battering the whole Maltese Islands. There was no telling whether the Twenty would order the destruction of the planet or how it would work. It didn't take special senses as an Atlantean to work out that they hadn't come off well as a nation today. This could be the only time they had.

He kissed her slowly, pushing her up against the rock that made up the base of the islet. *You want to complete the bond?* she projected, reading him perfectly.

He pulled out of the kiss and nodded. There were no serpent-like slits to her eyes. She was completely at ease as he nodded. *And I wanted to thank you properly for choosing me.*

Phoebe put her head on an angle, as if she was surprised.

There is nothing to worry about anymore, Drew. Didn't you hear her? All former bonds are gone. It's just us now.

Drew knew Phoebe was right, but he guessed he still couldn't believe she'd chosen him over the Murr, built like a god with the power of a king.

Phoebe showed him the turquoise ring that would be purple if they were destined mates. *Why do you need it; to prove to the world?* Her eyes looked sad.

Drew shook his head. No, he didn't. Phoebe had spent a lot of time with Vionne over the last months. If something was going to happen between them, it would have done so already. *Vionne won't fight me now.* Something had changed in him. *This is for me, Phoebe. I need to experience it ... with you,* he added guiltily.

Her eyes flickered orange and her pupils narrowed with emotion. He didn't want to open up old wounds at the reminder of Isla breathing for him first. That wasn't his intention. He'd never breathed for anyone else. *I want you to be my first,* he said, pushing a tendril of hair behind her ear.

She softened in his arms and her eyes returned to normal. He'd hurt her terribly with Isla. It had been to open his gills in order to breathe underwater and unavoidable to save her, but he'd still hurt her. It had only been afterwards that he'd learned the solemnness of the bond. It was a gift he'd taken far too lightly from Isla and from her. No wonder Darres wanted to kill him. *I've never done it. Can you help me?* he said.

Instead of Phoebe kissing him this time, he felt the icy mist enter him and make its way down his throat. It went on for so long he felt every seeking frond as it spread throughout his body. It travelled through veins and tingled along neural pathways, setting off small explosions of pleasure as it went.

Then it reached his heart. It encased it, until it felt like it could no longer beat. Then it exploded outwards and he knew very little after that. Just absolute joy. Pleasure. Love.

His mind awoke to Phoebe kissing him as they floated in the water near the seabed. Their shimmering, thin Murr clothes that barely covered them were easily removed and Phoebe's cool, silken skin slid perfectly against his. Igniting every nerve where she touched. His heart raced as he stared into her eyes, sloe with need. *Now open yourself and do the same for me,* she whispered in his mind. *Just find it in you. It's there, you just have to let it out.*

He knew what was meant to happen, but he had no idea where it came from—or if he was even capable. He closed his eyes. She was moving against him and the sea was gently swaying them. His skin was already alive from her essence all over him. He began to kiss her, slowly pushing inside her and losing himself. Except he wasn't just in tune with her, they became the rhythm of everything around them.

Then he felt it. A small ball of heat in the center of his chest. It grew and rotated like a ball of fire that grew hot and uncomfortable. He almost cried out, then he opened his eyes to see Phoebe's, pupils open, warm and welcoming.

Let it go, Phoebe said and formed a seal around his lips with her own.

It was enough.

Everything escaped from him with the climax of his life. He was lost, but she stayed right there with him and absorbed everything. They remained locked together and sank slowly to the sand.

It was, without doubt, the most satisfying, liberating feeling he'd ever experienced. Almost as exquisite as receiving. It fulfilled a fundamental need he didn't even know he had. He wanted to process what had just happened, but Phoebe was already kissing down his chest in small nips and his stomach clenched at the sting of sharp teeth. *Again,* she whispered before taking him in her mouth and he threw back his head.

"STAY THERE!" Jay said, ordering Tia to stay with the kids. Then he marched off in search of Dante's study. She, of course, flipped him off and did nothing of the sort, following along. However, she was sensible enough, given his current mood to stay back, but not too far as to lose him. Filfla was a labyrinth.

The feeling coursing through his veins was all too familiar and strangely invigorating. Biting anger, tampered down into knife-edged focus, made him feel alive. He and Dante were going to butt heads like they always did and blood was very definitely going to flow. It wasn't until that long, purpose-filled walk through endless corridors that it hit him it was what he lived for. It was one of the only times he ever felt something—that and sex with Tia. It shocked him with the emptiness of it. Not much to show for a life.

Tia had seen them beating down on each other a hundred times, except, this time, it wasn't over her—not directly. It would be over Dante's other great love: the kingdom. The world was bloody ending in twenty-four hours. All the other couples would be in each other's arms and they would rather kill each other than be in Tia's.

Jay sensed he was being followed and shot a look behind him. He swore. Ruby had joined the procession to Dante's study as well. Guilt piled onto the already frayed edges of his anger. He hadn't given Ruby a single thought. Even after all this time, his mind automatically defaulted to Tia. He was an appalling husband and couldn't blame Ruby for hating him. She was sidelined and ignored whenever it came to anything relating to Tia and Dante: the two great loves of his life.

Jay continued to follow the lights in the ceiling and, at

last, came to a guard stationed outside a door. "Is he in there?" was all he said.

The guard nodded and stepped out of the way. He was a Santalini that Jay knew well.

"Don't let them in." He took a breath, reached for the handle and went inside.

CHAPTER 37

ante sat behind his desk, scotch in hand, and watched Jay stalk into the room and sit heavily in the chair in front of him. Jay's anger crackled around him in a static halo. It was the only emotion easy to read about him and even that had taken him years to perfect. "Jay." He pushed a glass he'd already poured towards him.

The whole thing reminded him of the night of his wedding celebration, all those years ago, when they'd found out they were both in love with the same woman: Tia. Dante had been drunk and belligerent, waiting for a fight. Jay had been as in the dark as he was, but still tried to instill reason. Tonight he didn't know how he felt. He wasn't even sure he wanted to hear Jay's explanation.

"You OK now?" Jay said.

The reference to his health calmed Dante a little. He nodded. Tia's breath had got him back on his feet. "As soon as the Orb voided all other bonds, I felt back to normal." And he did. It was miraculous. Not having the ties to the other sisters had freed him from a huge weight he hadn't realized he'd been carrying.

Dante watched that calculating mind of Jay's whirring. He knew that meant his bonds had all been severed too—particularly Tia's. "How do *you* feel?" he threw back maliciously.

A flicker of a frown went across Jay's face and then it was gone. "Normal, I guess. A little relieved. Sad, maybe."

An honest answer that pricked Dante's conscience. Then he salvaged his anger. "You breathed with all of them, Jay. You must have known I'd feel it?"

Jay bobbed his head. "I didn't think about it."

Dante's anger bubbled up in him a notch, knowing that Jay was completely telling the truth. When Jay made up his mind about something, he was single-minded; confident and unwavering in the outcome. It was why he was so good in business. However, he wasn't letting him off the hook that easily. They'd danced this merry cha-cha of theirs for far too long. It was time to have it out. "No? How did you feel about it?" That was what he wanted to know.

Dante had gotten better at controlling his volatile temper over the years. Being king had seen to that. But there was something about Jay that always took them right back to childhood, when his father had brought his brat around to play with them.

"Malleven was a loose cannon, getting more unstable by the day. He was holding the kids over the girls. I had to do something … just in case."

Jay wasn't answering his question. "Why didn't you let me know?"

"It wouldn't have worked. It had to be a take-over Malleven didn't see coming."

Dante slammed his hands down on the desk and stood up. His anger was pulsing through him from a throbbing vein at his temple, right down to the white of his knuckles.

Ruby and Tia pushed into the room.

Dante's eyes remained on Jay and he looked back, not

giving an inch. The absurdity made him laugh as it always did. They'd never truly grown out of their teenage years, not really. He pointed at Jay and looked over at the girls, who stood together terrified of what might happen. "There they are… two Santalinis, blameless in all this and made for each other. The kingdom will be disbanded, not because we couldn't get our act together but because of blood corruption, by the man ready to swoop in and steel it."

Tia went to take a step forward, but Dante held up a hand. "No!" The force of it kept her in her place. "He still hasn't answered my question." Dante walked around his desk and stood in front of Jay. "Through everything, I always thought you were my man." He began a slow stroll around the room. Jay remained still and listening. The girls watched his every move as if he would explode any minute. "So, I ask you again, Jay. How do you feel?" Everything in their life before had come down to this. It was more than rivalry. More than fighting over the woman they loved. Jay had to come clean about how he truly felt about everything. No more hiding.

JAY STOOD. He wasn't entirely surprised that Dante had taken this route of hurt, but he was that he seemed to have doubted him. He was suddenly so weary of it all.

Jay looked into Tia's worried face, then at Ruby, and held out an arm. She ran to him immediately and he gave Tia one last apology in his eyes, then faced Dante again. There was going to be no fight today, he simply had nothing left in him. It was something he knew had to come. He guessed he'd put it off as long as possible. Tia was Dante's. She would always be Dante's and he couldn't kid himself she was in anyway his, anymore.

Ruby seemed to know and hugged into his side. There

was nothing left to say but the truth. "A very long time ago, your father, Christian, came to my office in New York." He looked at Tia with a small, regretful smile. We were together then." Dante had bowed out. They had the children. He had the Bonaci business and a proper little family. It was the closest he ever came to perfect happiness. "He told me about the Darkly Begotten prophecy, that I was his son and that it was fulfilled in me."

The anger visibly drained from Dante's face; his eyebrows went up and he froze to the spot.

"Turned out he was right, just the wrong generation."

Dante moved to his sideboard in silence, passed him a drink and then one for each of them. The threat of violence ebbed away.

"He said I would ruin your kingdom like a cancer from within and you would grow to hate me for it," he said, glancing at Tia. Her eyes were glassy with tears and he quickly averted his eyes. "I tried everything to get away from you both, but you wouldn't allow it." He held out both of his arms with Ruby still hugged into his side. "Well, here we are, five years later and the old man was right." He turned and steered Ruby towards the door without looking at Tia and Dante again. Without turning, "In answer to your question, I feel empty. Just like I always have." He snatched open the door and the cool air hit him. It was time to go and enjoy what little time they had left.

Dante didn't move for a full minute after the door closed.

Tia muttered, "Oh my god."

It had all been maneuvered by his stepfather right from the beginning: battering his own self confidence and then planting this seed of division between them.

Dante sank into his chair as the implications hit him, one

after another. Culminating in the greatest of all: Tia. She would have stayed with Jay happily, perhaps even married him, without his intervention. His life would have been completely different.

Suddenly there wasn't enough air in the room. Tia ran to him and he felt her arms encircle him as he held his head in his hands. She felt stiff and cautious, as if she was in shock too. Of course she was. It was the biggest blow Jay could have delivered him. One he forced him to give.

Jay hadn't been trying to take his kingdom by breathing with the sisters, because he could have had it all the way back then and yet stepped out of the way. Tia, the kingdom, his whole fucking existence had been because Jay had magnanimously allowed him.

He groaned aloud.

Tia tightened her grip and began to sob into him as if something in him had died.

shaya didn't sleep. Deliberations went on between the Twenty and with the Orb well into the night.

"On all counts they have been found wanting?" Seti said. "Atlanteans are greedy, privileged and have abused their stronger position to oppress the peoples of the Earth. Annihilation seems the only fitting course of action."

"What of the Borge?" Ragnar said. "Only the Borge have kept the old ways."

Seti conceded. "And that only serves to prove it's because they've been cut off for most of their existence.

"What of the Humans?" Ashaya blurted, before she could stop herself. She wasn't sure if it was her tiredness or her hurt with Vionne, but she no longer cared what anyone thought anymore. "They weren't even included in the last hearing and this is their planet. How can they be to blame when they were here before us?"

"They were left as the ancient caretakers of this planet and have all but destroyed it," Seti replied, with an aura of puzzlement. It was clear he wanted this tied up.

"With Atlantean leadership showing them how. Have you

forgotten that we didn't seek other planets just to fill the universe with The Way, but for our constant need for energy? We are every bit as guilty as the Humans, but on a much larger scale. I ask you, who in the end is more reprehensible?" By the time she'd finished her tirade, she was shaking.

Ashaya felt rather than saw the smile in Seti's inner voice. She had simply added weight to his argument. Her thoughtless anger, arguably learned from the Atlanteans themselves, had undone any good she might have done. She fought not to scream in frustration as Seti observed her knowingly. "Perhaps Ashaya could sum up her stay with the Atlanteans as she knows them so well," he said, clearly mocking her.

"You have been in a unique position," the Orb said for the first time in several hours. "Please offer your valuable viewpoint."

Ashaya was still awe-struck by being in her presence. An unquantifiable living organism that had burst out of Atlas, found this world and made it a home, instinctively bringing order around itself. Its sole purpose, to bring physical and spiritual harmony to all things. All planets that held life descended from theirs and had an Orb of its own. This was Earth's. It identified as a she, or Mother Nature, and had done so for several million years. She guessed this was the nearest thing to Earth's idea of a god.

"Surely the facts speak for themselves. Everything of value has been viewed and weighed from above," Seti said.

The Orb was an entity of infinite wisdom and regarded Seti for a long moment. She always got the impression they were constantly scanned for intent and emotion. Seti's impatience was schooled, but it was clearly there. "You very wisely placed Ashaya to live among the Atlanteans for a reason, it would be of great interest for the record to know her findings," the Orb said. "I wish to learn of the reasonings of the heart and not just the mind."

Seti was left with no alternative but to bow his head and wave her on with a hand.

The Orb turned to face her and she almost buckled under the weight of her power. She knew the hologram was just a representation to make her more approachable, but she emitted something of which they were all aware and it was so strong it filled the room. "Let me put this to you, Ashaya. If the judging were up to you, how would you judge the Atlanteans?"

It was a clever question, that, if answered honestly, would completely reveal her emotion and bias for the accused. The evidence was damning and if they were doomed anyway, this was her last chance to say anything in their favor. It was suicide for her, but the Orb had put it to her to expose her for exactly that reason. She had been corrupted, just as the Atlanteans had been. They simply couldn't help themselves. Any argument she now made on their behalf would condemn them equally. She couldn't win. Without emotion and with the flickering of green lights, Ashaya knew that the Orb understood full well. She was hit by a wave of fatigue. Whatever she said, wouldn't look good. The Orb was a genius simply rounding up her final summing up.

Strangely, reaching that understanding felt quite liberating. The lightening of her heart made her remember something Dante had once said. "Beware anyone with nothing to lose." It occurred to her then that perhaps he'd known who she was all along. Nevertheless, she knew what he meant now. It gave a person great courage when they no longer cared, because everything had been taken from them anyway. That was the carelessness she felt right then.

"Not what you think, what you feel," the Orb prompted, proving she was right. Atlasians emitted feelings with pictures. To ask her that in such Human terms would only prove a point.

A calm settled over Ashaya. Then a wave started at her feet and swept up over her whole body and she gave rein to it such as she'd never done before. She turned a slow circle to take them all in. They faced her blankly, seeing only the facts put in front of them. They had wasted the greatest opportunity of a lifetime. They were no better than a person going on holiday only to take look at the place from the window and go back home again. Then to have the audacity to say they didn't like it. Ashaya swallowed her anger and took a deep breath. "We journeyed here and learned while we slept for hundreds of years. We absorbed everything we thought there was to know about this intriguing planet. Were you not filled with wonder at this great jewel, hanging in the velvet blanket of space?"

A couple of the Twenty looked at each other, not knowing where she was going with this.

"The physical Earth is not in question here," Seti said, prompting her to get on with it.

Green lights flickered and the Orb remained silent.

"Well, that's how I came to *feel* about the people of this planet." Ashaya began a slow stroll in front of them. "There are Humans, Atlanteans that are Human-like, Atlanteans very Borge-like, Borge very Human-like and even Atlasian-like, but I can confirm that none are Atlasian ... None!" she said, looking every single one of them in the eye while that sunk in.

It struck her that there was no shuffle of feet, or discomfort at her bluntness. They were everything opposite to the people she had grown to love on this planet. "I can already hear your thoughts: Everyone is tainted by the inferior Human gene. But I put to you that ten thousand years ago we left our own planet to strengthen our race. Yes, in power and dominion, but wasn't it also to grow in knowledge? The Earth was chosen for its large area of water, but we found a people genetically close to our own. Put there and forgotten eons before. They were a good people. Abandoned. Looking for a way to survive. They were interested in us. Treated us as gods. We traded. Built Atlantis and then we destroyed all that we'd built. We decided that we didn't want Earth to be Earth, but Atlas II. We had journeyed almost three hundred Human years across the universe to make a copy of what we'd left behind—even though it was a colony who'd become land dwellers." She paused and continued her slow walk. To them it was to let her argument sink in but, in reality, she was locking down emotion that threatened to spill out and ruin any headway she was making.

"A Human male, Lance McCabe, lies dying. He was born to a Human priestess of the wind, tied to our race through The Way of the Five Moons, to our Siren of the wind. Aquillo, an Incarnate, was destined to be with her by right of divining ring. He was injured protecting his Siren as he does in every incarnation of his existence. A Human gives his life for an Atlantean princess and a sect that originated from another planet. Our planet. Our people." She paused at the wobble in her mental voice.

She took a ragged breath. "What I'm trying to say is that the Fates approved this planet in the beginning and it still does. It has tied us to it in so many ways. The most obvious being Lance McCabe and Drew Stone, who is now the Bonaci prince."

"He was changed by the Nix Siren," Ragnar said, stonily.

"As was her prerogative," she threw back. "And let us not forget that, in doing that, a Bonaci prince became revealed that wasn't represented up until that point. Dante saw the genius of it in his council, where all families could have their say."

There was a flurry of mental picture conversations between the Twenty at that. She didn't blame them. Dante's methods had never been exactly orthodox. "A council that even included a representative from the Earth—the host planet. He had the vision to see integration as part of The Way," she said.

Their thought pictures flashed with scenes of anger and outrage at inferring that The Way was in any way responsible for the debacle that was the current state of the Earth. "That same Bonaci prince, the one you refuse to acknowledge and insist on seeing as Human, eliminated our biggest threat, the Scythians, and works tirelessly to rehabilitate the hate it promoted in its acolytes. Many now see that it is ignorance and misunderstanding that is our greatest threat."

"What are you suggesting?" the Orb said. "That we leave things as they are ... reveal ourselves to the general population?"

"No, of course not. But I do think that if we use our power to appoint a king—the right king—talks could continue to have a working relationship with the Human governments so that our ways can be encouraged and made available to all." It was met with a wall of absolute silence.

THE CONTRAST in noise struck Ashaya when she walked into the magnificent hall of Filfla. She always thought of it as the palace of happy noise. Atlas was so quiet. No air meant no vocal chords and no voices meant no laughter, not that could be heard by the ear, anyway. Laughter, she decided, was by far the most joyous product of interaction with humans. She really hoped that her colleagues felt it too.

Beautiful people conversed in huddles. Children ran around and whooped with excitement as they played a game of chase between them. Even the rescued boys sat and chatted animatedly on the sofas with the President of the United States. They were all learning to relax in the company of Atlanteans—even the president. Although his black-suited Secret Servicemen stood sentry a little way off.

They were soon spotted and the room fell silent. Dante put up his hand and twenty chairs were arranged for them by the fountain. Liveried servants helped them over the fountain wall and handed them their towels. Ashaya was seated next to Seti, directly in the middle.

She felt desperately sorry for the fear in their faces. "I won't draw this out. We have deliberated on the evidence through the night," Seti projected loudly. "And a verdict has been reached. It was a grave undertaking, as the survival of the peoples of the Earth hangs in the balance." He slowly stood and begun his familiar, slow walk in front of them. "There are wars, famine, natural disasters, brought on by greed and blatant tampering with the Fates. The Earth loses harmony with the Orb, who has equalized everything for millions of years. The result is the turmoil the world's people now endure." He stopped and looked out at the many faces. "President of the USA, Vionne Borge, Dante Dubonnetti and Jay Gardiner. You have been identified as the leaders to blame for the mess you are now in. Come forward and kneel to your people."

Dante, Jay and Vionne stood hesitantly, but none were as shocked as the president, who looked around him in alarm at being included in the proceedings. No doubt he thought he was only there as an observer. His Secret Servicemen instinctively closed in to protect him.

Vionne came forward and knelt and then Jay. Dante went to the president first and said something between the wall of men. They stepped out of the way and the president stood. He followed Dante, picking their way through the many sofas, to where Jay knelt next to Vionne. Many of the assembly whispered behind hands at the shocking, unprecedented sight, as Seti loomed over the four of them.

"Tell me a good reason why the Earth should be entrusted back to you?" he said, resuming his slow walk in front of them. "I could simply open my ship as an ark and take the deserving few back with me. It has been built for the task. The Orb would do the rest," he said with a flick of the hand.

Ashaya smiled. Without him realizing it, he was already moving and gesturing like their hosts. Then the smile disappeared from her face when she heard her name. "Ashaya, it seems, has become very fond of the Earth and its peoples. She has argued for a final hearing before sentence is passed."

"Vionne Borge, Dante Dubonnetti and Jay Gardiner! You have been responsible for the leadership of our people and are therefore ultimately responsible for them in this sorry state."

CHAPTER 39

$\mathcal{D}$ante wanted to argue that it was Malleven, the mad megalomaniac, who'd fucked it up for them all. Everyone else had just reacted to it. But he could see it was pointless. And perhaps their delicate sensibilities were offended way before that. It felt like when he and Jay were kids and been hauled up in front of the headmaster for drinking yet again and there was just too much shit under the bridge to avoid expulsion. No one ever asked why they drank.

"Dante Dubonnetti!"

His eyes shot to Seti's.

"You seem resigned to your fate. You are normally so demonstrative of your feelings."

Dante narrowed his eyes at his smart-arsed comment. The bloke was an asshole, and he never did much take to authority figures. If ever he was going to say his piece, this was it. "I think you made up your mind before you came here," he said flatly to audible intakes of breath from the crowd.

A muscle in Seti's jaw twitched. "Please, hold nothing back," he said, continuing in the same provocative vein.

Dante knew he was falling into his little trap, but by then he didn't give a shit. "I don't think any individuals are to blame. I think you are … that is, I mean Atlas."

Gasps, whispers and coughs came from behind him, and a few, "yeses," which he was sure came from Keenan and his boys.

"A little louder, Your Highness," Seti continued in his mocking tone. "For the record."

Dante looked at Ashaya, who implored him with her eyes to either shut up or keep it down in some way.

"A convenient answer for a male who lost his kingdom to another," Seti went on. "And if bonds were still counted you would have four to your best friend's five, would you not?"

Seti was baiting him now and Dante gave Ashaya a small smile to say she was safe. The poor guy had no idea he was playing the mind games he lived for and so he got to his feet and grinned. Seti would find the humor and malice in his demeanor a very unnerving mixture, of which he wouldn't know how to process. "I'm merely saying that a system that pits prince against prince to find Sirens hidden in the Human world is sick and perverse and encourages infighting and corruption. How was anyone to know any better? Do you have any fucking idea what the Sirens' lives were like?"

Tia whooped behind him in agreement and he turned to see her pushing through the crowd that had all stood and moved to cluster around them.

"I can tell you that for most of them it was unspeakable." He became lost in the many conversations he'd had with his wife, Tia, when she'd been at her lowest ebb, lost and devastated after harming herself. He remembered what she'd said to him like it was burned into his soul. "Not equipped for life, let alone to be a queen." Acid churned in his stomach just like it had when he'd first heard it. "And it was the same with each and every Siren when they recounted their stories to me."

He raised his eyes to Seti once more. "I wasn't just making a council by breathing with them all, but ensuring their safety, so they would never be lost and alone in the world again and would have the family support they'd all been so cruelly denied."

He saw no empathy reflected back in Seti's face, only an aura of curiosity. "So, you would be happy with your best friend and brother to take the crown if he fulfilled those criteria? As he clearly won by right of pledge of the most Sirens and, as we have learned, he is also one of five sons and qualifies on all counts."

Dante studied Seti like an adversary playing a clever game with him. He knew as well as he did that Jay was one hundred percent Human and would never be considered for the crown. He was just setting the stage to out him in front of everyone, to humiliate him and take him out of the running. He smiled maliciously. "First, it was a calculated decision of myself and the council at that time not to breathe with Lily. She was married to Malleven, who was a danger to the state. To complete the link would put them all in danger." He was becoming angry, so he dropped his eyes and took a breath. "I would prefer it if my accomplishments were judged over my long period of kingship."

Dante decided to address the Twenty as a whole and not enter this game of cat and mouse with Seti, who was determined to bait him. "I am the only one here to hold the kingdom for three years, despite many attempts to depose me."

"In history, Your Highness," Alfonzo added, from the sidelines.

Dante nodded a thanks to him. He noticed chairs had

been brought behind him so the rest of them could get up off their knees.

"So tell me, Dante Dubonnetti, apart from not taking control of your household—a den of blood corruption—your wife running wild because of your many infidelities, what did you accomplish during your *long* reign?" Seti said.

The Dante of old would have punched the guy out, or Jay would have done it for him. Jay was good like that. The ultimate economy of words. Instead of answering, Dante glanced across at his friend who gave him "the look." The one that said everything he'd just been thinking and he loved him for it. Everything else could go fuck itself.

Dante faced the council again with renewed resolve. "I initiated a council such as has never been seen before. A prince represented from every family, chosen by divining ring or First Breath to a Siren. So, in effect, the Fates chose them. That included the Human, Lance McCabe, for full representation of the humans." He acknowledged Ashaya with a smile. "I have a strong relationship with the Borge and Human United States government. We worked together on the relocation and rebuilding of Murrtaine and the destruction of the Scythians, even after Malleven was king." He glanced beside him and Vionne nodded and to the president on the other side of him, who did the same. "And, recently, both my wife and I have become students of The Way of the Five Moons." He took a ragged breath and sat down in his chair after to signify it was all he had to say.

"That's it?" Seti said. "That's what you believe constitutes a successful kingdom?"

Dante felt the tingle of anger rise up his spine. *What was it with this guy?* However, before he opened his mouth to argue, he felt the warm signature of Tia's presence in his mind. *Remember me?* she whispered seductively. *Remember, I'm always on your side.*

He felt her hands rest on his shoulders behind him. "Can I just say that my husband has always fought to be a fair and kind king. You think he has made bad decisions, but everything he did was because he loved us and wanted to hold us together."

Lacy came and stood next to her sister. "He was always good to me, only taking what he needed for the kingdom. He never overstepped or interrupted my relationship with my mate."

Then Isla appeared at his left shoulder. "I came already pregnant in an intolerable situation with a cruel and evil mate. You know him as the former king, Malleven Mancini. Dante accepted me and allowed me my free choice, without judgement; even though I chose the brother who wasn't his ideal choice for the kingdom. My happiness came first, and I happily pledge to him for that."

Lily appeared next, from where he didn't know. She'd been waiting anxiously for Lance's arrival. He would come as soon as the Murr doctors cleared him fit enough for travel. The poor girl looked like she hadn't slept for days. *Most of this is my fault,* she projected loudly. *I couldn't see Malleven for the person he was. I was a vain and gullible girl. And, because of that, I lost Dante the kingdom and almost my mate's life.* She burst into tears. *And I will never forgive myself.*

Strangely, it was Tia who comforted her the most and there had never been any love lost between those two.

Seti, unaffected by her tears, turned his attention to Phoebe, who hovered nearby to see if she was going to add to the circus.

She answered immediately. "She didn't lose the kingdom, I did." Everyone looked at her and whispered behind closed hands, but Phoebe didn't crumple. "I chose Malleven out of grief and spite. I wanted to hurt Dante, so he felt as badly as I did at losing Drew. Now I see what a terrible thing I did. I don't hate him." She turned to talk directly to Vionne. "Or you ... Because I have Drew."

It was a loud and clear message to Vionne that no one could fail to interpret. Then, after a beat for it to sink in, she faced the Twenty again. "Drew was Human, and he saw the worth in him," she said pointing at Dante.

Dante smiled a little sadly back at her. To her it was a revelation, but he'd known it all along and never held it against her. She held out her hands and came forward. "Listen, we were scared all the time under Malleven. He was a tyrant. We pledged to Jay as the next best thing, in an awful situation. No offence," she said with a quick glance to Jay.

"None taken," Jay said, straight back.

"Given the choice, we would all have chosen to go back to Dante."

Tia rubbed his shoulders as emotion reared up in him for a moment. He felt rather than saw all the sisters nod in agreement. Some muttered, "Yes," and, "That's true."

Seti put up a hand to silence them and turned to the rest of his Twenty. They stood in a huddle for quite a few minutes. Then Ashaya turned to the assembly. *I just want to say something before sentence is passed.*

She'd come a long way since Dante had met her. She's gone from the hard little protégé of Seti to a clever, confident woman. She knew her own mind and would not be browbeaten. He admired her as she stood with her chin up and a slight tremor in her hands.

As you all know now, it has been my assignment and great privilege to come and live among you. Not as a spy, not just as an observer, but to live and feel what it is to be you.

I have seen love and great sacrifice from Human, Atlantean and Borge. Boys not even from our kind, rescued and given a loving home. Children, she projected, looking straight at Jay.

Cared for, no matter their parentage. Then at Dante. *Loved, no matter their lineage.*

Yes, there has been a blurring of the lines. A mixing of the ways. A tainting of the pure blood of Atlas. But this is not Atlas. It is a world of sea and of land. Of a people who live alongside us in hardship, who simply need a voice, she said, gazing at the president. Dante could swear she actually smiled.

VIONNE HUNG on every word as Ashaya spoke, heart swelling and rejoicing with pride. She was right. He'd never heard it put quite like that; as only a total outsider could see them. He'd lain under the shadow of falling short of Atlas' mark his whole life. It was the benchmark they all lived by—including the Humans that knew of their existence. What she was proposing was a bold and different way and he was sure it sung to each and every one of them.

Dante Dubonnetti saw and embraced this ethos. He came from a royal family but chose the Human world until just the last few years. Fate saw to it that he was first to find his Siren. We must listen to that. She did a slow turn like a seasoned speaker. *Otherwise, what is the point ... He created a council, perfect in its concept, because it included a Human. His best friend is Human. One of his Sirens is mated to a Human.*

Get to the point of what you are proposing, Seti projected, right over the top of her.

It didn't fluster her or make her lose her momentum. Ashaya merely faced him and bowed, showing perfect deference to his seniority. *I propose that we reinstate Dante Dubonnetti, along with the council he created and the strong ties with the US and UK governments. All bonds are now redundant except for immediate mates, giving the kingdom a chance without the constant challenges and distraction of that for the first time. With a continued audit every five hundred years where their progress can be observed, I think it can work.*

DANTE HAD BARELY GOT to know the girl really, but she'd spoken as eloquently as if she'd known him her whole life. He guessed she kind of did if she'd studied them throughout her journey there. It blew his mind that someone could have spent several Human lifetimes travelling just one journey.

Duly noted, Seti said. It was hard to tell whether he agreed or disregarded it. *Christian Dubonnetti,* he called.

The old goat stepped out of the semi-circle of onlookers. A blush of excitement in his cheeks. This was his moment and he was seizing it with relish.

You are father to both of these men? Seti asked.

"Only one by blood," Christian said, letting his eyes fall on Dante just long enough to sneer.

And you can vouch for Jay Gardiner's claim to the throne?

"I can," Christian said, bowing his head theatrically.

And yet the Sirens openly support your other son, Dante, Seti said.

Dante's eyes lifted to Seti in surprise. He was testing him, not Christian. Sweat trickled down his neck and he imperceptibly shook his head at him. There was no way he wanted Jay's true lineage exposed in front of all these people. Seti went on regardless, even though he had understood him perfectly.

"The same Sirens freely gave Jay Gardiner their breath. He is king by right of five Sirens to his four, and he also has an heir," Christian went on.

Seti held his hands behind his back and walked slowly to stand directly in front of Jay by the time Christian had stopped speaking. *Is this true?*

Dante knew it was another test to weigh up Jay. The ruse saddened him. Jay's Human genes meant he would never be allowed to lead the race, but he would have made a good king. He smiled at Jay's guarded answer. "It would appear so."

Seti looked at the collection of Sirens all still standing around Dante. *And if I were to grant the throne to Jay Gardiner, you would support him?*

Dante didn't want to look and put pressure on them, so he closed his eyes. He inwardly smiled as it was Tia who spoke. "In place of Dante, if we couldn't have him, we would support Jay."

And there it was at last. His heart broke with joy, if that was possible. Because that was exactly how it felt. Tia stating for the world to hear that he was first choice. Jay had always won in all things. He held his forehead to mask his emotion. Others may have thought it was bitter disappointment at losing the crown. They couldn't be more wrong. It was joy, vindication, validation, love, futility, regret, sadness, all rolled into one tidal wave of emotion that swept through him in quick succession.

Tia hadn't finished. "But if that is the case, I will remain with my husband."

As a sob threatened to break out of his body, his eyes met Jay's. He'd been watching him, completely unaffected by the show around them. His eyes were dewy and knowing. A little sad, but proud for him too. He gave him a small nod as if to say: he had this, and it was OK. It pained Dante's heart. In that moment, he knew Jay had made his peace and let go of Tia a long time ago.

Tia's hands gripped into his shoulders to ground him. She knew. Of course she did, and he felt her kiss the top of his head.

Jay turned his head away to look at Seti, still standing in

front of him. The world suddenly went quiet. Jay blinked and Dante just lipread the word "What?" from Jay.

In light of the facts, I hereby reinstate the kingdom, to Jay Gardiner.

There was a single beat of silence where everyone was stunned. No one reacted, until Christian danced and whooped for joy. "Yes," he hissed, loudly and clapped his hands. "Long live the king!"

There followed a few lackluster claps in the crowd.

Dante, still in shock, gaped openmouthed at Jay and then Seti, who was clearly enjoying himself. *What will your first act as king be?* Seti asked.

Dante frowned. It was such a peculiar thing for Seti to say. The whole thing was fast taking on all the characteristics of a trippy nightmare. For one unsettling moment he questioned whether or not he was asleep or drugged. Jay was staring at Seti and Seti was staring back in some weird standoff. He wondered if some internal conversation was going on. It seemed he was right when Seti eventually gave him a single nod.

Seti turned and said something to one of his Twenty, who carried over a flat wooden box. He opened it and took out a thin gold circlet. A crown once worn by medieval kings. Then he held it out to Jay. Not to place it on to his head but just to hold it. It was bizarre.

Dante looked around him to see if anyone had any more of a clue what was going on than he did, and saw they were watching in the same awe and confusion as he was. Everyone had somehow gone down the same rabbit hole of his crazy dream.

Jay took the crown, stood up and walked over to him. All he could do was stare as he seemed to have lost all motor skills. Jay leaned forward and placed the crown on his head.

Dante continued to look up at him in stunned silence. "A crown for the true King of the Atlantean nation," Jay said. "As it should be," Jay whispered more quietly, so only he could hear him.

CHAPTER 40

*J*ay squeezed his shoulder and stepped back, which was the closest thing to a hug from him. That act alone was enough to leave him reeling.

A buzz of electricity went through the crowd behind him.

"No!" Christian wailed. "He's been drugged. Compelled! This can't be allowed. He doesn't know his own mind."

Delissi came forward and whispered something to Seti, who nodded.

"Arrest those men!" Delissi shouted, pointing at Christian and Marco next to him. "They are guilty of treason."

Dante watched the guards drag his stepfather and brother off for past crimes, still unable to move or articulate a word.

Thank you, Jay, Seti said, and Jay bowed and returned to his seat.

Whatever gamble Seti had just played, he'd executed it masterfully. He'd guessed what Jay would do, without revealing he could never be king, no questions asked. He'd therefore satisfied all sides in one go. He had to admire him for that.

Seti then went to the President of the United States, who

immediately straightened in his chair. He'd been as absorbed by what was going on as the rest of them. *Mr President,* Seti projected. *Do you think you could work with this king?*

The president, looking a little on the back foot, nodded and managed to splutter the words. "Sure … we've done great work together already. It will continue." He quickly gathered himself together. "My biggest concern is the weather patterns."

The Orb will be satisfied. She will now reset, and Earth's climate will settle in response, Seti said.

The last person in the line-up was Vionne. Dante was the most nervous about him. He had neither a Siren nor a seat on the council. *Are you content to remain Lord Advocate of Murrtaine?*

There was a moment where their eyes met and Dante wondered if he would protest, but he merely nodded his head. *He is a good and able king,* he projected.

Dante gave him a single nod in thanks and looked to Ashaya in the hope she would finally say something, then to Seti who'd stepped back and looked as unsettled as he was. It was now or never. "Can I make a suggestion here?" Dante said, making the heat of all eyes fall back on him. "That you leave one of your Twenty here to oversee things. Perhaps one already accustomed to living with us?"

Vionne's eyes shot to his.

She would never get to see her family again in her lifetime? Seti directed to her in the form of a question.

Dante pushed on, sensing Seti wavering. "May I suggest that she makes a new family here, one that's not too dissimilar to home … with the Borge perhaps?

Vionne was looking from him to Ashaya with every word in astonishment. He didn't think he'd ever seen the big guy move so much. He almost laughed. The idiot had held off from what was right under his nose for a Siren that didn't want him anyway. He just needed a shove in the right direction.

Ashaya had the look of a frightened dear and Vionne—the big lummox, was just sitting there thinking of all the lame excuses, no doubt, he'd come up with along the way. "I know you vowed to your father to marry a Siren, but wouldn't he find such a worthy female equally acceptable?" He grinned at the male he'd come to view as a close and loyal friend. He deserved this, if only he'd allow himself the slack to enjoy it.

Suddenly, a wave of love and gratitude emanated from Vionne as he finally stood and knelt in front of Ashaya. *I would if she would do me the honor and have me?*

At last. Dante wanted to punch the air. Not sure what the Atlasians would make of it, he contented himself by grinning and clapping, to which everyone joined in. Vionne was a loved and respected guy and everyone that knew him wanted to see him happy.

Ashaya held out her hand and looked at Seti, as if asking some kind of permission. A long look was passed between them and she turned back to Vionne. *You should know that although my mother is dead now, she came from this planet. She was born here over five hundred years ago.*

Dante was not expecting that. His brain raced to interpret what it was she was actually saying.

She belonged to the last generation of Sirens.

A horrible realization was creeping through Dante's veins as he began to see where she was going with this.

Ashaya leaned forward and touched the side of Vionne's face. *She was in love with your father.*

VIONNE'S MIND went into freefall. Memories of his father's last conversation with him tumbled through his head. It was just after he'd vowed to marry his Siren. His father had rambled on about meeting his own Siren and losing her and how it had broken his heart. He and his brothers had put it down to the confusion of an old and dying man. *She died,* Vionne said lamely. He was so shocked he couldn't say any more than that.

She almost did, Ashaya said. *The Twenty before us were observing at the time and because one of the Sirens had been executed by the humans and there were no longer five, it was decided to take them back with them to Atlas in suspended sleep. They would have withered away without the healing powers of our technology.*

At first, he jumped, in horror, to the conclusion she was his half-sister, but she read him perfectly and shook her head and added, *On her return to Atlas, she met and mated my father and I came into being. But she never forgot her time here and spoke of your father often. It was the reason I had a special interest in this planet. It has always been an ambition to be one of the Twenty and come here. I guess I wanted to find the family that might have been mine.* She looked down sadly and said quietly, *And, of course, you ... I had to meet you.*

Vionne didn't wait a moment longer. He stood and scooped her up in one fluid move, kissing her in front of the whole assembly. He heard a few whistles and "ahs" and many clapped, but he was lost in the sensation of her.

DANTE FELT A BIZARRE, reckless kind of hopefulness go through the room. He felt the same. Like somehow everything was going to come out right in the end.

Vionne finally put Ashaya down and came over, pulled him in and touched foreheads with him. It was the closest form of acceptance any Murr could give. It was usually reserved for very close family and friends. He was bewildered and honored.

Then Seti shook his hand in a very Atlantean way, albeit a little stiffly, but Dante appreciated the gesture. It proved the guy had a soul after all. "Thank you," he said, and really meant it. He couldn't believe how things had turned out. He just had to ask, though, "What did you say to Jay, before he gave me the crown? You made quite a play there," Dante said, still a little surprised and in awe. It could have blown up in his face.

There was still a smugness about the guy that he would never fully understand. *I simply asked him if he would leave Tia alone when he gave you his crown.*

Dante grinned. "And what did he say?" He half laughed, already knowing his response.

A strange vernacular, Seti said, looking up for the answer somewhere. *Not on your life, or something similar. I'm not sure what it means exactly. But I took it to be a negative answer.*

Dante laughed loudly at that and at the guy's obvious sense of humor. Who knew? He bowed and excused himself after that. He went and found Jay talking with a group of guards and pulled him into a tight hug, which he hated.

Then he remembered a last thing that hadn't been resolved as he saw Seti walking away. "Hey! What about JJ and the Darkly Begotten thing?"

Chatter hushed around them as everyone turned for the answer to that. Tia and Lacy came and stood either side of him to listen.

Seti turned back around. He seemed to compose himself as if what he had to say wasn't easy. It worried Dante more than words. The room fell silent and his guts churned in sudden dread at what it could be.

We have achieved a wondrous thing here today, Seti began.

It sounded like, "You've had the good news, now here's the bad, that I was hoping I wouldn't have to give you."

We have found a real way to move forward. Great things will happen, bridging the gap between the races.

Dante wanted to shout at him to get on with it, when he heard the, *however.*

The cost of the taint you have welcomed is the Darkly Begotten generation foretold to you many millennia ago. JJ is the outcome of that.

Dante looked at Tia and gripped her hand. Her face was hard and furious, ready to protect her son.

But Seti looked directly at her as if he knew. *He is a miracle, it is true. But he should not have been your eldest son.* His eyes tracked to Dante. *Xavier is the true and rightful heir. But JJ is an eldest son too,* he said, his eyes falling on Jay.

Dante saw then what he was driving at. Tia had two eldest sons in her womb at the same time because they had different fathers.

So you see, the succession is not set. Two eldest sons of two kings. Dante's heart sank. It was the cost of the little stunt Seti had pulled earlier to keep Jay's heritage quiet. There would be trouble down the line.

He looked across at Jay, whose mind was rapidly working through the same process as he was. "So what are you saying we do?" Jay said, looking between them. It was typical Jay to want a definitive answer today. He was always a man of action that needed a plan.

The prophecy says they will fight. Brother against brother. The dark and the light, Seti said, nodding to Phoebe at her possible future role.

Seti sighed deeply, as if he took no pleasure in what he' had to say. Then he looked sympathetically at Dante and Jay. *Enjoy your victory while it lasts because prophecy will always be fulfilled.*

CHAPTER 41

Dante saw to it that the Great Hall of Filfla was done up like a spring gala. With the help of his cousin, the Maltese prime minister, flowers were sent in from all over Malta for the wedding. They were floor to ceiling, interwoven into the vines that formed the many pillars of the great room. Seats were cleared to the side and an aisle formed of white rose petals that ran through the middle, from the magnificent steps to the panoramic window. Dante stood on a white canopied podium and looked out at all the beautiful, expectant faces, so proud of them all. The venue was certainly worthy of such an ancient and noble race.

Vionne waited, nervously, just off to the left, as was the custom, with all four of his brothers, in the shimmering grey, gossamer suits of the Borge. Then the music changed and Dante's eyes went to the newly erected DJ decks. To Tia, who winked, and the very human wedding march began.

Everyone turned. Ashaya came from behind the pyramid of steps on Seti's arm and took everyone's breath. Dante glanced at Vionne and swore he grew another foot in pride.

She looked radiant in the pale yellow of the priestesses of the Five Moons. Her silky black hair was down to just past her chin and crowned with a garland of white flowers. The alabaster color of her skin contrasted exquisitely with the coal black of her eyes. The black ribbons that represented the many stripes of her people were intricately woven from her neck down the length of her bare arms. More flowers circled her wrists and were visible around her ankles. She walked barefoot, gracefully, with everyone marveling at her alien beauty. The dress parted showing the ribbons crisscrossing the length of her legs. The effect was complete. She was a stunning, ethereal vision from another world.

Dante watched the president's reaction. He was as mesmerized by the spectacle as they were. He was the first ever outsider to witness something like this—a mark of the new times.

Seti walked with Ashaya, proudly wearing the grey suit of the Twenty, with just a small gold crescent moon broach on his shoulder to distinguish his position. It seemed fitting that he gave her away. He was her commanding officer and had made this possible, after all. Now things had been settled, he didn't seem nearly as bad. The remaining eighteen followed in perfect identical formation behind them. They continued their slow walk down the aisle, splitting off at the front to make way for the others.

Dante grinned. Darres' boys followed, carrying more garlands. They were tall and kind of gangly, not yet grown into their legs. They would hate all this pomp and be aching to get away to play with his own boys. Then, behind them, came the boy he had been made aware of that was rescued. He was part of the procession and a little bewildered, looking around for a familiar face. It threw up a number of questions. Then his heart warmed when his own daughter,

Alexia, pushed out from the crowd and went and held his hand the rest of the way. He'd need details later.

Seti passed Ashaya's hand to Vionne's when they reached the front and left them gazing into each other's eyes. "Took you some time, but you got there in the end," Dante said and got a few chuckles in the crowd. "Well, I'm glad you did."

Dante looked around at all the smiling faces, waiting on what he would say. He didn't want to make a long speech. He just wanted a moment to absorb how far they'd all come. "Welcome," he said, looking at them all. "It is my great honor and privilege to have you all here today to celebrate the first marriage of an Atlasian and a Borge, and out of water," he tacked on, to more chuckles. "Seriously, this is a momentous occasion. As with all marriages, it should be celebrated." He found Tia and smiled. Then he picked out Lacy and Keenan, Isla, then Phoebe. "But this one is special because it crossed huge obstacles and boundaries to happen at all. Even lightyears," he said, smiling kindly at Ashaya. "It signifies new beginnings, not just for the two here, but for us all. Where we can celebrate our differences instead of being afraid of them. Learn from them and even love them." He took a deep breath, his heart so full he could barely speak. "So it is with great pleasure that I bring you all here today to witness the marriage of Vionne Borge, Prince and Lord Advocate of Murrtaine and the Siren Princess Ashaya of Atlas.

Vionne's eyes went straight to his at the word, Siren.

Doesn't being the daughter of one make her one too? he said, privately, to Vionne's mind. He knew it was the one thing that had held him back all this time. *I think you kept your word.*

Vionne nodded imperceptibly and looked back at Ashaya. If he didn't know better, he would have thought he was fighting back emotion.

Dante inwardly chuckled and went straight on with the

vows. "Do you, Vionne Borge, take Ashaya of Atlas as your mated female through your journey on Earth and into the ether together?"

I do, Vionne said, confidently, to the whole assembly.

Dante turned to Ashaya and asked the same question proudly. "Do you, Ashaya, forgo your home of Atlas to continue life's journey on Earth with Vionne Borge, as your mated male, till you enter the ether together?

I do, she said, without hesitation.

"Then it is with great happiness that I pronounce you married under the blessings of the Five Moons, the Orb and the power vested in me as King of the Atlantean nation. You may kiss each other."

Vionne crushed Ashaya in a kiss that erupted the crowd into cheers and a snowstorm of rose petals. Dante had never seen everyone so happy. Couples hugged and the children whooped, squealed and gathered huge handfuls of petals to continue throwing them up in the air. It became joyful pandemonium.

A great party was held in Filfla after that. Dante sent a proclamation that the wedding, the continuation of the race and the kingdom was to be celebrated throughout the whole Atlantean world. Future possible conflicts were exactly that: a long way off.

The president shook Dante's hand, stunned and over-whelmed but happy, and left by helicopter. Off to process what he'd learned and deal with other pressing matters, with the promise of continued talks. Dante himself waved him off.

Another helicopter immediately took its place on the landing pad and a much-thinner Lance was helped out. He wasn't alone. Dante shook his hand warmly, thanking him for all he'd done protecting Lily and the race. "It's good to see you're on the mend," Then he turned his attention, amused, to the tall, scruffy Aussie surfer girl next to him that he recognized as a close friend of Lily's and part of his crew. "Shona?"

"G'day," she said immediately, getting under Lance's arm to help him walk off. "I can't leave this galah for five flamin' minutes."

Dante laughed and walked along with them, listening patiently to Shona's good-natured chiding and telling Lance off for getting himself hurt without her around to keep an eye on things. "You know I was surfin' Pipe and had to come all the way here when I heard?"

Guards surrounded them and helped negotiate the long passageway to the lift that took Lance down to the Great Hall.

Lily almost knocked him over when she ran to him. Then she hugged Shona tightly, then Lance again.

"Will you stay on my council?" Dante asked, when Lily finally let him go. The guy had been through a lot and he wouldn't blame him if he put two fingers up to it all after Malleven, but he nodded.

"I may have to take up wind-surfing, though. There're no waves around here."

Dante laughed at the horror on Shona's face. He was a good guy and Lily was ecstatically happy to have him back. The freaky gold in his eyes had gone too. Lance seemed to read his mind. "The last of the gold came out in the Murrs' healing machine," he said.

Dante nodded. It was good news. He didn't want any remnant of Malleven left to haunt them.

Can I speak to you privately, Lance? I have news of my own, I can't wait to tell you, Lily said, touching the side of Lance's face.

Lance grinned, a little unsure. "What is it, Tiger?"

Dante went to walk off as she seemed nervous and they

had a lot to sort out. But before he could move off, Lance shouted, "Pregnant! What? How?" Lance said, picking Lily up and putting her down quickly with the pain from his healing wound.

Dante spun back around and openly stared at the both of them. His mind raced and a heavy weight sunk onto his chest that he couldn't shift.

The doctors say it was being underwater that set it off. Lily was grinning, the happiest Dante had ever seen her. He didn't have the heart to burst their bubble. He knew Sirens could gestate babies for a long while until they began to grow, often only starting when the mother spent time in water. They could hold more than one pregnancy, from more than one father. JJ was proof of that. Dante walked back over, pulled Lily into a hug and looked at Lance's knowing eyes over the top of her head. He was terrified of the same thing. Dante winked to lighten the moment. It wasn't ideal and a conversation for later, but it wasn't the end of the world. He loved little JJ, but, he had to admit, he didn't relish the idea of Malleven's DNA still walking the earth.

The music was switched off for Seti and the rest of the Twenty to bid a surprisingly emotional goodbye. They couldn't delay going back to Atlas any longer. They would never see them again. It would take five hundred years for them to get back and a new party to arrive. The distance was staggering.

"Wait!" Tia called after Seti, as he stepped over the fountain wall. "You never actually told us why we have our powers with music?" It was so true, it almost made him laugh. Sailors through history had died for the Sirens' song.

Seti froze, unnaturally still, as he thought about it. Then he straightened up in the shallow waters. *The question should be, why were you never permitted to sing?*

Tia turned and frowned at Dante, to see if he got what he was saying.

Then Seti addressed him directly. *If ever you should need Atlas all you need is to call. All it requires is ten hands and a perfect note.* Dante thought the guy actually smiled. He put up a final hand of farewell and disappeared into the fountain.

"What does that actually mean?" Tia said, irritated by Seti's cryptic answer.

A slow smile crept across Dante's face as he remembered the Sirens and mates' handprints in the pedestal of the Orb room of Murrtaine. "You just have to sing and they'll come," he said simply, to which Tia tutted and flounced off at the unsatisfactory answer.

Dante laughed.

"You finally got your Siren," Dante said, turning to Vionne and shaking his hand.

I can't thank you enough, Vionne said. He seemed to be smiling all the time now he'd learned how to do it.

"I hear your people move into New Murrtaine tomorrow, so you're both leaving us."

Vionne couldn't speak first of all. He was overcome by emotion, which was highly unusual for a Murr. *I still can't believe it ... my father.*

Dante embraced him to save his embarrassment. Ashaya saw and put her hand on his back. She was an amazing woman and perfect for Vionne. "He would have been so proud," he said, patting his back. "Life has a habit of coming full circle."

Vionne pulled apart and nodded just as Darres' boys shot past with the other Murr youngster who'd been part of the procession. Dante nodded in his direction. "And who is the new addition?" Vionne pulled Ashaya into his side and she looked up at him adoringly. Vionne shook his head as if he still couldn't believe it himself. *It was my brother Darres who first put the idea in my head and then we discussed it,"* he said, lost in Ashaya's eyes.

He has a need for a mother and father and we thought, well, we are in need of a son, Ashaya said, finishing his sentence for him.

Dante knew of the disaster that had killed several Murrs and guessed the little guy was the product of that. "That's just grand," he said, his heart swelling for them.

Vionne bowed and Ashaya took his arm. They were swamped with well-wishers. Recently reunited Sebastian and Naomi, the Sirens' mother and father, were the last in a long line to congratulate them. Then Ashaya seized the opportunity to lead him to the privacy of their room.

Dante took a moment, then continued his way, circulating, shaking hands and receiving slaps on his back. He found Phoebe sitting in Drew's lap surrounded by a loud group of boys, alive with laughter and chatter. They were arguing over an arcade game with two motorbikes on springs he'd had installed for the party. Another group were gathered around a console with a screen the size of a blackboard.

Phoebe pulled out of a kiss when they sensed him approach. Dante waved them on with a regal hand. "We'll talk about your academy when you're less busy," he said. "It's a good idea."

Drew grinned and looked around him as an idea formed in his mind. "You sure you don't want me and Lance to play a set?"

Phoebe burst out laughing and Dante gave him a warning look. He still had nightmares of Phoebe's coming-out party that got trashed the last time Drew's band played. Several guards ended up in the hospital. "No, you're grand," he said, dryly.

Two of his children ran between them, chased by Darres and Isla's boys. Dante scanned the crowd and found the two of them standing quietly off to the side. They were completely content in each other's company and perfectly suited to each other. He went over and kissed Isla's cheek and shook Darres' hand. "You will live in Murrtaine?"

They both nodded.

"And you won't kill Drew?" he said to Darres, trying not to grin.

"That, I can't promise," the big Murr said, but he sensed amusement beneath the hard exterior. Even he had a sense of humor.

"Thank you," he said to Isla.

"Look after her," Dante said as parting words to them both. He had so much respect for this Siren. She was his favorite after Tia, but he'd never hurt the others by saying it aloud.

Dante turned and there was his real father, the Duke Ormond Delissi, in front of him. Delissi bowed and held out his hand to him. "Your Highness," he said.

Dante paused for a long moment before he took Delissi's hand and searched his eyes. All along, he'd never known where he stood. Traitor or spy. Good or bad guy. Although there had always been something honest and knowing in his eyes. "How did you know?" Dante said, eventually.

"I didn't," the duke said, looking mystified. "I merely saw to it that the correct procedures were followed and trusted in the Fates to do the rest. You could say: I had faith. Looks like I was right," Delissi said with a small smile. "Atlantis has its rightful, true king, undisputed at last."

For the second time that day Dante felt the weight of emotion in his throat and the sting of tears behind his eyes. However, when he went to take the hand he'd left hanging too long, his father pulled him into a tight embrace. His breathing was hard into his shoulder as if he too fought to hold down years of recrimination, love and tears, where no one ever got to see them. It was the first real hug from any father he'd ever had. Christian was never worth a light. "I am so proud to call myself your father," Delissi said quietly in his ear.

It was almost his undoing, so Dante pulled away and nodded a little awkwardly, but a new bond of understanding was there. They could never let the outside world know; it would weaken their positions, but there was no longer any doubt of allegiance. "You will remain my man in Washington, DC?" Dante said, voice gruff with emotion.

Delissi inclined his head. "As long as Your Highness needs me, and my legs remain sound enough to carry me," he said, smiling and holding up his black cane.

Dante smiled and felt an arm link through his. He turned and it was Tia carrying JJ on her hip. "And come and be a grandfather whenever you can," he said, relieving Tia of the child's weight.

His father's face lit up with joy. His career had meant that he'd never had a home life or a family. "I wouldn't miss that for the world," he said. He then bowed and took his leave to follow the president back for debriefing on what it all meant for the two nations. Dante reluctantly said goodbye. He would enjoy getting to know his father at last.

When he was out of sight, JJ asked to get down and ran to join the others. He seemed to have reverted to being an ordinary little boy. "I'm worried about him," Tia said, hugging into his side. "God knows what effect Malleven has had on him." Jay joined them and the three of them looked on at the joyful group of their five children.

"Lily's pregnant," Dante said, flatly, knowing they would all join the dots.

"There'll be trouble," Jay said.

"We'll sort it out, the three of us," Dante said, grinning.

Jay rolled his eyes.

Taking in the happiness, dancing and laughter of Human, Atlantean and Borge, all mixing in together, it was hard to think that they couldn't.

EPILOGUE

Twenty years later: Malta

Jay put the finishing sentence to the long letter that explained fully the reason he was going, to his son. He wondered wistfully that he'd never had more children with Ruby. They'd just had the one, a girl, and he knew she wasn't his. She was accepted and they'd never once spoken about it. It was the tax he was willing to pay for loving another woman. *Tia,* the love and the curse of his life.

He laughed to himself and folded the piece of paper that laid out his whole story: how the cancer he had because he was undoubtedly Human was ravaging his body. It had been the final middle finger from Christian, who'd been executed all those years ago. It was pointless fighting it as it was one fight he wasn't going to win. He put the letter in the envelope, sealed it and propped it on the nightstand next to the one he'd written for Ruby.

She stirred in the bed and instinctively turned towards him. "Sleep," he whispered and kissed her bare shoulder. "It's still early."

Ruby smiled lazily and snuggled down, clearly relishing that she didn't have to leave her warm cocoon too soon.

Jay smiled and watched her sleep. She'd been a good wife in the end. She'd loved and stuck by him and he did love her in his way. JJ was now at college with Dante's four, and they were all strong individuals; ready to take on and make their own way in this strange and messed-up world.

He was doing the right thing. Murrs had no cancer so there was no cure for it and there was no way he'd put the people he loved through a long treatment of chemo just for it to possibly buy him six months and then have to watch him wither away. *No,* this was the one thing he could control and he was grabbing it with both hands. Dante, of course, had known, and hadn't said a word in twenty years. The proof of his DNA came as no surprise, meaning he'd known all along. He smiled with a wave of nostalgia at the memory of his being king for five minutes. Dante could have blown away his bid simply by announcing it and had chosen to keep it quiet. He'd understood that he needed to be part of their world if he wasn't going to be with Tia. They'd started out arguing, fighting and pulling Tia between them in their childish power games. And now Dante was offering her to him for one last time. It wasn't for what you'd think. He was sacrificing her for Jay's final goodbye and only the three of them would understand.

He closed the door to the villa quietly, got in his shiny red sports car and drove to the north where a boat was waiting to take him to the small uninhabited, rocky island where he would meet Tia.

Jay had ordered him not to, but he'd come anyway. Dante was waiting for him, alone on the dock. "Tia's on the boat and Keenan is your driver." Dante had recreated the day he'd spent with Tia, exactly. The day they'd finally reached an understanding that had carried them through life without killing each other. A single blast of laughter escaped him. He had not planned saying goodbye to his close friend, Keenan. "You're an asshole," Jay said, pulling Dante into a hug.

Jay never had demonstrated feelings well, but he guessed he could allow him just this once. They kissed each other's cheek and there were tears in both of their eyes. Dante had the sense to not say a word. He couldn't bear it and would simply have walked off. Besides, nothing needed to be said. Dante knew him that well.

He simply took in his friend's face and nodded a thanks. He'd never been religious. Not as a Human or as an Atlantean, with all the Five Moons crap Dante and Tia practiced, but he did believe in the Ether. It was the universe, space, or the place where all energy came from and went back to. He could get on board with that. And, for him, Tia was the only key for them all to be together in it. The idea had come to him many years ago when she'd done it for one of her friends, saving him from a terrifying death.

He looked over at Tia, alone and sitting at the bow of the boat. "Is she OK?" he asked.

Dante didn't bother to lie. "She understands why."

Jay nodded and studied Tia's beautiful profile. She hadn't aged a day over thirty, nor had Dante. That was why this was the right decision. Their lifespans would be five times that of his. At least this way it wasn't goodbye for ever.

Sirens had this wonderous gift of spirit through the giving of their breath, but they could take a life too. If they wanted, they could absorb a person's spirit into their own and carry it with them for ever. Jay realized what a great sacrifice Dante was making in allowing it. But he guessed Dante loved him too, and, this way, when their time came, the three of them would join the Ether together and never be apart.

Jay gave his old friend one last smile, touched the side of

his face and walked towards the boat. His heart smashed against his ribcage at the finality of it. He was actually doing it and would never look on his dearest friend's face again. Like someone about to jump off a cliff. Then he counted in his head and waited for Dante's last wisecrack.

"Don't take the piss, Jay."

And there it was. It made him laugh out loud, he couldn't help it. Jay turned and continued to walk backwards to take a last look at the tall figure with the rock star good looks and shoulder-length hair holding it together with a joke to let him go. Dante knew it was exactly what he needed.

"Can't promise," Jay called back. "What do you expect when you leave her unattended?" His final word wavered in his throat and he turned and leaped across to the boat.

Keenan had the sense to keep his mouth shut and Jay never looked at Dante again. They moved off and Jay sat in the shade while they chugged gently towards the little island. When they got there, Jay just shook Keenan's hand, jumped out and swam the small distance to the island. He'd spoken to him briefly, explaining, the day before. He'd made it clear he didn't want sappy goodbyes. He had also made him swear not to tell anyone—particularly Ruby.

Tia jumped in after him and they were swept up by a friendly wave, onto the table-like rock. Keenan threw them a small bag of food and provisions for the day and the boat moved slowly away. From there, they climbed the rest of the way up the small hill where he held Tia's hand in silence and they watched the boat go out of sight.

It was a beautiful day and the sun reflected on the tips of the small waves exactly like the last time they were there. Little boats went by and people waved. There were fisherman and windsurfers and an occasional small plane overhead. It was his favorite place in the world, with his favorite person. A perfect place to spend his last day. He gradually got her to talk and they told old stories of the three of them and laughed. They sunbathed and slept until there was nothing left to say. "The sea has diamonds, remember?" he said, referring to the last time they'd been there and made their no-sex pact. The light, the smell of the water, everything was perfect at this time of day. It was why he'd chosen this time to do it.

He looked at his watch. "It's 5 o'clock." He'd arranged with Keenan to collect Tia at 5.30. He didn't want to drag it out and he didn't want her left alone any length of time there.

She shook her head, already crying. "I can't do it, Jay."

"You can," he said, harshly. "I was never going to do old age, was I? You know me better than that." He left off; while they hardly aged at all. She would work that out for herself.

She got a hold on herself, which he knew she would, and she managed a small, wan smile. He held her face, made her look up at him and spoke a little softer. "If you don't, this thing inside me will do it for you, except it will take away the person I am … the person you love."

Her eyes closed slowly and tears tracked through the salt on either side of her face at the reality of that.

"I need you, Tia. I've never asked you for much, but I need you to do this last thing for me."

Dante had passed on to her what he needed her to do. The answer was perfect. She'd done it once before when she'd gone to Antarctica with her scientist friends. Dante had allowed her to go, thinking it was the safest place on Earth. Unfortunately, Human forces tracked her down and attacked them. Her friend, Ben, fell into a fissure and became crushed between the moving ice. Tia had been devastated, but absorbed his spirit to save him from a horrifying death. That was what he was asking from Tia today, as hard as it was for her to do.

She tried to speak, but a sob escaped her. She struggled to

pull herself together, crumbling again and again. "What shall I say to the kids?"

"You can tell them in time, but, for now, tell them it was a tragic accident so they can grieve and move on with their lives. Then, later, you can explain that you saved me just like you did for your friend on the ice and that I'm safely with you."

Tia looked at him a long moment until he kissed her reverently on the mouth. "Do you ever feel him?" he asked, not sure if he wanted her to say yes or no.

She shook her head. "Sometimes I hear a whisper or a shift of his spirit that sparks a memory. I don't think he's conscious."

It was a relief in a way. The bond had been bad enough, without hearing Tia's internal monologue.

"The priestesses say that I'll just carry you to the Ether where you will be free when my time comes," Tia said, rubbing her thumb under his eye to catch a tear he hadn't even felt fall.

Jay saw the devilish thought the moment it entered her eyes. "Dante will assume we'll have sex."

He laughed and pulled her down to sit with him in his lap. "Yeah, he will." Honestly, he hadn't thought of that when he'd planned the day. They'd made their pact and stuck to it for over twenty years. Their relationship had grown stronger because of it. She'd been right about that. He guessed she knew him the most out of anyone. Part of Dante and even Ruby, never entirely believed they could keep their hands off each other. It saddened and amused him at the same time. It said a lot about what they thought of his character. "It's time," Jay said, pulling her head into his shoulder so he could control his heartrate. He looked out at the little boats trundling by. They were both stalling and time was ticking on. He wanted the privacy before Keenan got back.

Jay felt the sobs shake her body. "Come on," he said, putting her away from him so he could hold her face. "Breathe for me one last time and then do it," he said, looking intently into her eyes. Her face was wet with tears and her nose was running. He marveled that she was forty-three and her face looked as gorgeous and youthful as it ever did. He passed her his discarded t-shirt. "Without the snot, though, eh."

They both laughed and she wiped her whole face with it while she wailed harder, then got a hold and looked at him again and swallowed hard.

Jay moved in slowly to cover her mouth with his and groaned. It had been a very long time. The Atlasians had cancelled all bonds not belonging to mates. He'd even managed to satisfy his blood thirst with Ruby alone, so he didn't cause Dante any more trouble. It felt like when they'd first met all over again.

Her spirit eased into his bones like a comfy pair of slippers. A cool, seeking mist and it was yesterday again. Making its slow progress to his heart, its tentacles wrapped itself around it, over and over, so tightly he thought he would die from that alone. Then his whole body shook as she pushed him gently backwards to lay flat on the dusty ground. His world exploded. His vision filled with colored light and his body convulsed until it bathed in ecstasy and the euphoria that followed. When he floated back down to Earth, he whispered, "Now, babe."

Her lips neared and he took one last look into those large green, luminous eyes and he heard her song for the first time. It was beautiful. A Siren's song, calling his soul.

. . .

TIA STOOD LOOKING up at the moon, holding Dante's hand, raw and stripped of emotion. "It's not fair," she said on a ragged breath.

"That we live long lives?" Dante let out a long, exhausted, breath. "Jay always knew we would live longer than him. He never spoke of it. It was just one of those things he accepted. If it hadn't been cancer, he would have found another way."

Tia scowled up at her husband, not because he was wrong but because he was right. "Well, he's a selfish bastard," she said, feeling the deep cut in her heart that she would no longer get to tell him.

Dante didn't argue, just pulled her into the heat of his body and she was glad. He was shielding her from his own emotion. They'd cried enough together when she'd got back and now he was sad and quiet, dealing with the loss of a brother he loved as much as she did.

The air had suddenly turned chilly. "Shh," he said. Knowing her tears were coming again even before she did. "He is with us always and we have JJ and the children." He pulled her chin up to look at him and solemnly kissed her. Then he looked deeply in her eyes. "And we'll all be together again."

GLOSSARY

Characters in family groups:

Bonaci

Alfonzo Bonaci—Head of the Bonaci royal family and uncle to the Sirens

Sebastian Bonaci—Brother to Alfonzo and father to the Sirens

Luca Bonaci— Half-brother to the Sirens

Dino Bonaci—Full brother to Luca and half-brother to the Sirens

Tia Storm— Siren—First wife and most compatible to Dante — queen—bonded to Jay

Lacy Rain—Siren—Mated and most compatible with Keenan Santalini and second wife to Dante

Isla Snow—Siren—Mated to Darres Borge, third wife to Dante (Most compatible with Malleven)

Lilian Gale—Siren—Mated and most compatible with Lance McCabe—bonded to Cesaré Florianna by First Breath and therefore the only Siren not married to Dante

Phoebe Ray—Siren—Mated to Drew Stone, fourth wife to

Dante—bonded to Malleven by First Breath—Most compatible eventually with Vionne Borge

Royal Children
Xavier—Son of Dante and Tia
Alexia—Daughter of Dante and Tia
Roman—Son of Dante and Tia
Zander—Son of Dante and Tia
JJ—Son of Jay and Tia

Borge
Darl—Lord Advocate of Murrtaine and father to Vionne, Dax, Caan, Axyl and Darres
Vionne Borge—Murr and eldest son and successor to Darl
Dax Borge—Son of Darl, brother to Vionne
Caan Borge—Son of Darl, brother to Vionne
Axyl Borge—Son of Darl, brother to Vionne, Dax, Caan, twin of Darres and ruler of Murrla
Darres Borge—Son of Darl, twin of Axyl, brother to Vionne, Dax and Caan—mate to Isla Snow
Naomi—Wife to Sebastian Bonaci—mother to Sirens

Royal children
Keefa—Son of Darres and Isla Snow
Dannon—Son of Darres and Isla Snow
Loki—Adopted son of Ashaya and Vionne

Dubonnetti
Dante Dubonnetti—King and most compatible mate and married to Tia Storm (and all other Sirens except Lily)
Duke Ormond Delissi—Biological father to Dante and Ambassador for the Atlanteans in Washington, DC
Christian Dubonnetti—Stepfather to Dante and head of the Dubonnetti royal family

Marco Dubonnetti— Half-brother to Dante and Jay
Gardiner
Paulo Dubonnetti—Half-brother to Dante and Jay Gardiner
Antonio Dubonnetti—Half-brother to Dante and Jay
Gardiner—lover to Malleven Mancini
Stephan Dubonnetti—Youngest—half-brother to Dante and
Jay Gardiner
Joseph Brincat—Prime Minister of Malta and cousin to
Dante

Florianna

Cesaré Florianna—Head of the Florianna— bonded to Lilian
Gale by First Breath – king's right hand on his council
Sandro Florianna—Eldest brother to Cesaré
David, Roberto and Mario—Brothers to Cesaré
Malleven Mancini—Cousin to Cesaré—most compatible
with Isla Snow, married to Lilian Gale, bonded to Phoebe
Ray—challenger for the Kingdom

Santalini

Andreas—Elder of the Florianna royal family and uncle to
Keenan Santalini
Keenan Santalini—Most compatible with and mated to
Lacy Rain
Ruby Santalini—Sister to Keenan and married to Jay
Gardiner
Marius Santalini—Eldest brother to Keenan
Adriano, Drago and Louis—Brothers to Keenan
Reeve Santalini—Fellow guard and cousin to the brothers

The Humans

Jay Gardiner—Protector/Lover bonded to Tia Storm—
married to Ruby Santalini
Lance McCabe—Most compatible mate with Lilian Gale—

reincarnated from the male heir of the sect of the Five Moons (Incarnates)
Drew Stone—Mate to Phoebe Ray (later Bonaci)

The Scythians
Lord Croll—High Priest and commander
Seville—Mentor/Trainer and handler to Drew Stone

The boys
Justin—Head boy in Drew's six
361—Boy in Drew's six
Luke, Mike, Gus, David—Part of Drew's six boys at the camp.

The Atlasians
Ashaya—One of the Twenty judges and love interest with Vionne
Seti—Commander of the Twenty
Ragnar—One of the Twenty

Those filling council seats and whom they represent
Dante Dubonnetti—King and head of council representing the Dubonnetti
Cesaré Florianna—King's right hand and representing the Florianna
Keenan Santalini—Representing the Santalini
Darres Borge—Representing the Borge/Murrs
Lance McCabe—Representing the Human population
Sebastian and Alfonzo Bonaci—Representing the Bonaci in the absence of a Bonaci mate.

Protectors
Sean McPhearson—Protector to Tia Storm
Cash Reynolds—Protector to Tia Storm
Connor—Protector to Phoebe Ray

River—Lily's Protector and Lance's band mate
Nathan—Lily's Protector, Lance's brother by adoption and fellow band mate
Shona—Lily's Protector and part of Lance's surfer crew

The Magi
Nasr—High Priest
Ghazi—Protector of Phoebe and nemesis to Malleven

Terms particular to the Atlanteans:

Divining ring—worn by all princes and forged particularly for them. Can only have one wearer. Forged from the Orb itself. Determines whether a Siren is nearby and the wearer's status to her by its color:
Opaque white—default resting color
Turquoise/green—a Siren is nearby
Purple—the Siren nearby is the wearer's most compatible mate
Red—the wearer is excluded or disqualified from bonding with the Siren nearby. They should not marry or mate a Siren for fear of displeasing the Orb

Elixir—Potion taken by princes and those Humans in contact with a Siren to prevent an extreme reaction or even death in the event of breathing her essence.

First Breath—The breath passed from a Siren for the very first time. Her power passes to the recipient only on the very first exchange. Usually reserved for the king.

Murrla—satellite Murr city situated near Antarctica.

Scythians—Ancient warlike religious order of fighter

monks rumored to kidnap small boys to indoctrinate and train them. Human supremacists, their sole aim is to destroy the Atlantean nation.

The Arawans—the sect or The Way of the Five Moons—is the ancient religion of Atlanteans. Came with them from Atlas.

The Magi—ancient order of magicians and alchemists of which Malleven belongs. Mainly Human in origin but have worked alongside the Atlantean nation since the beginning of their colonization.

The Orb—the ancient power source of Atlanteans. Believed to rest beneath Murrtaine and came with their ancestors from Atlas.

Atlas—home planet of the Atlantean ancestors.

Ether—viewed as a heavenlike place where all energy comes from and returns to.

COMING IN 2021:

The new NIGHT SHADES series: **The Blackwood Curse**
To start reading:
Or to learn more, visit:

www.stedman.com

CONTACT T

To receive your two 21st Century Sirens Novellas and be the first to know anything relating to T's books, leave your details here: https://mailchi.mp/d18c89c14f50/tstedmannovellas
And please don't forget to leave a review wherever you bought your book, I really appreciate the feedback.
Much love,
T
https://tstedman.com
https://www.facebook.com/TStedman1author
https://twitter.com/AuthorTStedman

www.ingramcontent.com/pod-product-compliance
Lightning Source LLC
Chambersburg PA
CBHW031927110726
47902CB00001B/69